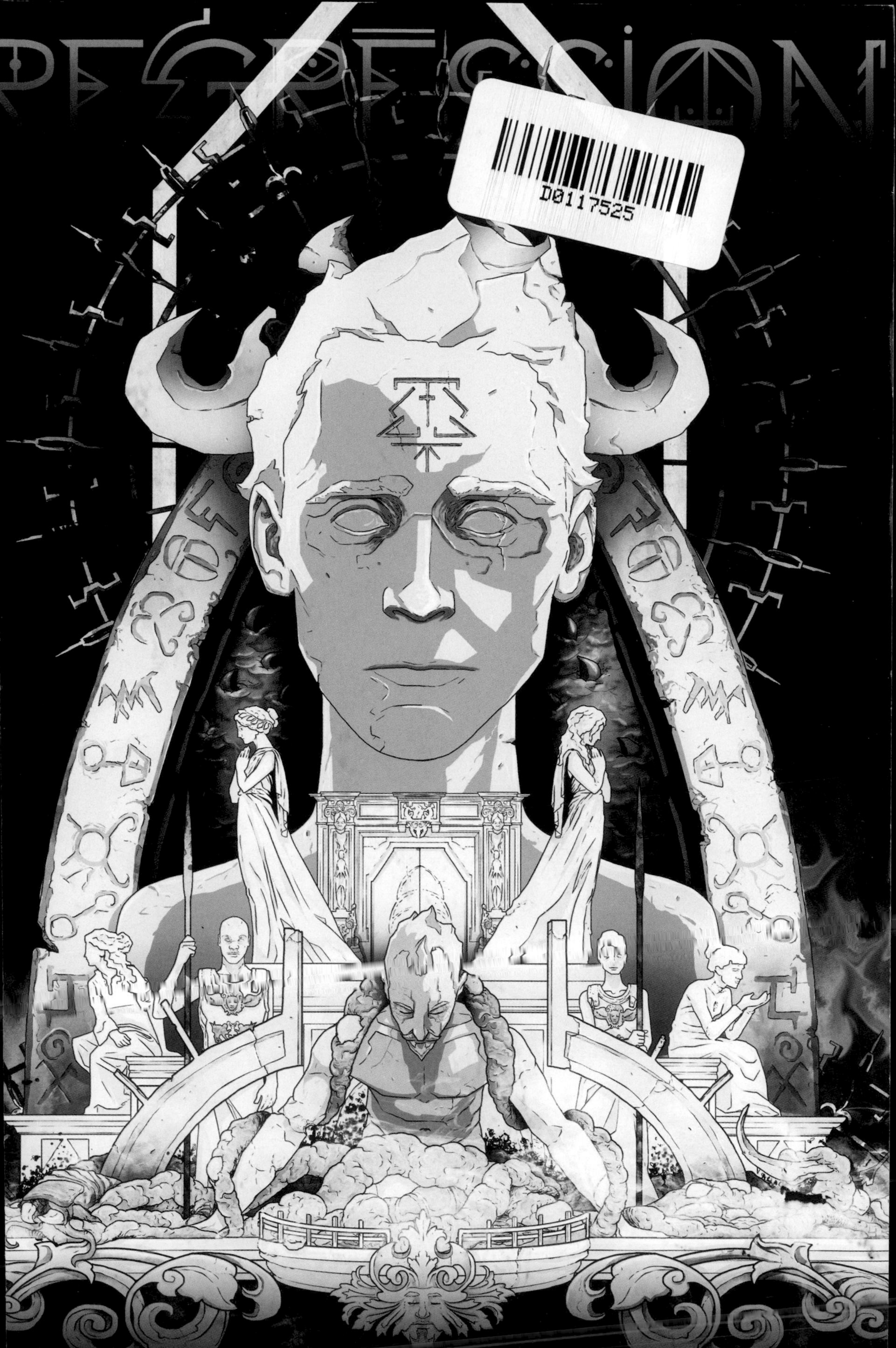

VOL. 1: WAY DOWN DEEP

IMAGE COMICS, INC. / ROBERT KIRKMAN: CHIEF OPERATING OFFICER / ERIK LARSEN: CHIEF FINANCIAL OFFICER / TODD MCFARLANE: PRESIDENT / MARC SILVESTRI: CHIEF EXECUTIVE OFFICER / JIM VALENTINO: VICE PRESIDENT / ERIC STEPHENSON: PUBLISHER / COREY MURPHY: DIRECTOR OF SALES / JEFF BOISON: DIRECTOR OF PUBLISHING PLANNING & BOOK TRADE SALES / CHRIS RO___ DIRECTOR OF DIGITAL SALES / JEFF STANG: DIRECTOR OF SPECIALTY SALES / KAT SALAZAR: DIRECTOR OF PR & MARKETING / BRANWYN BIGGLESTONE: CONTROLLER / KALI DUGAN: SENIOR A___ COUNTING MANAGER / SUE KORPELA: ACCOUNTING & HR MANAGER / DREW GILL: ART DIRECTOR / HEATHER DOORNINK: PRODUCTION DIRECTOR / LEIGH THOMAS: PRINT MANAGER / TRICIA RAM___ TRAFFIC MANAGER / BRIAH SKELLY: PUBLICIST / ALY HOFFMAN: EVENTS & CONVENTIONS COORDINATOR / SASHA HEAD: SALES & MARKETING PRODUCTION DESIGNER / DAVID BROTHERS: BRAND___ MANAGER / MELISSA GIFFORD: CONTENT MANAGER / DREW FITZGERALD: PUBLICITY ASSISTANT / VINCENT KUKUA: PRODUCTION ARTIST / ERIKA SCHNATZ: PRODUCTION ARTIST / RYAN BREW___ PRODUCTION ARTIST / SHANNA MATUSZAK: PRODUCTION ARTIST / CAREY HALL: PRODUCTION ARTIST / ESTHER KIM: DIRECT MARKET SALES REPRESENTATIVE / EMILIO BAUTISTA: DIGITAL SALES R___ RESENTATIVE / LEANNA CAUNTER: ACCOUNTING ANALYST / CHLOE RAMOS-PETERSON: LIBRARY MARKET SALES REPRESENTATIVE / MARLA EIZIK: ADMINISTRATIVE ASSISTANT / **IMAGECOMICS.C**___

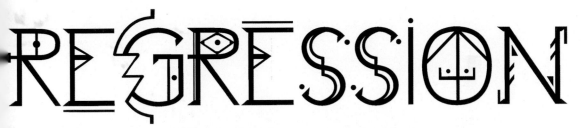

REGRESSION

CULLEN BUNN
STORY

DANNY LUCKERT
ART

MARIE ENGER
COLORS/LETTERS

JOEL ENOS
EDITOR

RESSION, VOL. 1: WAY DOWN DEEP. FIRST PRINTING. NOVEMBER 2017.
LISHED BY IMAGE COMICS, INC. OFFICE OF PUBLICATION: 2701 NW VAUGHN ST., SUITE 780, PORTLAND, OR 97210. PRINTED IN THE USA. FOR INFORMATION REGARDING THE CPSIA ON THIS NTED MATERIAL CALL: 203-595-3636 AND PROVIDE REFERENCE #RICH-768296. FOR INTERNATIONAL RIGHTS, CONTACT: FOREIGNLICENSING@IMAGECOMICS.COM. ISBN: 978-1-5343-0337-9.

ONE

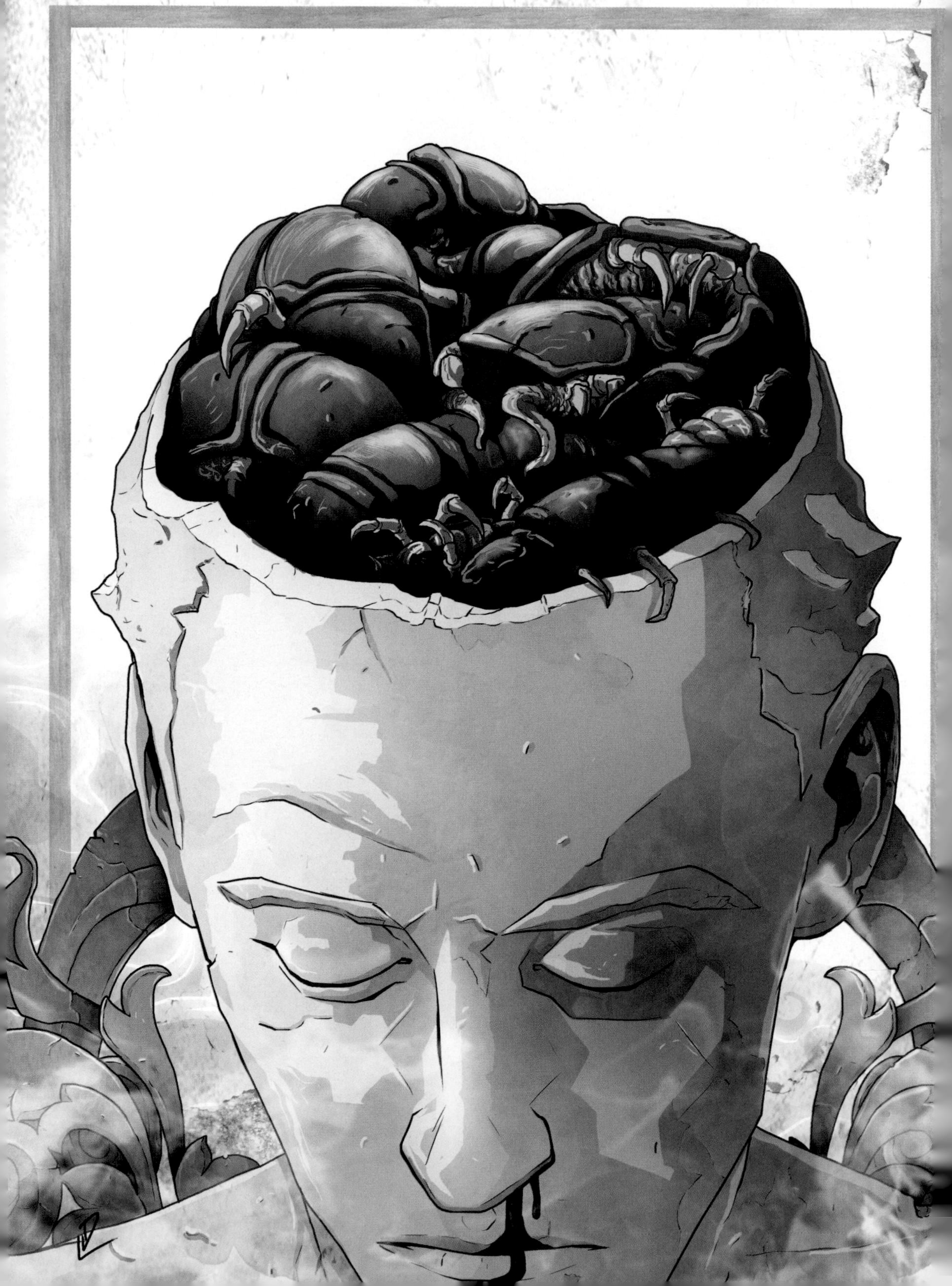

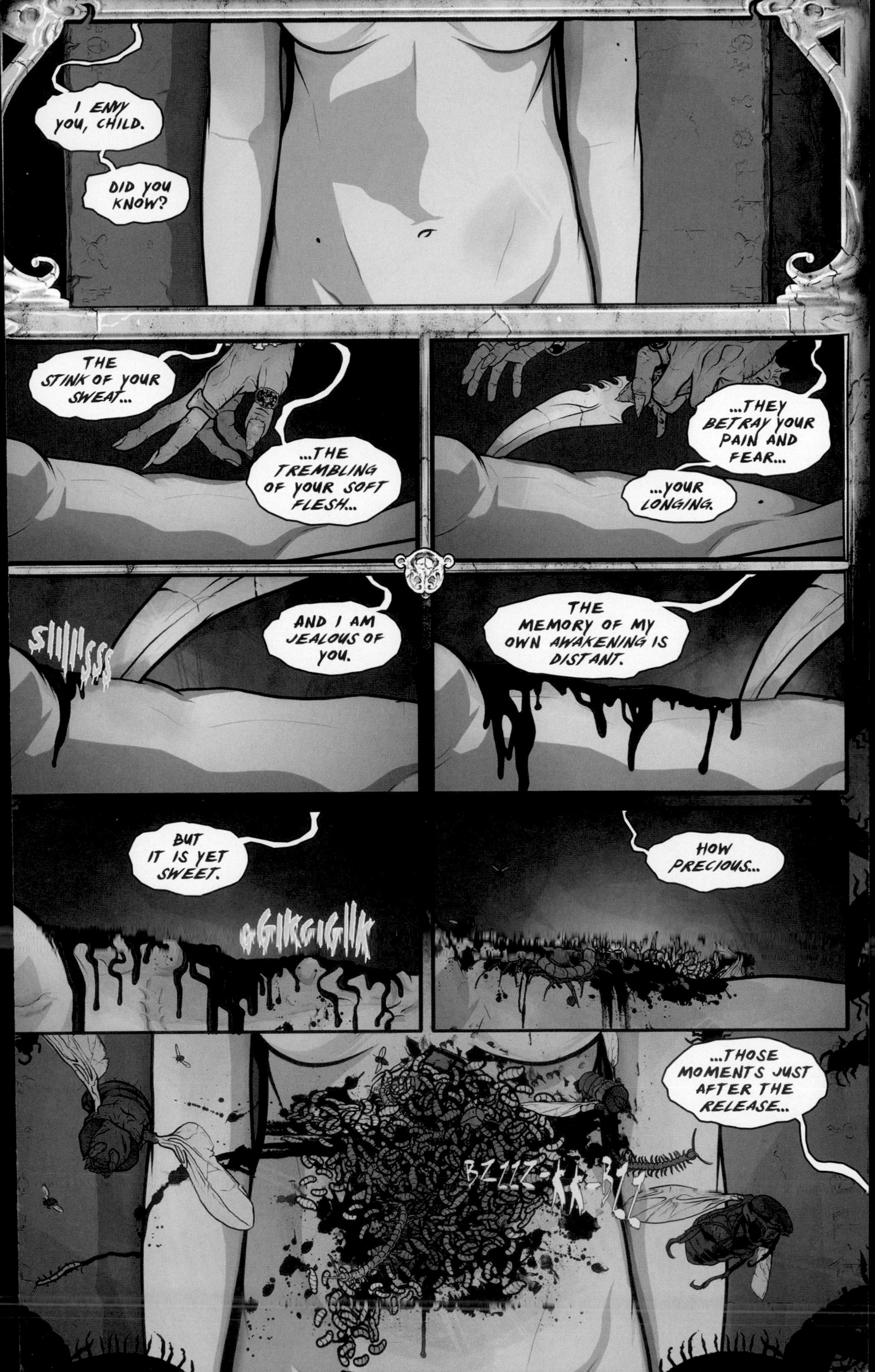
I ENVY YOU, CHILD.
DID YOU KNOW?
THE STINK OF YOUR SWEAT...
...THE TREMBLING OF YOUR SOFT FLESH...
...THEY BETRAY YOUR PAIN AND FEAR...
...YOUR LONGING.
SIIIISSS
AND I AM JEALOUS OF YOU.
THE MEMORY OF MY OWN AWAKENING IS DISTANT.
BUT IT IS YET SWEET.
GGIKGIGIIK
HOW PRECIOUS...
...THOSE MOMENTS JUST AFTER THE RELEASE...
BZZZZ-KK-BZZ

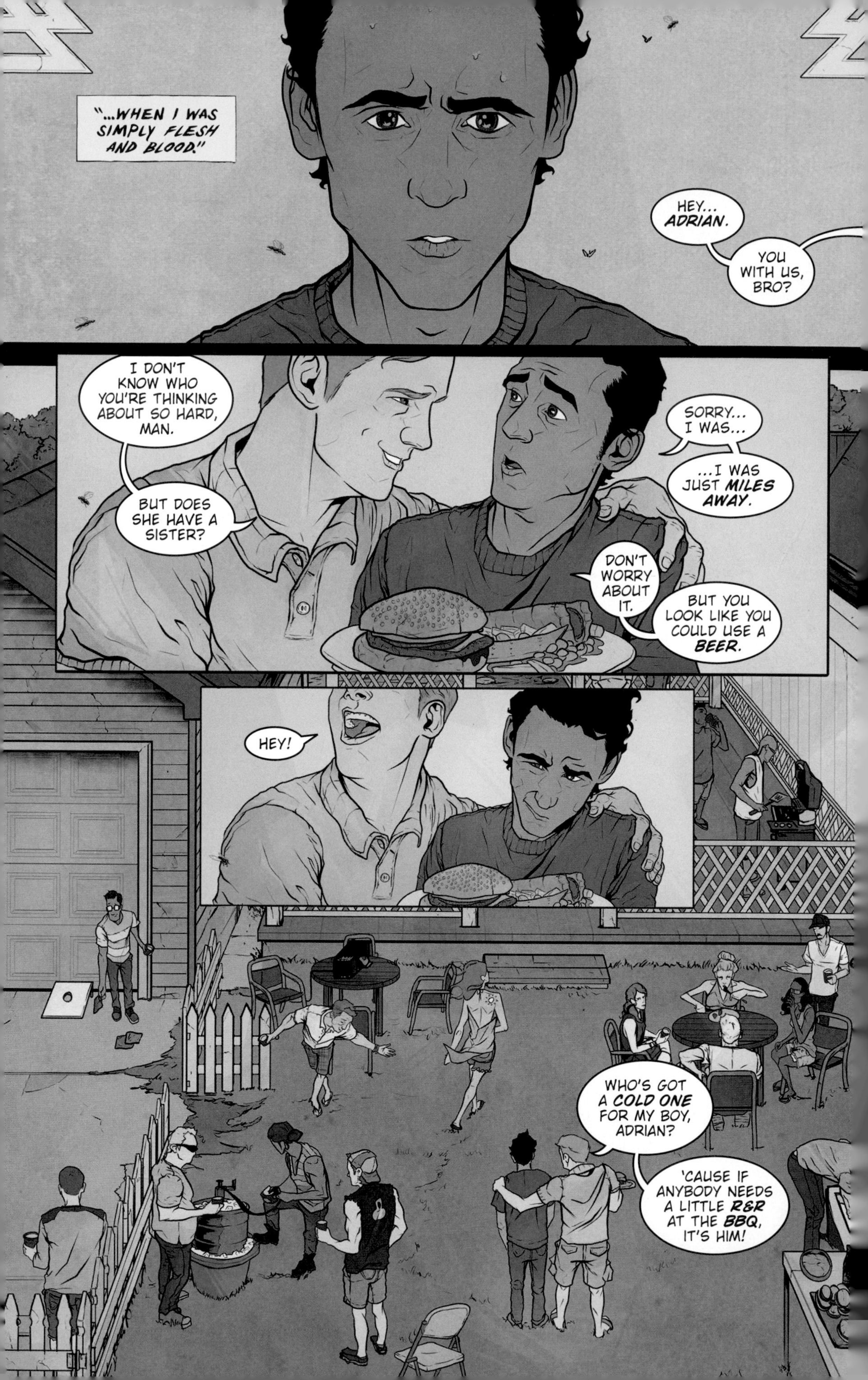
"...WHEN I WAS SIMPLY FLESH AND BLOOD."
HEY... ADRIAN.
YOU WITH US, BRO?
I DON'T KNOW WHO YOU'RE THINKING ABOUT SO HARD, MAN.
BUT DOES SHE HAVE A SISTER?
SORRY... I WAS...
...I WAS JUST MILES AWAY.
DON'T WORRY ABOUT IT.
BUT YOU LOOK LIKE YOU COULD USE A BEER.
HEY!
WHO'S GOT A COLD ONE FOR MY BOY, ADRIAN?
'CAUSE IF ANYBODY NEEDS A LITTLE R&R AT THE BBQ, IT'S HIM!

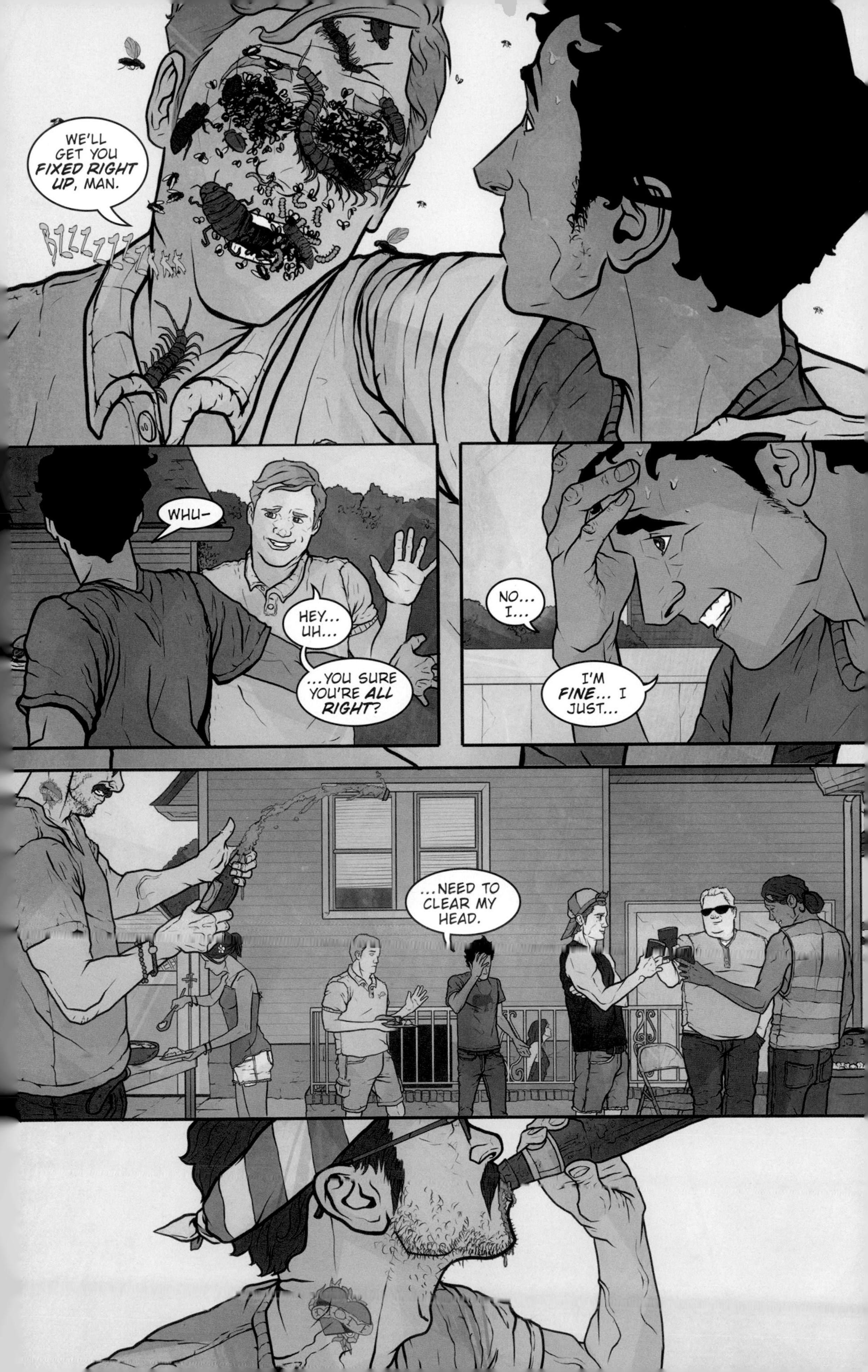
WE'LL GET YOU FIXED RIGHT UP, MAN.
BZZZZZZZCKKK
WHU-
HEY... UH...
...YOU SURE YOU'RE ALL RIGHT?
NO... I...
I'M FINE... I JUST...
...NEED TO CLEAR MY HEAD.

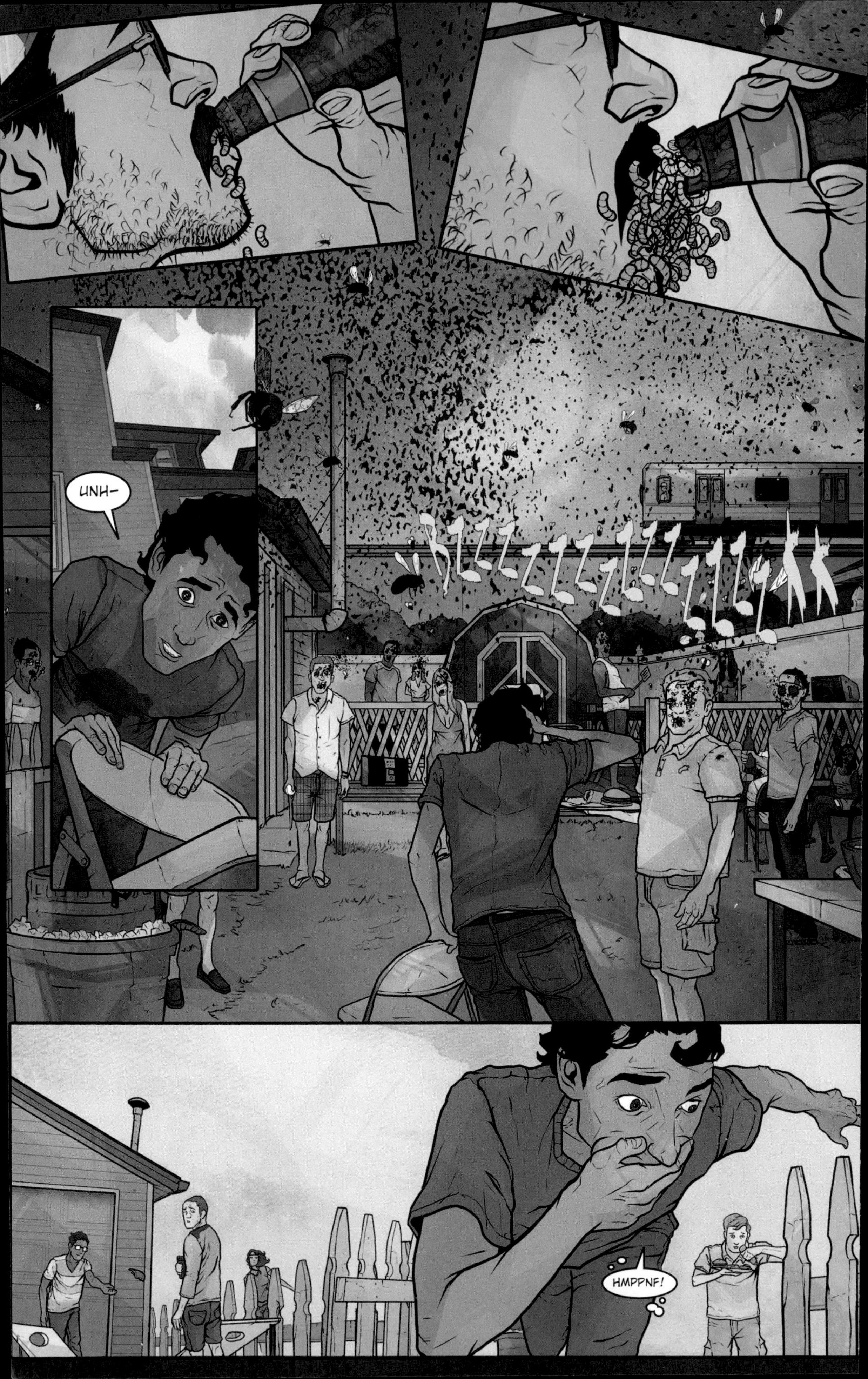
UNH-
BZZZZZZZZZZZZZZZZZZKK
HMPPNF!

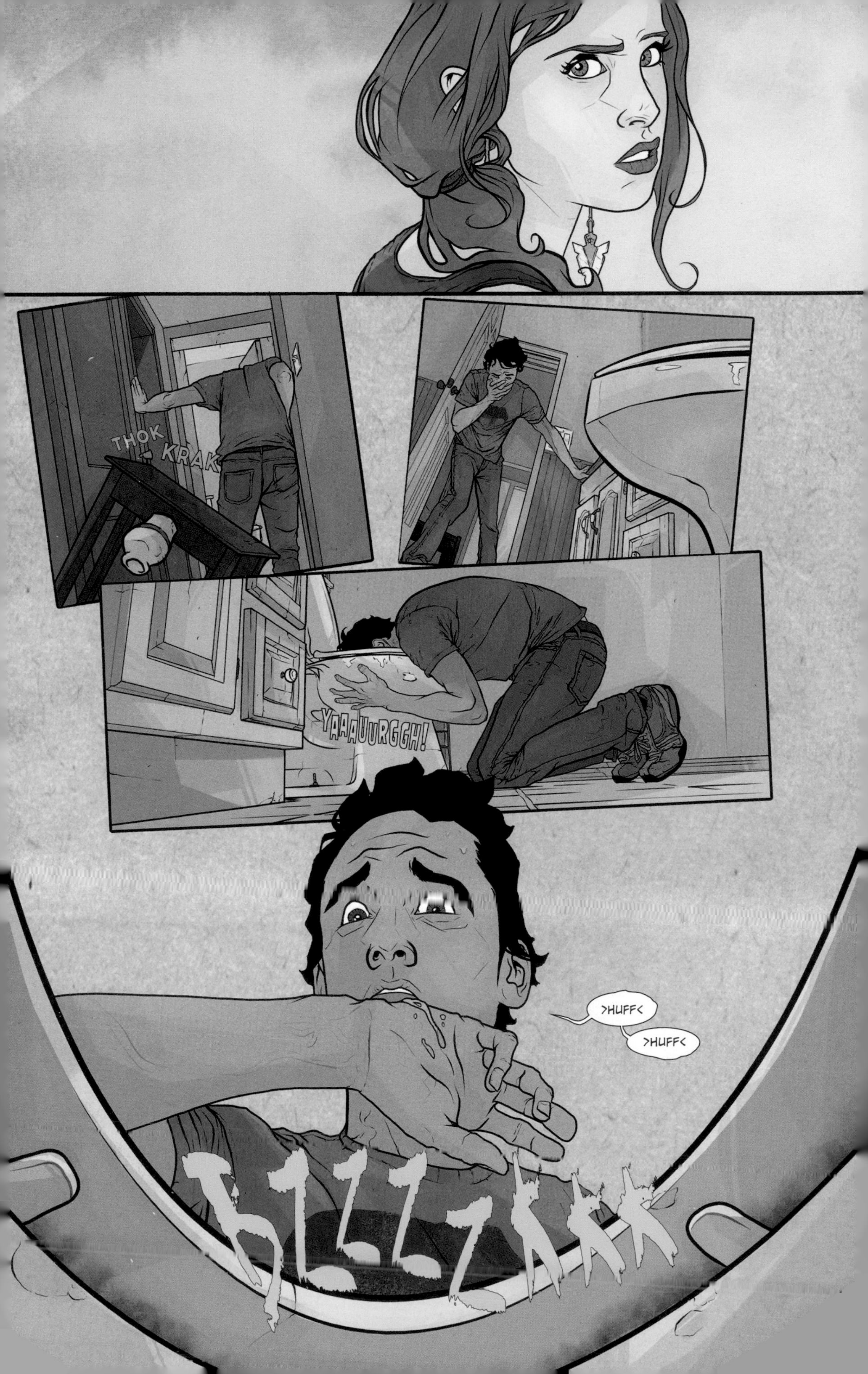
THOK
KRAK
YAAAUURGGH!
>HUFF<
>HUFF<
SHZZZKKK

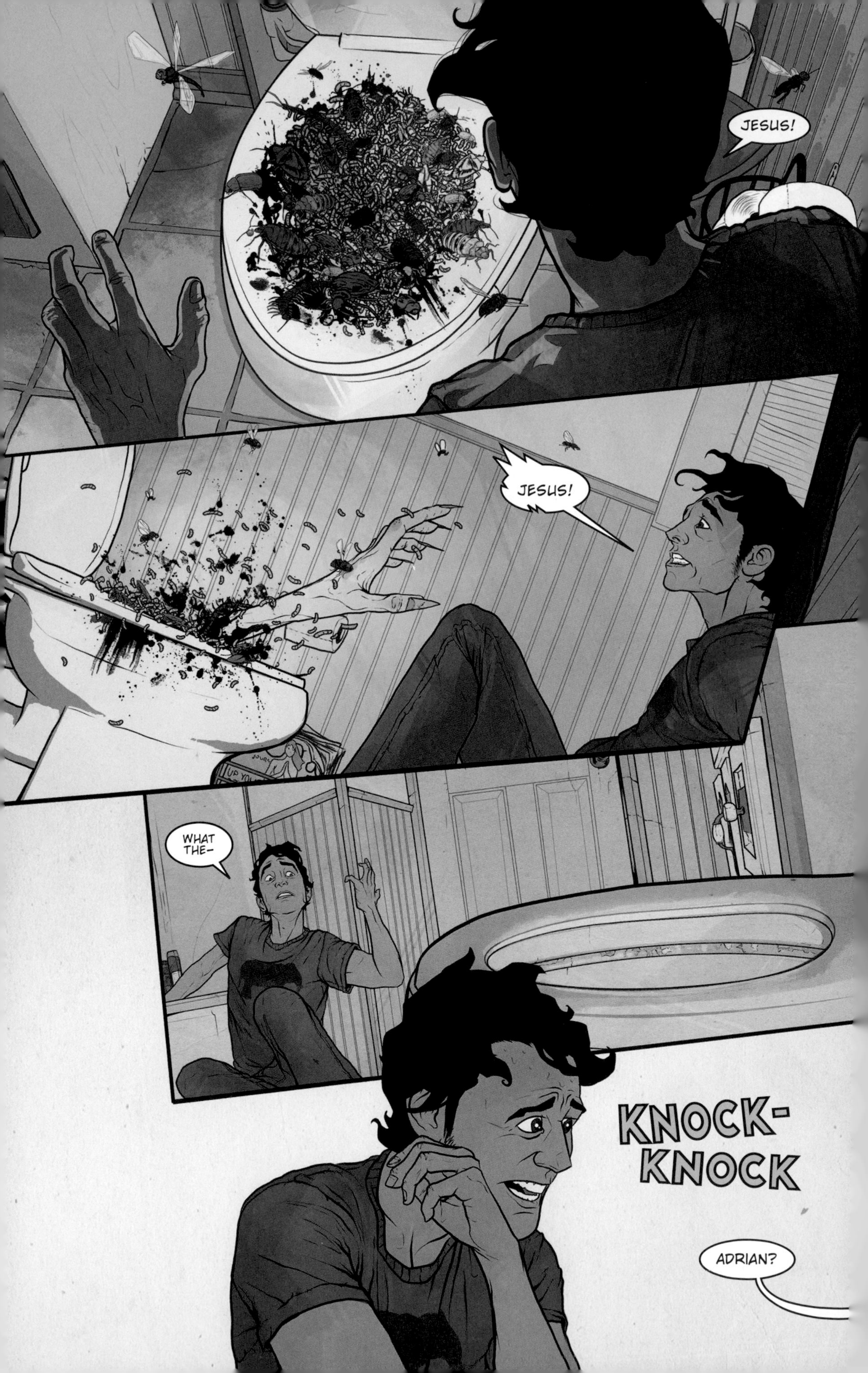
JESUS!
JESUS!
WHAT THE-
KNOCK-KNOCK
ADRIAN?

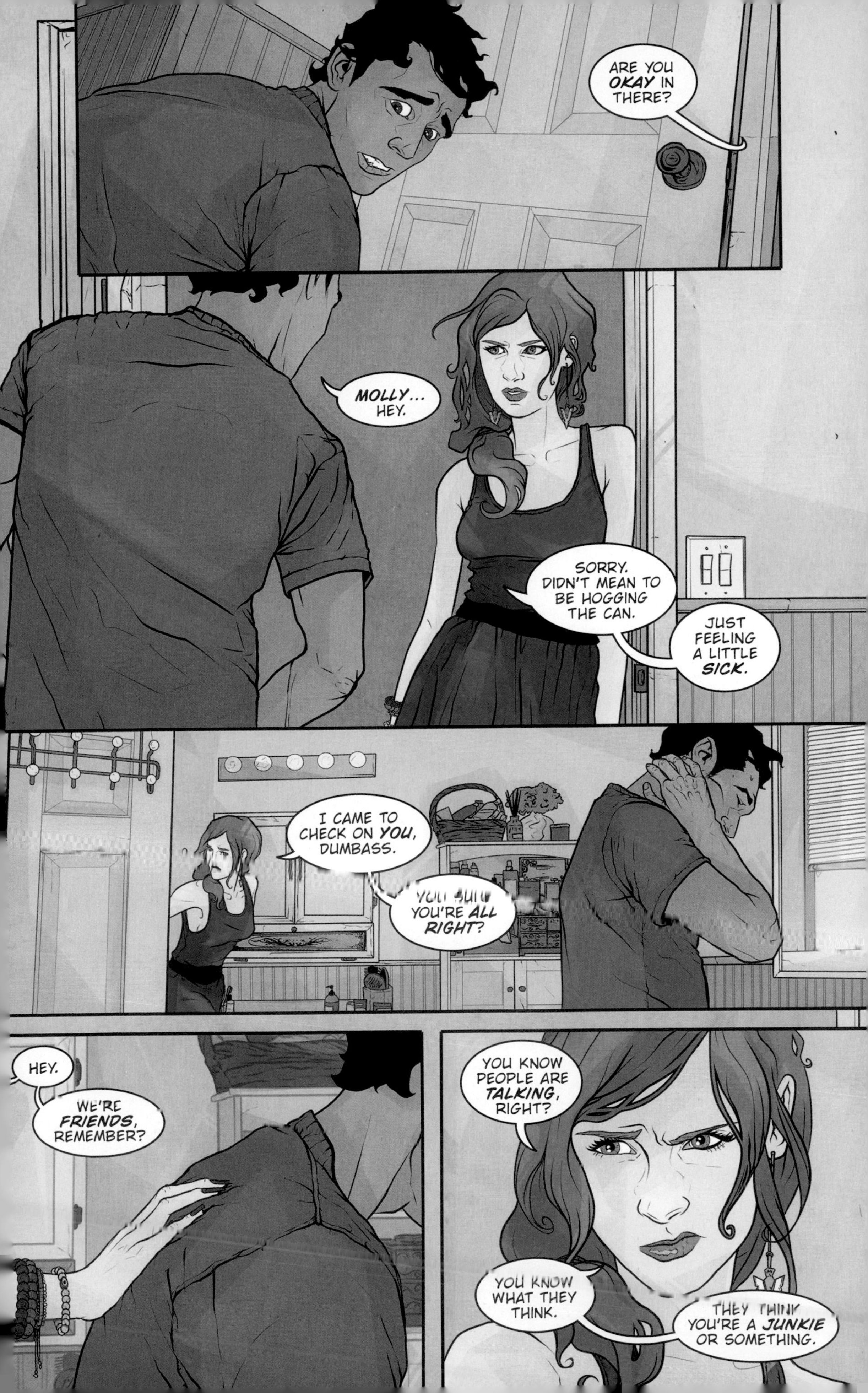
ARE YOU OKAY IN THERE?
MOLLY... HEY.
SORRY. DIDN'T MEAN TO BE HOGGING THE CAN.
JUST FEELING A LITTLE SICK.
I CAME TO CHECK ON YOU, DUMBASS.
YOU'RE ALL RIGHT?
HEY.
WE'RE FRIENDS, REMEMBER?
YOU KNOW PEOPLE ARE TALKING, RIGHT?
YOU KNOW WHAT THEY THINK.
THEY THINK YOU'RE A JUNKIE OR SOMETHING.

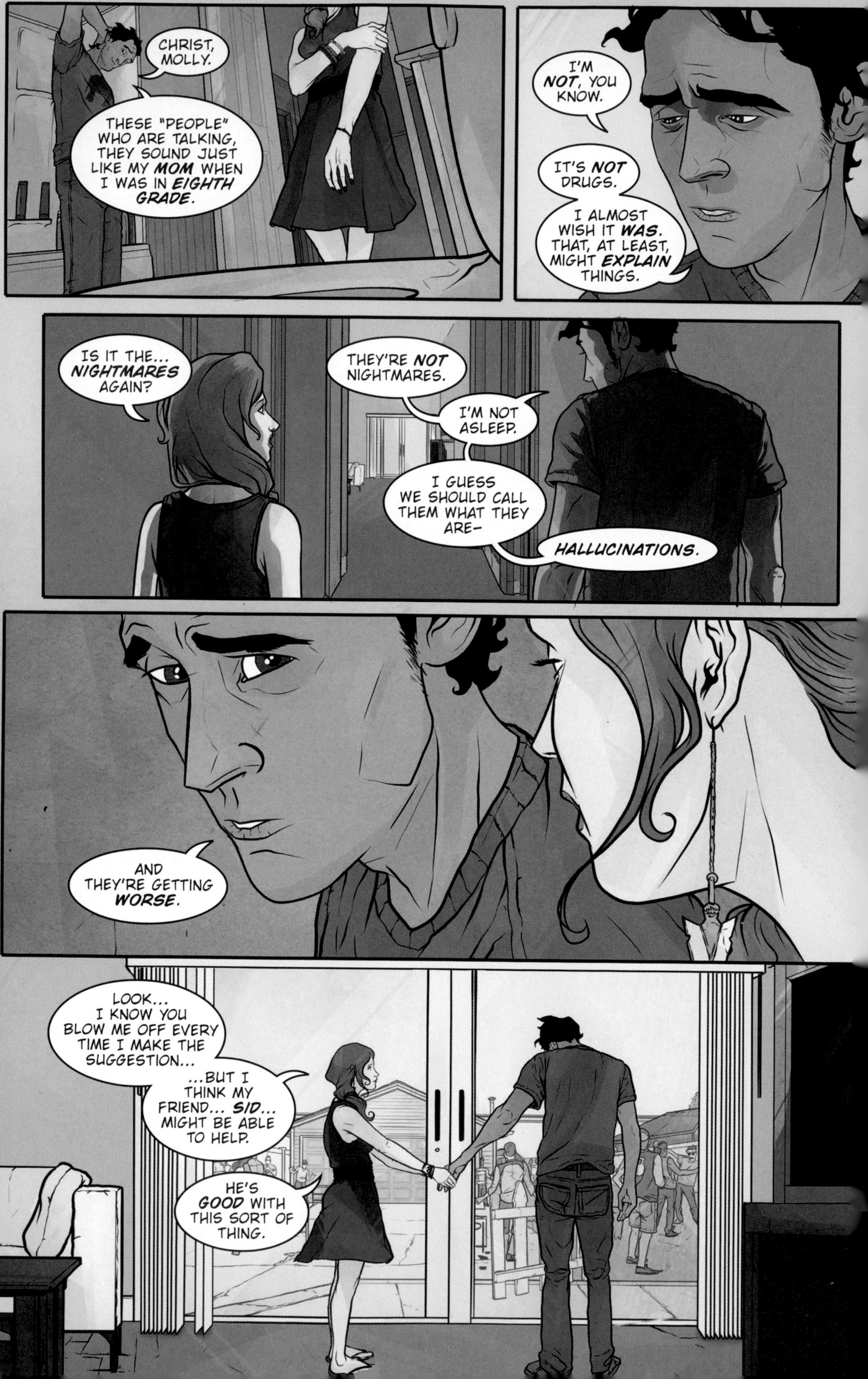
CHRIST, MOLLY.
THESE "PEOPLE" WHO ARE TALKING, THEY SOUND JUST LIKE MY MOM WHEN I WAS IN EIGHTH GRADE.
I'M NOT, YOU KNOW.
IT'S NOT DRUGS.
I ALMOST WISH IT WAS. THAT, AT LEAST, MIGHT EXPLAIN THINGS.
IS IT THE... NIGHTMARES AGAIN?
THEY'RE NOT NIGHTMARES.
I'M NOT ASLEEP.
I GUESS WE SHOULD CALL THEM WHAT THEY ARE-
HALLUCINATIONS.
AND THEY'RE GETTING WORSE.
LOOK... I KNOW YOU BLOW ME OFF EVERY TIME I MAKE THE SUGGESTION...
...BUT I THINK MY FRIEND... SID... MIGHT BE ABLE TO HELP.
HE'S GOOD WITH THIS SORT OF THING.

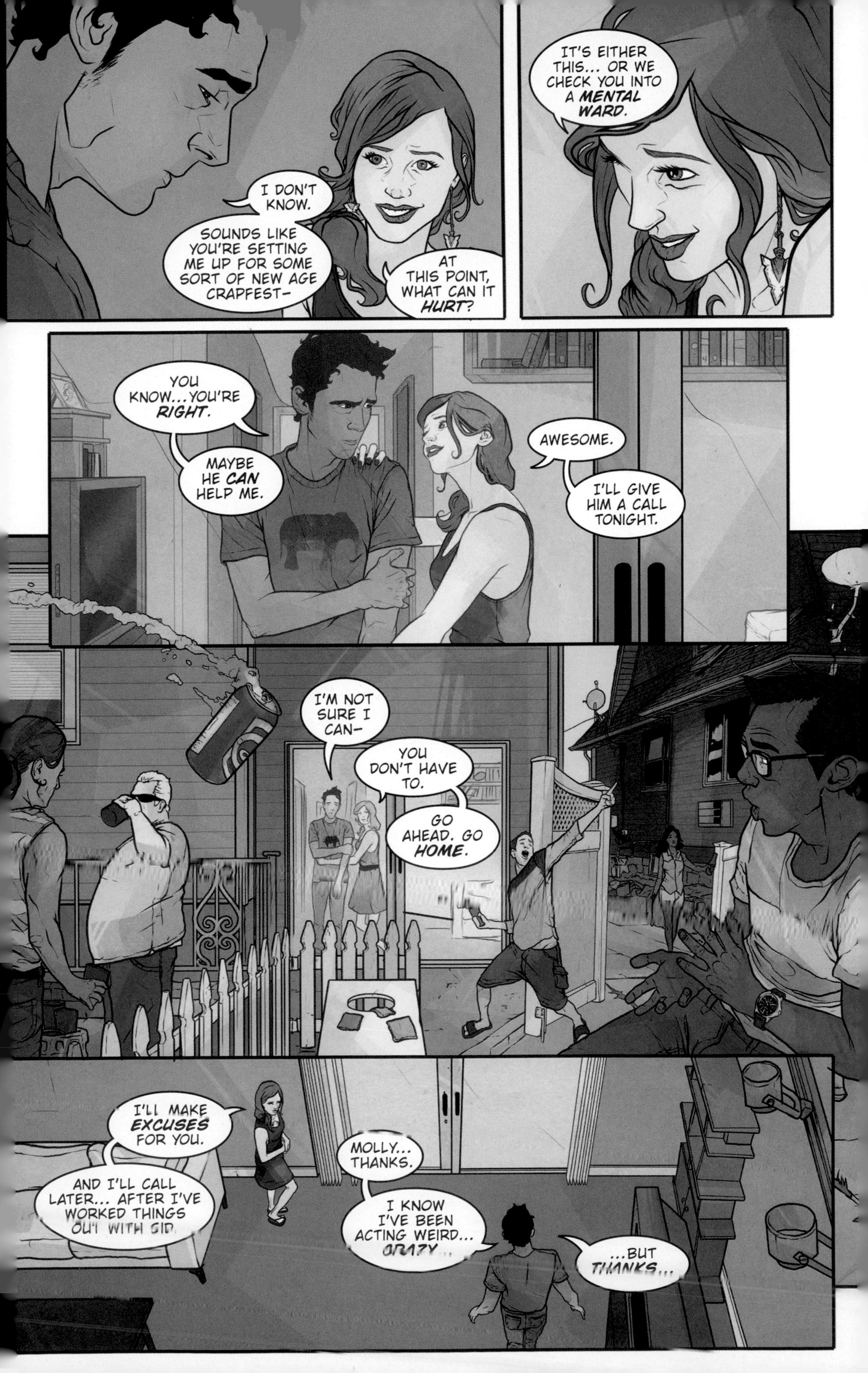
I DON'T KNOW.
SOUNDS LIKE YOU'RE SETTING ME UP FOR SOME SORT OF NEW AGE CRAPFEST-
AT THIS POINT, WHAT CAN IT *HURT*?
IT'S EITHER THIS... OR WE CHECK YOU INTO A *MENTAL WARD*.
YOU KNOW... YOU'RE *RIGHT*.
MAYBE HE *CAN* HELP ME.
AWESOME.
I'LL GIVE HIM A CALL TONIGHT.
I'M NOT SURE I CAN-
YOU DON'T HAVE TO.
GO AHEAD. GO *HOME*.
I'LL MAKE *EXCUSES* FOR YOU.
AND I'LL CALL LATER... AFTER I'VE WORKED THINGS OUT WITH SID.
MOLLY... THANKS.
I KNOW I'VE BEEN ACTING WEIRD... CRAZY...
...BUT *THANKS*...

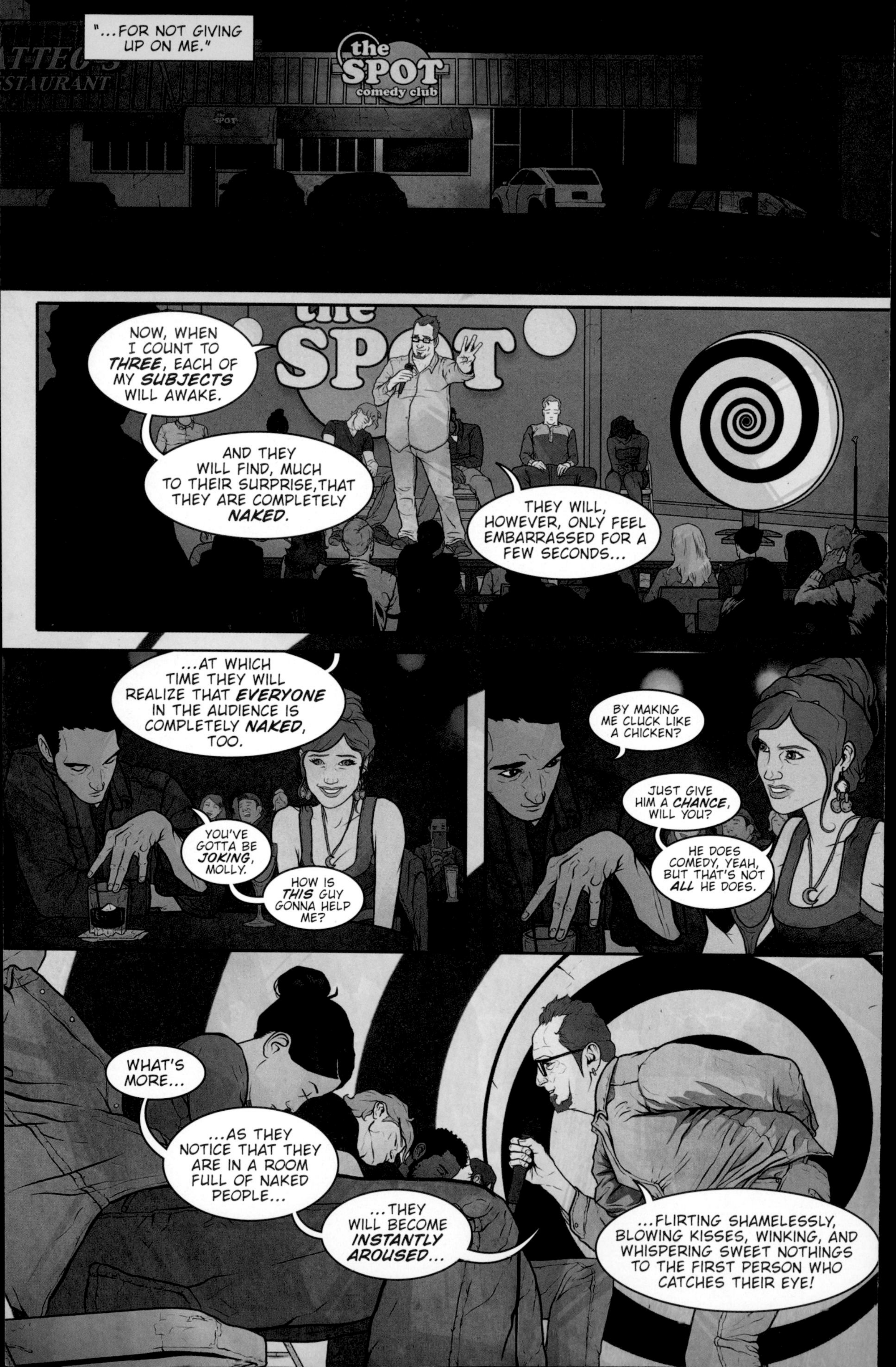
"...FOR NOT GIVING UP ON ME."
the SPOT comedy club
NOW, WHEN I COUNT TO THREE, EACH OF MY SUBJECTS WILL AWAKE.
AND THEY WILL FIND, MUCH TO THEIR SURPRISE, THAT THEY ARE COMPLETELY NAKED.
THEY WILL, HOWEVER, ONLY FEEL EMBARRASSED FOR A FEW SECONDS...
...AT WHICH TIME THEY WILL REALIZE THAT EVERYONE IN THE AUDIENCE IS COMPLETELY NAKED, TOO.
YOU'VE GOTTA BE JOKING, MOLLY.
HOW IS THIS GUY GONNA HELP ME?
BY MAKING ME CLUCK LIKE A CHICKEN?
JUST GIVE HIM A CHANCE, WILL YOU?
HE DOES COMEDY, YEAH, BUT THAT'S NOT ALL HE DOES.
WHAT'S MORE...
...AS THEY NOTICE THAT THEY ARE IN A ROOM FULL OF NAKED PEOPLE...
...THEY WILL BECOME INSTANTLY AROUSED...
...FLIRTING SHAMELESSLY, BLOWING KISSES, WINKING, AND WHISPERING SWEET NOTHINGS TO THE FIRST PERSON WHO CATCHES THEIR EYE!

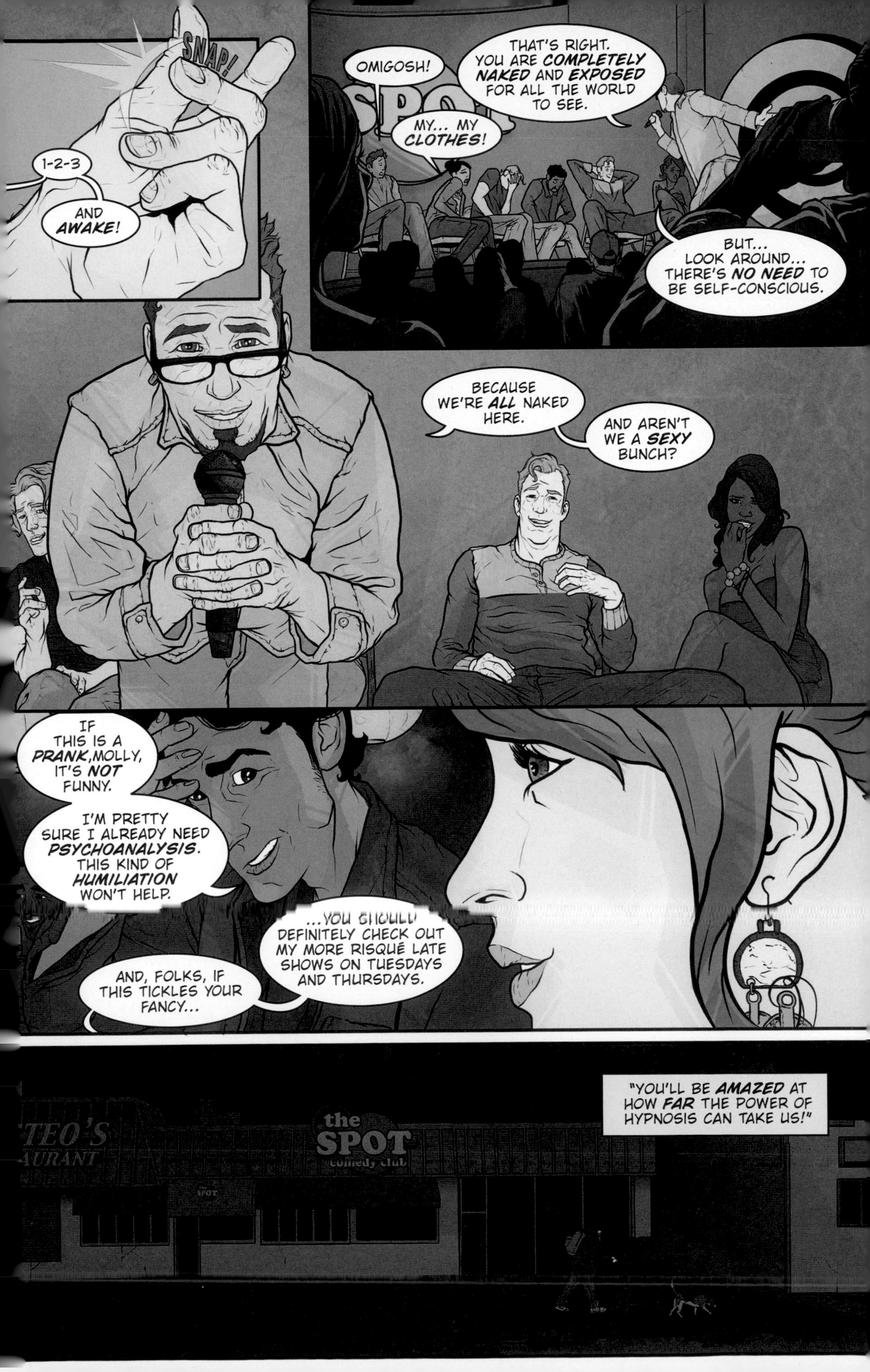
SNAP!
1-2-3
AND AWAKE!
OMIGOSH!
THAT'S RIGHT. YOU ARE COMPLETELY NAKED AND EXPOSED FOR ALL THE WORLD TO SEE.
MY... MY CLOTHES!
BUT... LOOK AROUND... THERE'S NO NEED TO BE SELF-CONSCIOUS.
BECAUSE WE'RE ALL NAKED HERE.
AND AREN'T WE A SEXY BUNCH?
IF THIS IS A PRANK, MOLLY, IT'S NOT FUNNY.
I'M PRETTY SURE I ALREADY NEED PSYCHOANALYSIS. THIS KIND OF HUMILIATION WON'T HELP.
AND, FOLKS, IF THIS TICKLES YOUR FANCY...
...YOU SHOULD DEFINITELY CHECK OUT MY MORE RISQUÉ LATE SHOWS ON TUESDAYS AND THURSDAYS.
the SPOT comedy club
"YOU'LL BE AMAZED AT HOW FAR THE POWER OF HYPNOSIS CAN TAKE US!"

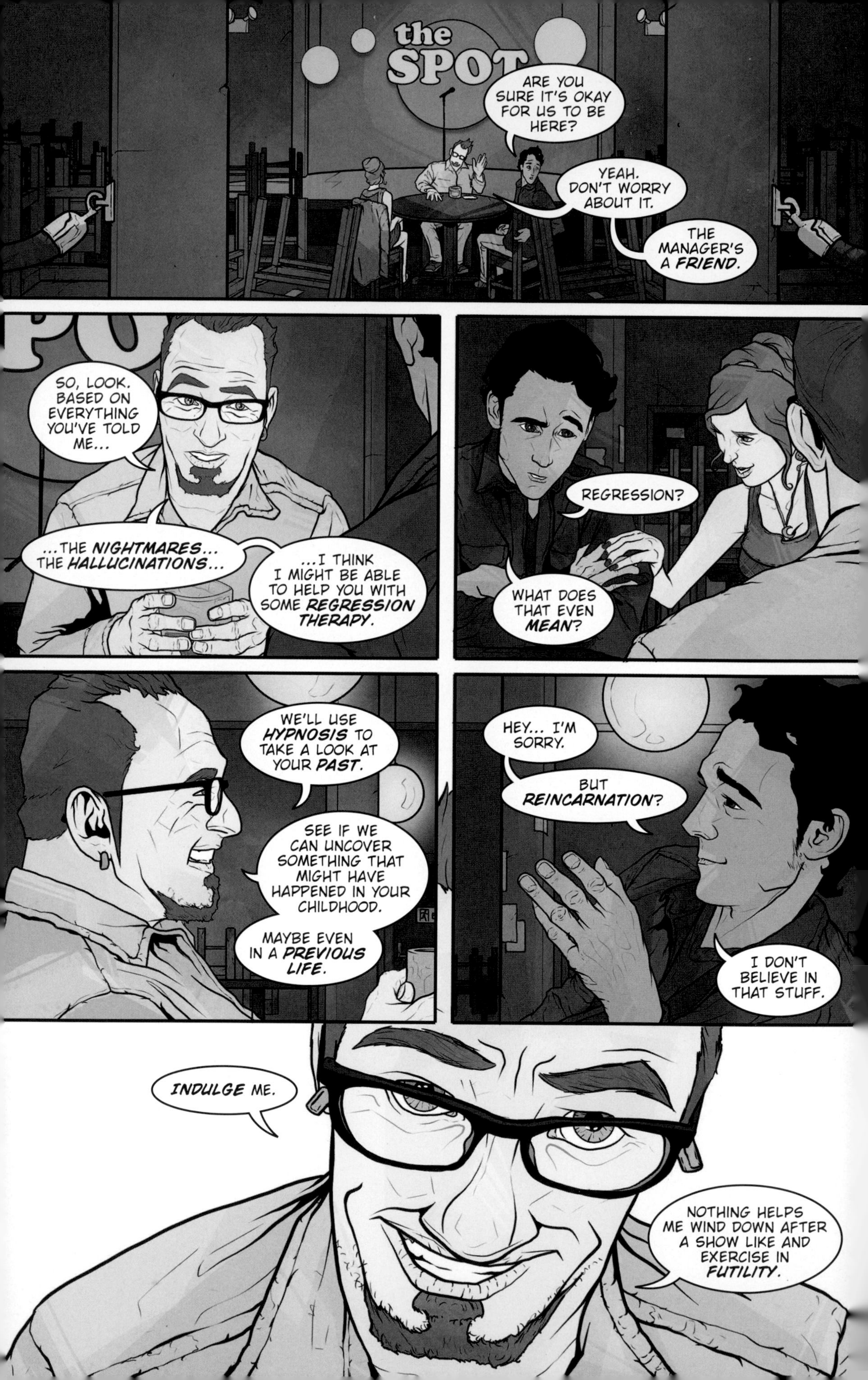
the SPOT
ARE YOU SURE IT'S OKAY FOR US TO BE HERE?
YEAH. DON'T WORRY ABOUT IT.
THE MANAGER'S A FRIEND.
SO, LOOK. BASED ON EVERYTHING YOU'VE TOLD ME...
...THE NIGHTMARES... THE HALLUCINATIONS...
...I THINK I MIGHT BE ABLE TO HELP YOU WITH SOME REGRESSION THERAPY.
REGRESSION?
WHAT DOES THAT EVEN MEAN?
WE'LL USE HYPNOSIS TO TAKE A LOOK AT YOUR PAST.
SEE IF WE CAN UNCOVER SOMETHING THAT MIGHT HAVE HAPPENED IN YOUR CHILDHOOD.
MAYBE EVEN IN A PREVIOUS LIFE.
HEY... I'M SORRY.
BUT REINCARNATION?
I DON'T BELIEVE IN THAT STUFF.
INDULGE ME.
NOTHING HELPS ME WIND DOWN AFTER A SHOW LIKE AND EXERCISE IN FUTILITY.

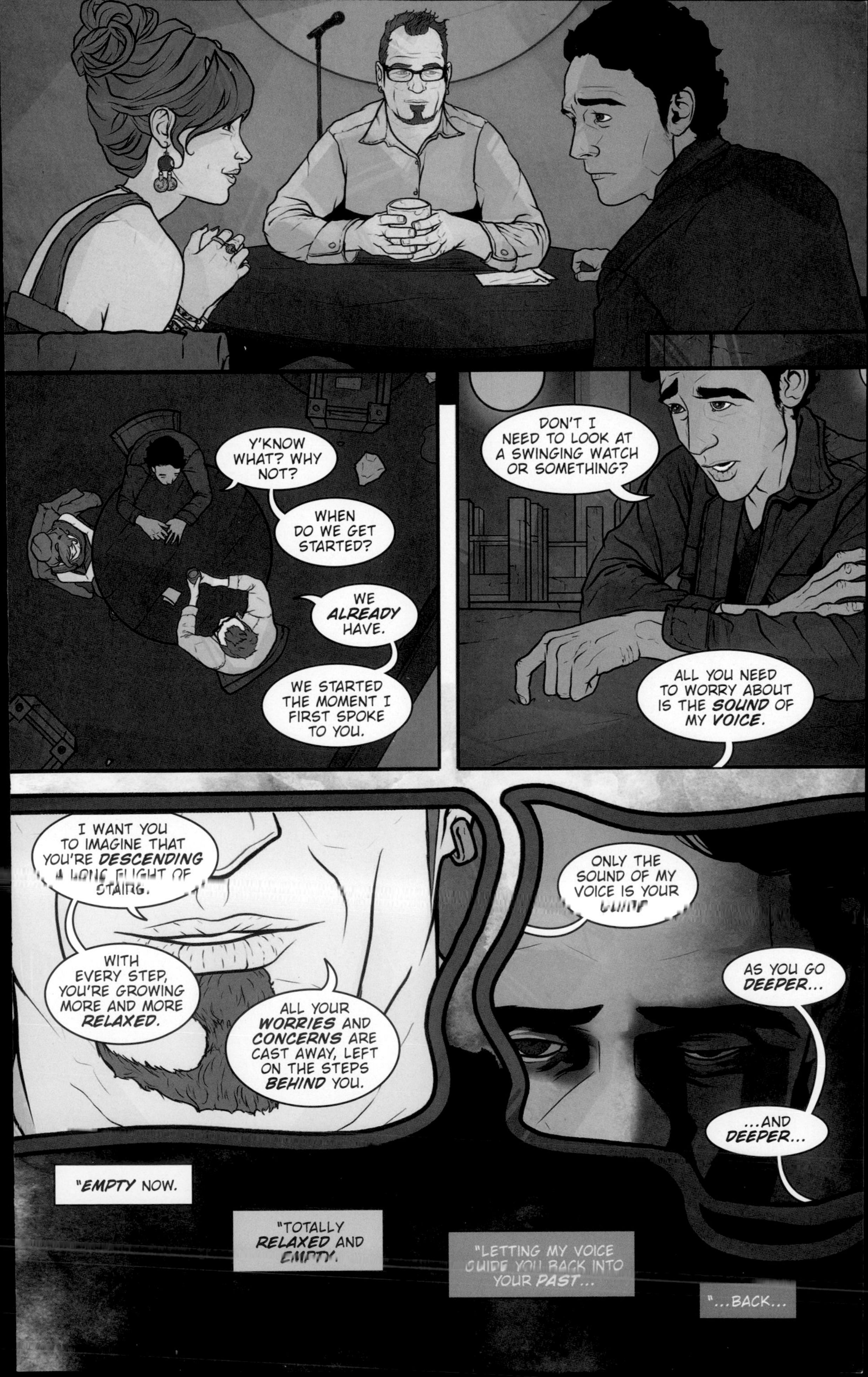
Y'KNOW WHAT? WHY NOT?
WHEN DO WE GET STARTED?
WE *ALREADY* HAVE.
WE STARTED THE MOMENT I FIRST SPOKE TO YOU.
DON'T I NEED TO LOOK AT A SWINGING WATCH OR SOMETHING?
ALL YOU NEED TO WORRY ABOUT IS THE *SOUND* OF MY *VOICE*.
I WANT YOU TO IMAGINE THAT YOU'RE *DESCENDING* A LONG FLIGHT OF STAIRS.
WITH EVERY STEP, YOU'RE GROWING MORE AND MORE *RELAXED*.
ALL YOUR *WORRIES* AND *CONCERNS* ARE CAST AWAY, LEFT ON THE STEPS *BEHIND* YOU.
ONLY THE SOUND OF MY VOICE IS YOUR
AS YOU GO *DEEPER*...
...AND *DEEPER*...
"*EMPTY* NOW.
"TOTALLY *RELAXED* AND *EMPTY*.
"LETTING MY VOICE GUIDE YOU BACK INTO YOUR *PAST*...
"...BACK...

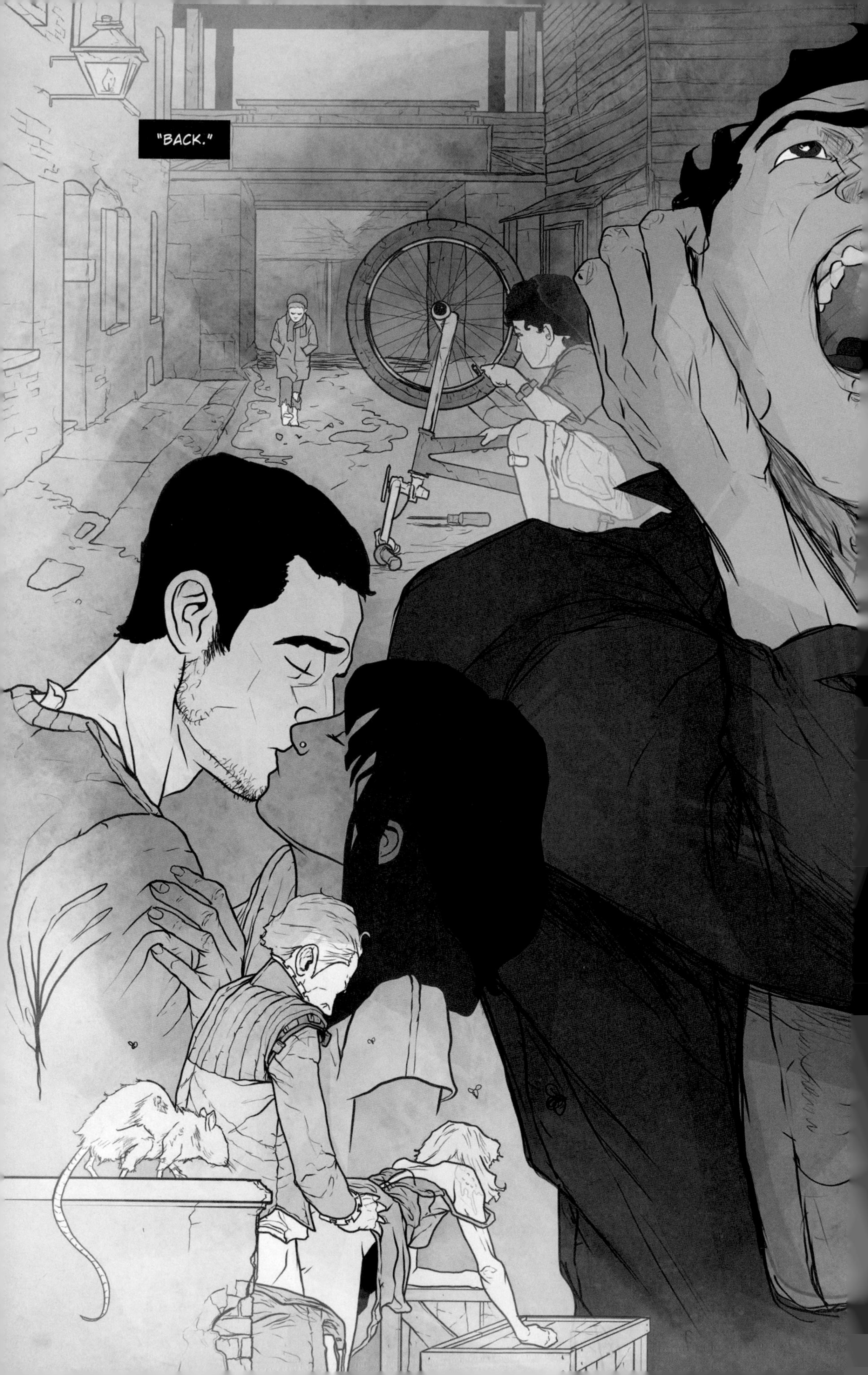
"BACK."

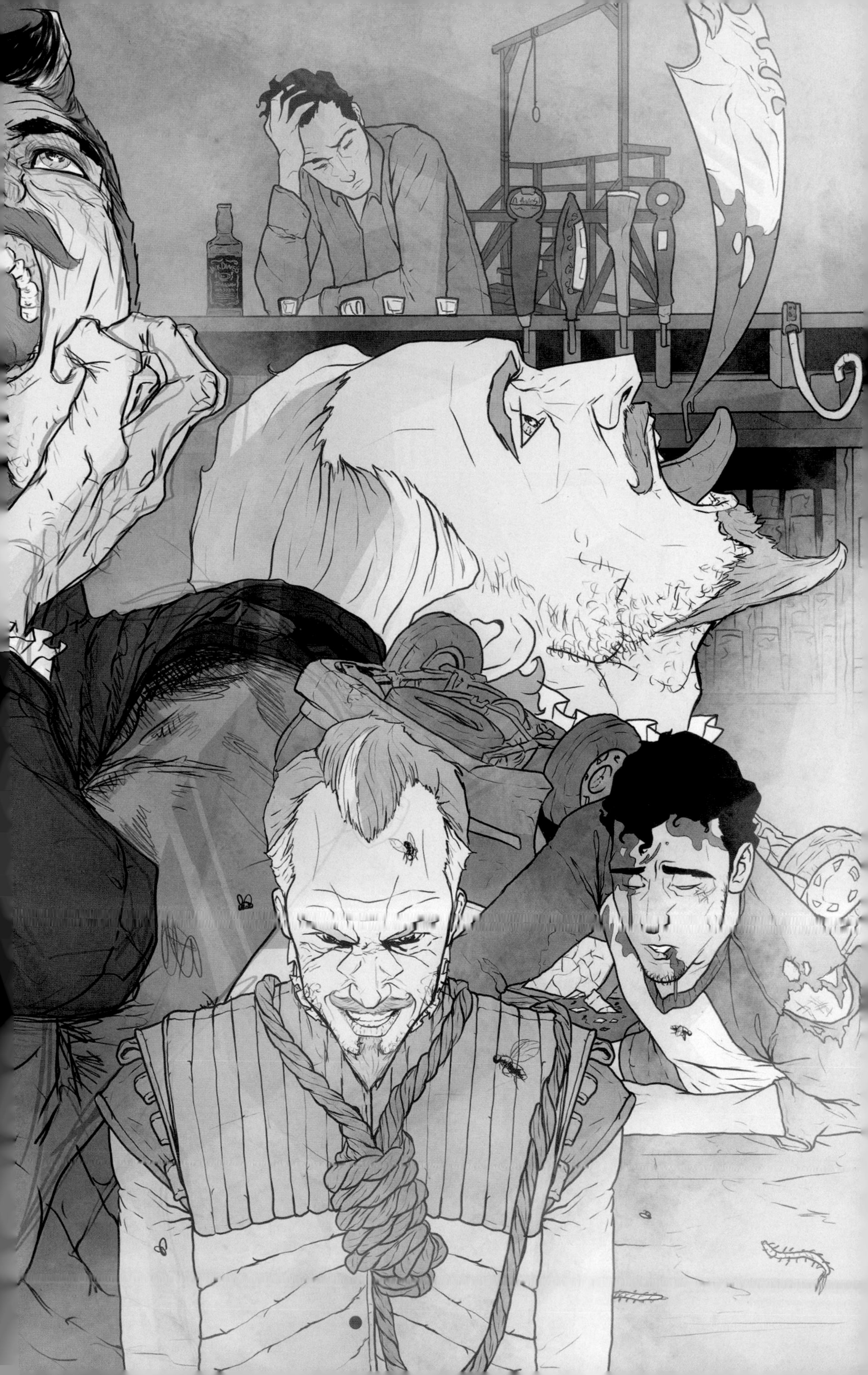

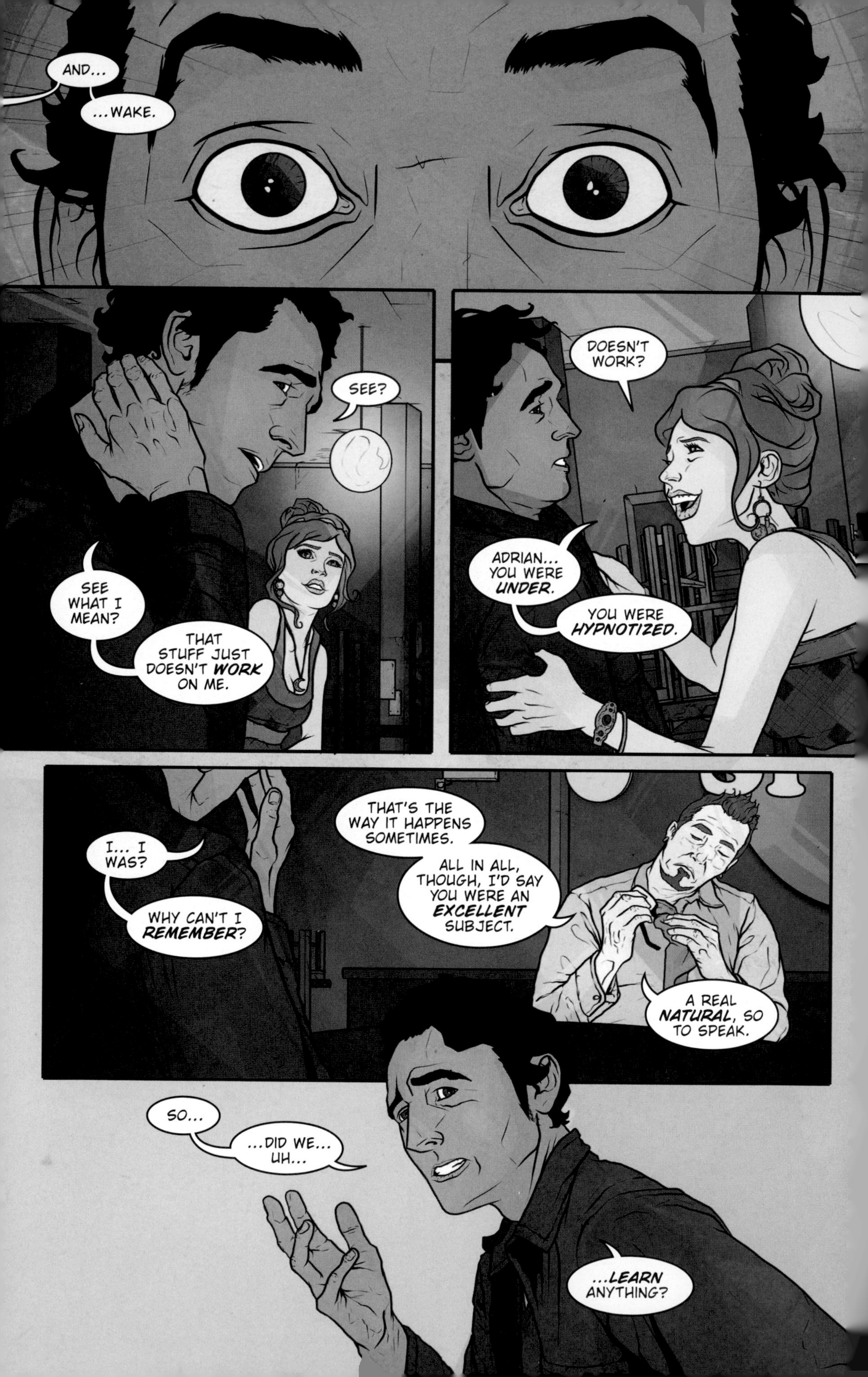
AND...
...WAKE.
SEE?
SEE WHAT I MEAN?
THAT STUFF JUST DOESN'T **WORK** ON ME.
DOESN'T WORK?
ADRIAN... YOU WERE **UNDER**.
YOU WERE **HYPNOTIZED**.
I... I WAS?
WHY CAN'T I **REMEMBER**?
THAT'S THE WAY IT HAPPENS SOMETIMES.
ALL IN ALL, THOUGH, I'D SAY YOU WERE AN **EXCELLENT** SUBJECT.
A REAL **NATURAL**, SO TO SPEAK.
SO...
...DID WE... UH...
...**LEARN** ANYTHING?

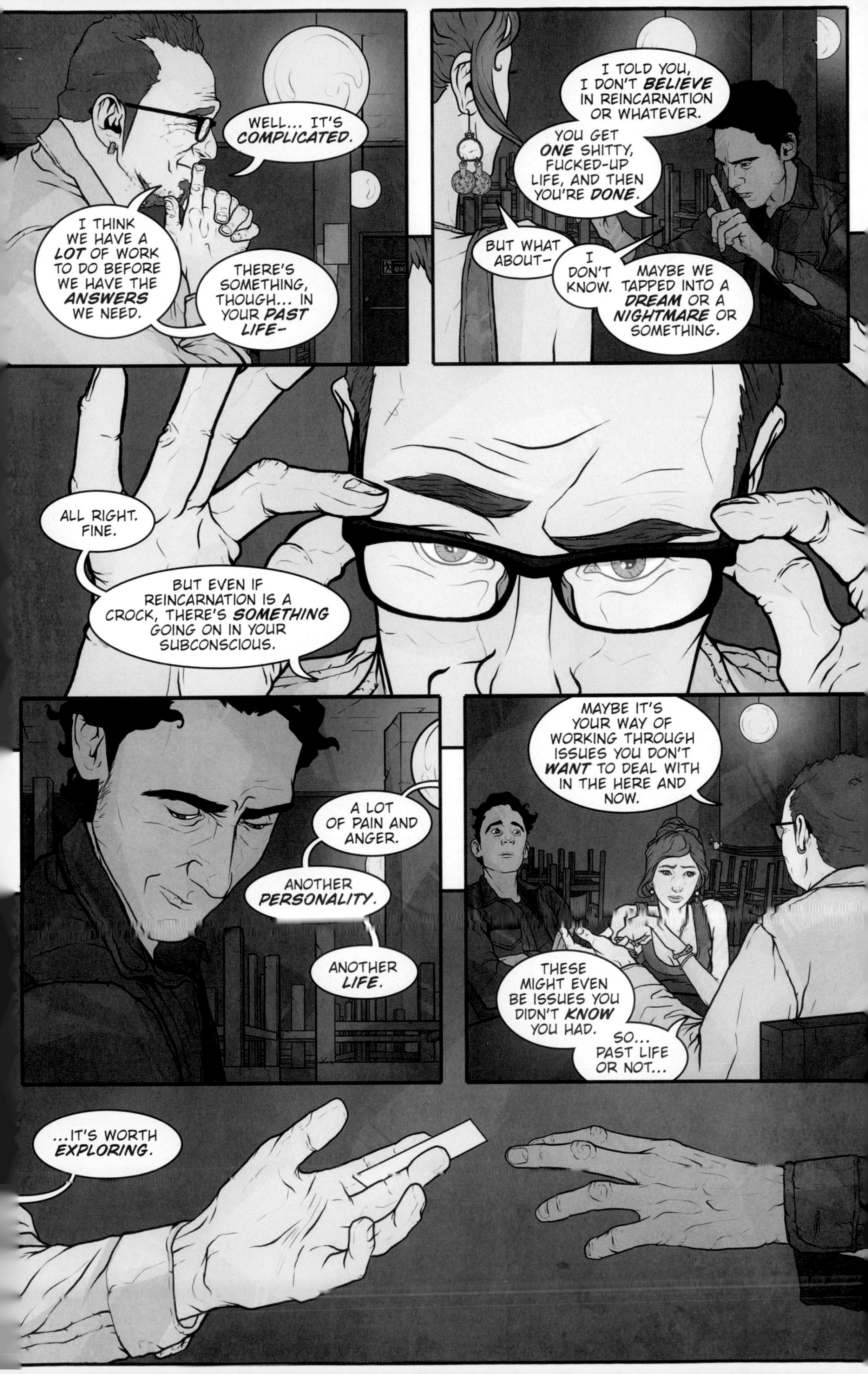
WELL... IT'S COMPLICATED.
I THINK WE HAVE A LOT OF WORK TO DO BEFORE WE HAVE THE ANSWERS WE NEED.
THERE'S SOMETHING, THOUGH... IN YOUR PAST LIFE-
I TOLD YOU, I DON'T BELIEVE IN REINCARNATION OR WHATEVER.
YOU GET ONE SHITTY, FUCKED-UP LIFE, AND THEN YOU'RE DONE.
BUT WHAT ABOUT-
I DON'T KNOW.
MAYBE WE TAPPED INTO A DREAM OR A NIGHTMARE OR SOMETHING.
ALL RIGHT. FINE.
BUT EVEN IF REINCARNATION IS A CROCK, THERE'S SOMETHING GOING ON IN YOUR SUBCONSCIOUS.
A LOT OF PAIN AND ANGER.
ANOTHER PERSONALITY.
ANOTHER LIFE.
MAYBE IT'S YOUR WAY OF WORKING THROUGH ISSUES YOU DON'T WANT TO DEAL WITH IN THE HERE AND NOW.
THESE MIGHT EVEN BE ISSUES YOU DIDN'T KNOW YOU HAD.
SO... PAST LIFE OR NOT...
...IT'S WORTH EXPLORING.

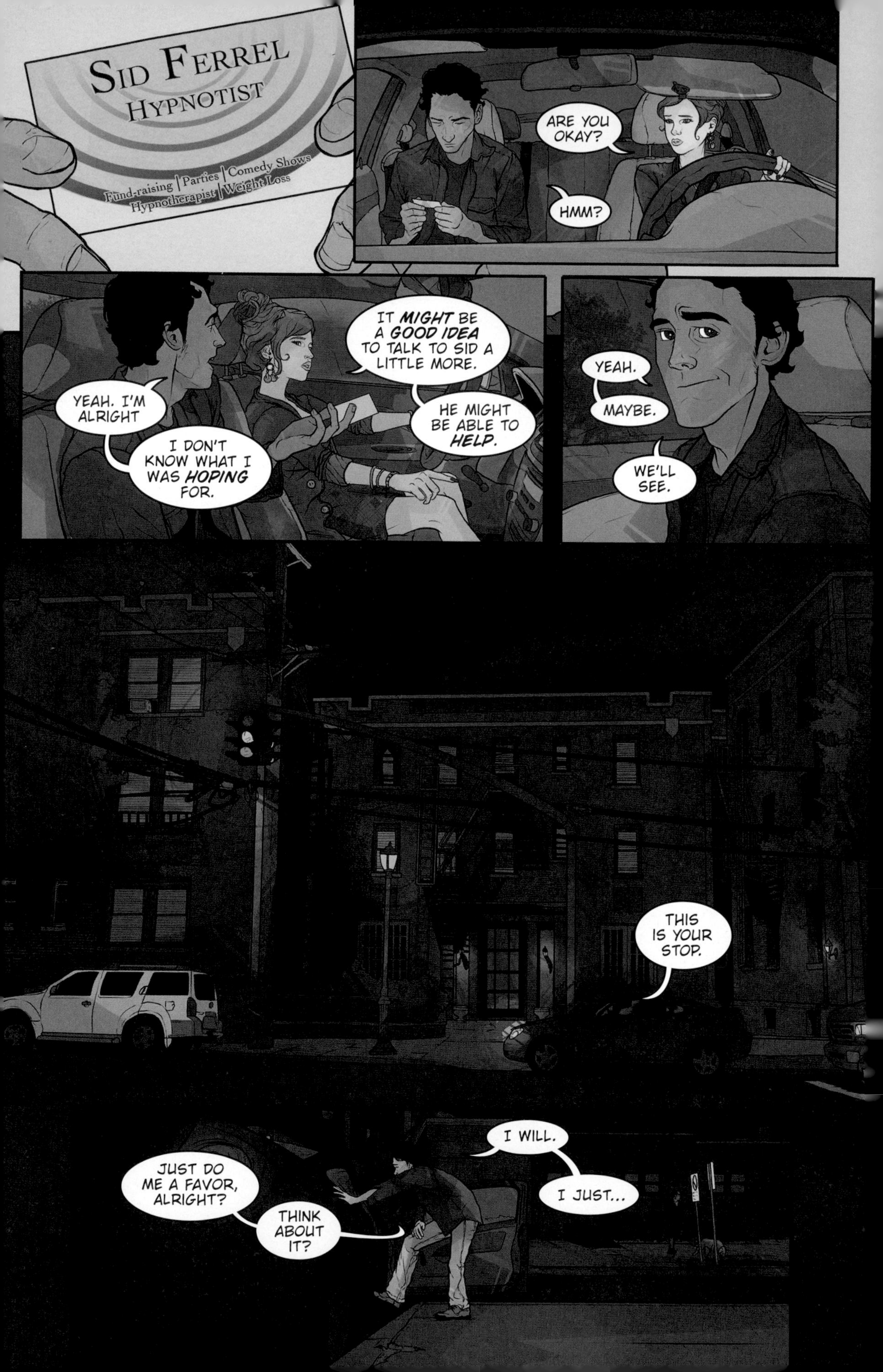
SID FERREL
HYPNOTIST
Fund-raising | Parties | Comedy Shows
Hypnotherapist | Weight Loss
ARE YOU OKAY?
HMM?
YEAH. I'M ALRIGHT
I DON'T KNOW WHAT I WAS HOPING FOR.
IT MIGHT BE A GOOD IDEA TO TALK TO SID A LITTLE MORE.
HE MIGHT BE ABLE TO HELP.
YEAH.
MAYBE.
WE'LL SEE.
THIS IS YOUR STOP.
JUST DO ME A FAVOR, ALRIGHT?
THINK ABOUT IT?
I WILL.
I JUST...

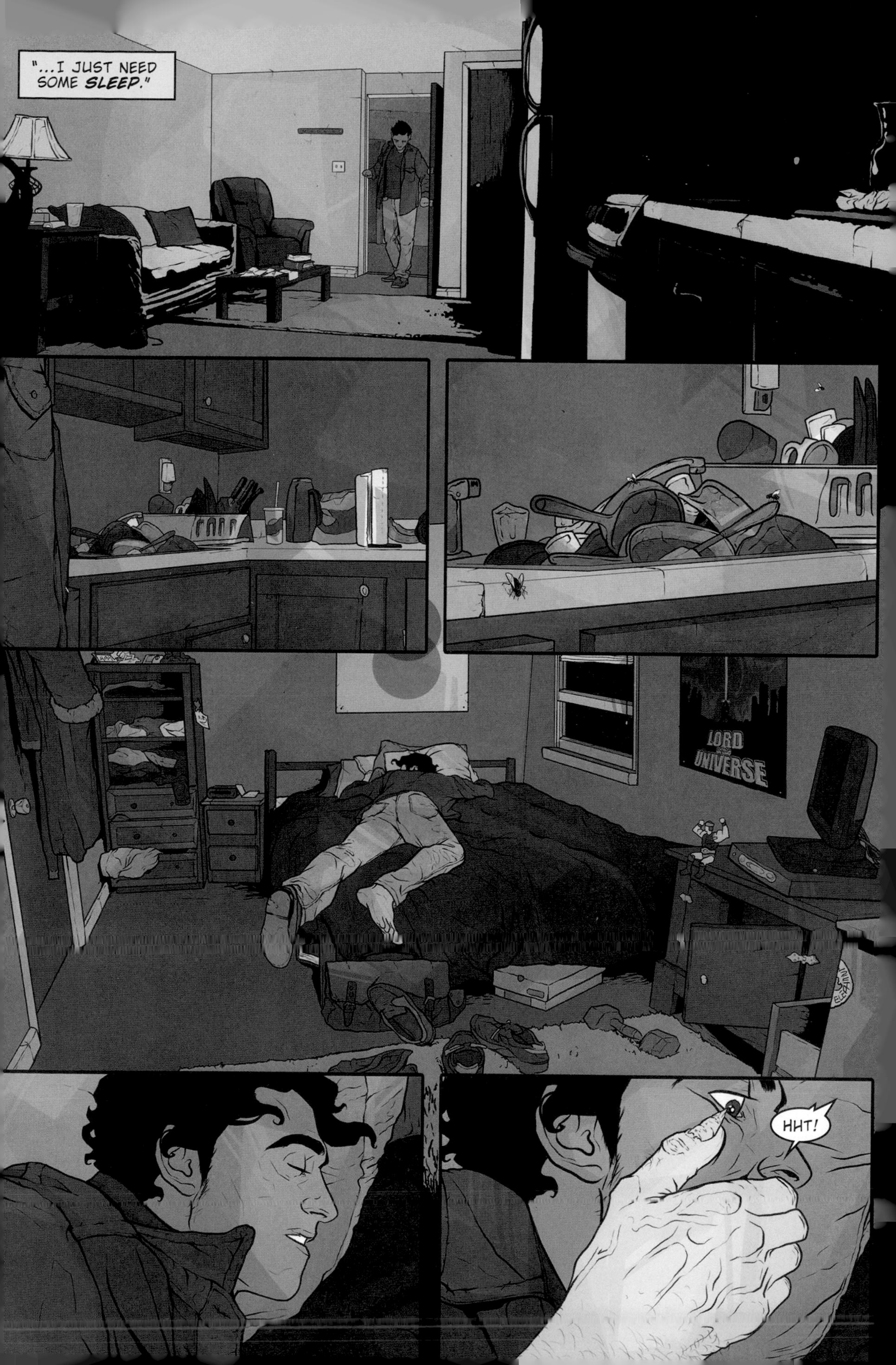
"...I JUST NEED SOME SLEEP."
LORD UNIVERSE
HHT!

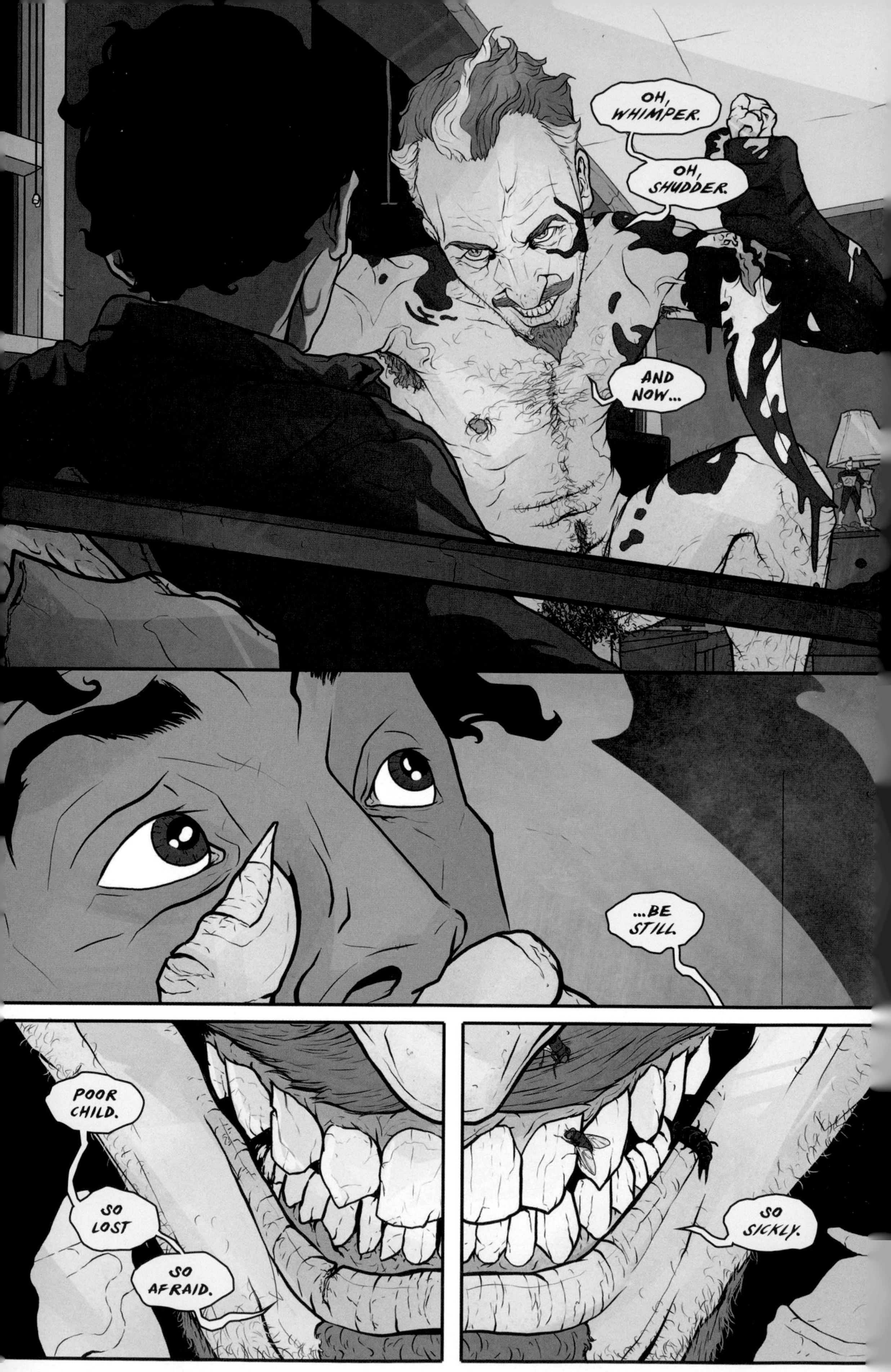
OH, WHIMPER.
OH, SHUDDER.
AND NOW...
...BE STILL.
POOR CHILD.
SO LOST
SO AFRAID.
SO SICKLY.

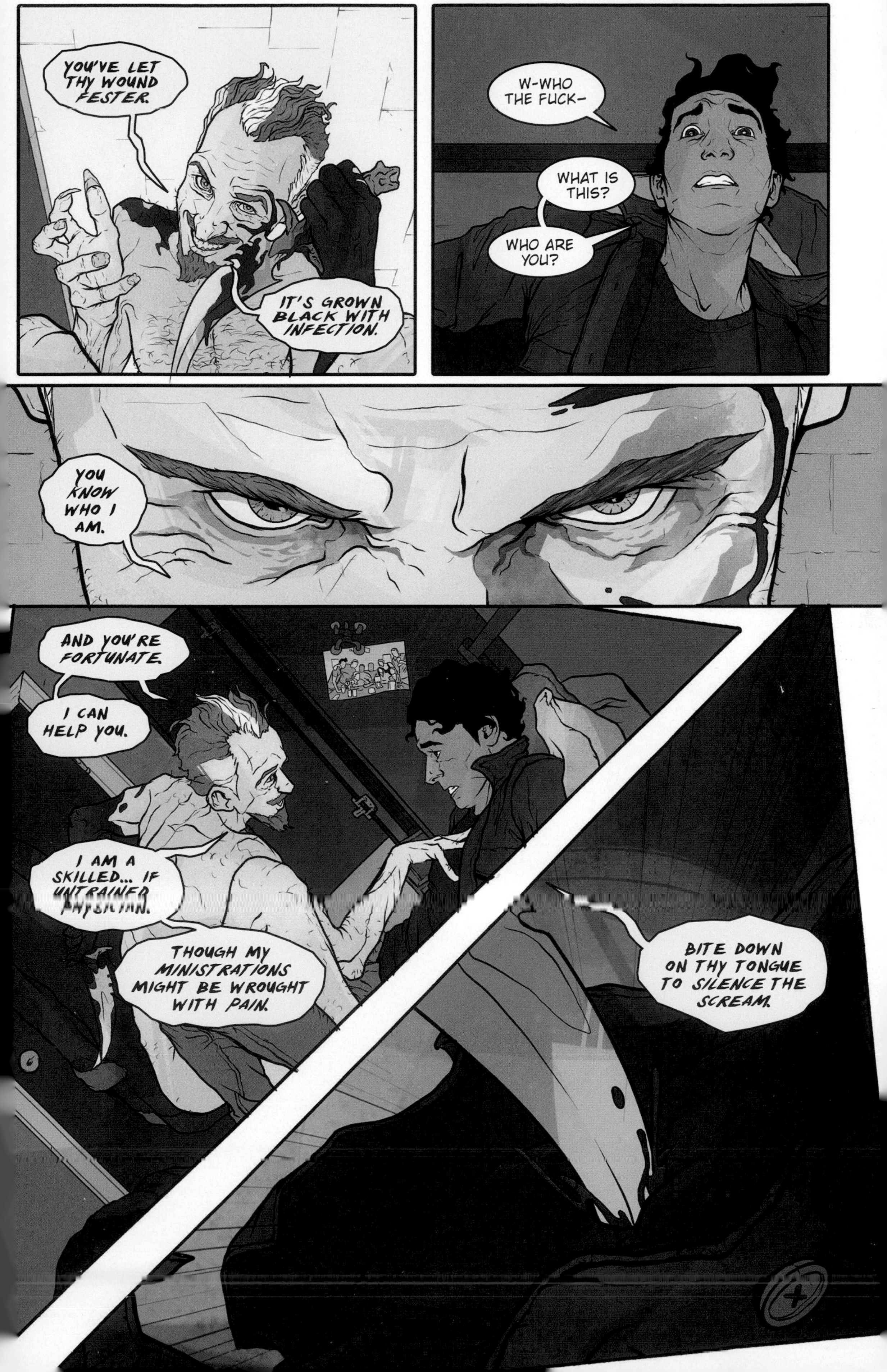
YOU'VE LET THY WOUND FESTER.
IT'S GROWN BLACK WITH INFECTION.
W-WHO THE FUCK-
WHAT IS THIS?
WHO ARE YOU?
YOU KNOW WHO I AM.
AND YOU'RE FORTUNATE.
I CAN HELP YOU.
I AM A SKILLED... IF UNTRAINED PHYSICIAN.
THOUGH MY MINISTRATIONS MIGHT BE WROUGHT WITH PAIN.
BITE DOWN ON THY TONGUE TO SILENCE THE SCREAM.

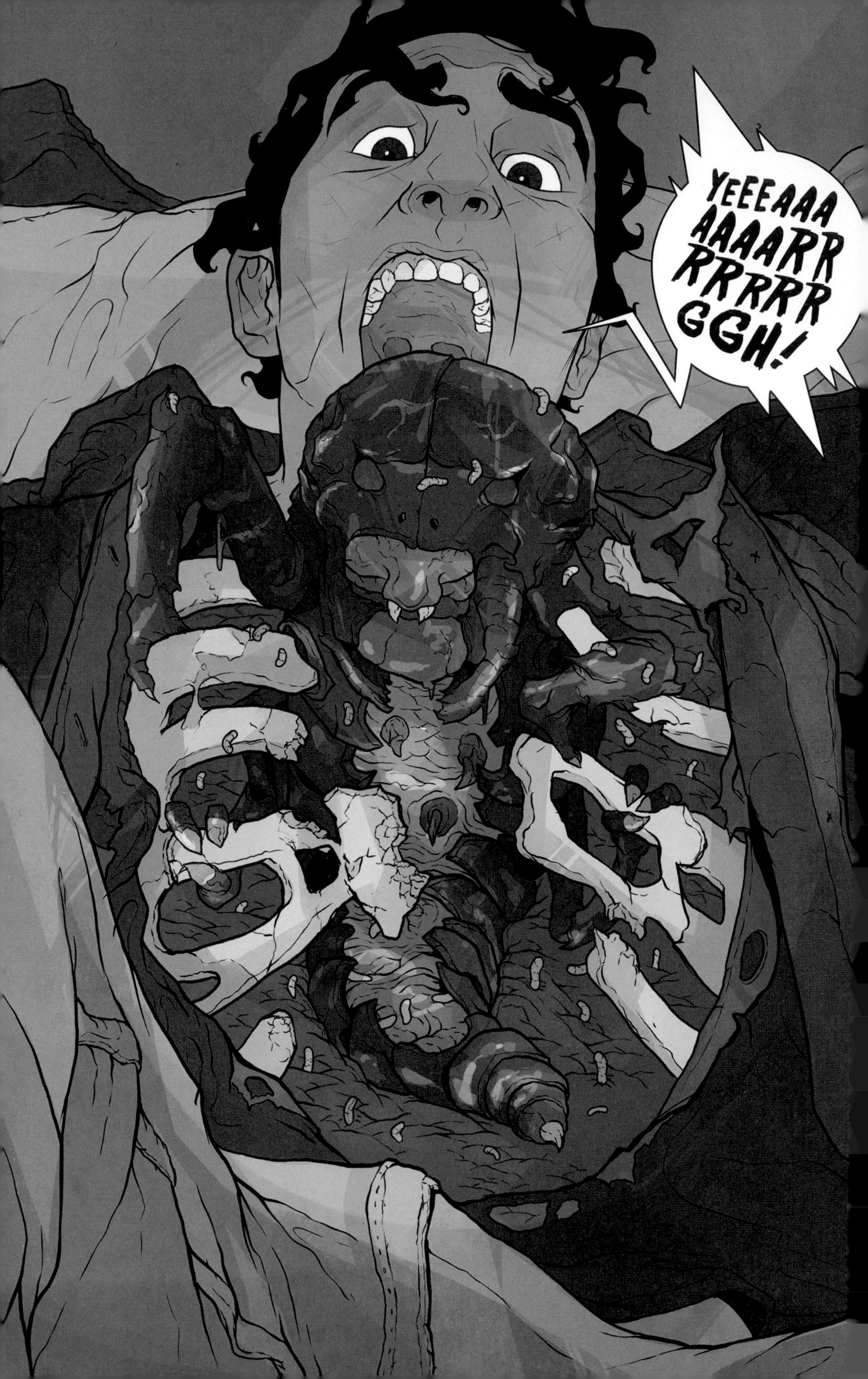
YEEEAAA AAAARR RRRRR GGH!

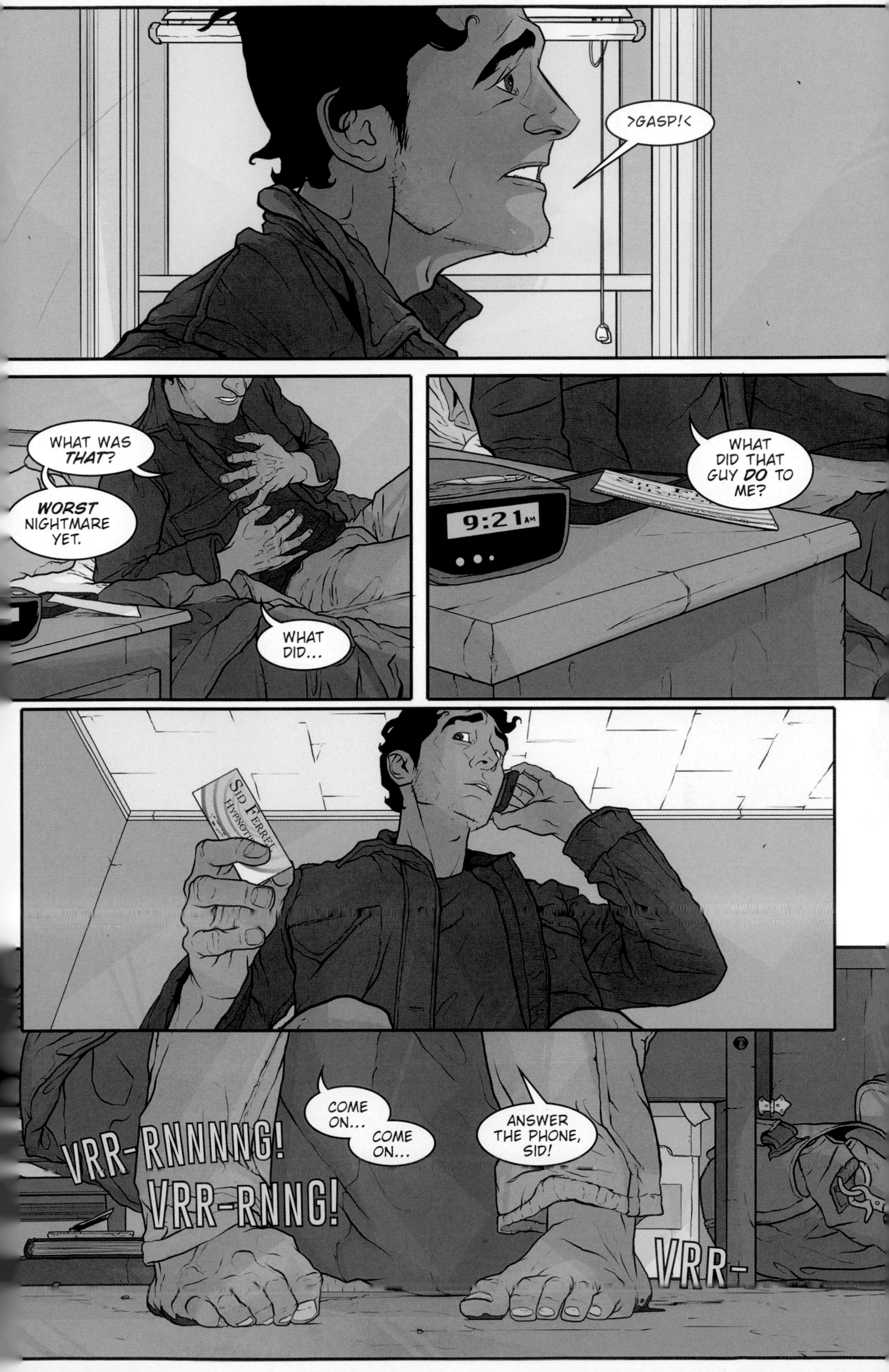
>GASP!<
WHAT WAS THAT?
WORST NIGHTMARE YET.
WHAT DID...
WHAT DID THAT GUY DO TO ME?
9:21 AM
SID FERREL HYPNOTI
VRR-RNNNNG!
VRR-RNNG!
COME ON...
COME ON...
ANSWER THE PHONE, SID!
VRR-

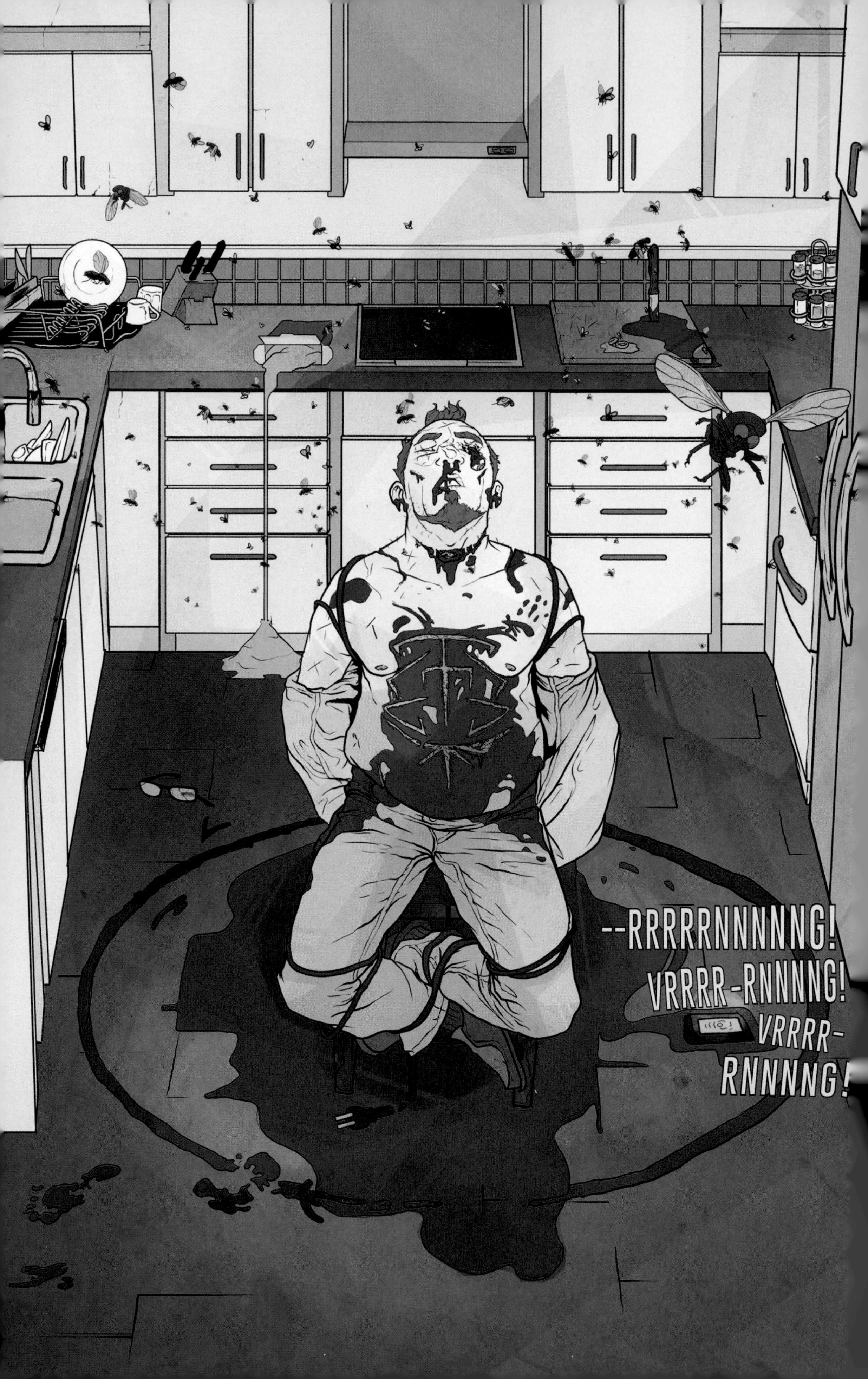
--RRRRRNNNNNG!
VRRRR-RNNNNG!
VRRRR-
RNNNNG!

TWO

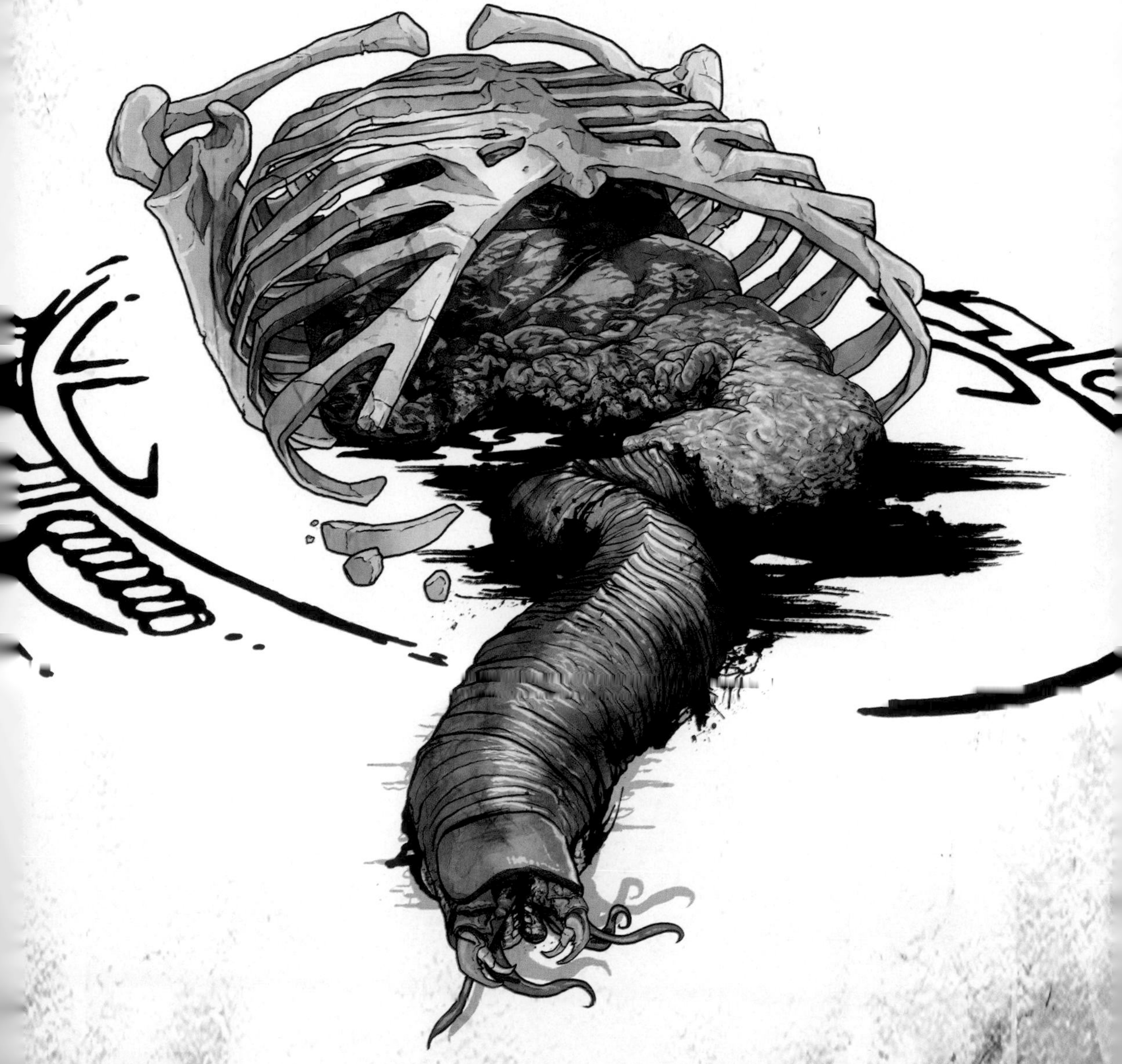

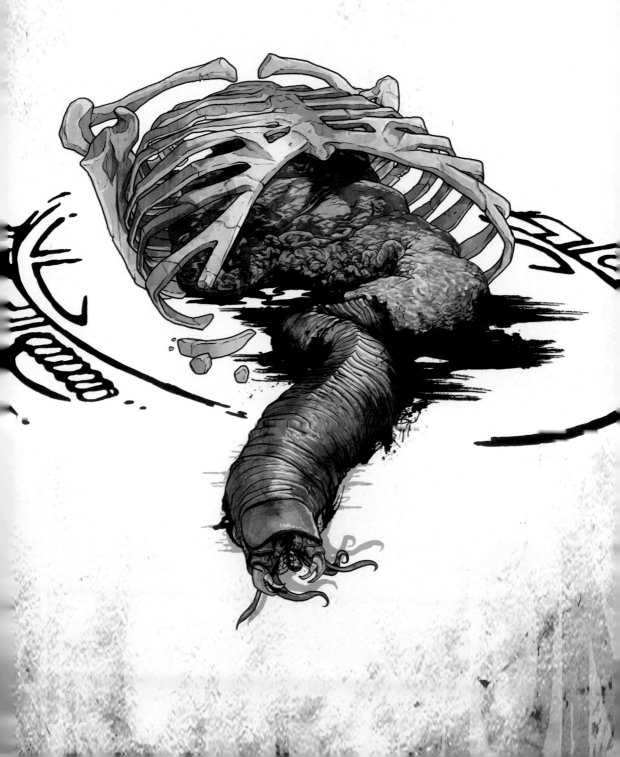

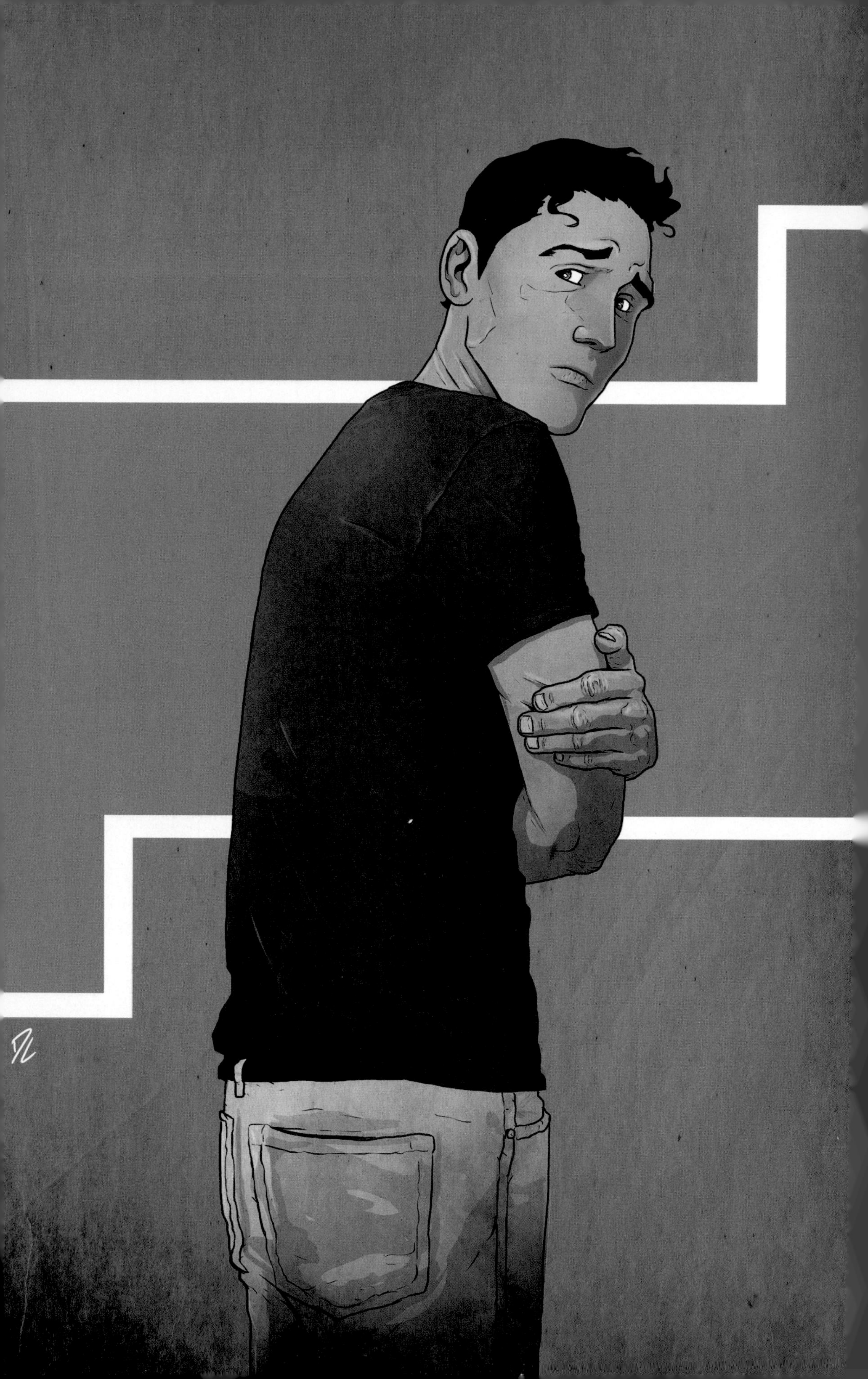

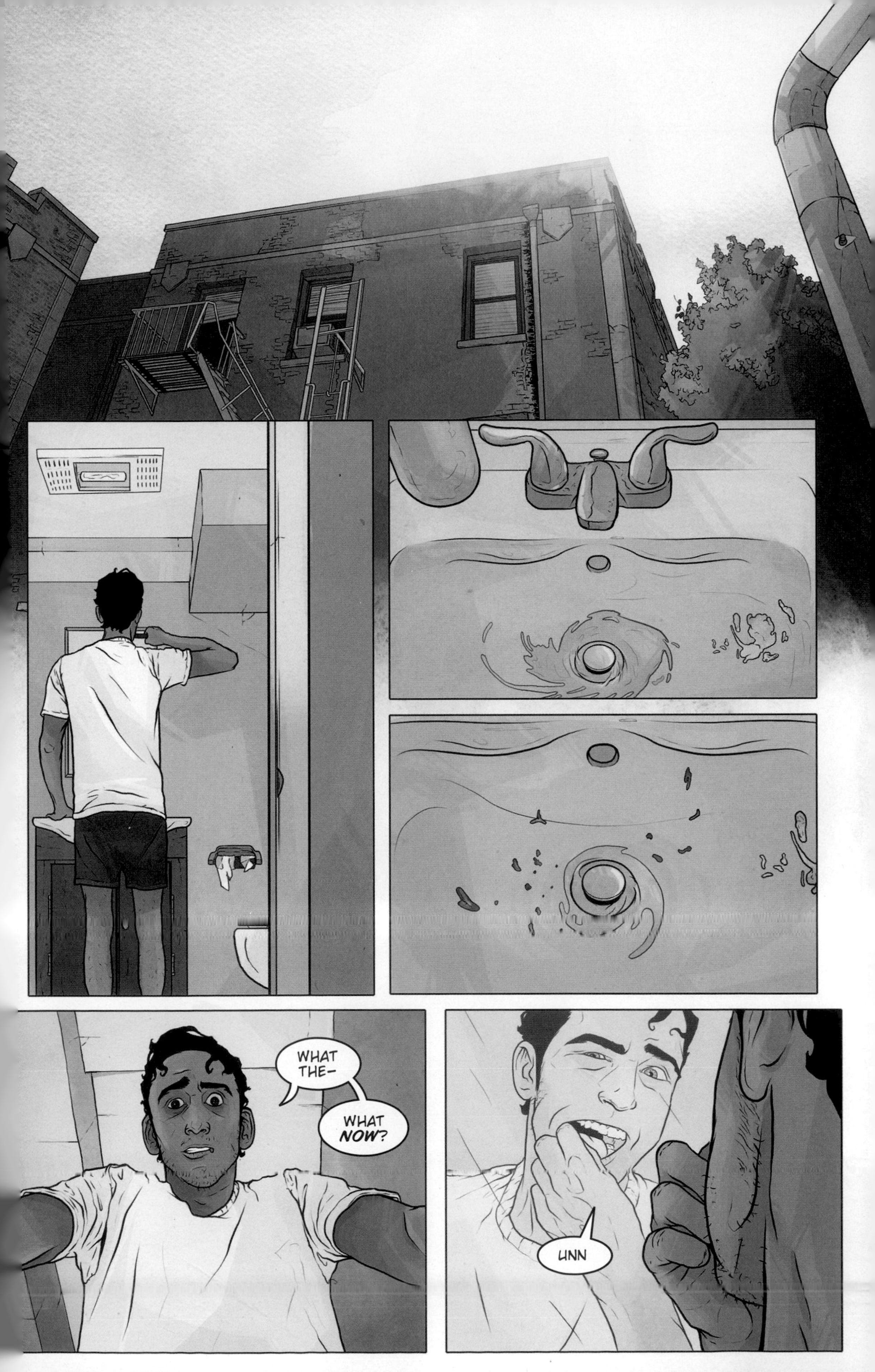
WHAT THE-
WHAT NOW?
UNN

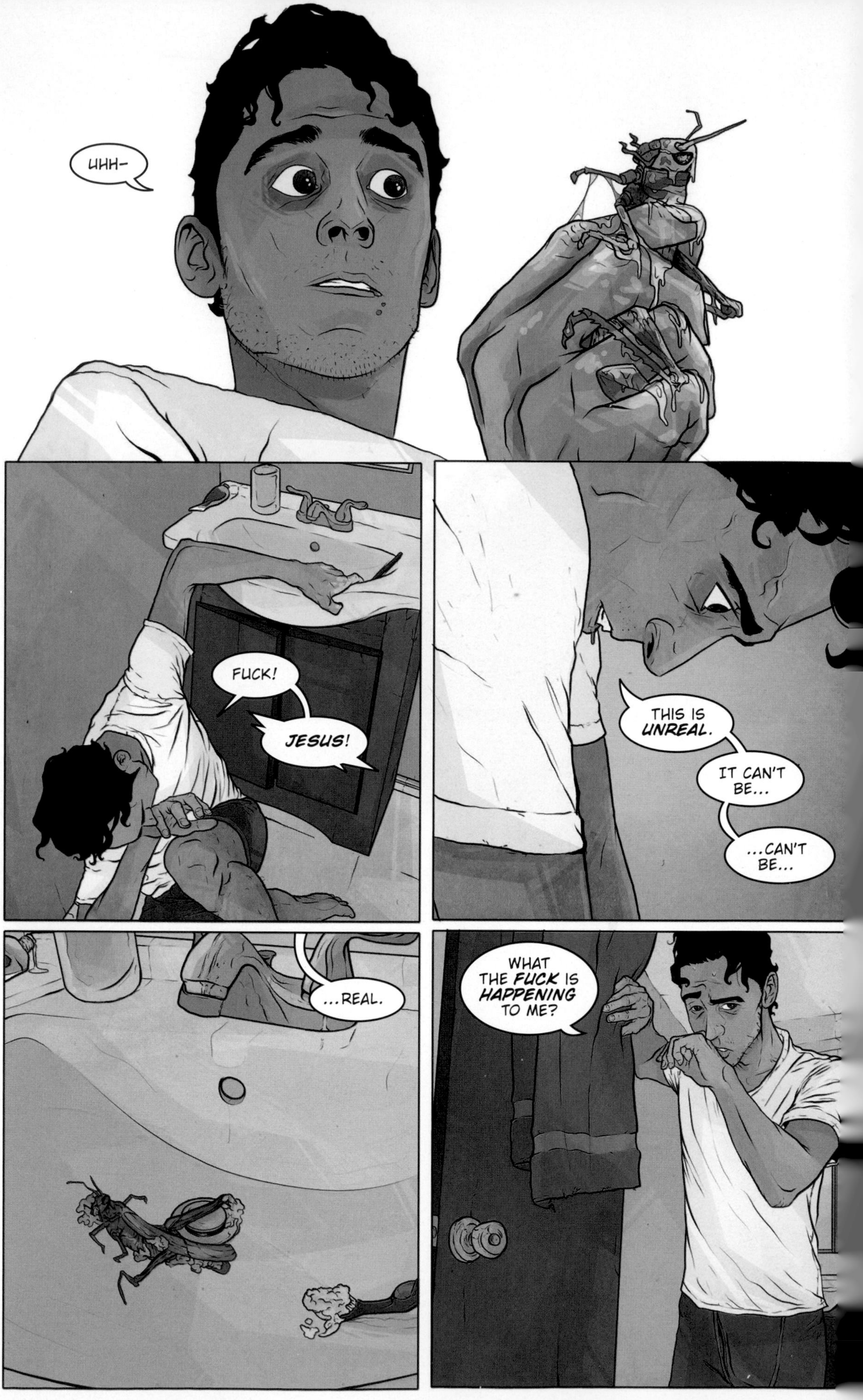

UHH-
FUCK!
JESUS!
THIS IS UNREAL.
IT CAN'T BE...
...CAN'T BE...
...REAL.
WHAT THE FUCK IS HAPPENING TO ME?

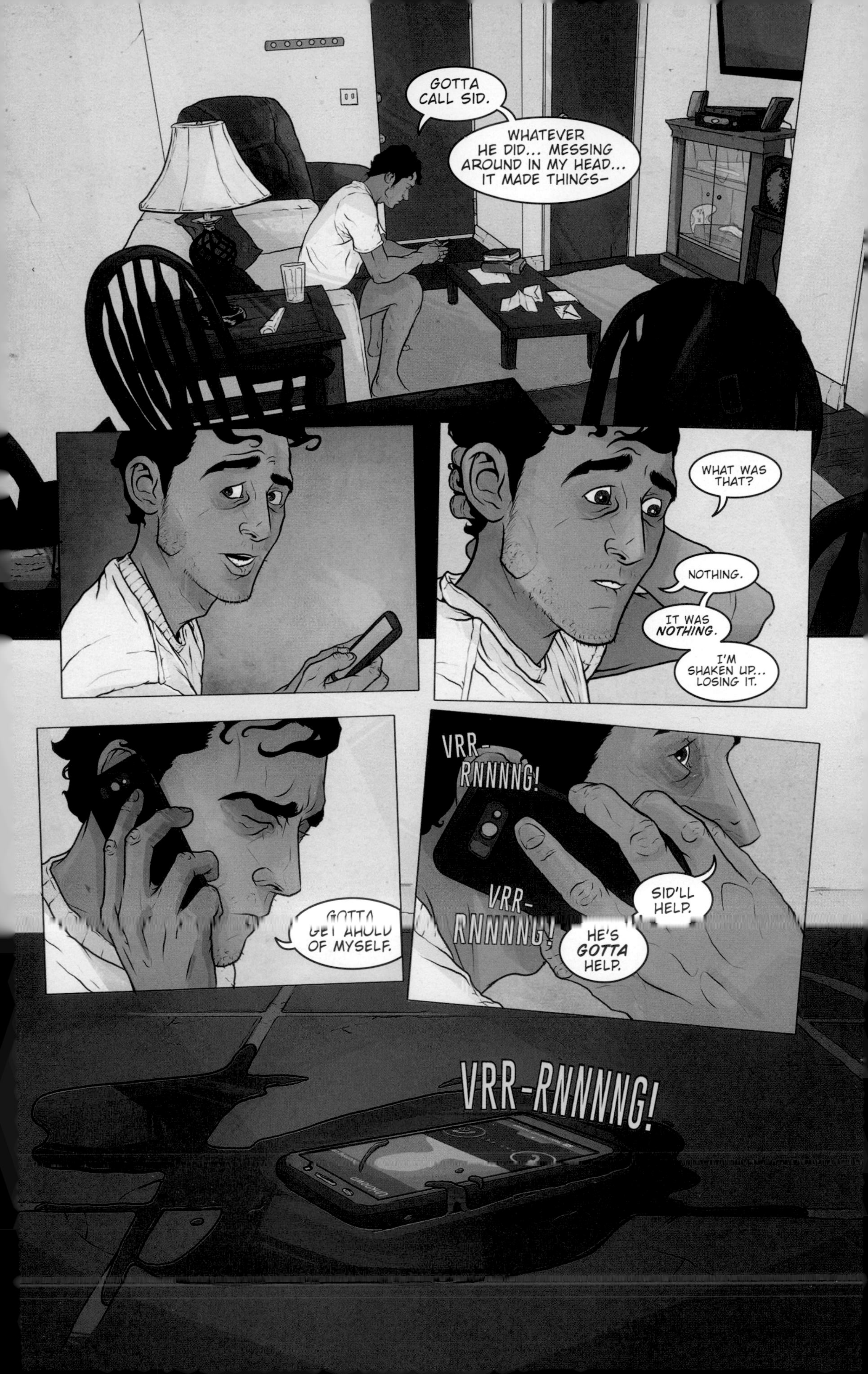
GOTTA CALL SID.
WHATEVER HE DID... MESSING AROUND IN MY HEAD... IT MADE THINGS–
WHAT WAS THAT?
NOTHING.
IT WAS *NOTHING*.
I'M SHAKEN UP... LOSING IT.
GOTTA GET AHOLD OF MYSELF.
VRR-RNNNNG!
VRR-RNNNNG!
SID'LL HELP.
HE'S *GOTTA* HELP.
VRR-RNNNNG!

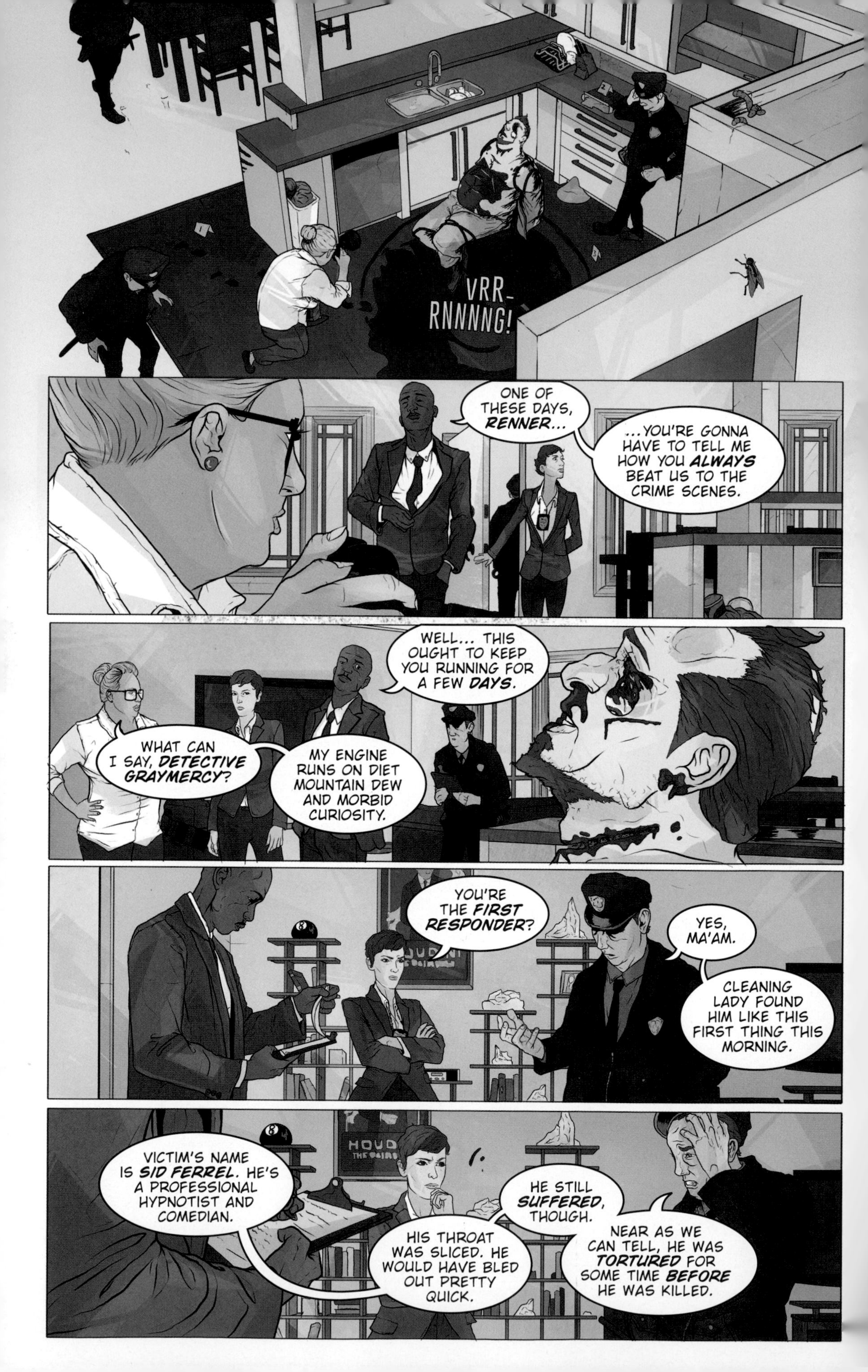
VRR-
RNNNNG!
ONE OF THESE DAYS, RENNER...
...YOU'RE GONNA HAVE TO TELL ME HOW YOU ALWAYS BEAT US TO THE CRIME SCENES.
WELL... THIS OUGHT TO KEEP YOU RUNNING FOR A FEW DAYS.
WHAT CAN I SAY, DETECTIVE GRAYMERCY?
MY ENGINE RUNS ON DIET MOUNTAIN DEW AND MORBID CURIOSITY.
YOU'RE THE FIRST RESPONDER?
YES, MA'AM.
CLEANING LADY FOUND HIM LIKE THIS FIRST THING THIS MORNING.
VICTIM'S NAME IS SID FERREL. HE'S A PROFESSIONAL HYPNOTIST AND COMEDIAN.
HIS THROAT WAS SLICED. HE WOULD HAVE BLED OUT PRETTY QUICK.
HE STILL SUFFERED, THOUGH.
NEAR AS WE CAN TELL, HE WAS TORTURED FOR SOME TIME BEFORE HE WAS KILLED.

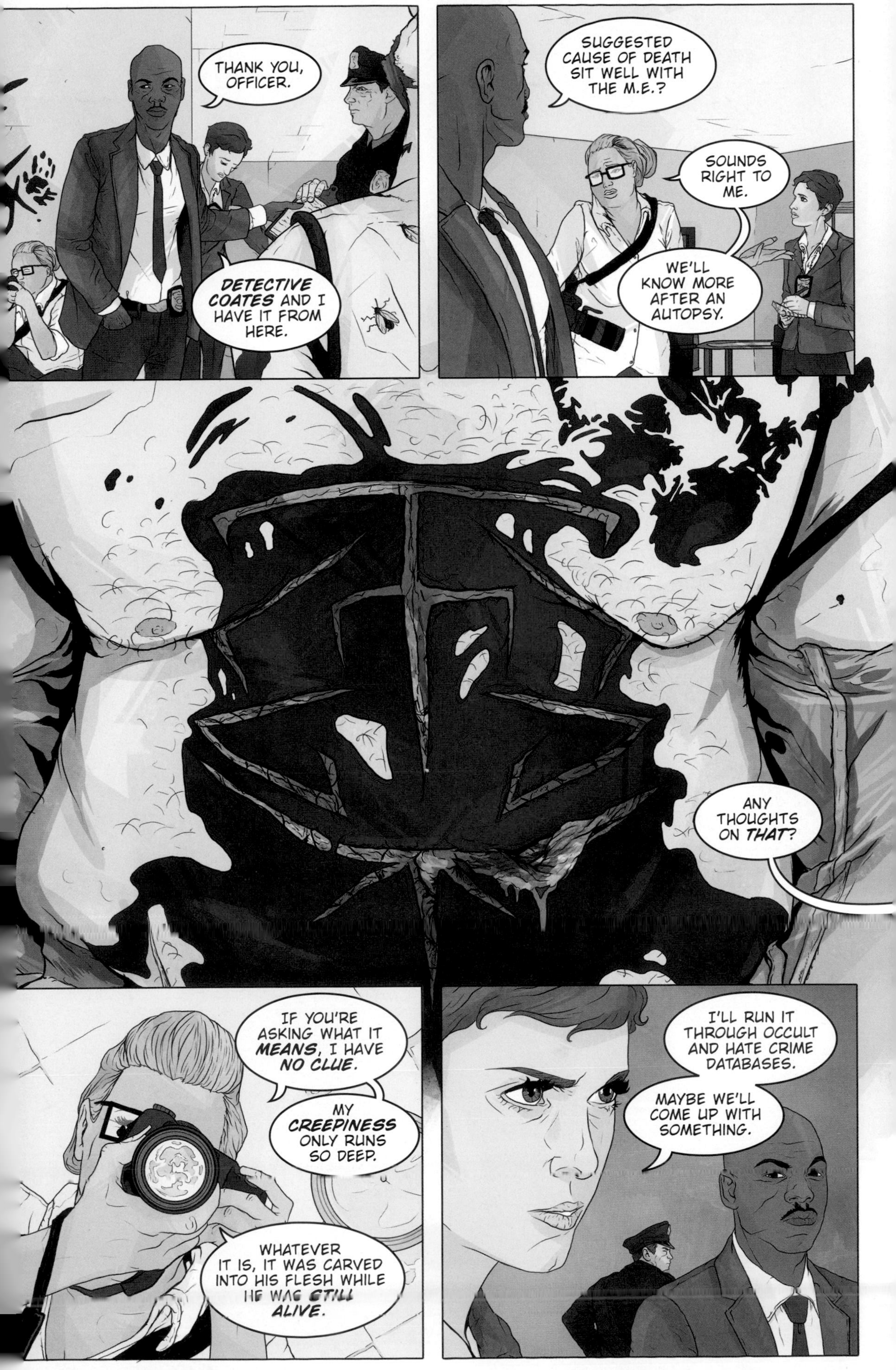
THANK YOU, OFFICER.
DETECTIVE COATES AND I HAVE IT FROM HERE.
SUGGESTED CAUSE OF DEATH SIT WELL WITH THE M.E.?
SOUNDS RIGHT TO ME.
WE'LL KNOW MORE AFTER AN AUTOPSY.
ANY THOUGHTS ON THAT?
IF YOU'RE ASKING WHAT IT MEANS, I HAVE NO CLUE.
MY CREEPINESS ONLY RUNS SO DEEP.
WHATEVER IT IS, IT WAS CARVED INTO HIS FLESH WHILE HE WAS STILL ALIVE.
I'LL RUN IT THROUGH OCCULT AND HATE CRIME DATABASES.
MAYBE WE'LL COME UP WITH SOMETHING.

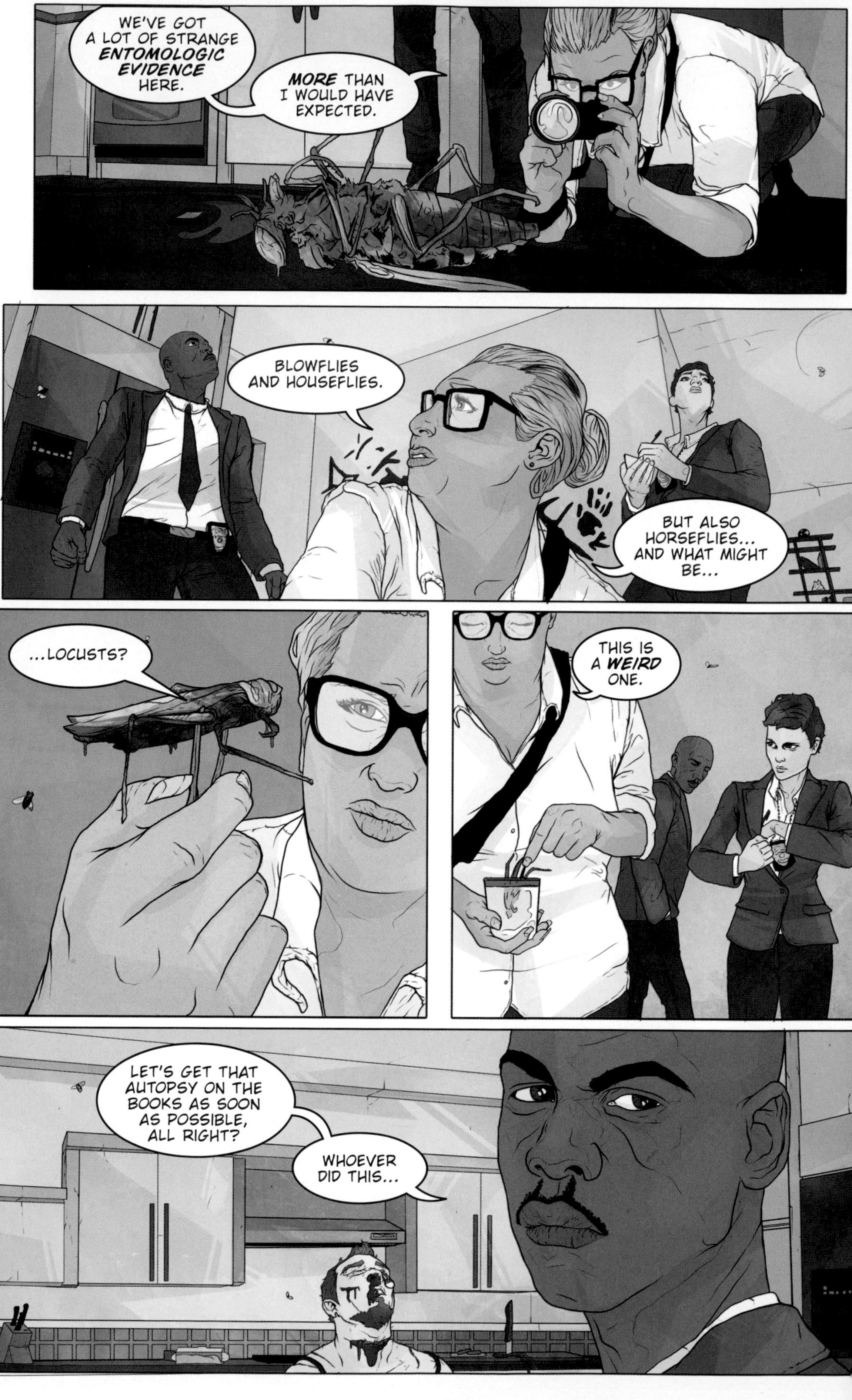
WE'VE GOT A LOT OF STRANGE ENTOMOLOGIC EVIDENCE HERE.
MORE THAN I WOULD HAVE EXPECTED.
BLOWFLIES AND HOUSEFLIES.
BUT ALSO HORSEFLIES... AND WHAT MIGHT BE...
...LOCUSTS?
THIS IS A WEIRD ONE.
LET'S GET THAT AUTOPSY ON THE BOOKS AS SOON AS POSSIBLE, ALL RIGHT?
WHOEVER DID THIS...

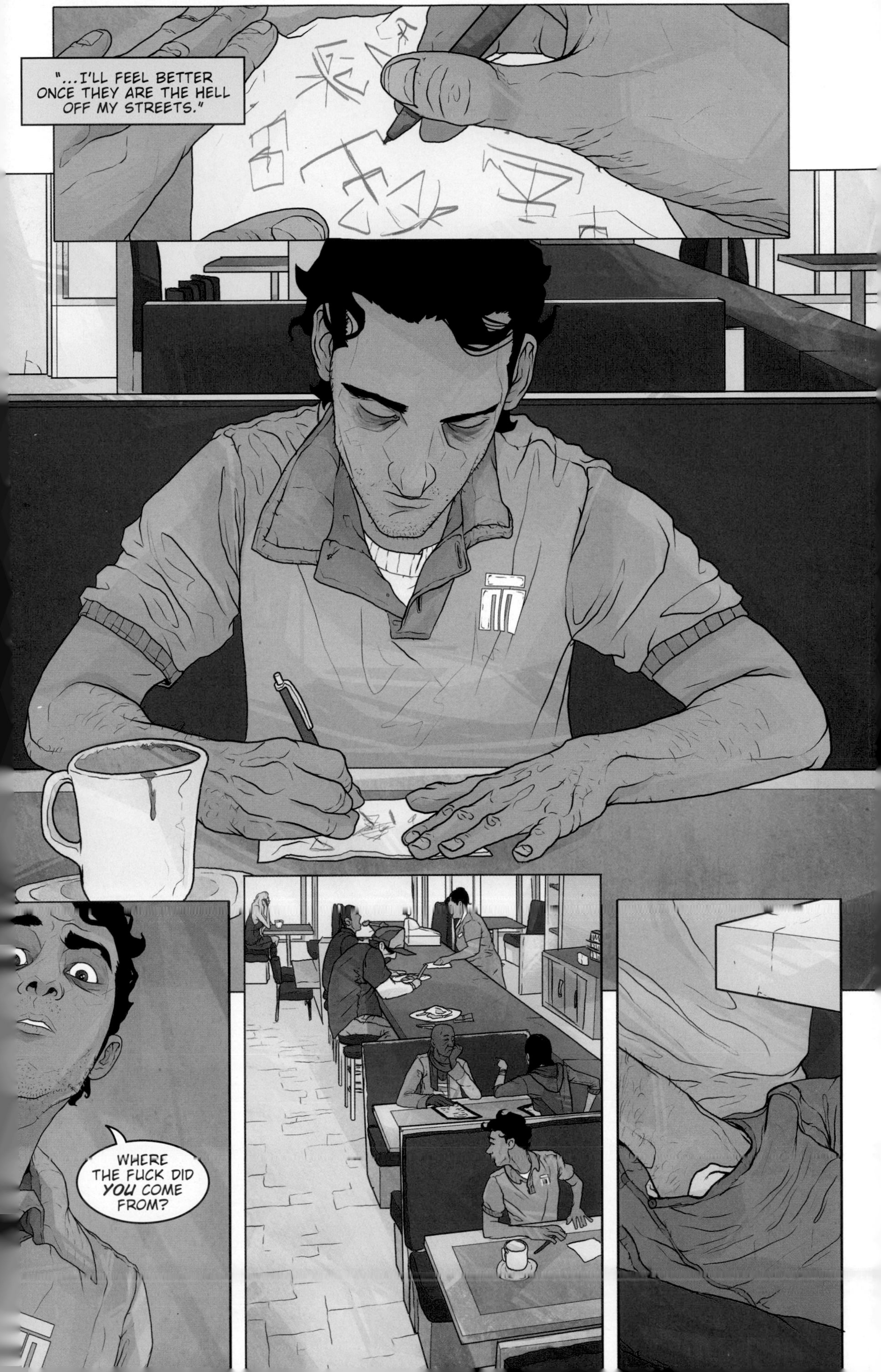
"...I'LL FEEL BETTER ONCE THEY ARE THE HELL OFF MY STREETS."
WHERE THE FUCK DID *YOU* COME FROM?

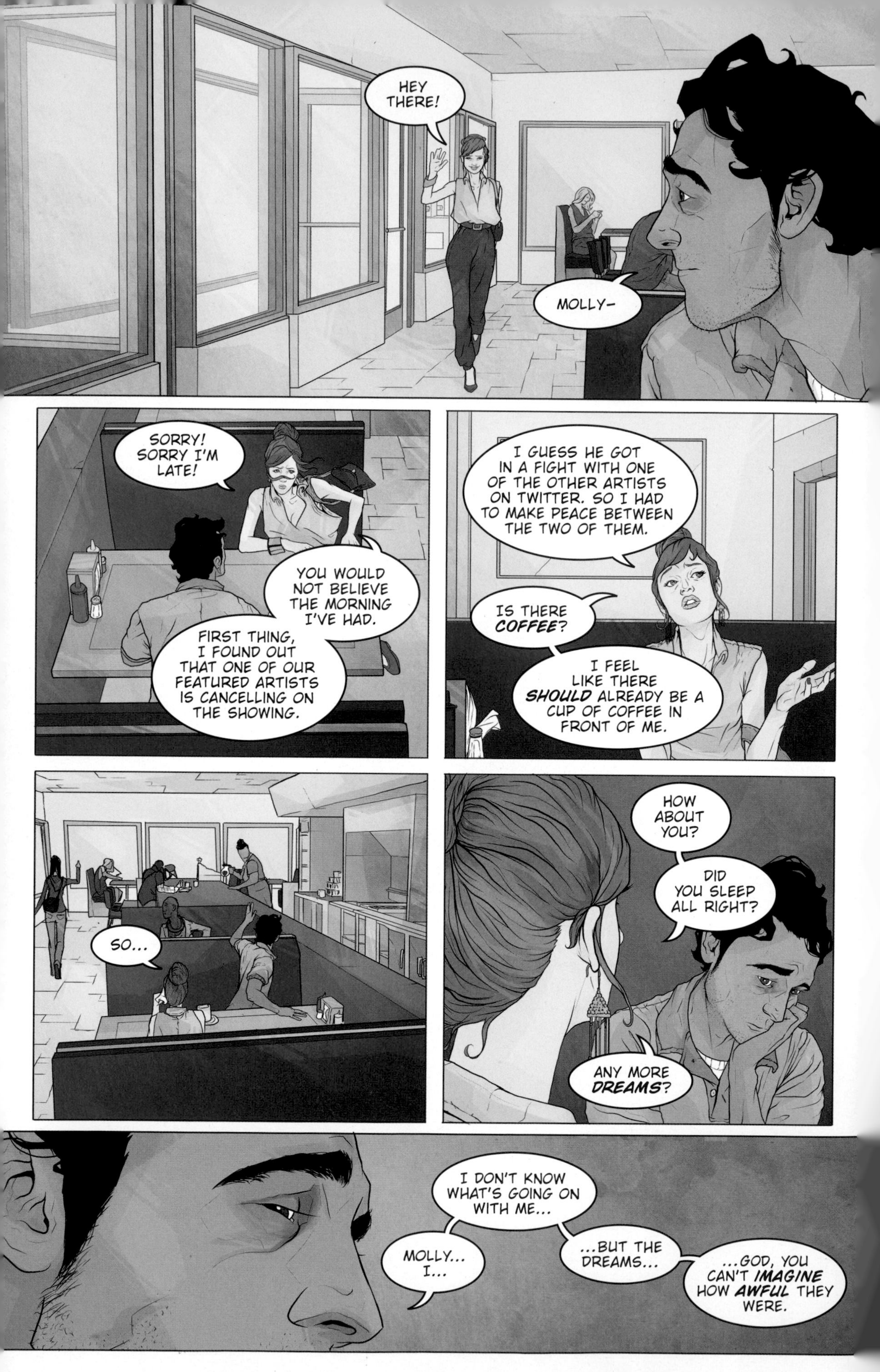
HEY THERE!
MOLLY–
SORRY! SORRY I'M LATE!
YOU WOULD NOT BELIEVE THE MORNING I'VE HAD.
FIRST THING, I FOUND OUT THAT ONE OF OUR FEATURED ARTISTS IS CANCELLING ON THE SHOWING.
I GUESS HE GOT IN A FIGHT WITH ONE OF THE OTHER ARTISTS ON TWITTER. SO I HAD TO MAKE PEACE BETWEEN THE TWO OF THEM.
IS THERE **COFFEE**?
I FEEL LIKE THERE **SHOULD** ALREADY BE A CUP OF COFFEE IN FRONT OF ME.
SO...
HOW ABOUT YOU?
DID YOU SLEEP ALL RIGHT?
ANY MORE **DREAMS**?
MOLLY... I...
I DON'T KNOW WHAT'S GOING ON WITH ME...
...BUT THE DREAMS...
...GOD, YOU CAN'T **IMAGINE** HOW **AWFUL** THEY WERE.

YOU WERE *THERE*. YOU *SAW* WHAT HAPPENED.

WHAT DID THAT GUY—SID—DO TO ME?

THERE WASN'T MUCH TO IT, REALLY.

HE SAID THIS WAS JUST THE *FIRST STEP* TO A MUCH DEEPER REGRESSION.

FIRST STEP?

MOLLY, I FEEL LIKE I'M LOSING MY MIND!

WHAT DID I *SAY*?

IF THIS WAS A *PAST LIFE REGRESSION*, MAYBE I SAID A *NAME* OR *SOMETHING*?

ADRIAN... I'M NOT SUPPOSED TO...

SID SAID I SHOULD LET THOSE ANSWERS COME TO YOU *ON THEIR OWN*.

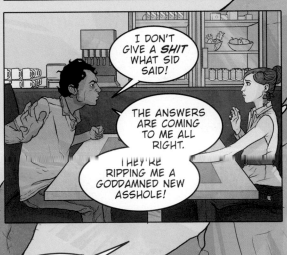

I DON'T GIVE A *SHIT* WHAT SID SAID!

THE ANSWERS ARE COMING TO ME ALL RIGHT.

THEY'RE RIPPING ME A GODDAMNED NEW ASSHOLE!

YOU TOOK ME TO THAT GUY, MOLLY!

YOU *SAID* HE COULD *HELP*!

BUT HE... YOU...

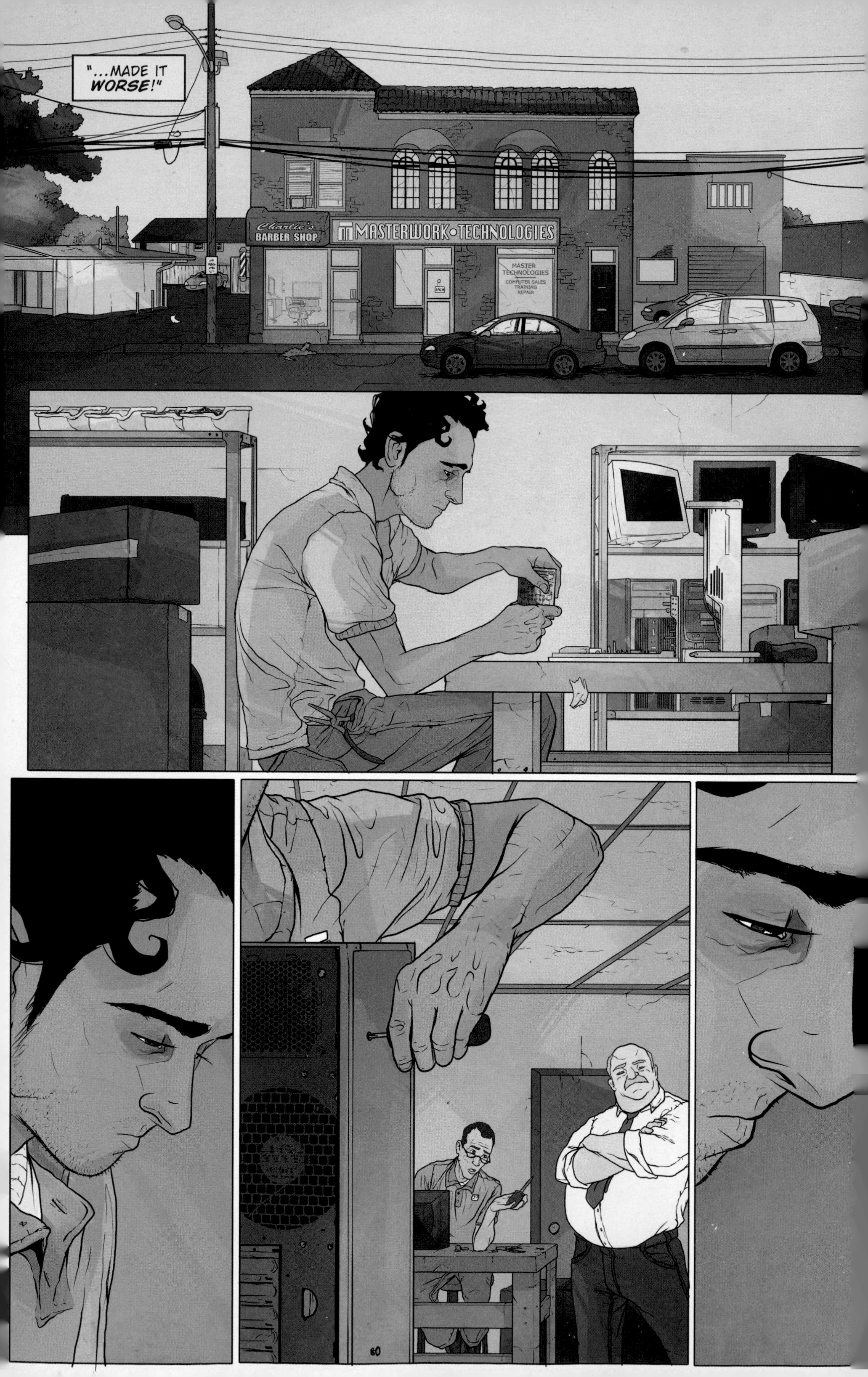
"...MADE IT *WORSE!*"
Charlie's BARBER SHOP
MASTERWORK•TECHNOLOGIES
MASTER TECHNOLOGIES
COMPUTER SALES
TRAINING
REPAIR

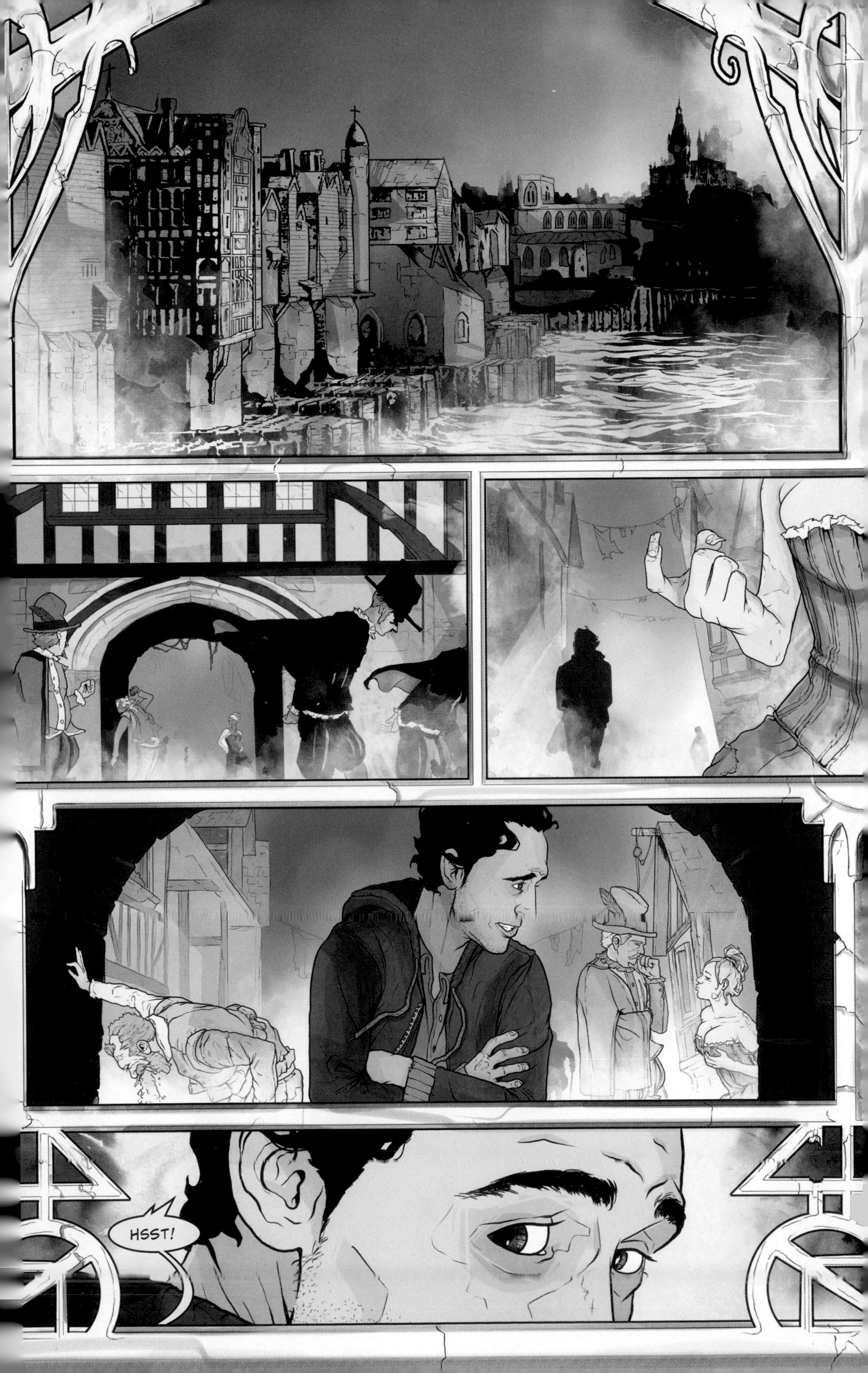
HSST!

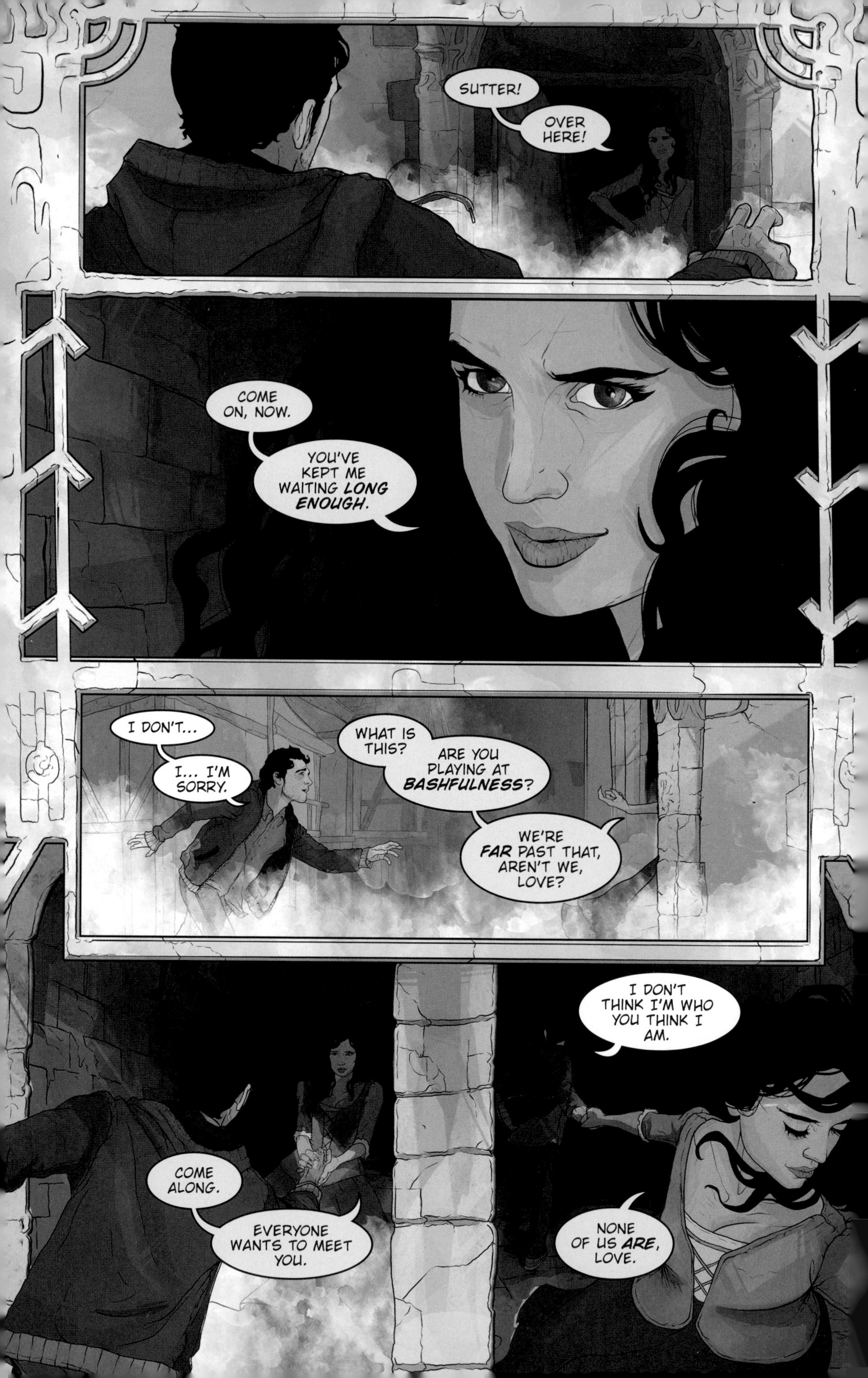
SUTTER!
OVER HERE!
COME ON, NOW.
YOU'VE KEPT ME WAITING **LONG ENOUGH**.
I DON'T...
I... I'M SORRY.
WHAT IS THIS?
ARE YOU PLAYING AT **BASHFULNESS**?
WE'RE **FAR** PAST THAT, AREN'T WE, LOVE?
I DON'T THINK I'M WHO YOU THINK I AM.
COME ALONG.
EVERYONE WANTS TO MEET YOU.
NONE OF US **ARE**, LOVE.

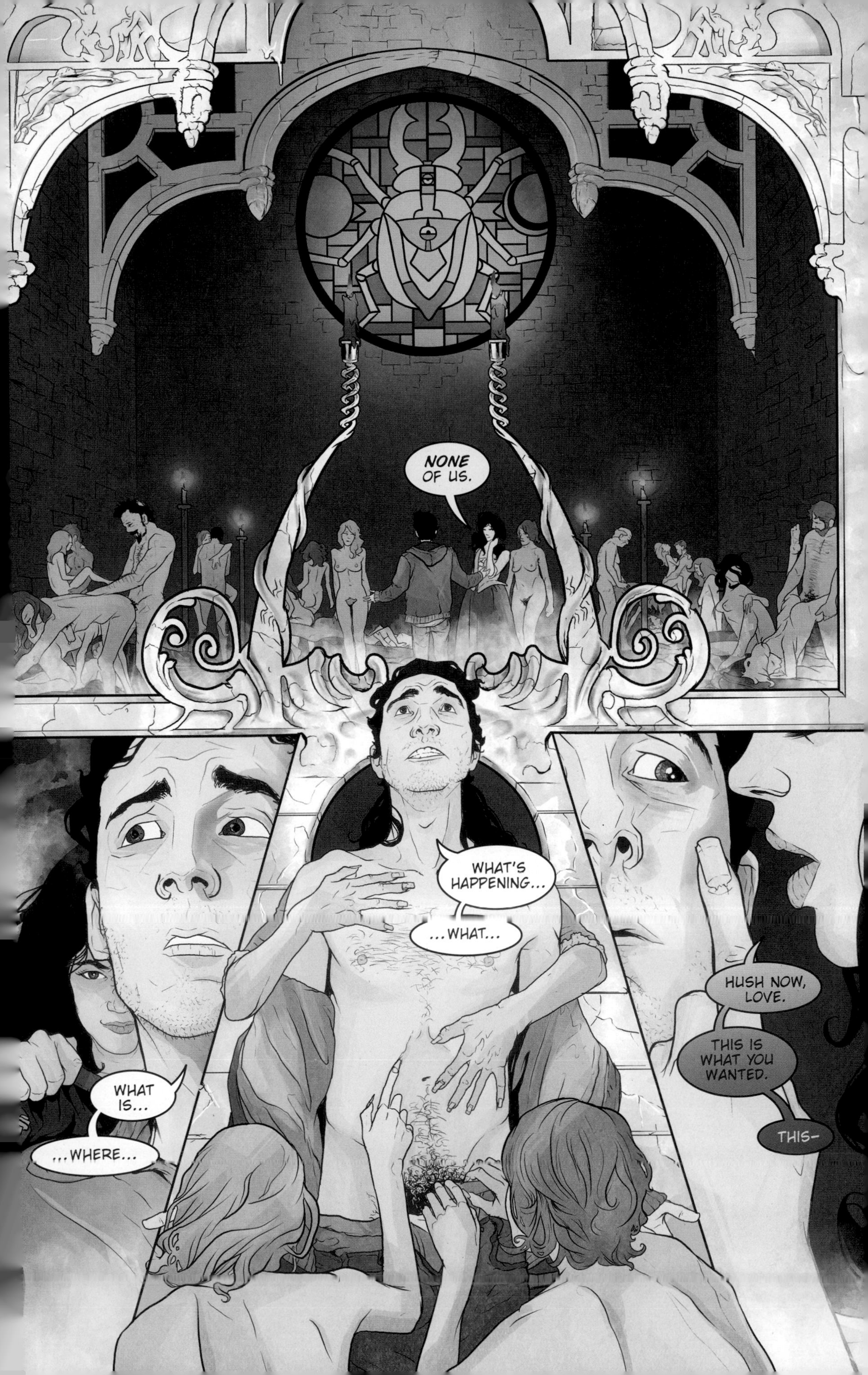
NONE OF US.
WHAT'S HAPPENING...
...WHAT...
WHAT IS...
...WHERE...
HUSH NOW, LOVE.
THIS IS WHAT YOU WANTED.
THIS-

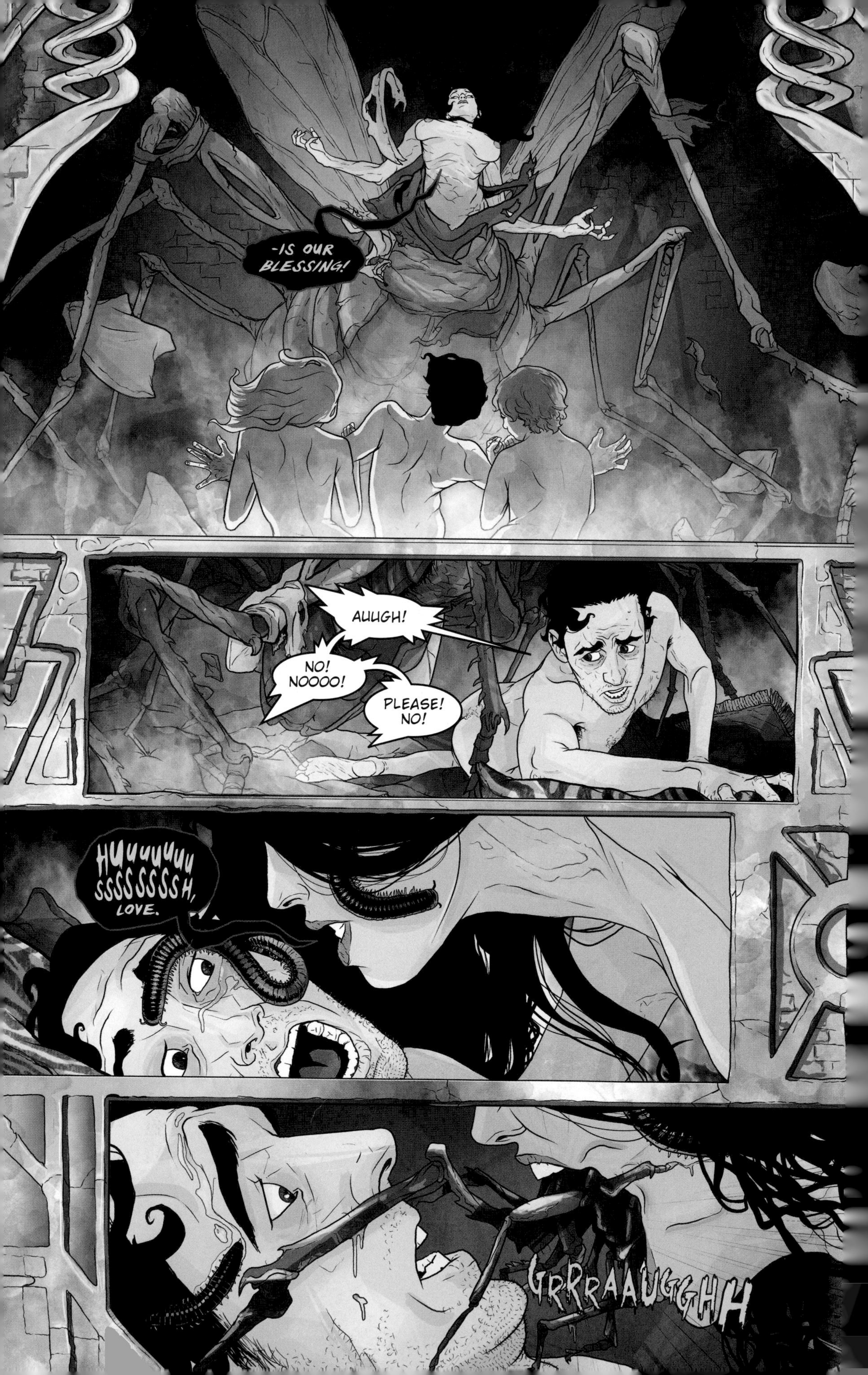
-IS OUR BLESSING!
AUUGH!
NO! NOOOO!
PLEASE! NO!
HUuuuuuu SSSSSSSSH, LOVE.
GRRRAAUGGHH

ADRIAN!

ADRIAN, ARE YOU *LISTENING* TO ME?

OH, EXCUSE ME! DID I *WAKE* YOU?

WHAT THE HELL IS THIS?

I DON'T *PAY* YOU TO TAKE *NAPS!*

IT WON'T HAPPEN AGAIN—

AH... LOOK...

I HAVEN'T BEEN SLEEPING WELL.

DAMN RIGHT, IT WON'T! AND IF YOU THINK I'M PAYING YOU *DIME-ONE* FOR THE LAST *HOUR,* YOU'RE OUT OF YOUR MIND!

I DON'T GIVE TO THE SALVATION ARMY COME CHRISTMAS TIME—

—AND I *DAMN SURE* WON'T HAVE SOME CHARITY CASE ON *MY* TIMECARDS!

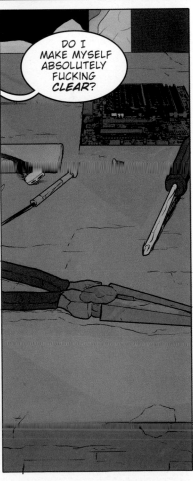

DO I MAKE MYSELF ABSOLUTELY FUCKING *CLEAR?*

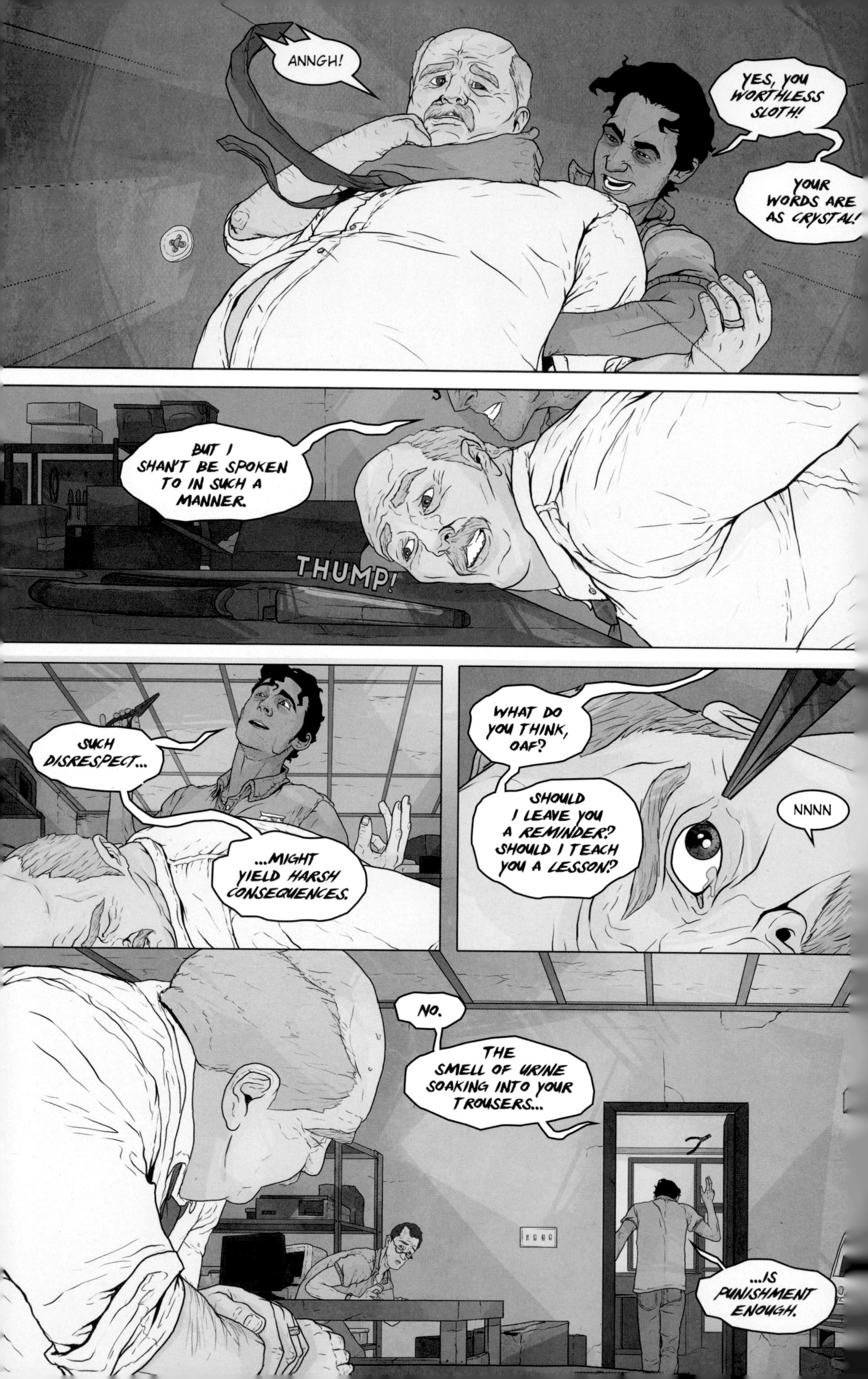
ANNGH!
YES, YOU WORTHLESS SLOTH!
YOUR WORDS ARE AS CRYSTAL!
BUT I SHAN'T BE SPOKEN TO IN SUCH A MANNER.
THUMP!
SUCH DISRESPECT...
...MIGHT YIELD HARSH CONSEQUENCES.
WHAT DO YOU THINK, OAF?
SHOULD I LEAVE YOU A REMINDER? SHOULD I TEACH YOU A LESSON?
NNNN
NO.
THE SMELL OF URINE SOAKING INTO YOUR TROUSERS...
...IS PUNISHMENT ENOUGH.

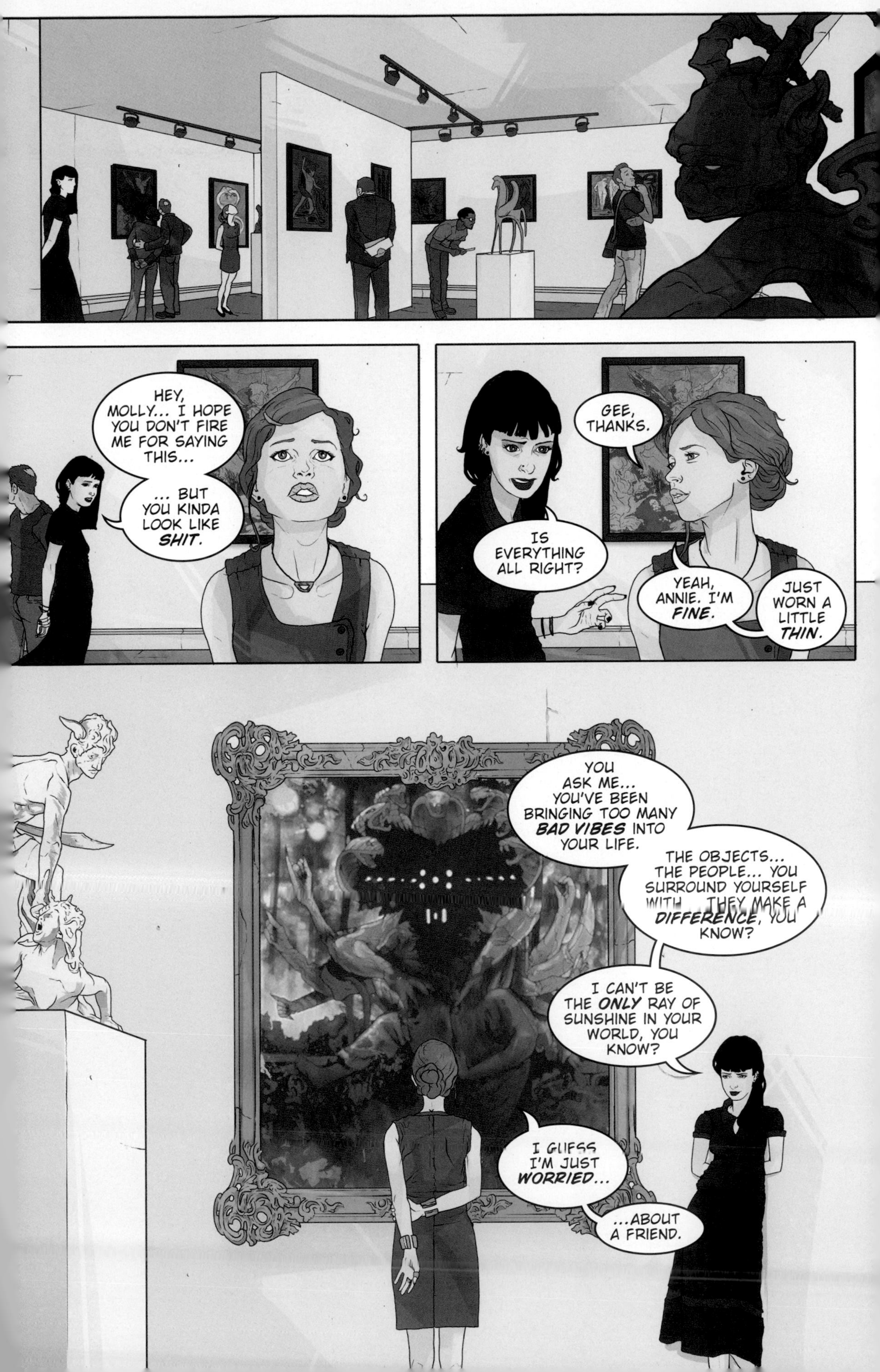

HEY, MOLLY... I HOPE YOU DON'T FIRE ME FOR SAYING THIS...
... BUT YOU KINDA LOOK LIKE ***SHIT***.
GEE, THANKS.
IS EVERYTHING ALL RIGHT?
YEAH, ANNIE. I'M ***FINE***.
JUST WORN A LITTLE ***THIN***.
YOU ASK ME... YOU'VE BEEN BRINGING TOO MANY ***BAD VIBES*** INTO YOUR LIFE.
THE OBJECTS... THE PEOPLE... YOU SURROUND YOURSELF WITH... THEY MAKE A ***DIFFERENCE***, YOU KNOW?
I CAN'T BE THE ***ONLY*** RAY OF SUNSHINE IN YOUR WORLD, YOU KNOW?
I GUESS I'M JUST ***WORRIED***...
...ABOUT A FRIEND.

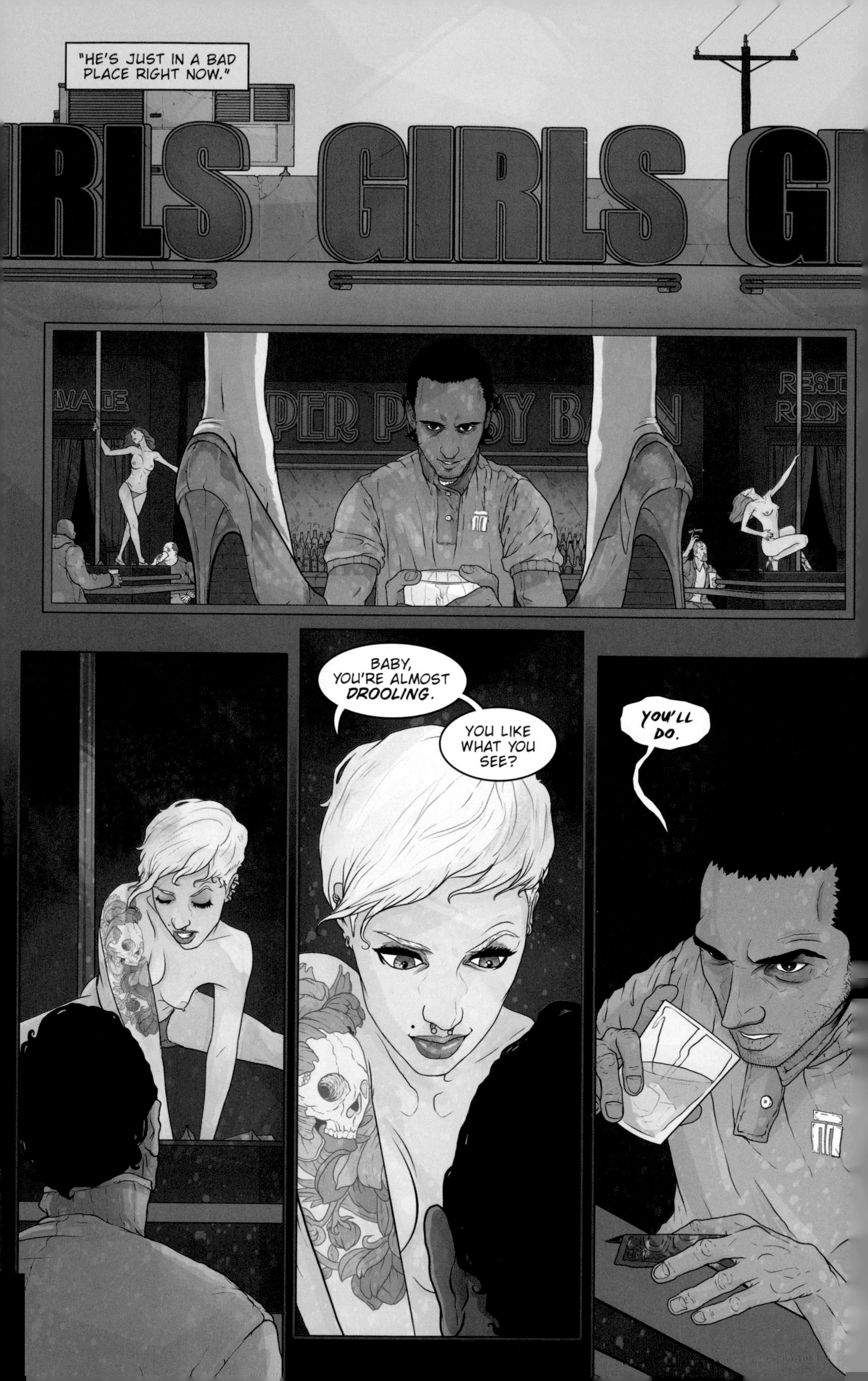
"HE'S JUST IN A BAD PLACE RIGHT NOW."
GIRLS GIRLS
BABY, YOU'RE ALMOST *DROOLING*.
YOU LIKE WHAT YOU SEE?
YOU'LL DO.

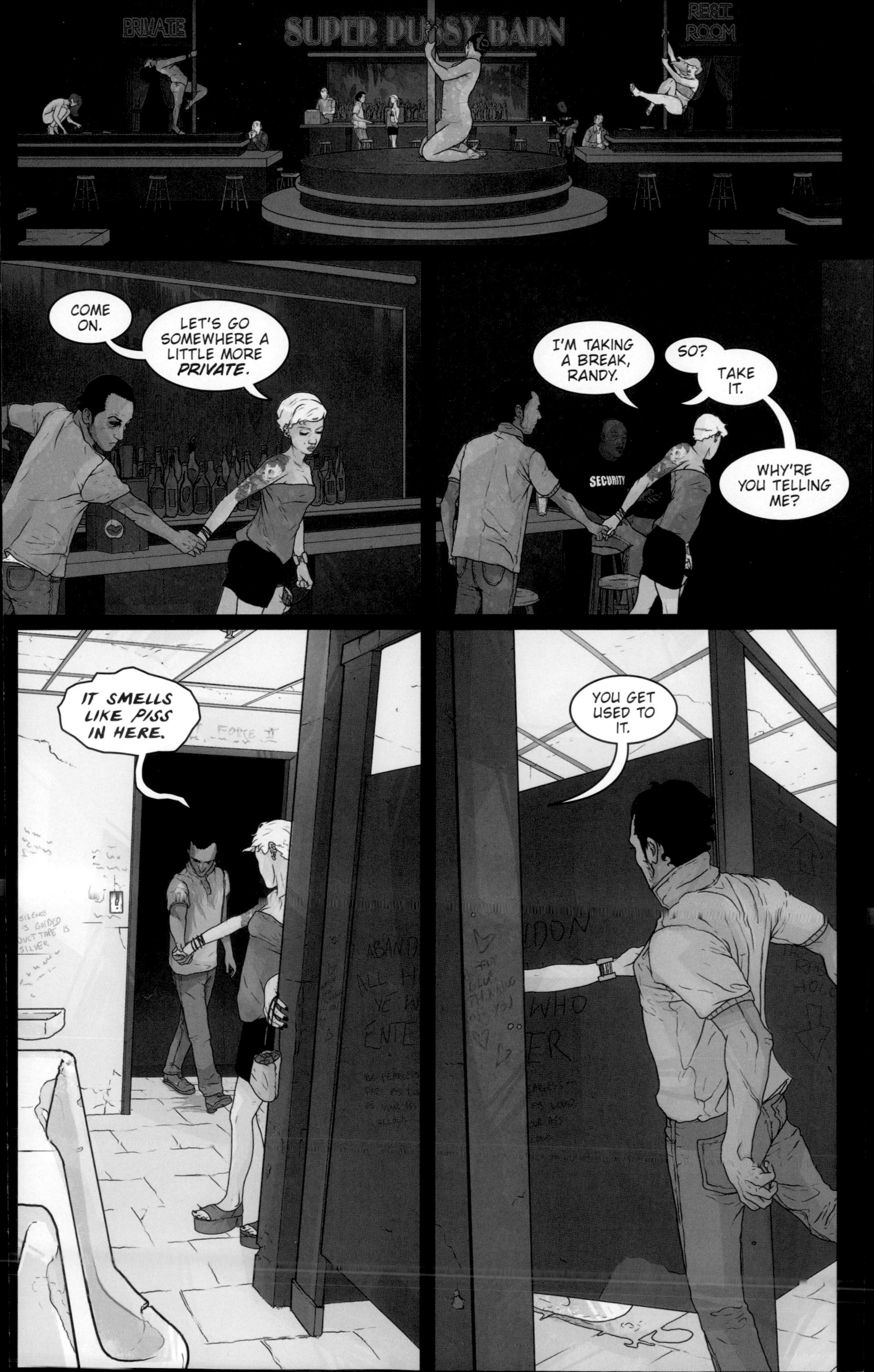
PRIVATE
SUPER PUSSY BARN
REST ROOM
COME ON.
LET'S GO SOMEWHERE A LITTLE MORE *PRIVATE*.
I'M TAKING A BREAK, RANDY.
SECURITY
SO?
TAKE IT.
WHY'RE YOU TELLING ME?
IT SMELLS LIKE PISS IN HERE.
YOU GET USED TO IT.

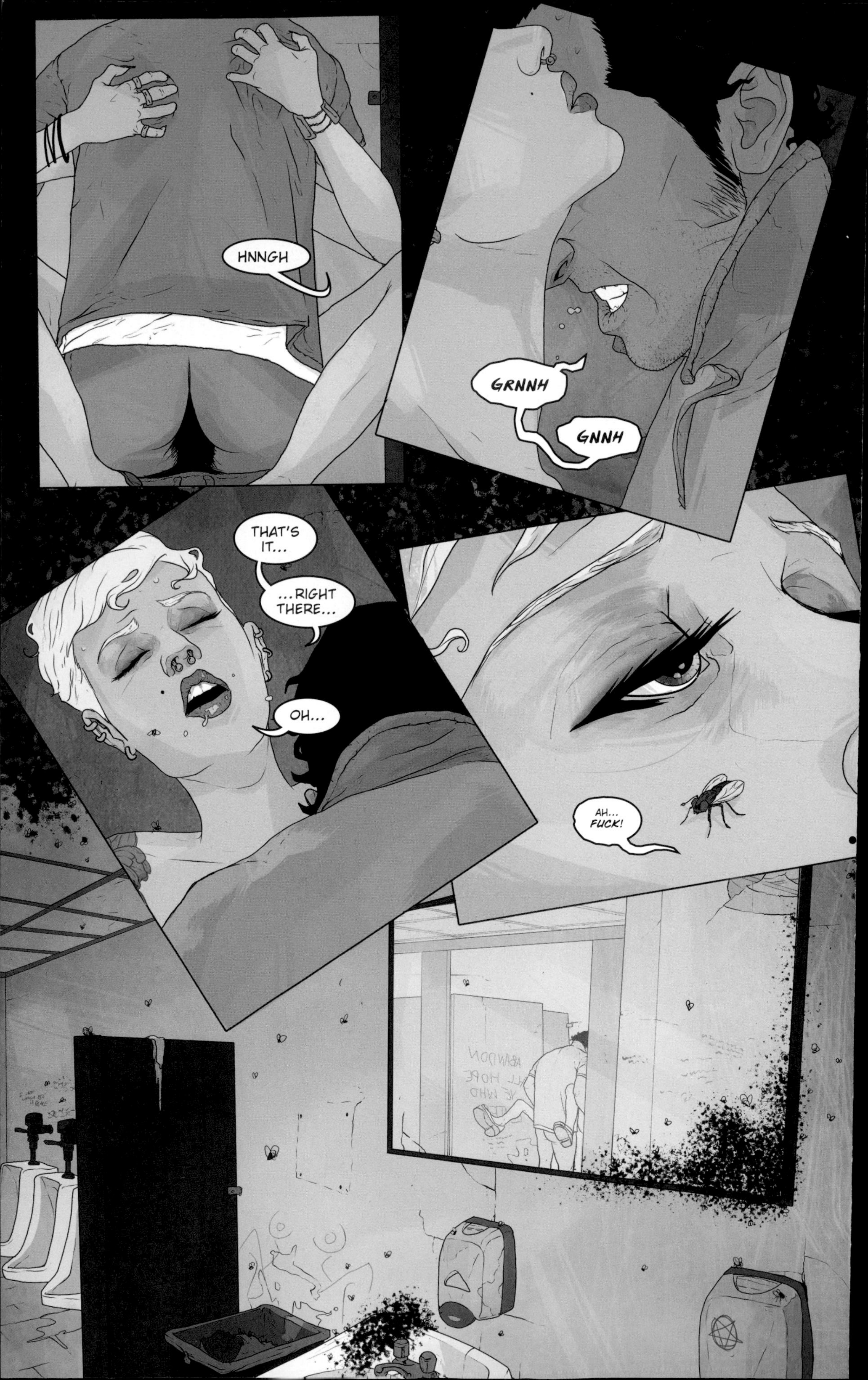
HNNGH
GRNNH
GNNH
THAT'S IT...
...RIGHT THERE...
OH...
AH... FUCK!

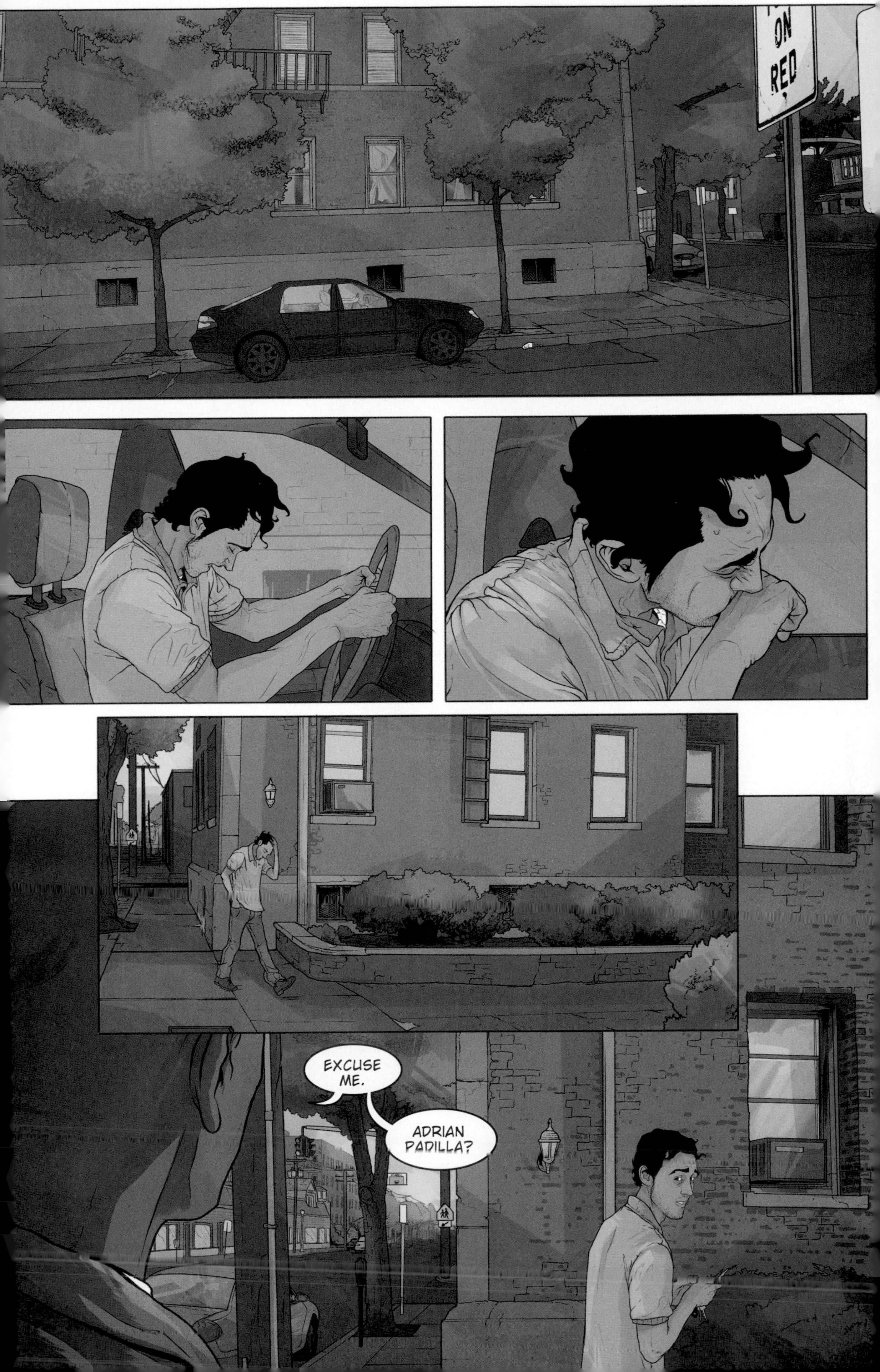
ON RED
EXCUSE ME.
ADRIAN PADILLA?

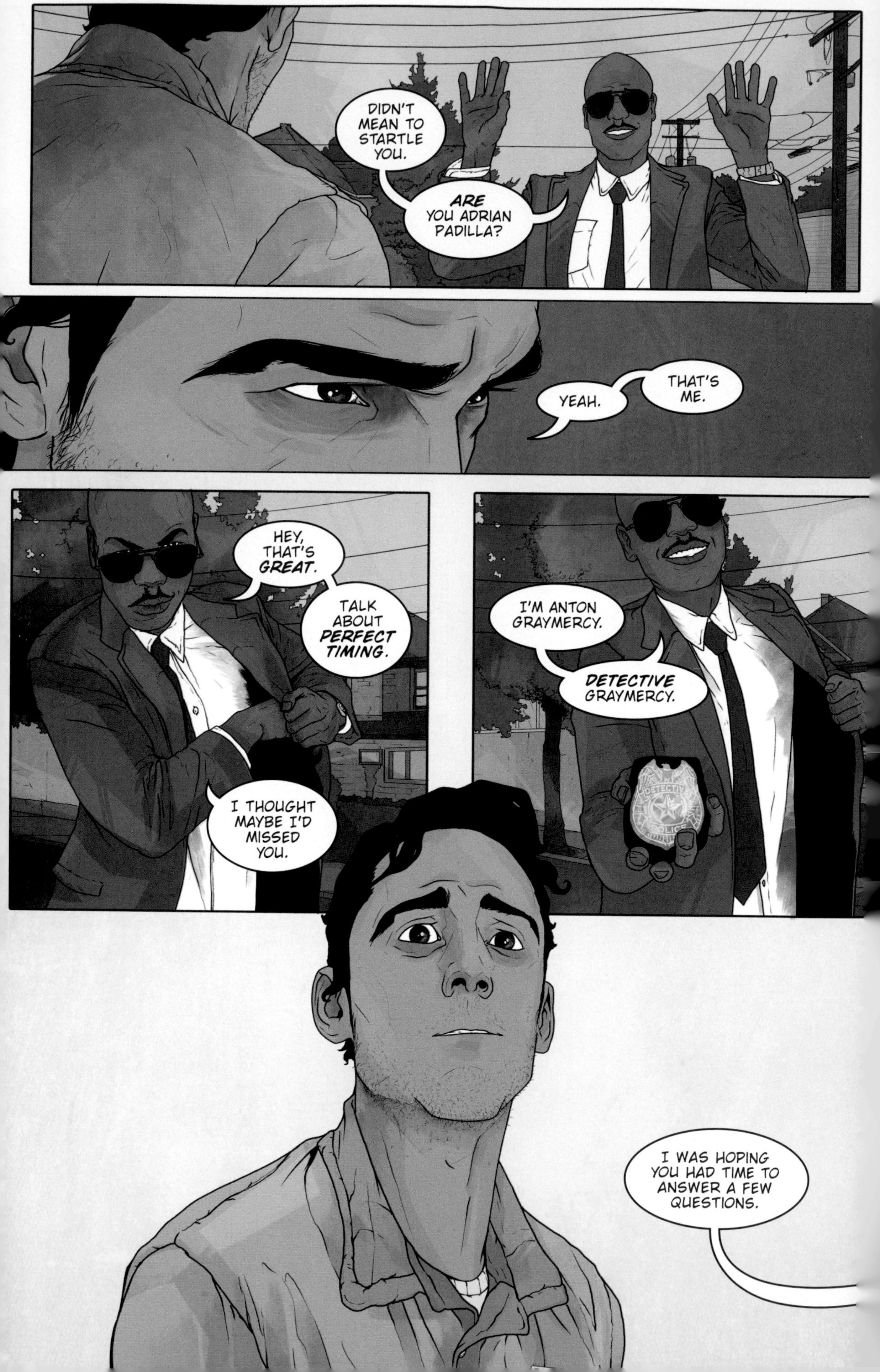
DIDN'T MEAN TO STARTLE YOU.
ARE YOU ADRIAN PADILLA?
YEAH.
THAT'S ME.
HEY, THAT'S GREAT.
TALK ABOUT PERFECT TIMING.
I THOUGHT MAYBE I'D MISSED YOU.
I'M ANTON GRAYMERCY.
DETECTIVE GRAYMERCY.
DETECTIVE
POLICE
I WAS HOPING YOU HAD TIME TO ANSWER A FEW QUESTIONS.

THREE

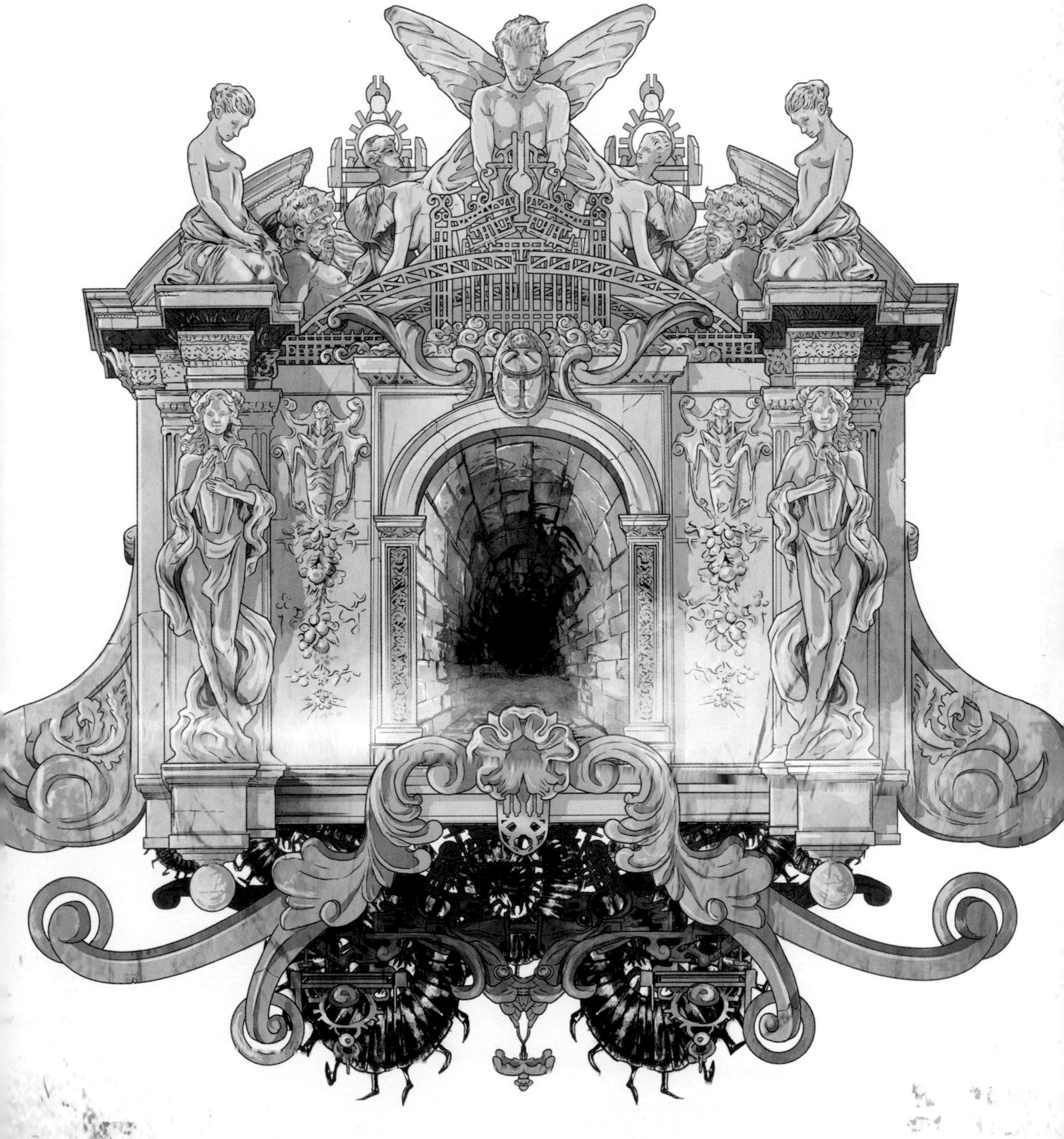

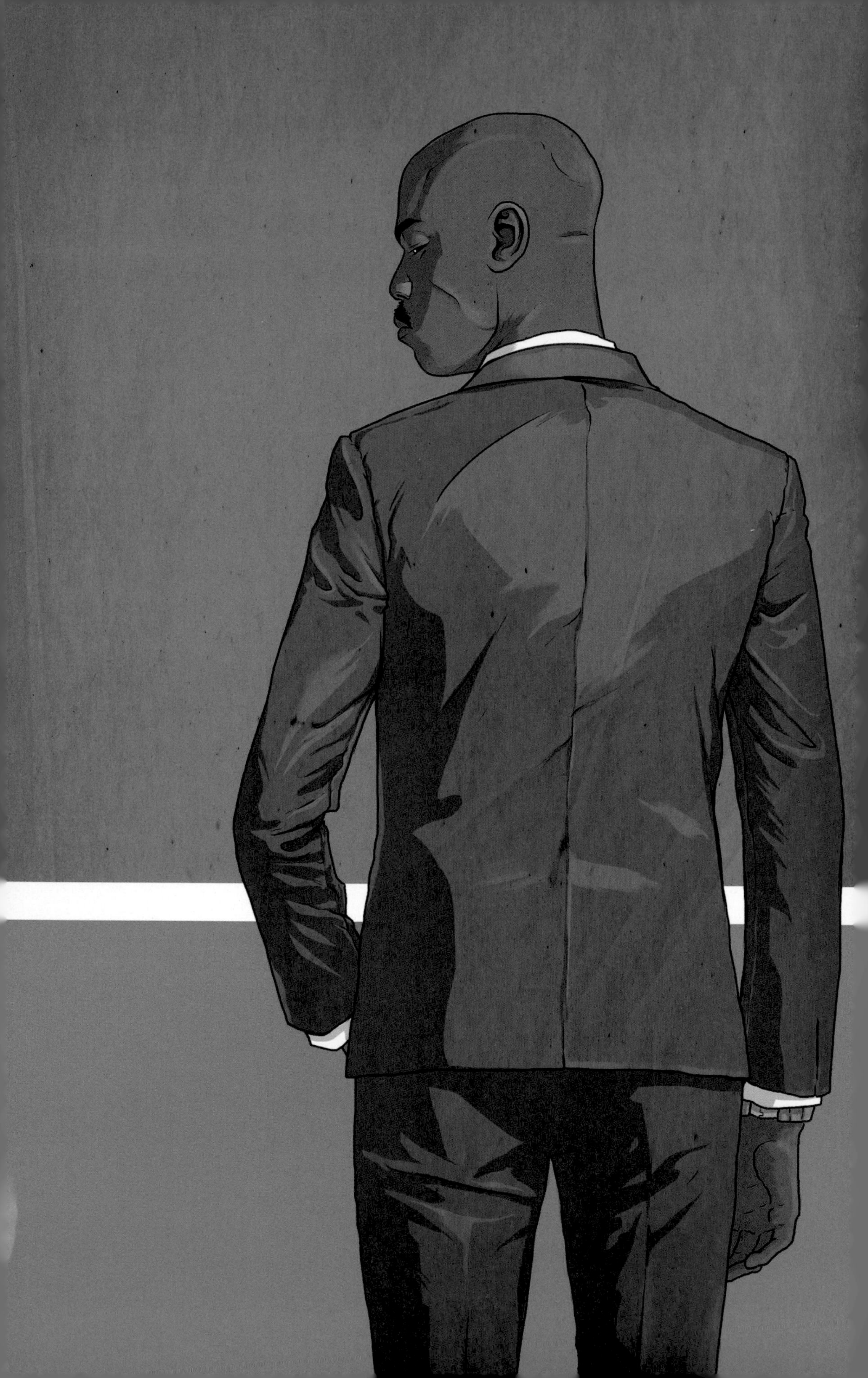

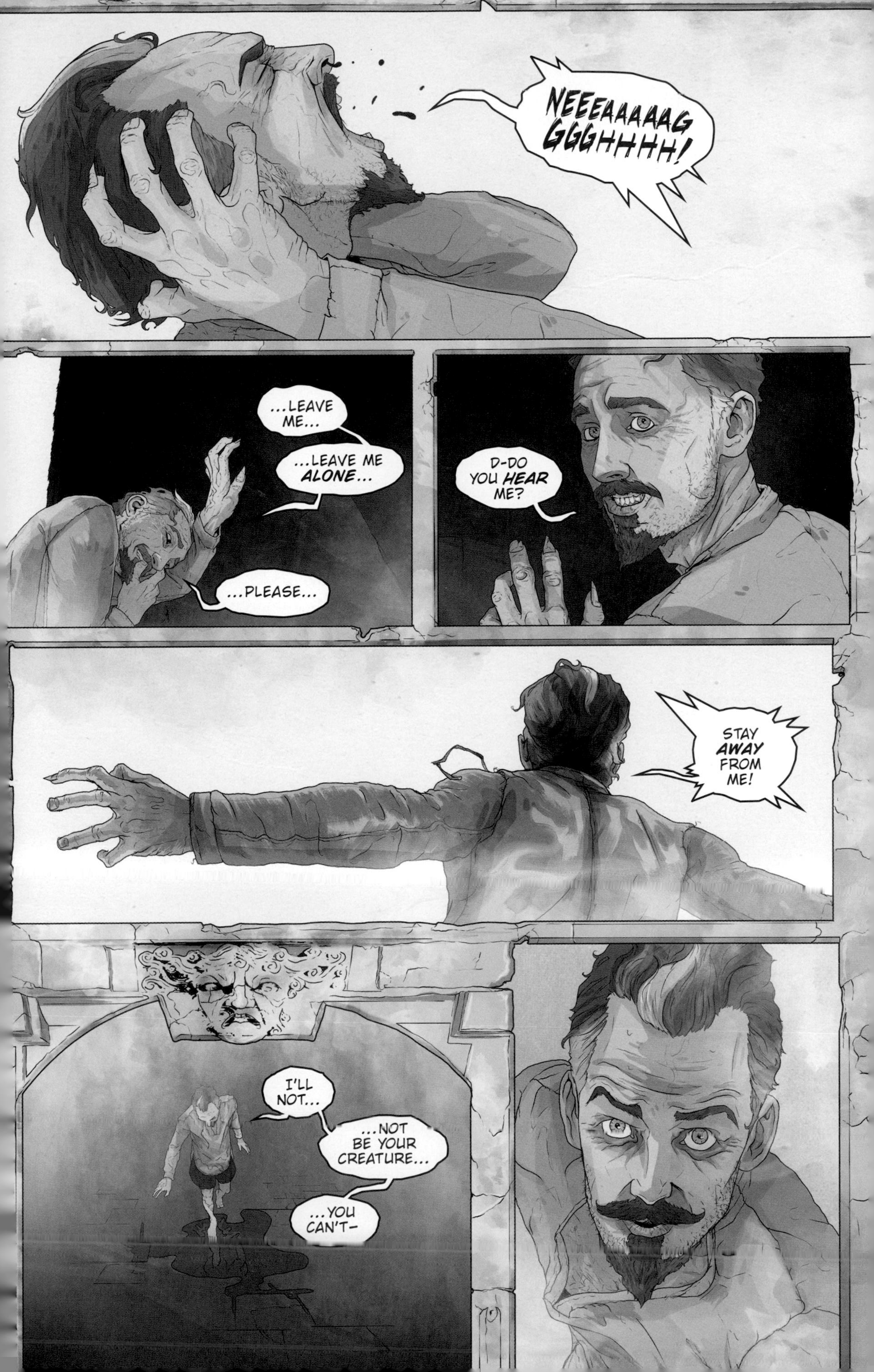
NEEEAAAAAG GGGHHHH!
...LEAVE ME...
...LEAVE ME ALONE...
...PLEASE...
D-DO YOU HEAR ME?
STAY AWAY FROM ME!
I'LL NOT...
...NOT BE YOUR CREATURE...
...YOU CAN'T-

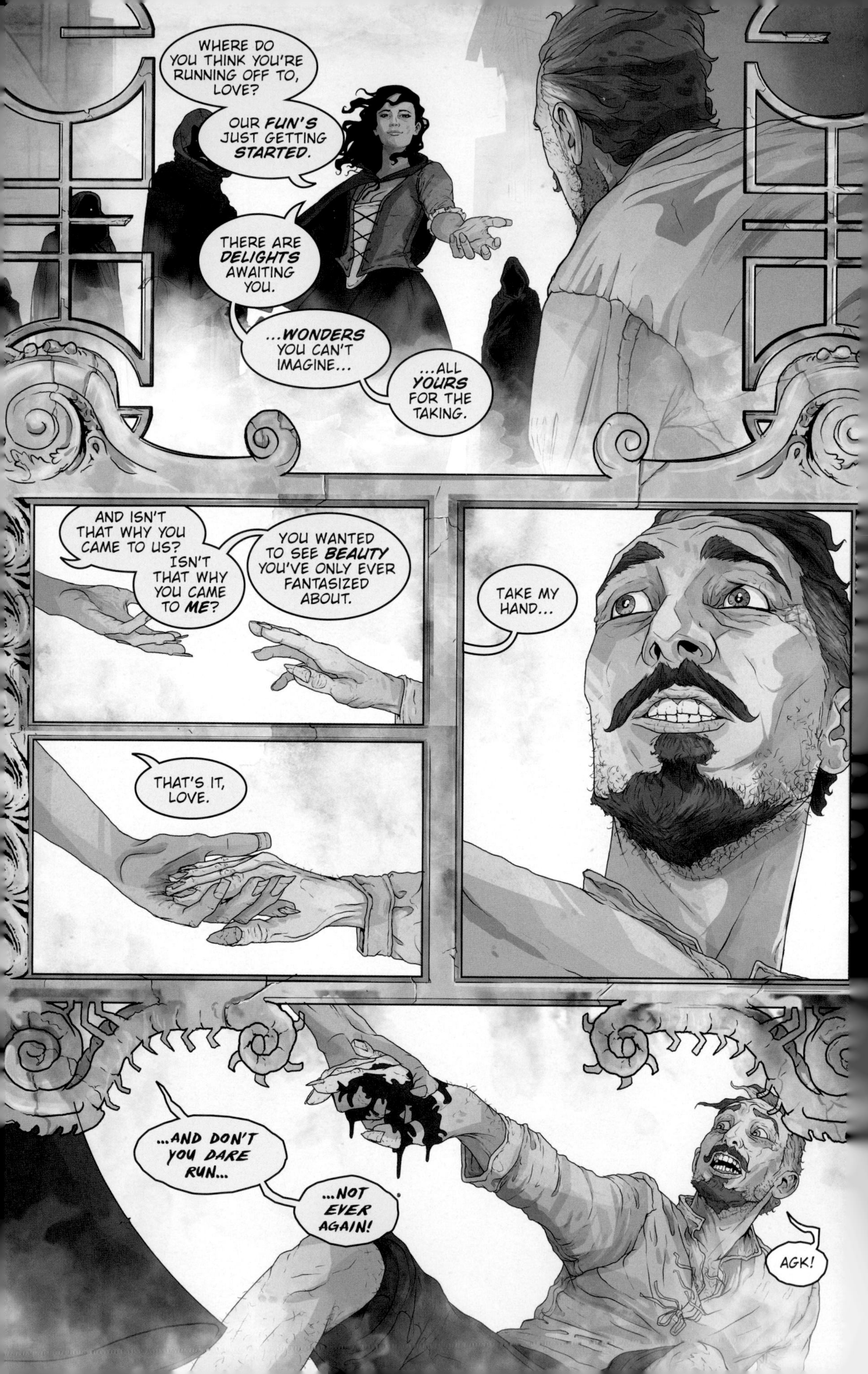
WHERE DO YOU THINK YOU'RE RUNNING OFF TO, LOVE?
OUR FUN'S JUST GETTING STARTED.
THERE ARE DELIGHTS AWAITING YOU.
...WONDERS YOU CAN'T IMAGINE...
...ALL YOURS FOR THE TAKING.
AND ISN'T THAT WHY YOU CAME TO US? ISN'T THAT WHY YOU CAME TO ME?
YOU WANTED TO SEE BEAUTY YOU'VE ONLY EVER FANTASIZED ABOUT.
TAKE MY HAND...
THAT'S IT, LOVE.
...AND DON'T YOU DARE RUN...
...NOT EVER AGAIN!
AGK!

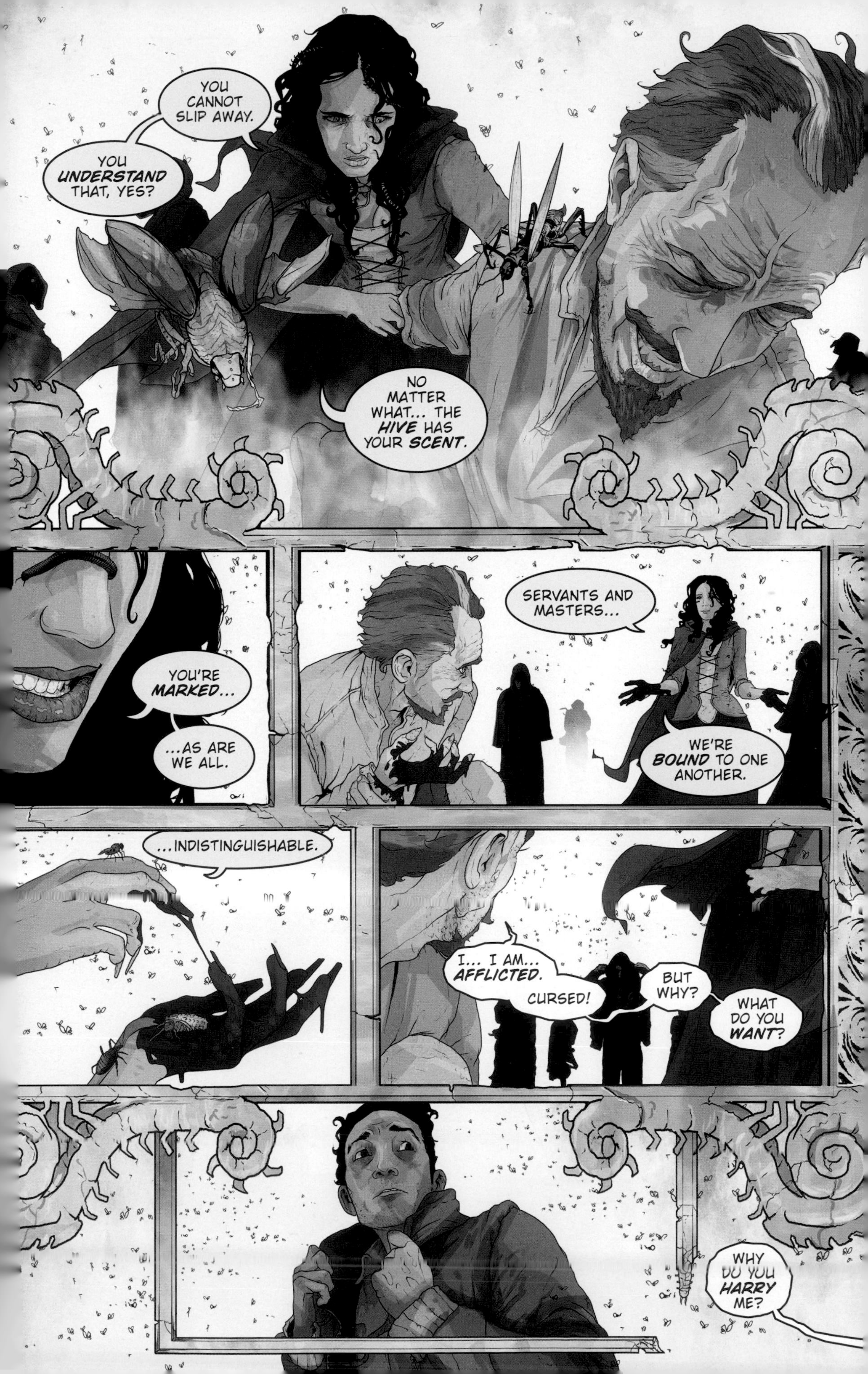
YOU CANNOT SLIP AWAY.
YOU *UNDERSTAND* THAT, YES?
NO MATTER WHAT... THE *HIVE* HAS YOUR *SCENT*.
YOU'RE *MARKED*...
...AS ARE WE ALL.
SERVANTS AND MASTERS...
WE'RE *BOUND* TO ONE ANOTHER.
...INDISTINGUISHABLE.
I... I AM... *AFFLICTED*.
CURSED!
BUT WHY?
WHAT DO YOU *WANT*?
WHY DO YOU *HARRY* ME?

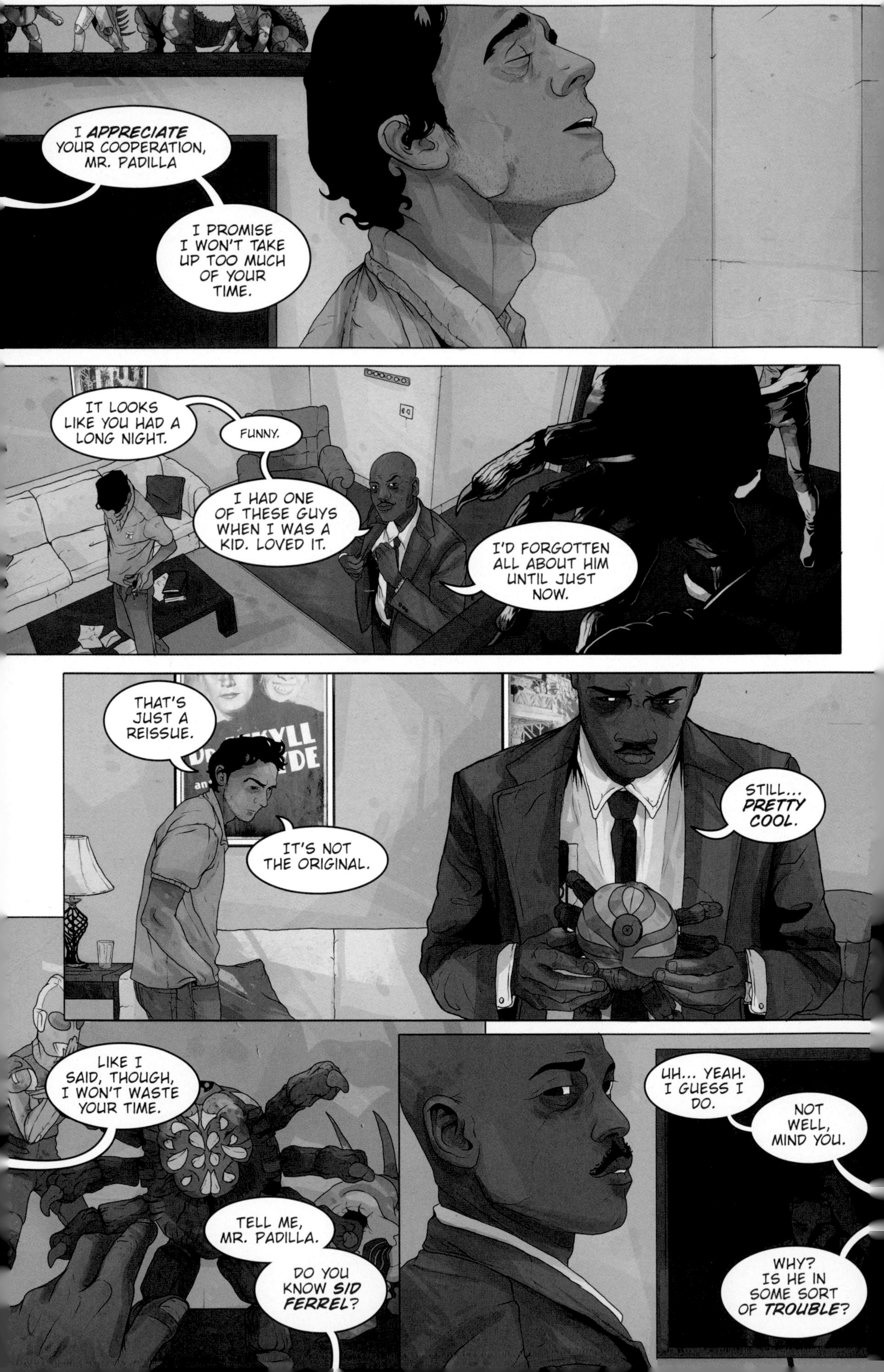
I APPRECIATE YOUR COOPERATION, MR. PADILLA
I PROMISE I WON'T TAKE UP TOO MUCH OF YOUR TIME.
IT LOOKS LIKE YOU HAD A LONG NIGHT.
FUNNY.
I HAD ONE OF THESE GUYS WHEN I WAS A KID. LOVED IT.
I'D FORGOTTEN ALL ABOUT HIM UNTIL JUST NOW.
THAT'S JUST A REISSUE.
IT'S NOT THE ORIGINAL.
STILL... PRETTY COOL.
LIKE I SAID, THOUGH, I WON'T WASTE YOUR TIME.
TELL ME, MR. PADILLA.
DO YOU KNOW SID FERREL?
UH... YEAH. I GUESS I DO.
NOT WELL, MIND YOU.
WHY? IS HE IN SOME SORT OF TROUBLE?

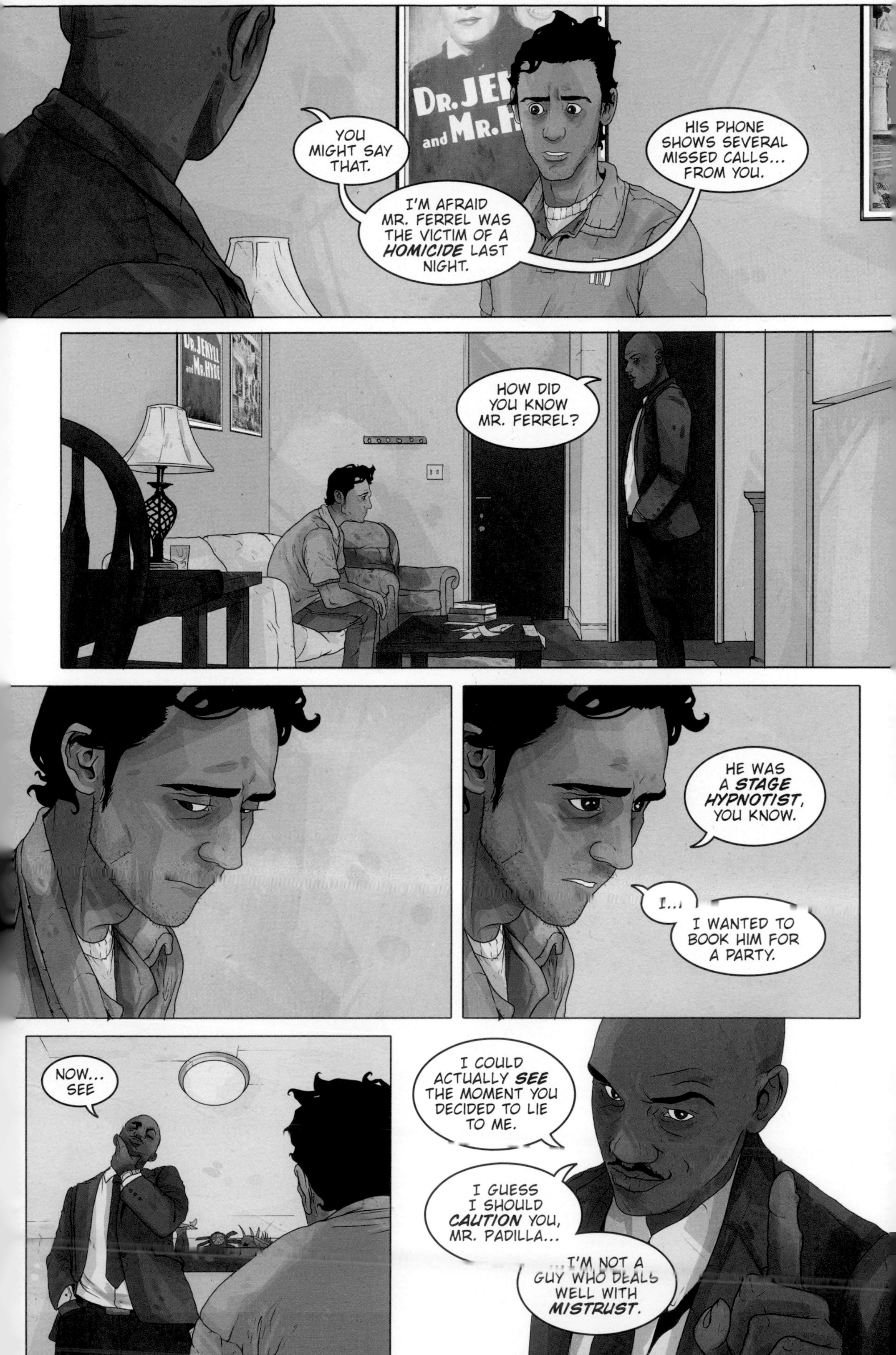
DR. JEKYLL and MR. HYDE
YOU MIGHT SAY THAT.
I'M AFRAID MR. FERREL WAS THE VICTIM OF A HOMICIDE LAST NIGHT.
HIS PHONE SHOWS SEVERAL MISSED CALLS... FROM YOU.
HOW DID YOU KNOW MR. FERREL?
HE WAS A STAGE HYPNOTIST, YOU KNOW.
I...
I WANTED TO BOOK HIM FOR A PARTY.
NOW... SEE
I COULD ACTUALLY SEE THE MOMENT YOU DECIDED TO LIE TO ME.
I GUESS I SHOULD CAUTION YOU, MR. PADILLA...
...I'M NOT A GUY WHO DEALS WELL WITH MISTRUST.

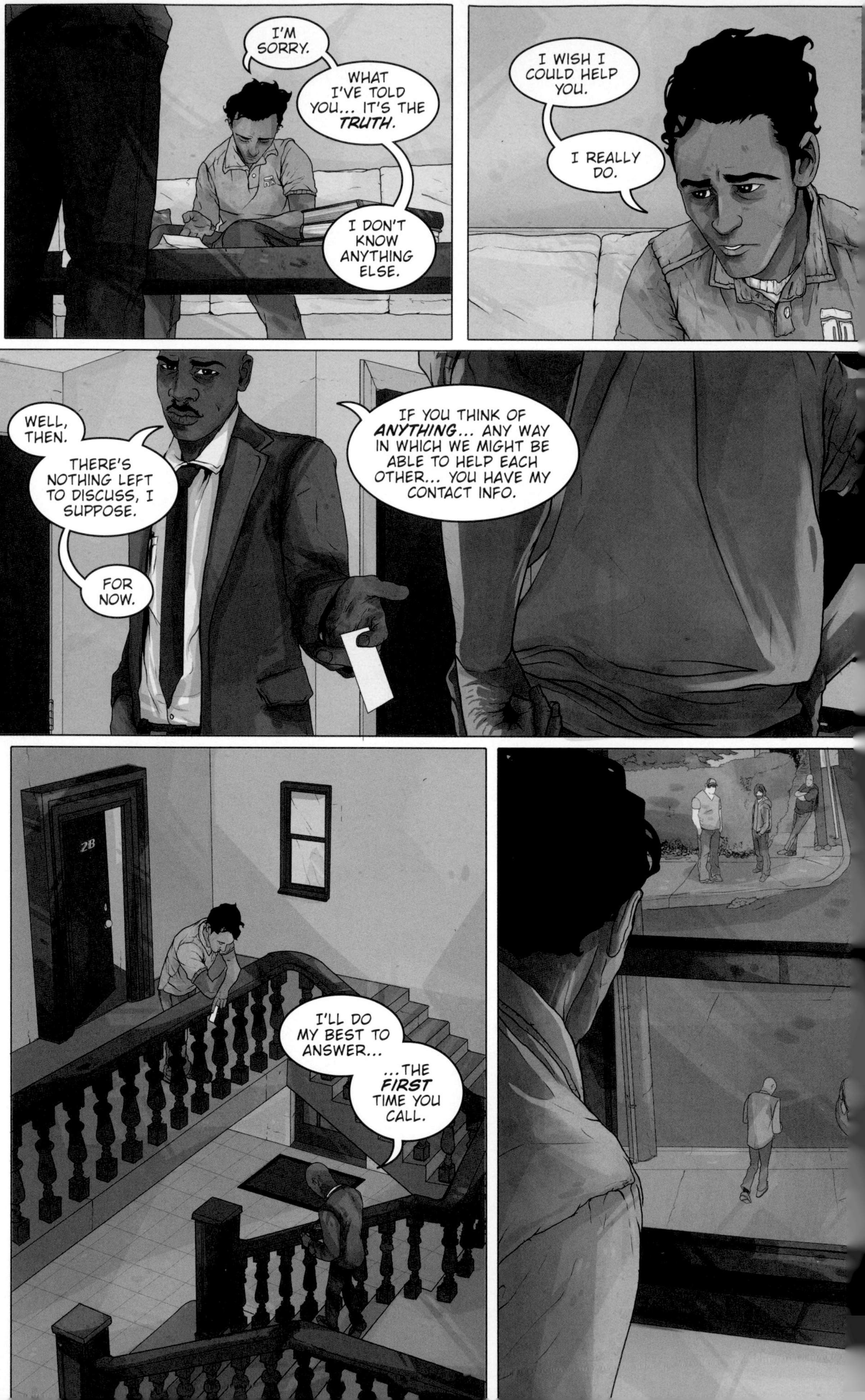
I'M SORRY.
WHAT I'VE TOLD YOU... IT'S THE TRUTH.
I DON'T KNOW ANYTHING ELSE.
I WISH I COULD HELP YOU.
I REALLY DO.
WELL, THEN.
THERE'S NOTHING LEFT TO DISCUSS, I SUPPOSE.
FOR NOW.
IF YOU THINK OF ANYTHING... ANY WAY IN WHICH WE MIGHT BE ABLE TO HELP EACH OTHER... YOU HAVE MY CONTACT INFO.
2B
I'LL DO MY BEST TO ANSWER...
...THE FIRST TIME YOU CALL.

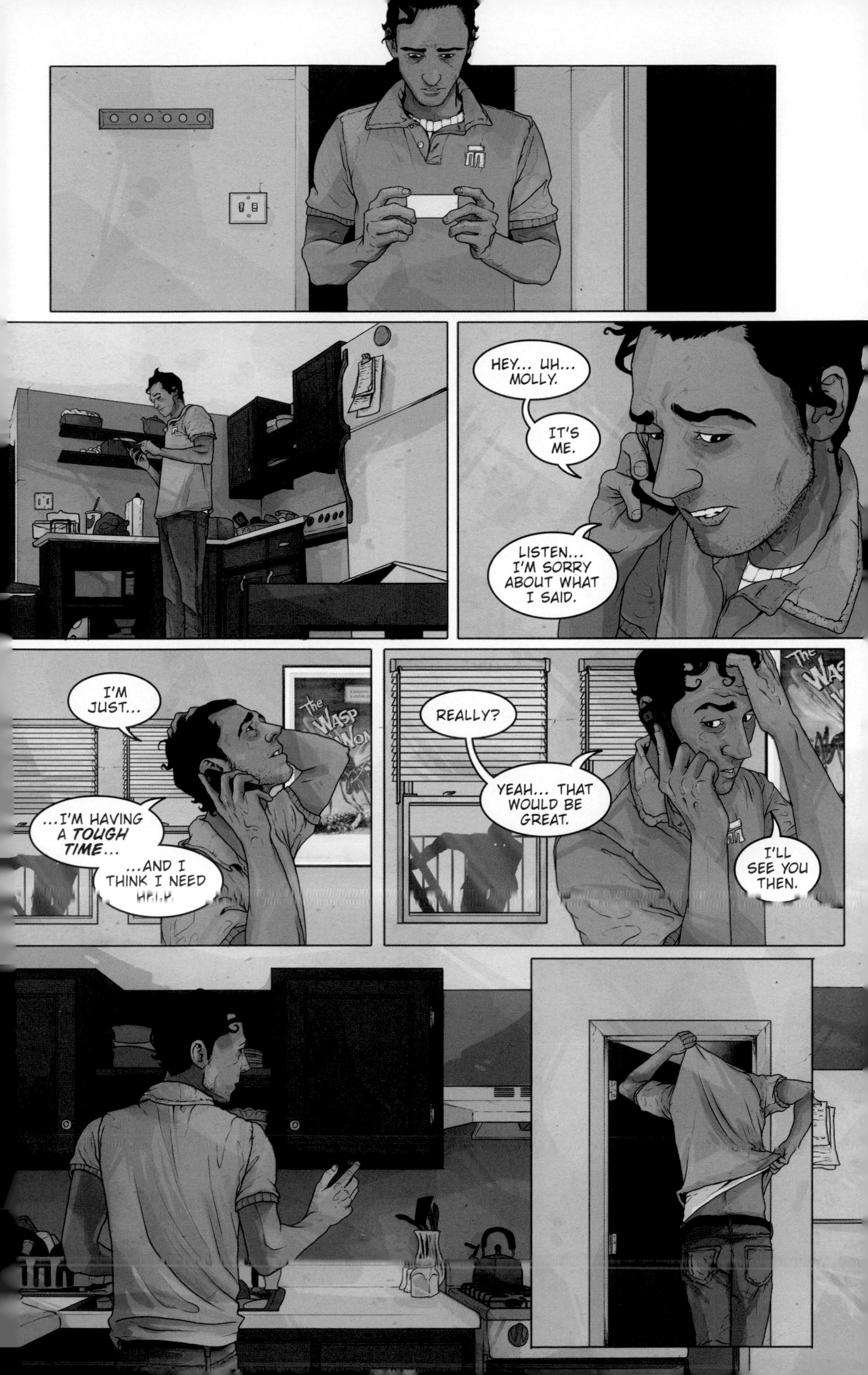

HEY… UH… MOLLY.
IT'S ME.
LISTEN… I'M SORRY ABOUT WHAT I SAID.
I'M JUST…
…I'M HAVING A TOUGH TIME…
…AND I THINK I NEED
REALLY?
YEAH… THAT WOULD BE GREAT.
I'LL SEE YOU THEN.

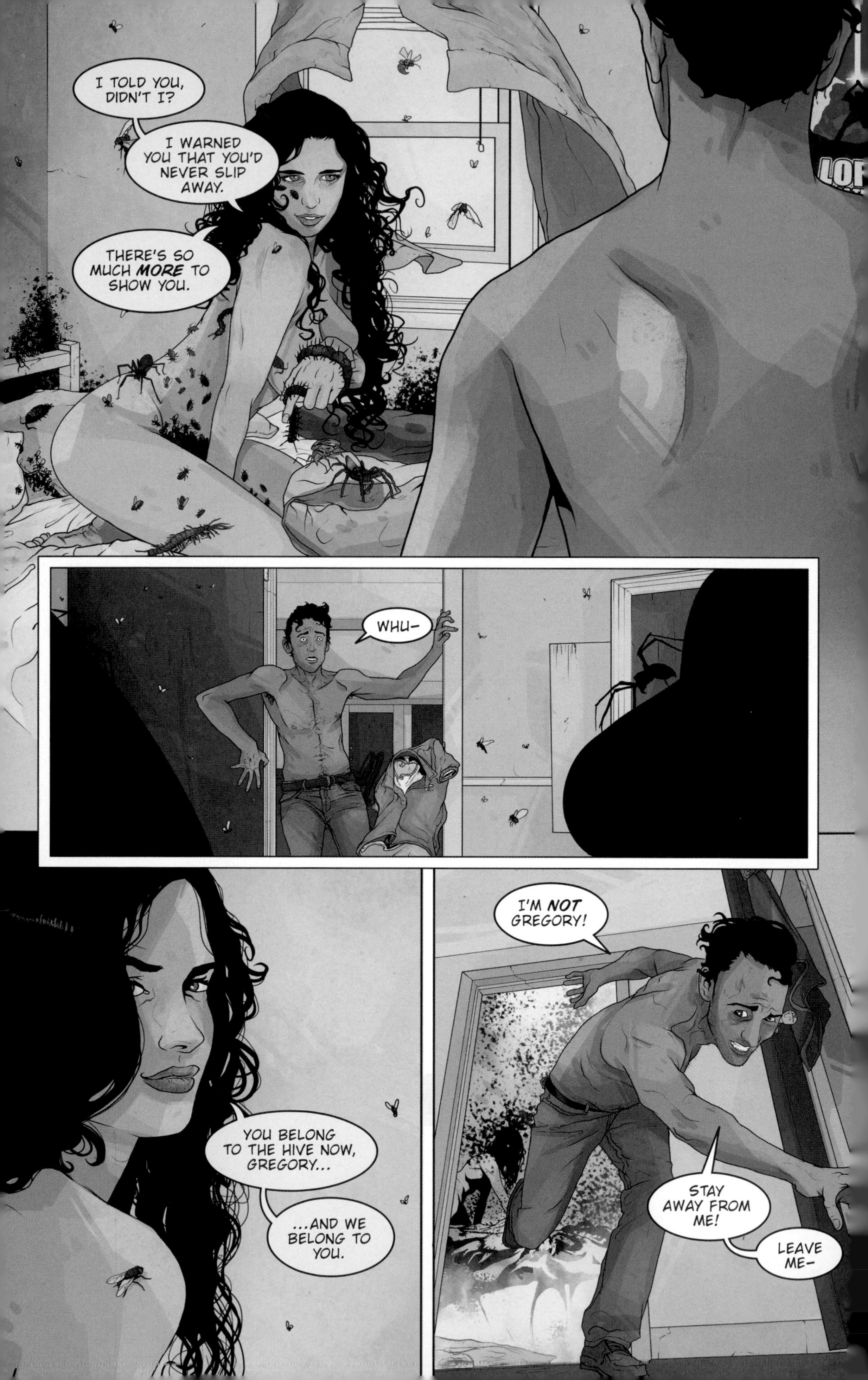
I TOLD YOU, DIDN'T I?
I WARNED YOU THAT YOU'D NEVER SLIP AWAY.
THERE'S SO MUCH MORE TO SHOW YOU.
WHU-
YOU BELONG TO THE HIVE NOW, GREGORY...
...AND WE BELONG TO YOU.
I'M NOT GREGORY!
STAY AWAY FROM ME!
LEAVE ME-

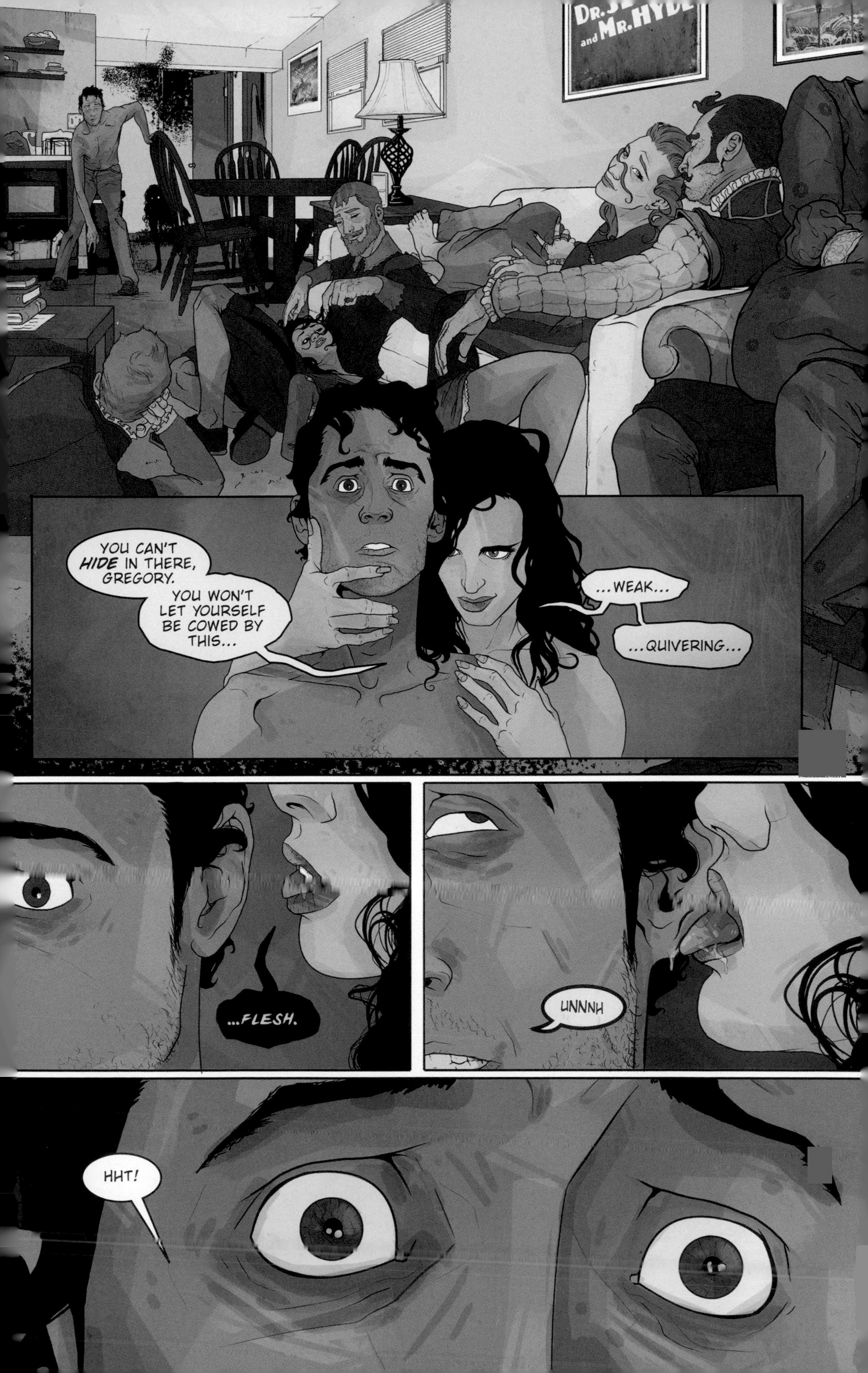
YOU CAN'T *HIDE* IN THERE, GREGORY.
YOU WON'T LET YOURSELF BE COWED BY THIS...
...WEAK...
...QUIVERING...
...FLESH.
UNNNH
HHT!

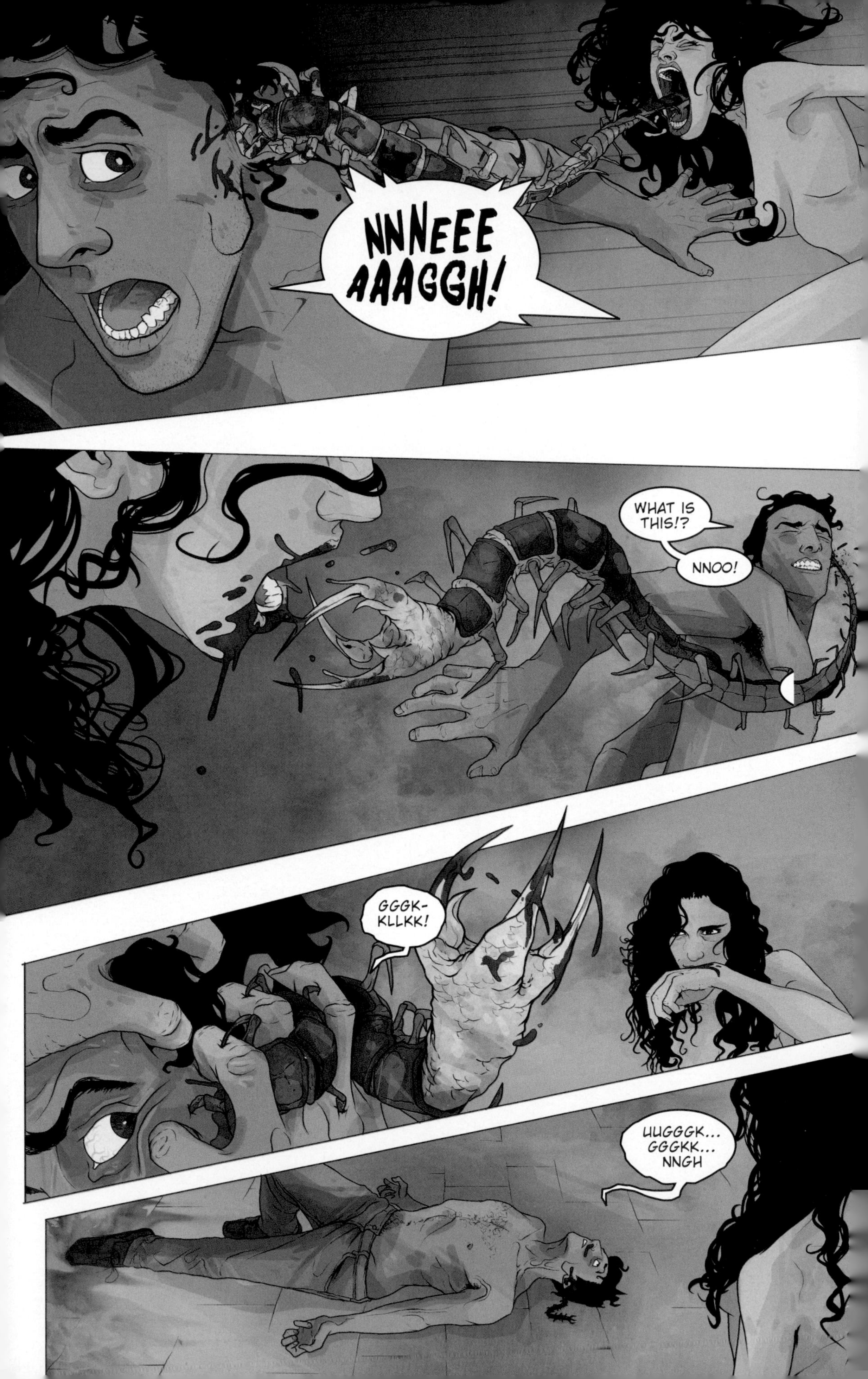
NNNEEE AAAGGH!
WHAT IS THIS!?
NNOO!
GGGK-KLLKK!
UUGGGK... GGGKK... NNGH

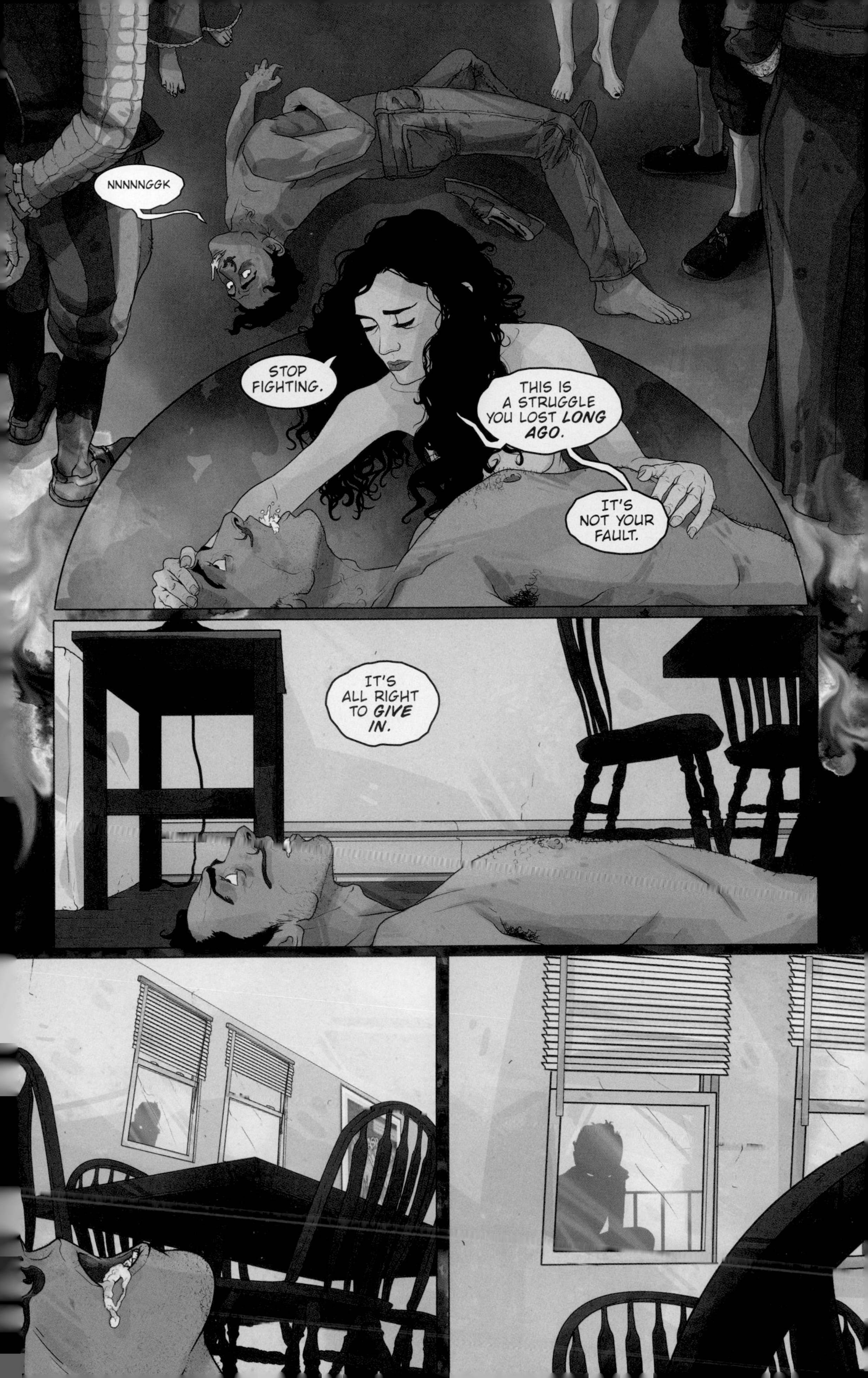
NNNNNGGK
STOP FIGHTING.
THIS IS A STRUGGLE YOU LOST LONG AGO.
IT'S NOT YOUR FAULT.
IT'S ALL RIGHT TO GIVE IN.

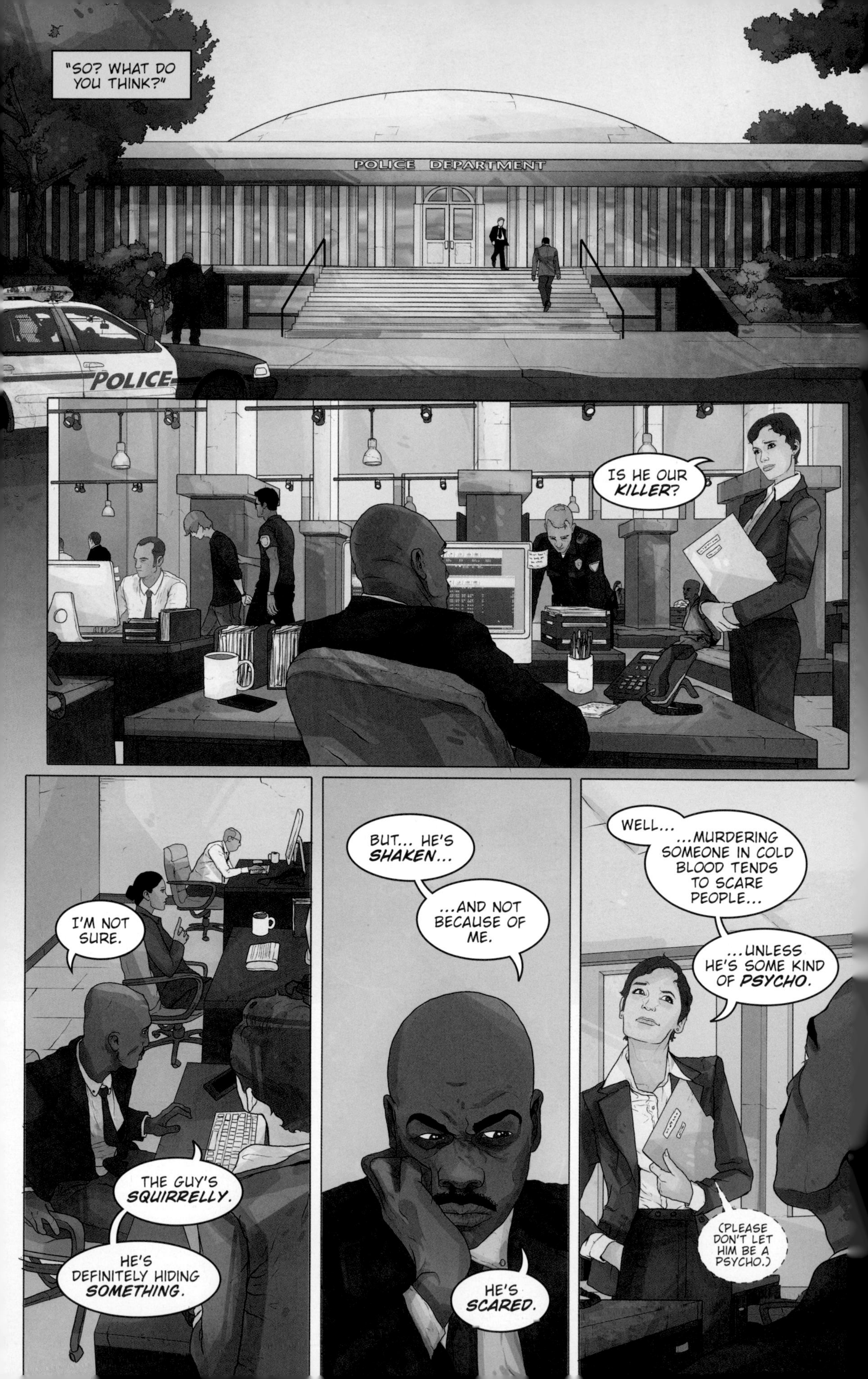
"SO? WHAT DO YOU THINK?"
POLICE DEPARTMENT
POLICE
IS HE OUR KILLER?
I'M NOT SURE.
THE GUY'S SQUIRRELLY.
HE'S DEFINITELY HIDING SOMETHING.
BUT... HE'S SHAKEN...
...AND NOT BECAUSE OF ME.
HE'S SCARED.
WELL...
...MURDERING SOMEONE IN COLD BLOOD TENDS TO SCARE PEOPLE...
...UNLESS HE'S SOME KIND OF PSYCHO.
(PLEASE DON'T LET HIM BE A PSYCHO.)

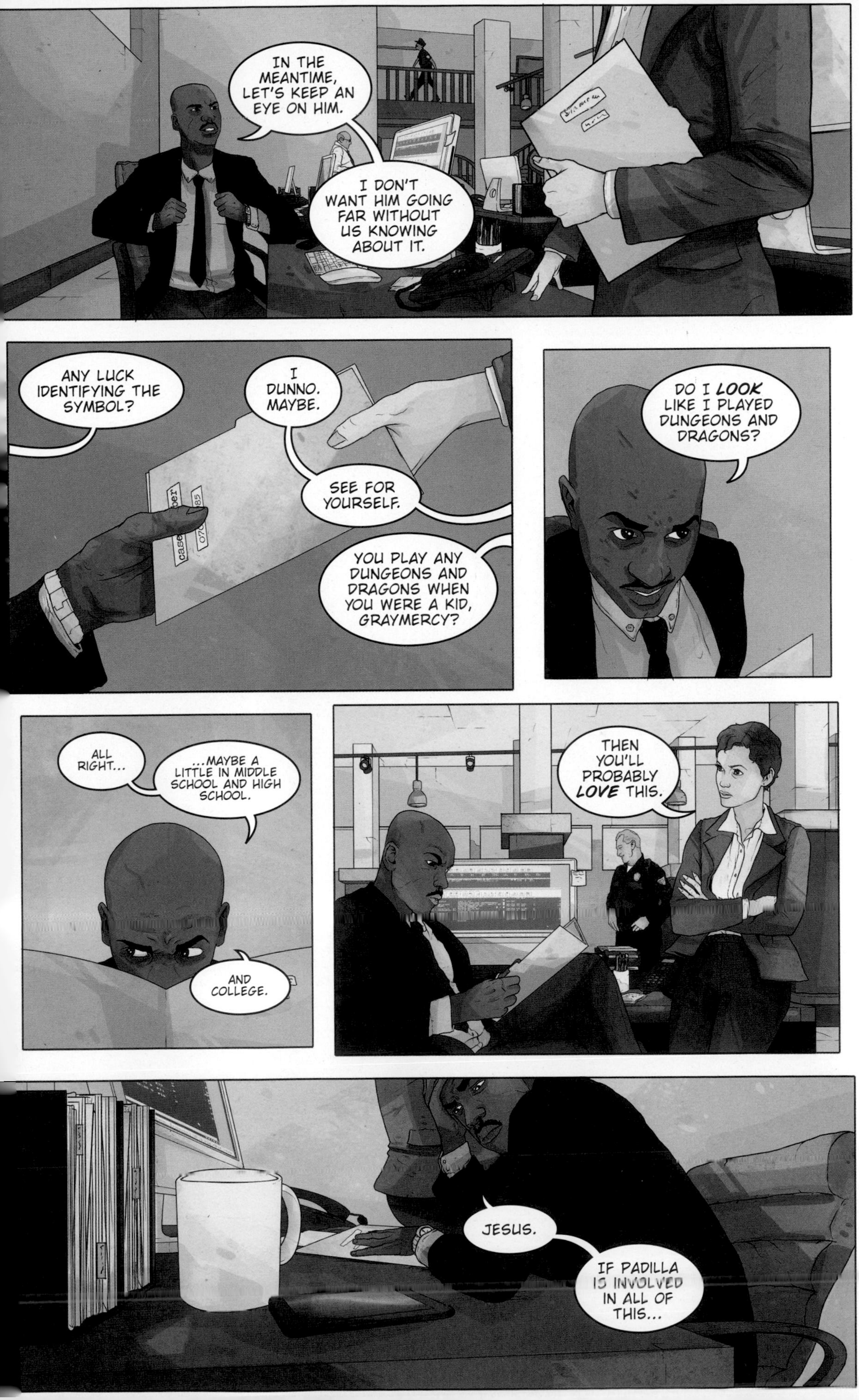
IN THE MEANTIME, LET'S KEEP AN EYE ON HIM.
I DON'T WANT HIM GOING FAR WITHOUT US KNOWING ABOUT IT.
ANY LUCK IDENTIFYING THE SYMBOL?
I DUNNO. MAYBE.
SEE FOR YOURSELF.
YOU PLAY ANY DUNGEONS AND DRAGONS WHEN YOU WERE A KID, GRAYMERCY?
DO I LOOK LIKE I PLAYED DUNGEONS AND DRAGONS?
ALL RIGHT...
...MAYBE A LITTLE IN MIDDLE SCHOOL AND HIGH SCHOOL.
AND COLLEGE.
THEN YOU'LL PROBABLY LOVE THIS.
JESUS.
IF PADILLA IS INVOLVED IN ALL OF THIS...

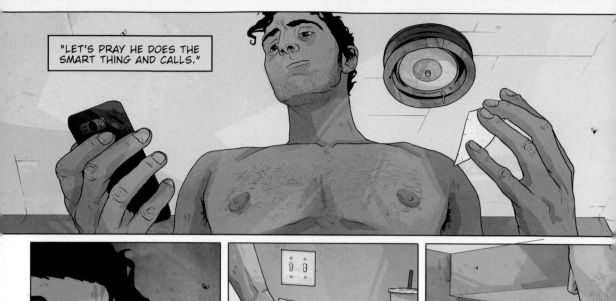

"LET'S PRAY HE DOES THE SMART THING AND CALLS."

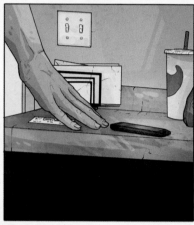

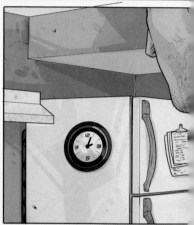

FUCK ME.

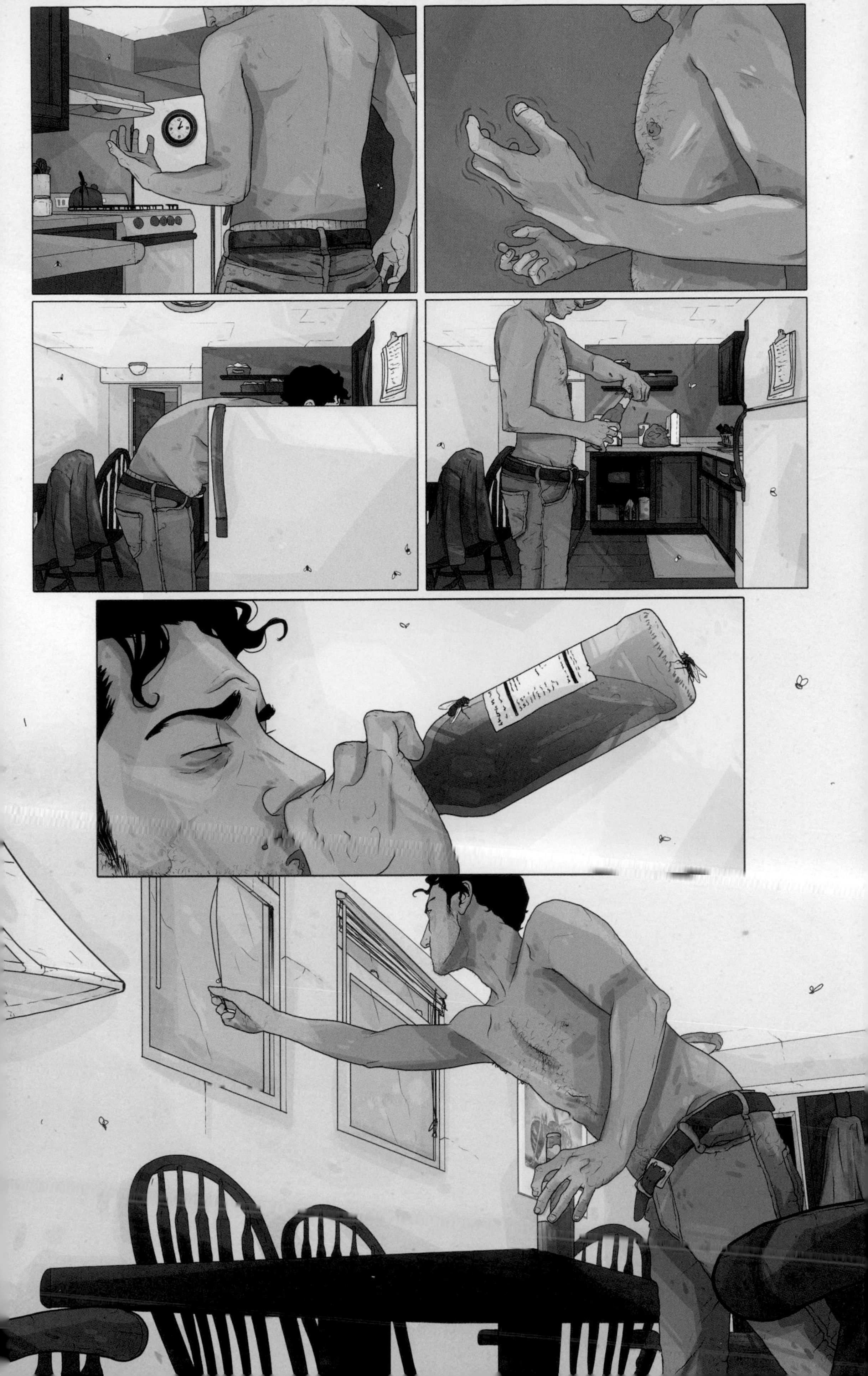

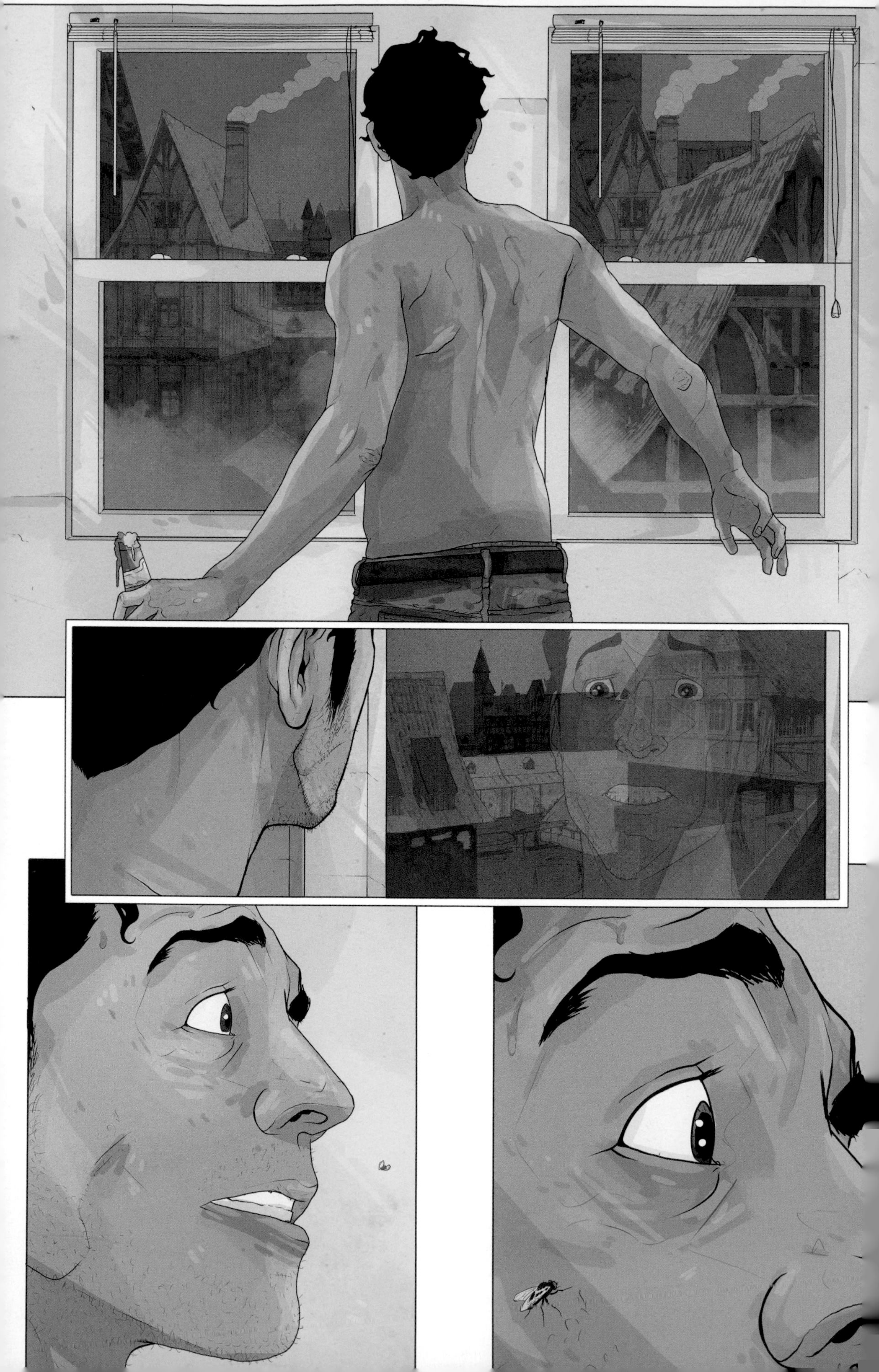

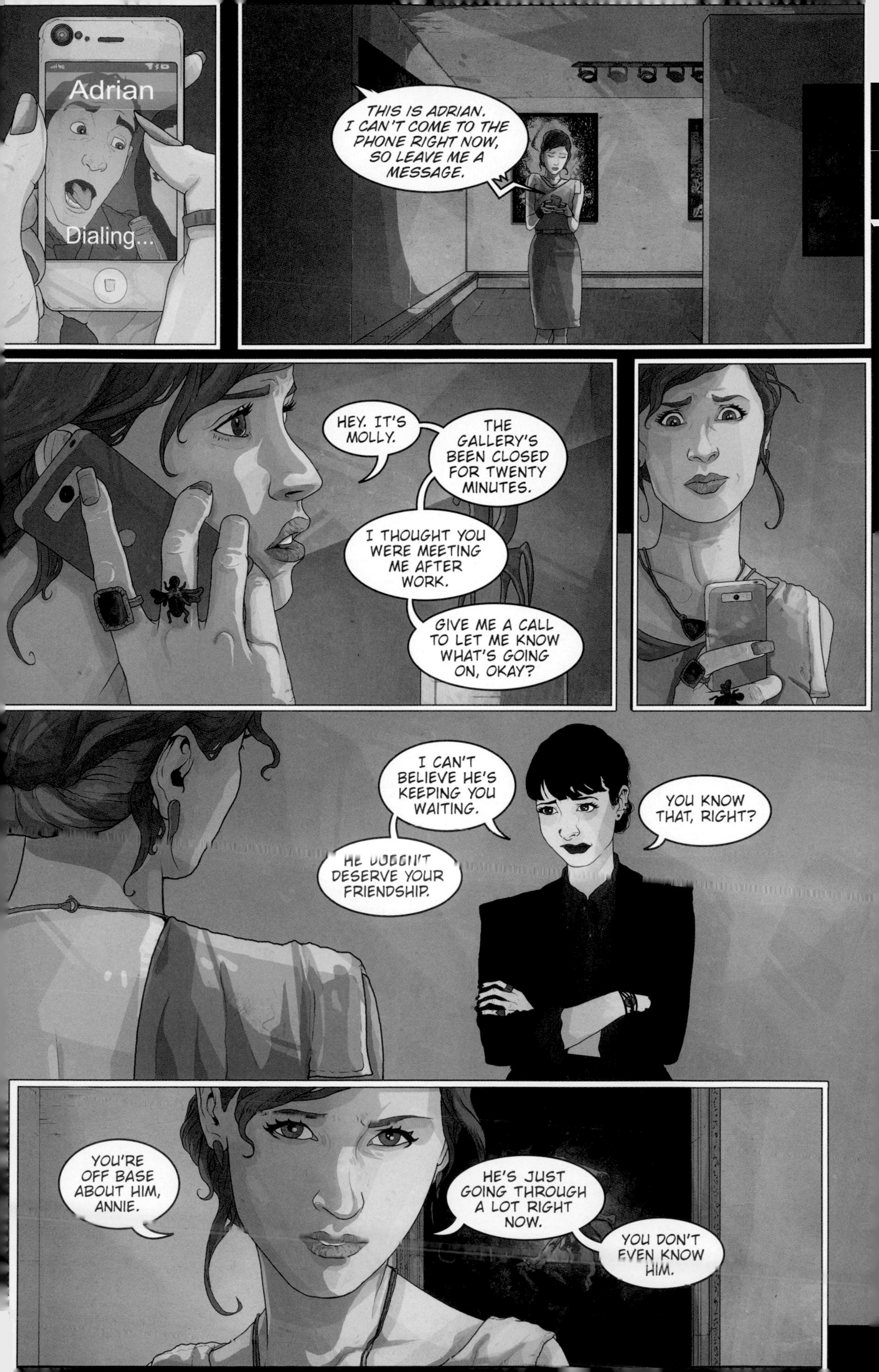
Adrian
Dialing...
THIS IS ADRIAN. I CAN'T COME TO THE PHONE RIGHT NOW, SO LEAVE ME A MESSAGE.
HEY. IT'S MOLLY.
THE GALLERY'S BEEN CLOSED FOR TWENTY MINUTES.
I THOUGHT YOU WERE MEETING ME AFTER WORK.
GIVE ME A CALL TO LET ME KNOW WHAT'S GOING ON, OKAY?
I CAN'T BELIEVE HE'S KEEPING YOU WAITING.
HE DOESN'T DESERVE YOUR FRIENDSHIP.
YOU KNOW THAT, RIGHT?
YOU'RE OFF BASE ABOUT HIM, ANNIE.
HE'S JUST GOING THROUGH A LOT RIGHT NOW.
YOU DON'T EVEN KNOW HIM.

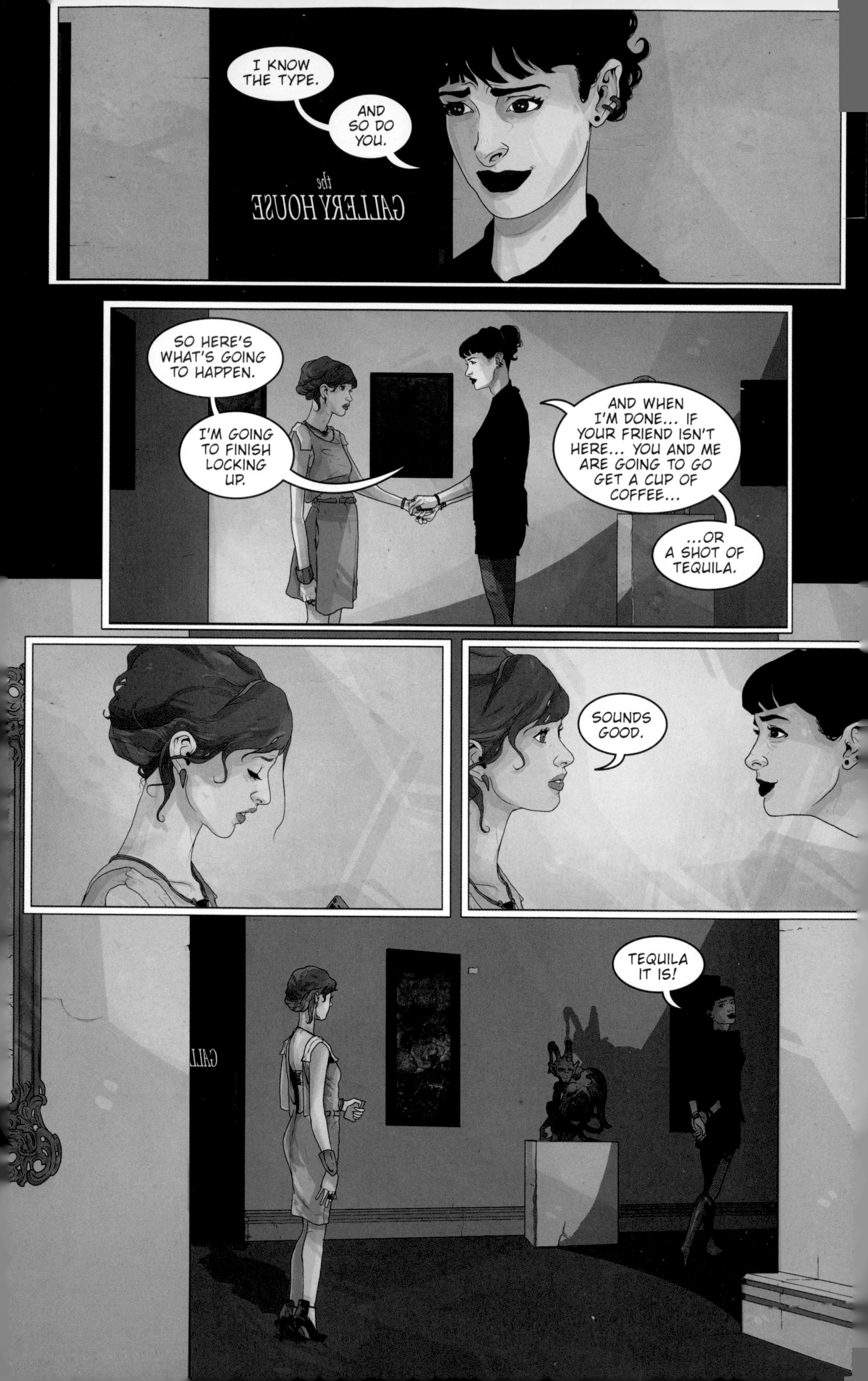
I KNOW THE TYPE.
AND SO DO YOU.
the GALLERY HOUSE
SO HERE'S WHAT'S GOING TO HAPPEN.
I'M GOING TO FINISH LOCKING UP.
AND WHEN I'M DONE... IF YOUR FRIEND ISN'T HERE... YOU AND ME ARE GOING TO GO GET A CUP OF COFFEE...
...OR A SHOT OF TEQUILA.
SOUNDS GOOD.
TEQUILA IT IS!

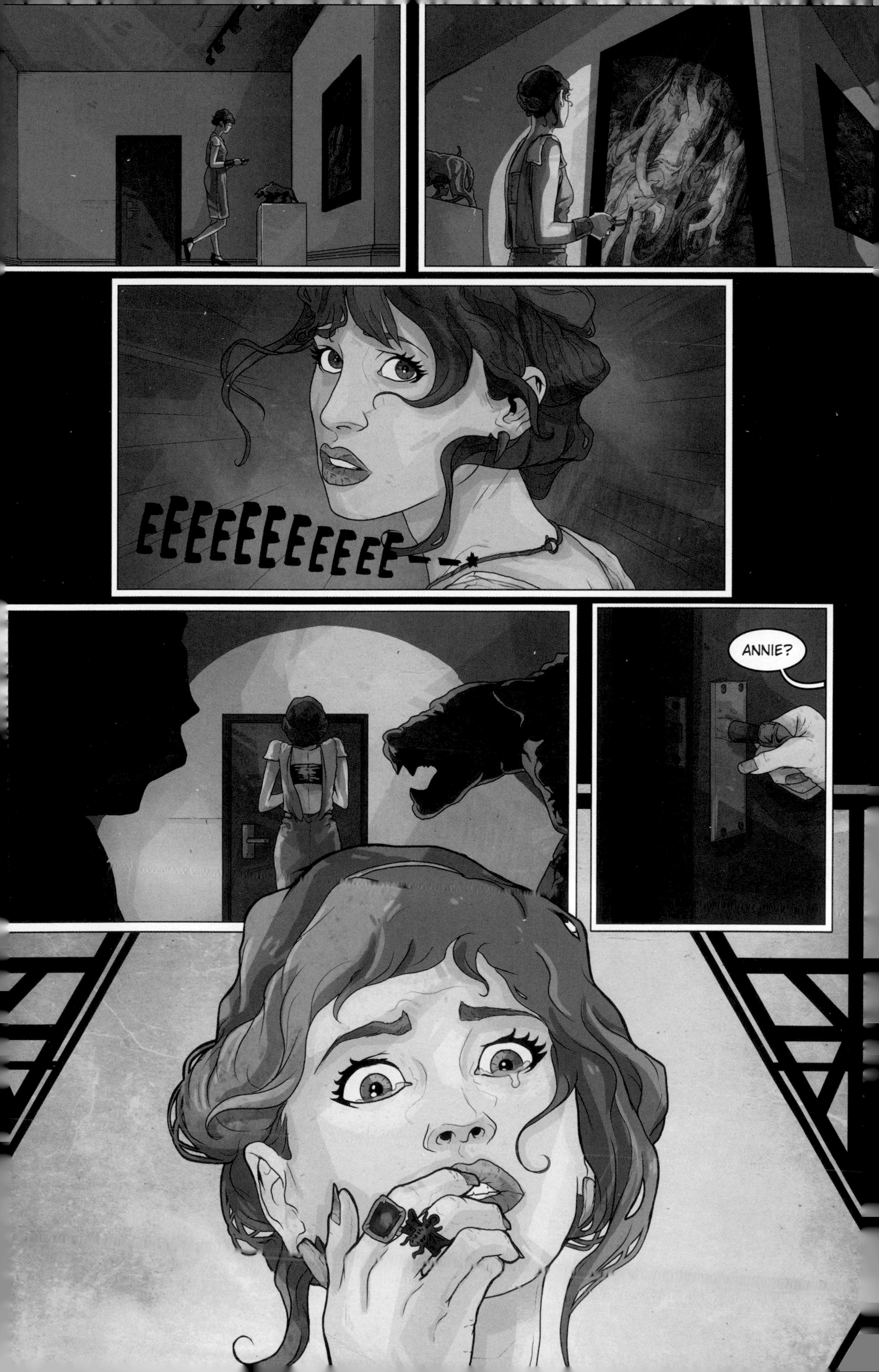
EEEEEEEEEEEE---*
ANNIE?

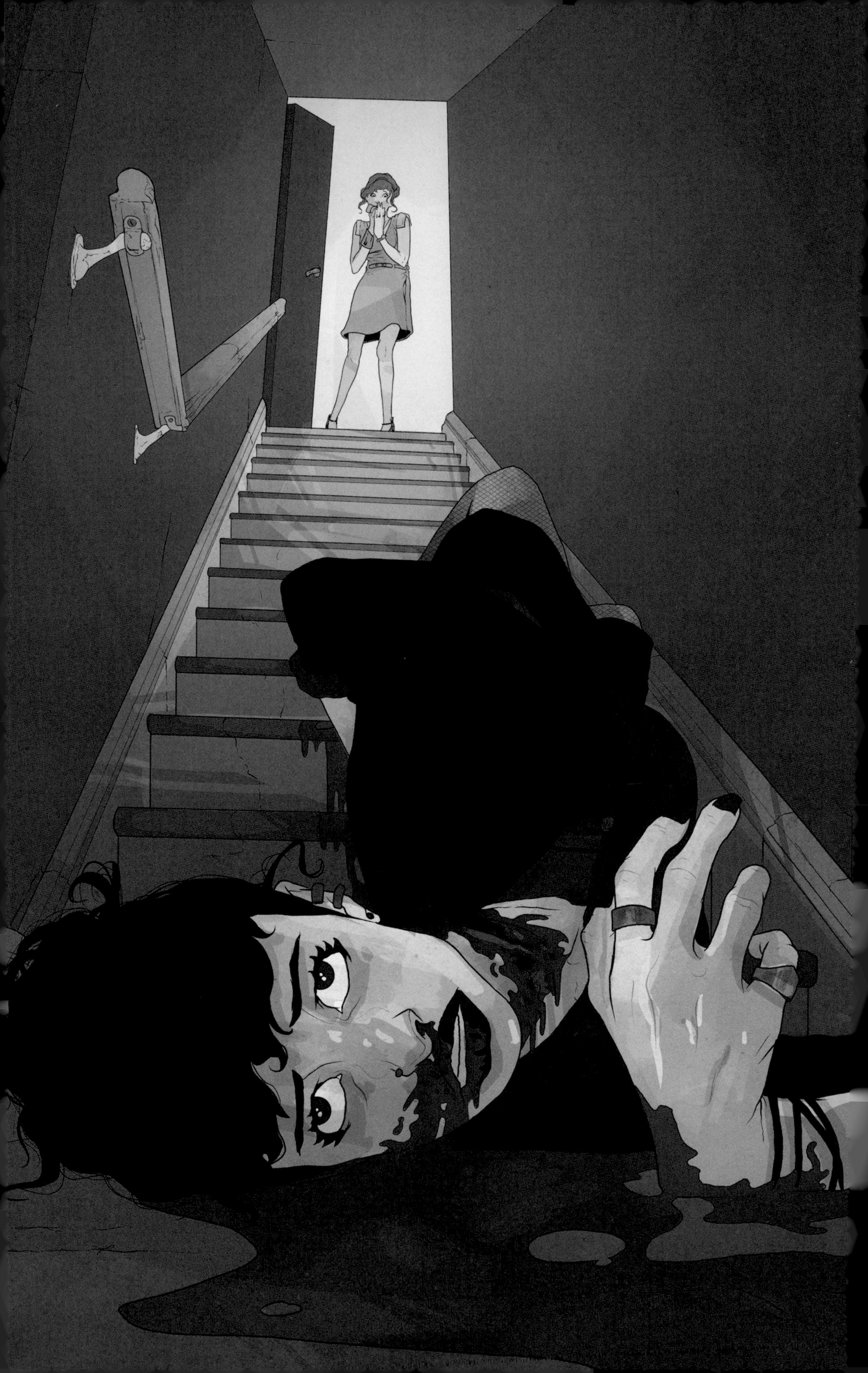

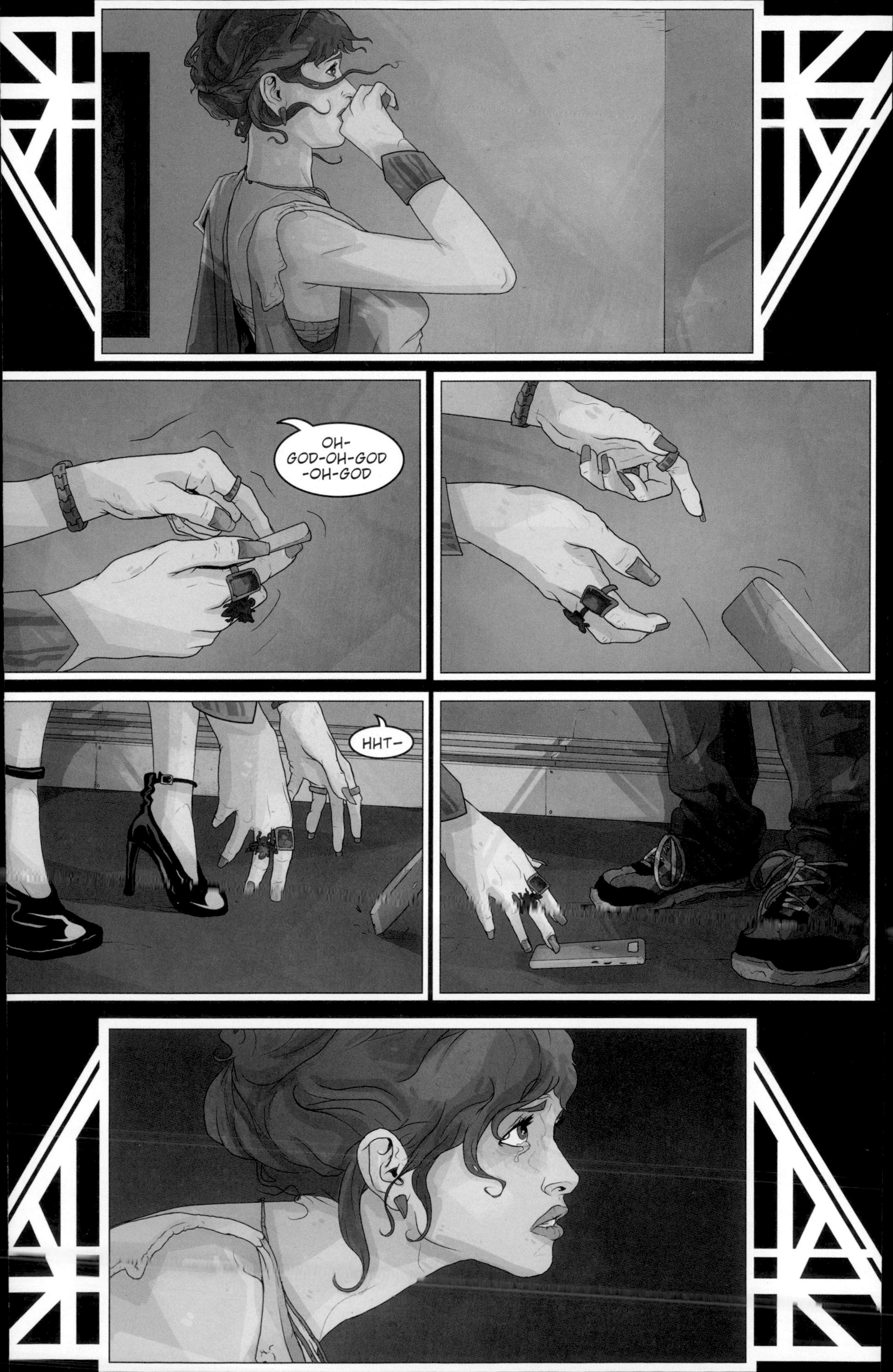
OH-GOD-OH-GOD-OH-GOD
HHT-

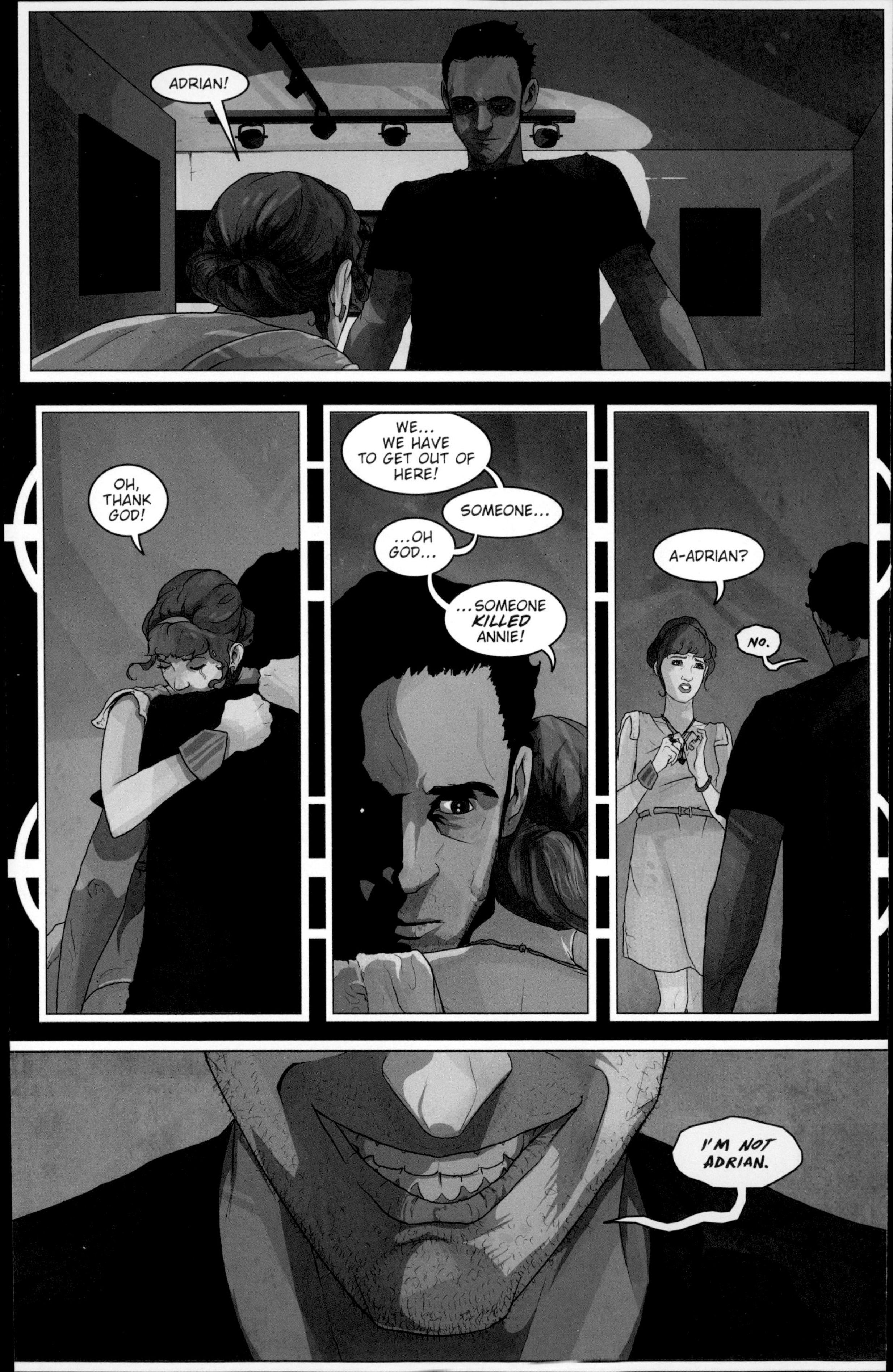
ADRIAN!
OH, THANK GOD!
WE... WE HAVE TO GET OUT OF HERE!
SOMEONE...
...OH GOD...
...SOMEONE *KILLED* ANNIE!
A-ADRIAN?
NO.
I'M NOT ADRIAN.

FOUR

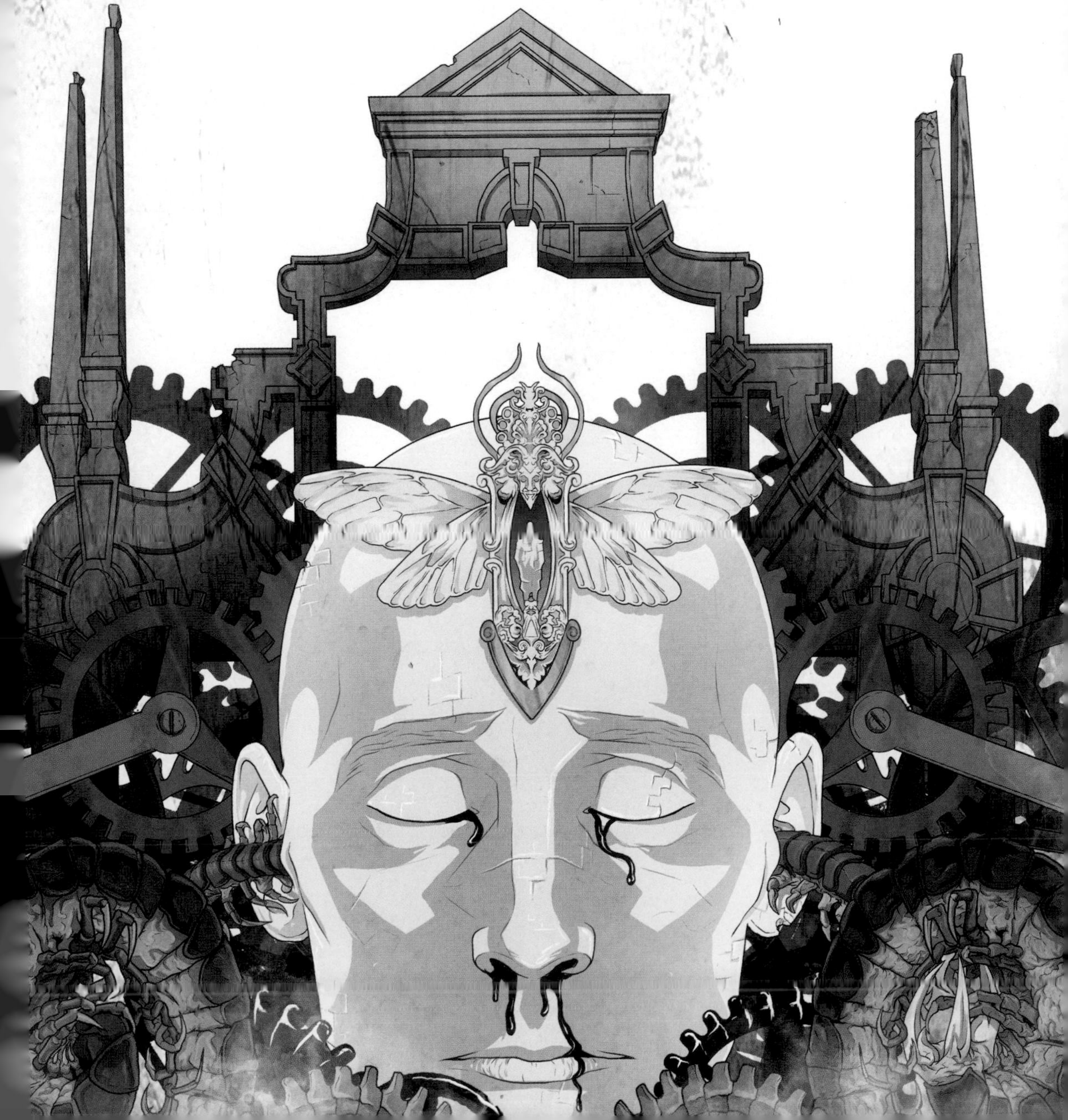

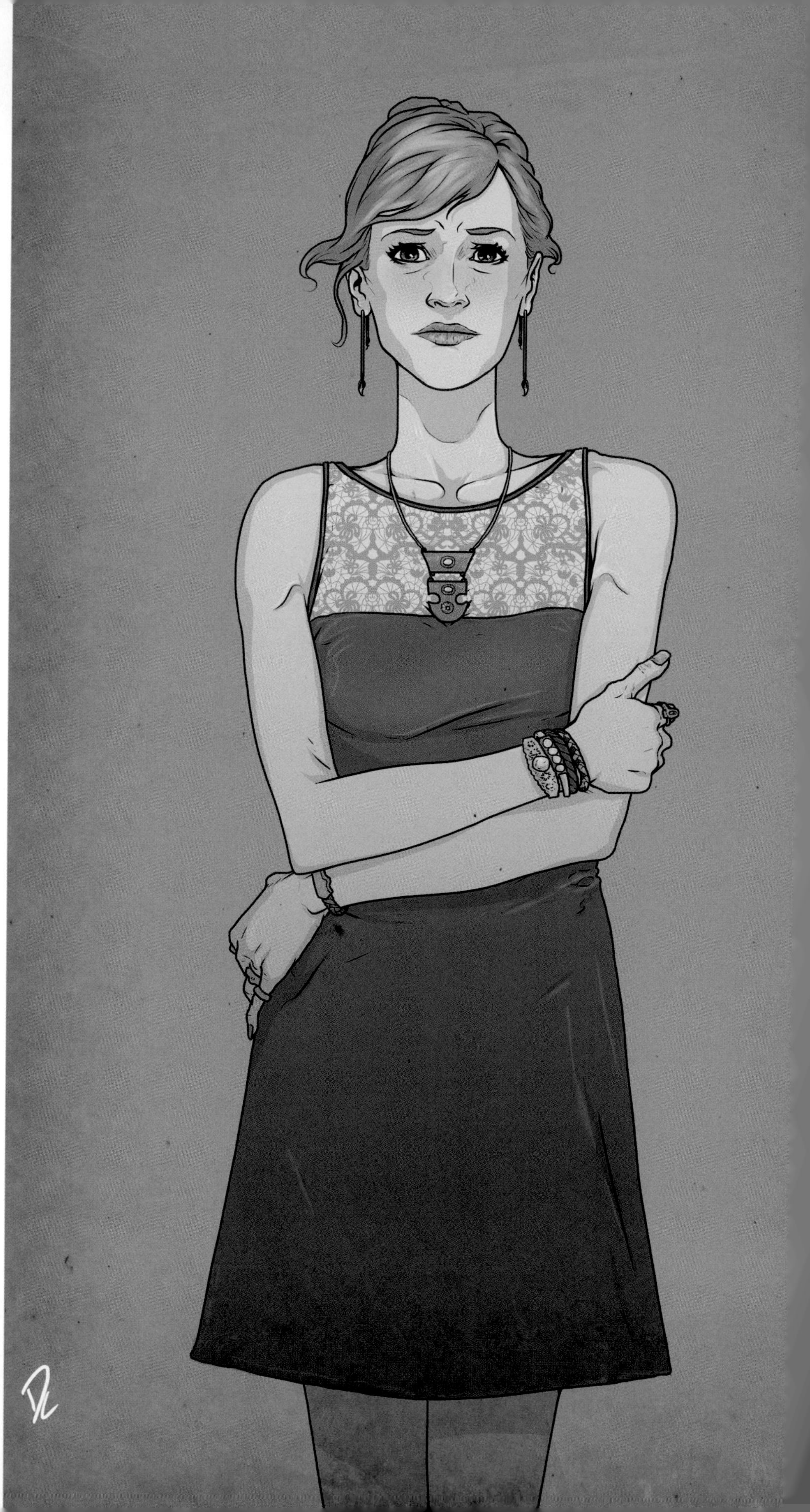

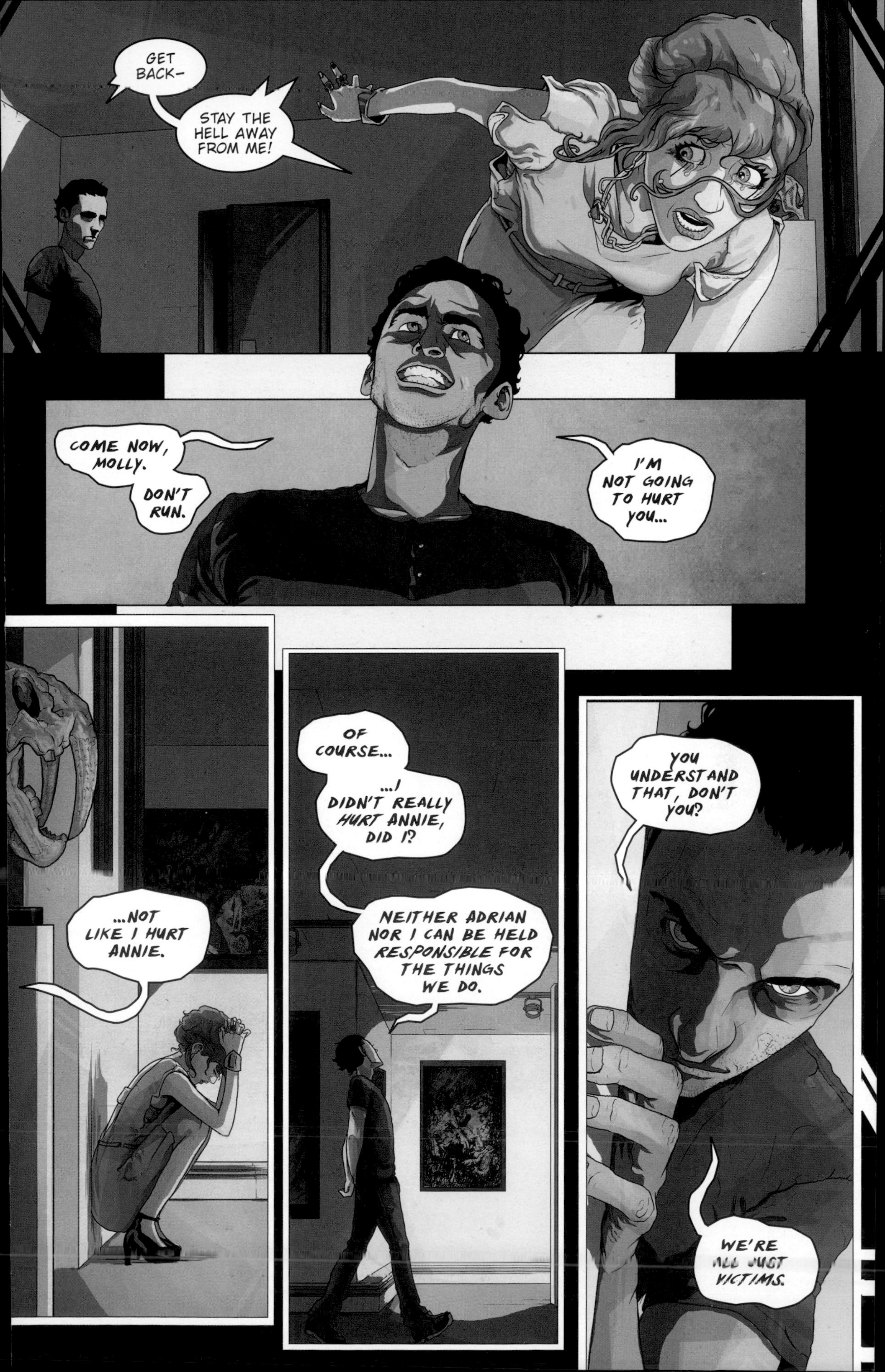

GET BACK–
STAY THE HELL AWAY FROM ME!
COME NOW, MOLLY.
DON'T RUN.
I'M NOT GOING TO HURT YOU...
...NOT LIKE I HURT ANNIE.
OF COURSE...
...I DIDN'T REALLY HURT ANNIE, DID I?
NEITHER ADRIAN NOR I CAN BE HELD RESPONSIBLE FOR THE THINGS WE DO.
YOU UNDERSTAND THAT, DON'T YOU?
WE'RE ALL JUST VICTIMS.

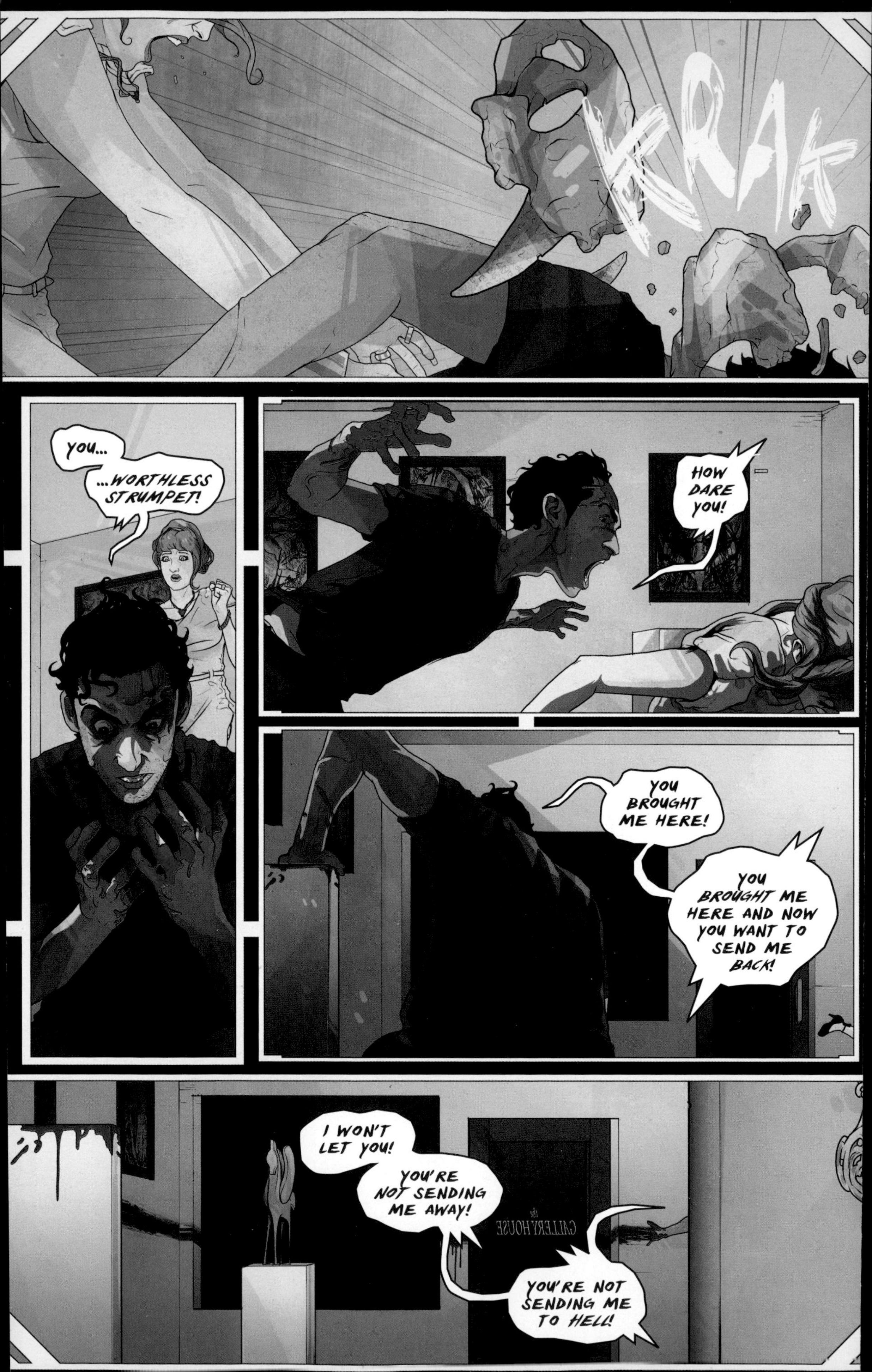

KRAK
YOU...
...WORTHLESS STRUMPET!
HOW DARE YOU!
YOU BROUGHT ME HERE!
YOU BROUGHT ME HERE AND NOW YOU WANT TO SEND ME BACK!
I WON'T LET YOU!
YOU'RE NOT SENDING ME AWAY!
YOU'RE NOT SENDING ME TO HELL!

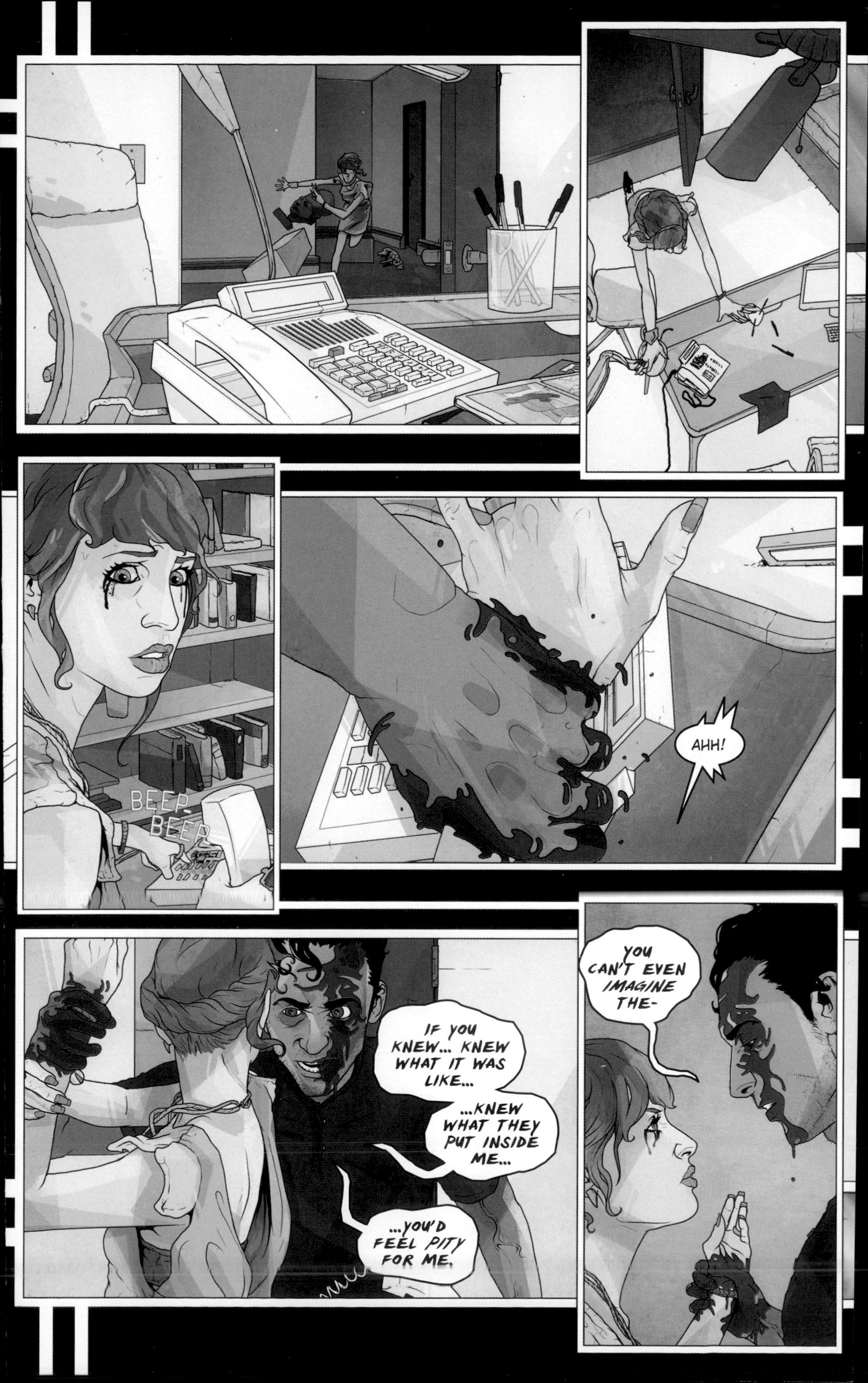
BEEP-
BEEP
AHH!
IF YOU KNEW... KNEW WHAT IT WAS LIKE...
...KNEW WHAT THEY PUT INSIDE ME...
...YOU'D FEEL PITY FOR ME.
YOU CAN'T EVEN IMAGINE THE-

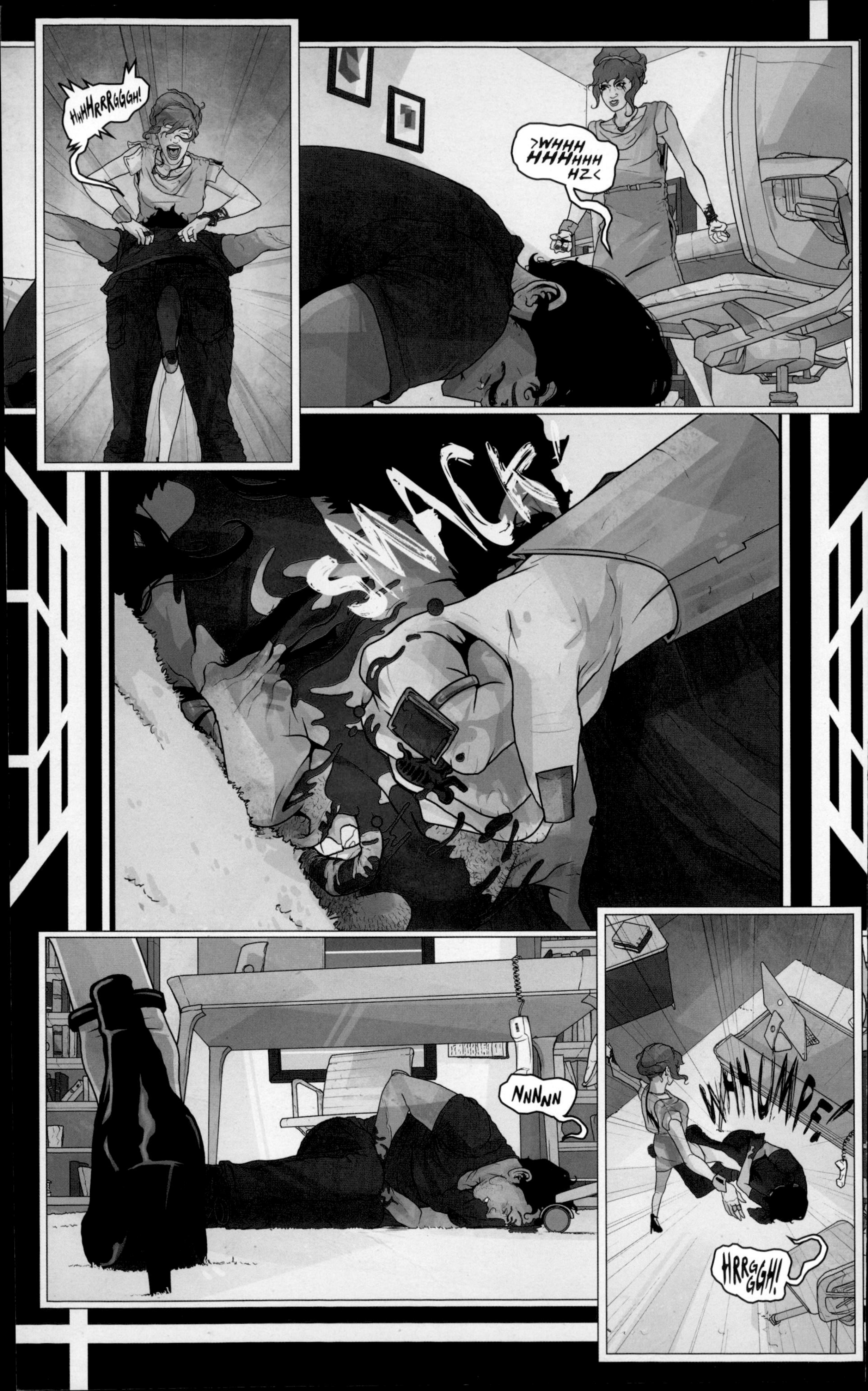
HHHHRRRGGGH!
>WHHH HHHHHH HZ<
SMACK!
NNNNN
WHUMPF!
HRRGGGH!

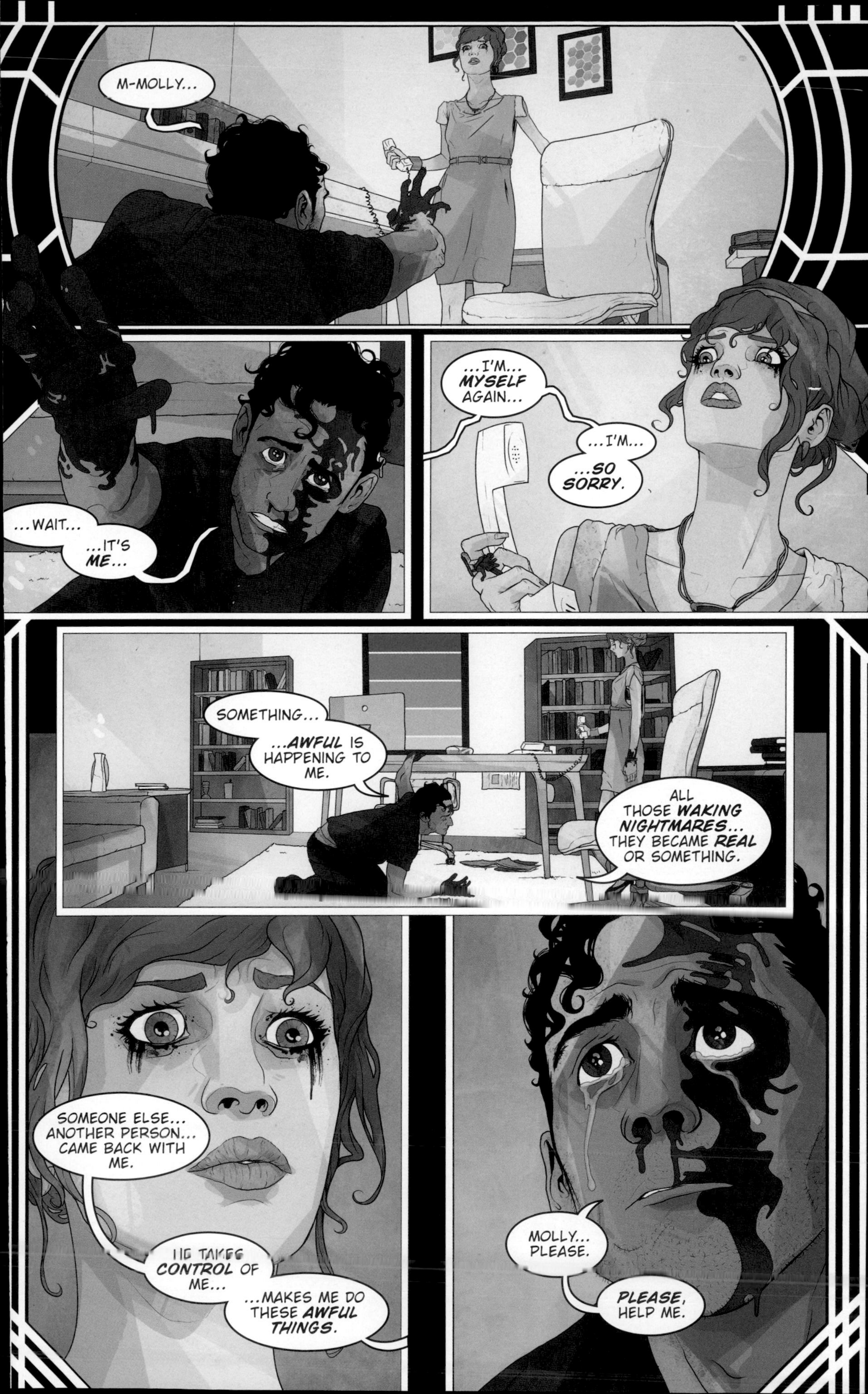
M-MOLLY...
...WAIT...
...IT'S ME...
...I'M... MYSELF AGAIN...
...I'M...
...SO SORRY.
SOMETHING...
...AWFUL IS HAPPENING TO ME.
ALL THOSE WAKING NIGHTMARES... THEY BECAME REAL OR SOMETHING.
SOMEONE ELSE... ANOTHER PERSON... CAME BACK WITH ME.
HE TAKES CONTROL OF ME...
...MAKES ME DO THESE AWFUL THINGS.
MOLLY... PLEASE.
PLEASE, HELP ME.

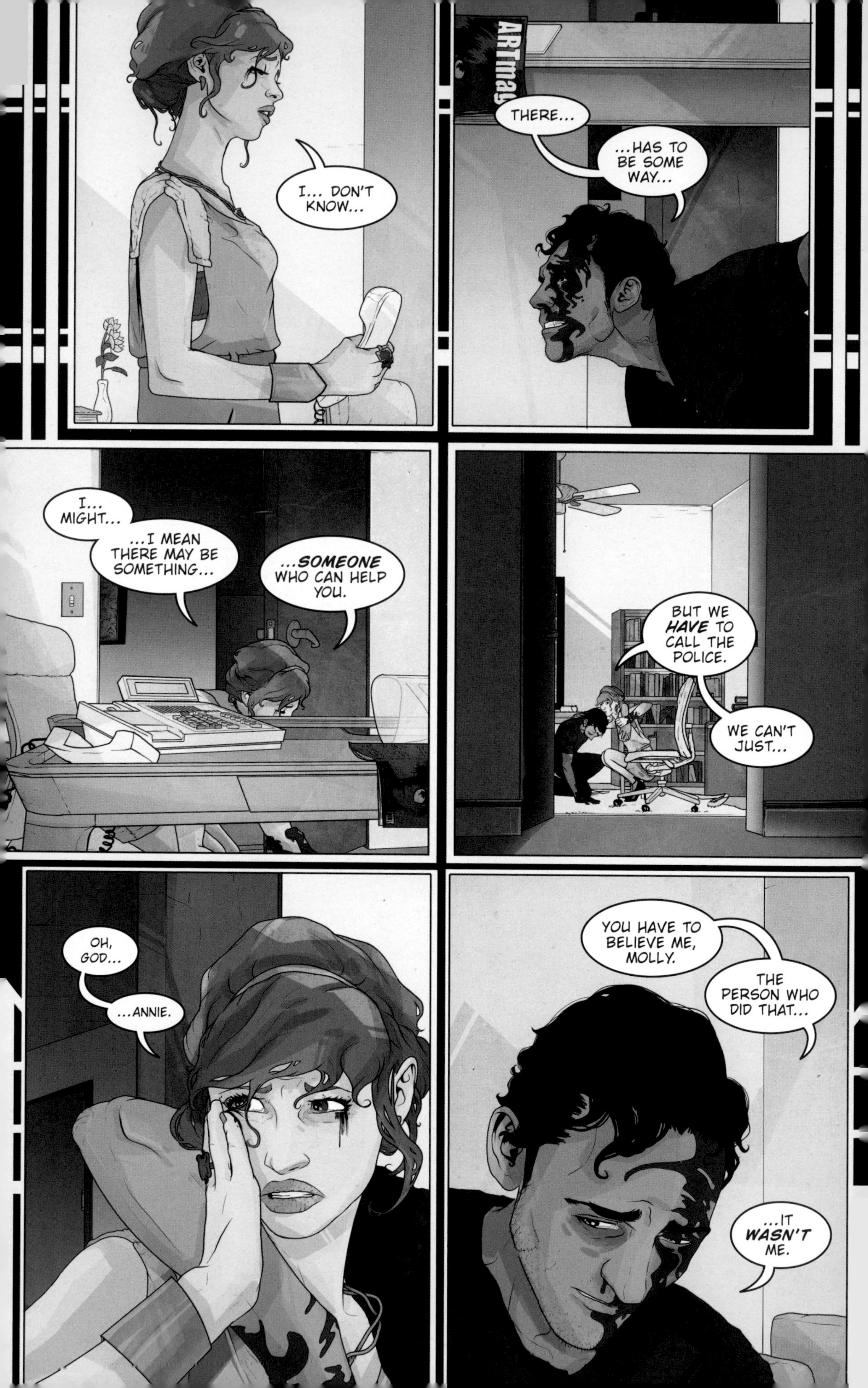
I... DON'T KNOW...
ARTmag
THERE...
...HAS TO BE SOME WAY...
I... MIGHT...
...I MEAN THERE MAY BE SOMETHING...
...SOMEONE WHO CAN HELP YOU.
BUT WE HAVE TO CALL THE POLICE.
WE CAN'T JUST...
OH, GOD...
...ANNIE.
YOU HAVE TO BELIEVE ME, MOLLY.
THE PERSON WHO DID THAT...
...IT WASN'T ME.

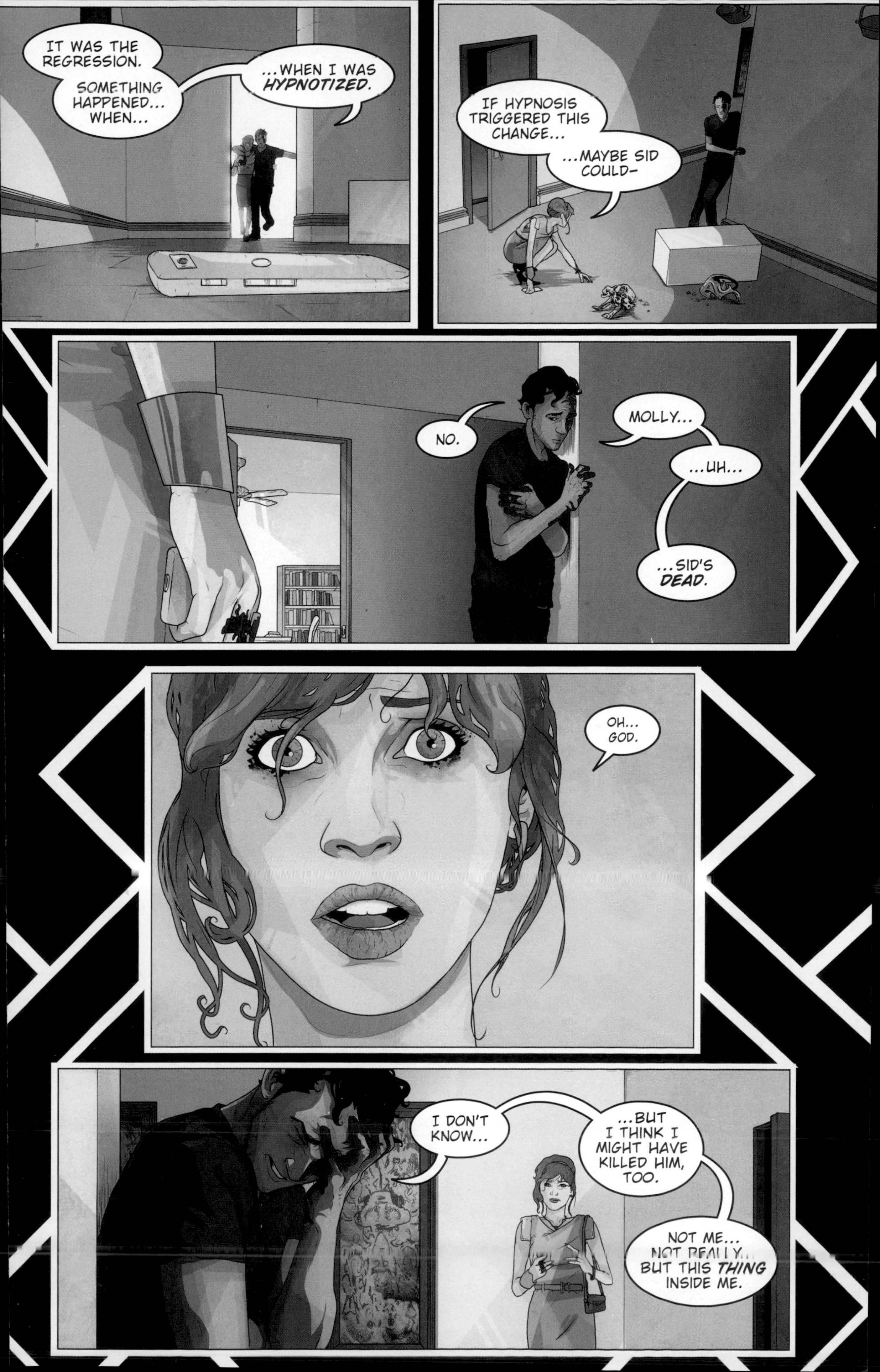
IT WAS THE REGRESSION.
SOMETHING HAPPENED... WHEN...
...WHEN I WAS *HYPNOTIZED.*
IF HYPNOSIS TRIGGERED THIS CHANGE...
...MAYBE SID COULD-
NO.
MOLLY...
...UH...
...SID'S *DEAD.*
OH... GOD.
I DON'T KNOW...
...BUT I THINK I MIGHT HAVE KILLED HIM, TOO.
NOT ME... NOT REALLY... BUT THIS *THING* INSIDE ME.

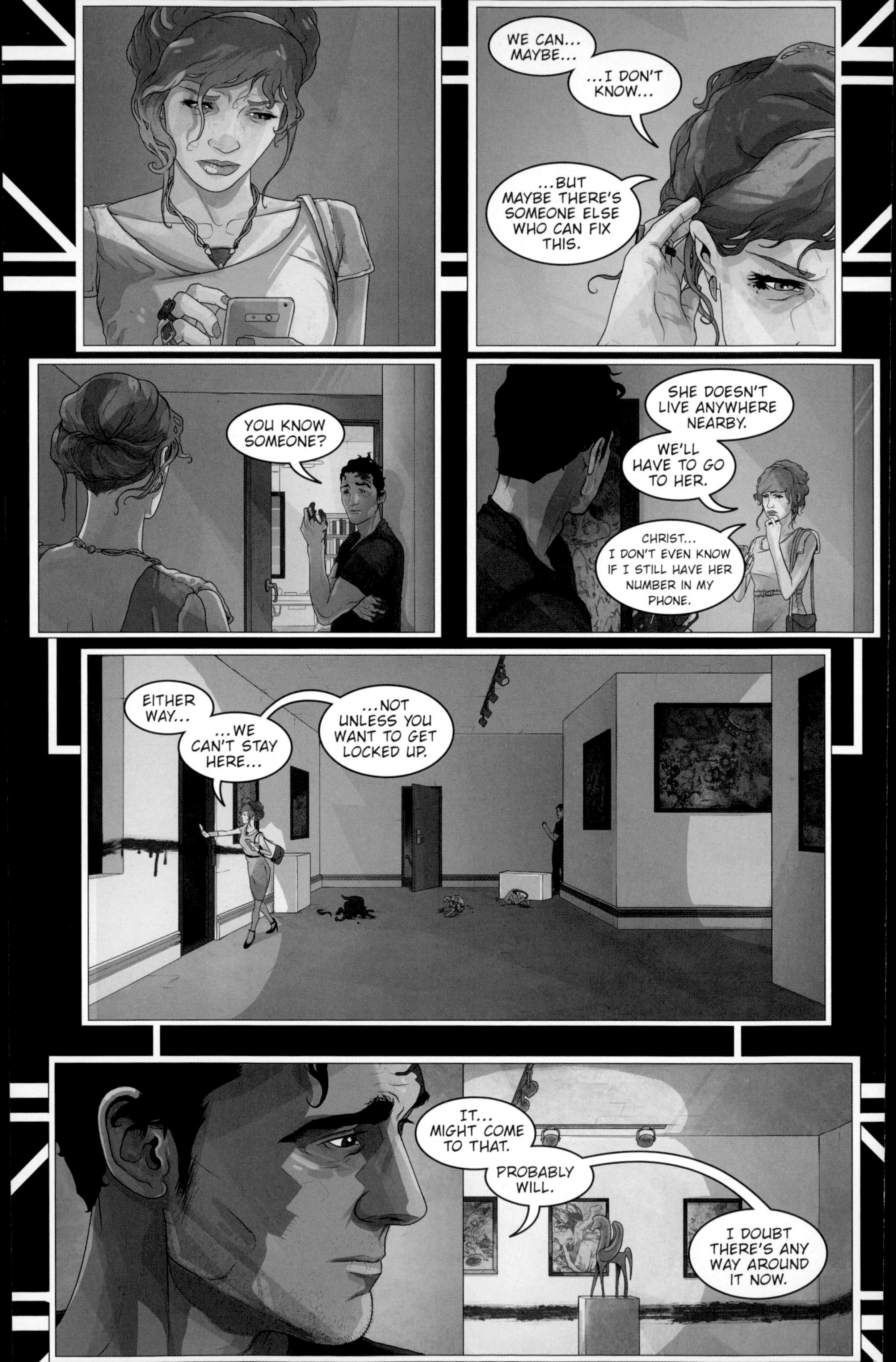
WE CAN... MAYBE...
...I DON'T KNOW...
...BUT MAYBE THERE'S SOMEONE ELSE WHO CAN FIX THIS.
YOU KNOW SOMEONE?
SHE DOESN'T LIVE ANYWHERE NEARBY.
WE'LL HAVE TO GO TO HER.
CHRIST... I DON'T EVEN KNOW IF I STILL HAVE HER NUMBER IN MY PHONE.
EITHER WAY...
...WE CAN'T STAY HERE...
...NOT UNLESS YOU WANT TO GET LOCKED UP.
IT... MIGHT COME TO THAT.
PROBABLY WILL.
I DOUBT THERE'S ANY WAY AROUND IT NOW.

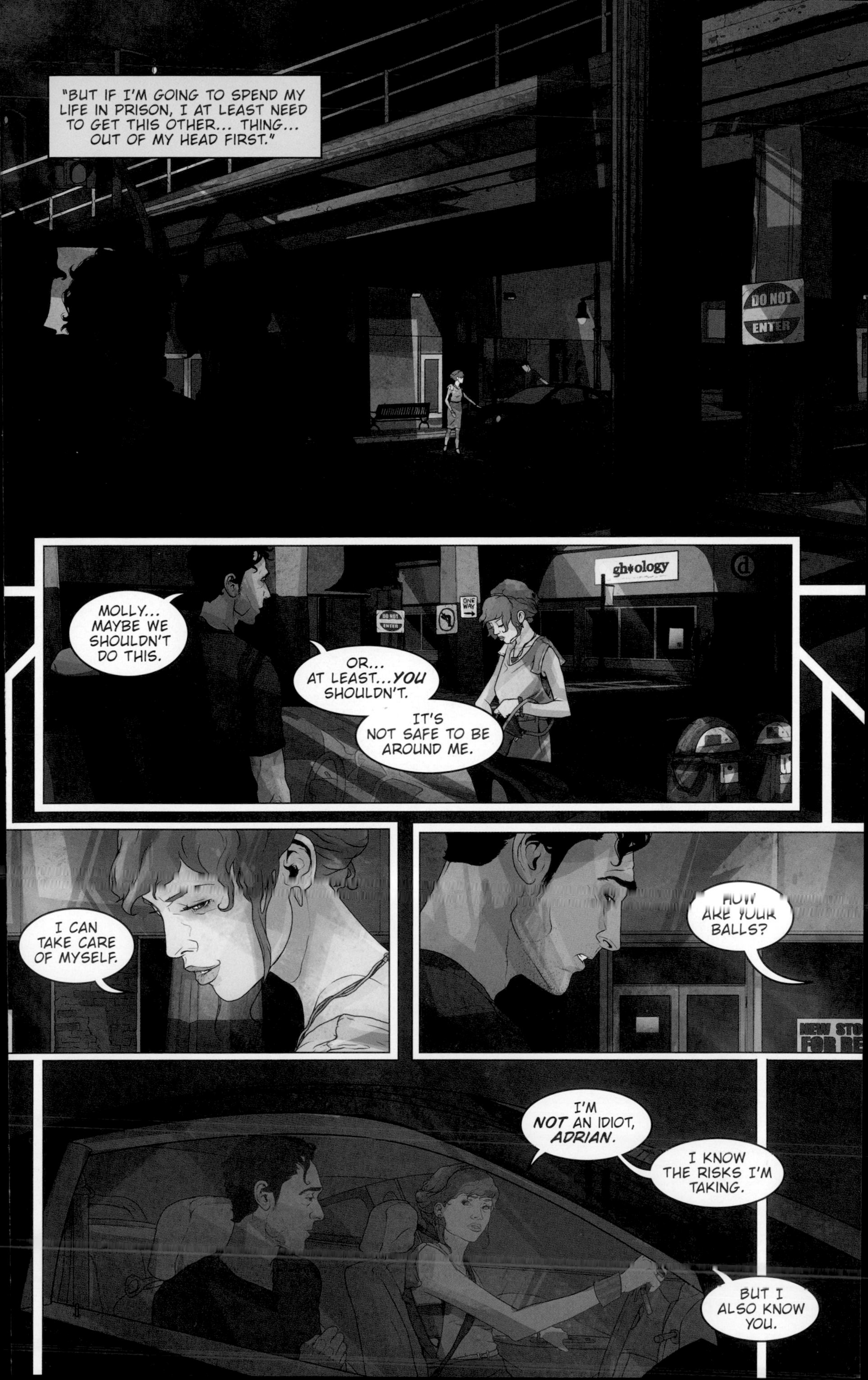
"BUT IF I'M GOING TO SPEND MY LIFE IN PRISON, I AT LEAST NEED TO GET THIS OTHER... THING... OUT OF MY HEAD FIRST."
DO NOT ENTER
gh*ology
ONE WAY
MOLLY... MAYBE WE SHOULDN'T DO THIS.
OR... AT LEAST...*YOU* SHOULDN'T.
IT'S NOT SAFE TO BE AROUND ME.
I CAN TAKE CARE OF MYSELF.
HOW ARE YOUR BALLS?
I'M *NOT* AN IDIOT, *ADRIAN.*
I KNOW THE RISKS I'M TAKING.
BUT I ALSO KNOW YOU.

WHEN I FIRST SAW YOU... ...IN THE GALLERY... ...I *KNEW* IT WASN'T YOU.

MAYBE NOT CONSCIOUSLY... ...NOT AT FIRST... ...BUT SOMEWHERE DEEP DOWN.

DOES THAT MAKE SENSE?

AS MUCH AS ANYTHING ELSE.

I CAN HEAR IT IN YOUR *VOICE.* IT'S *DIFFERENT.*

YOU DON'T SOUND THE SAME AS YOU DID WHEN YOU WERE COMING AFTER ME.

YOU SOUND *FRIGHTENED.*

WE'LL *BEAT* WHATEVER THE HELL THIS IS.

WHATEVER'S HAPPENING TO YOU... WE'LL FIGURE IT OUT.

I'M GOING TO HELP YOU THROUGH THIS.

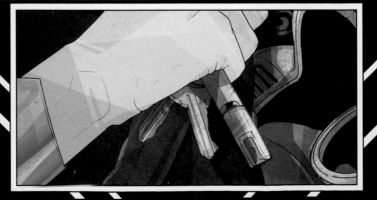

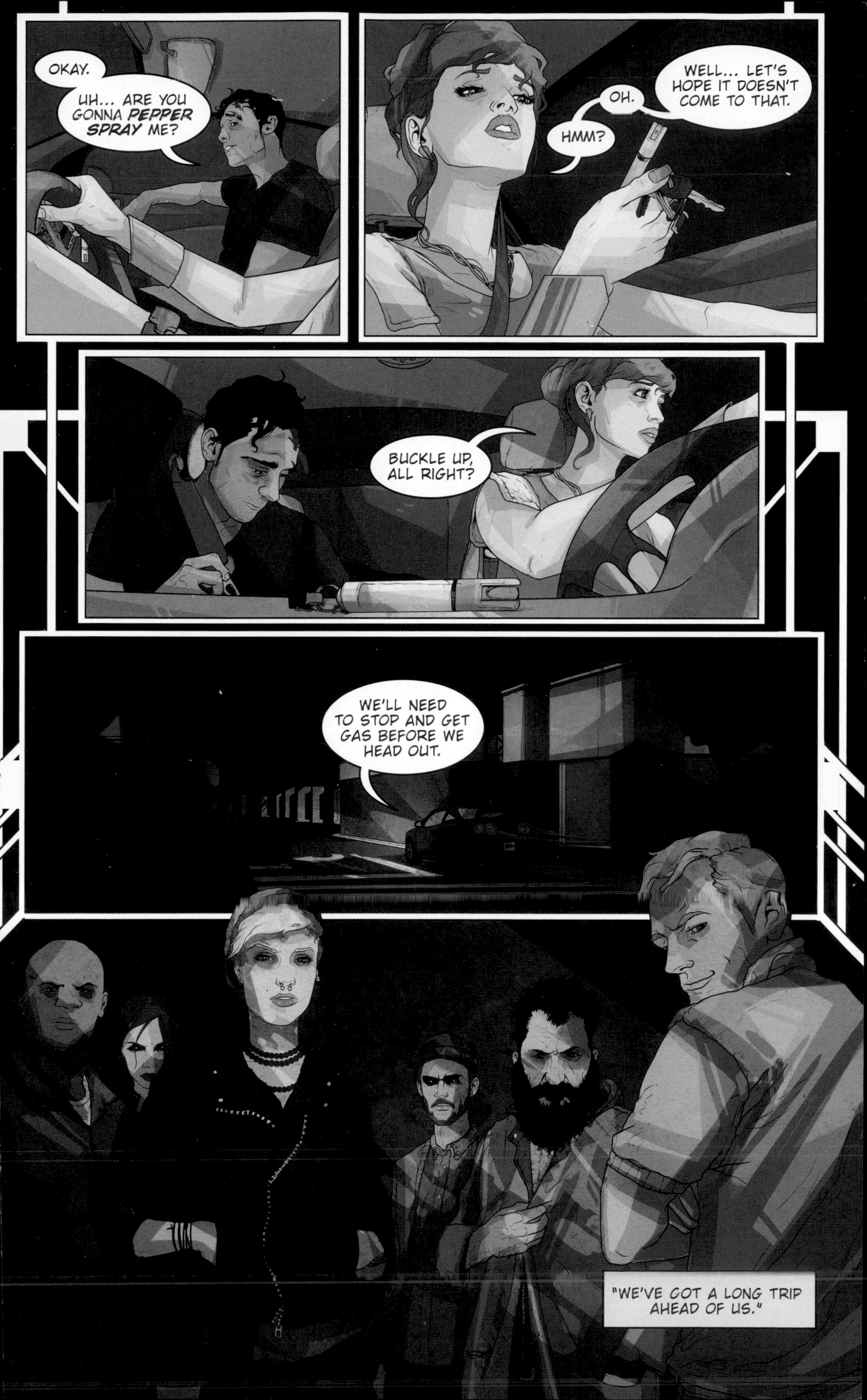
OKAY.
UH... ARE YOU GONNA PEPPER SPRAY ME?
HMM?
OH.
WELL... LET'S HOPE IT DOESN'T COME TO THAT.
BUCKLE UP, ALL RIGHT?
WE'LL NEED TO STOP AND GET GAS BEFORE WE HEAD OUT.
"WE'VE GOT A LONG TRIP AHEAD OF US."

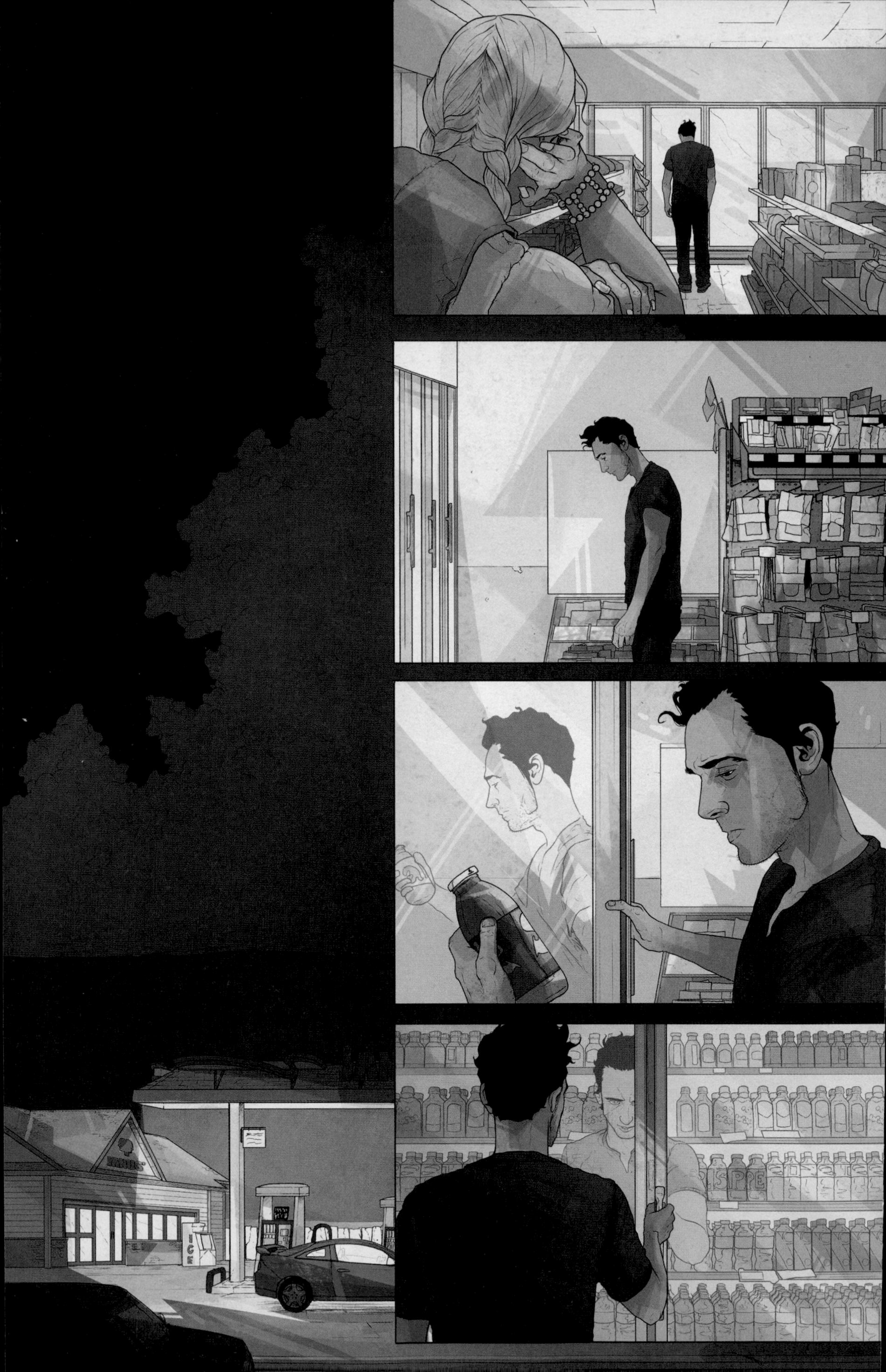
ICE

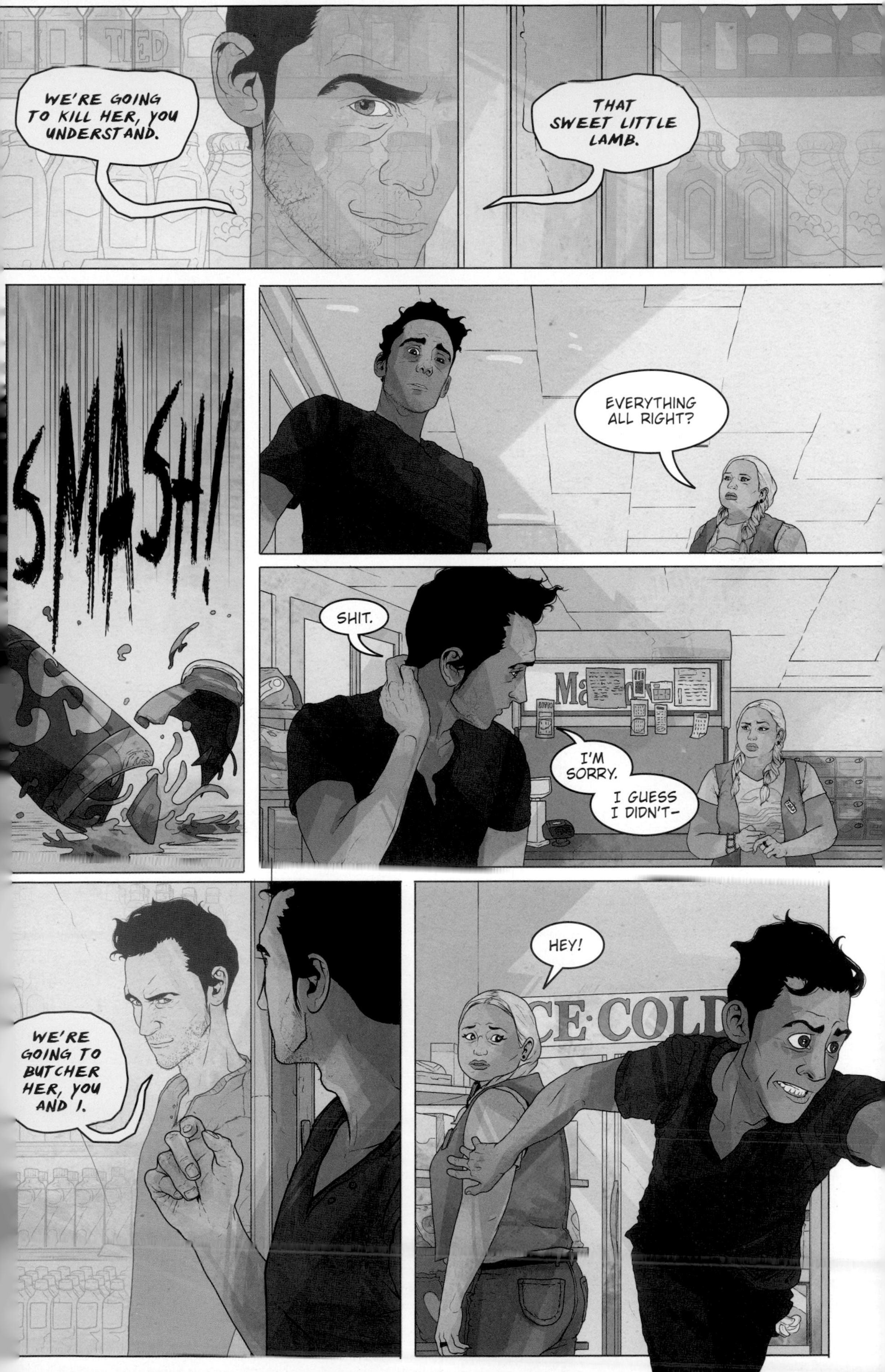
WE'RE GOING TO KILL HER, YOU UNDERSTAND.
THAT SWEET LITTLE LAMB.
SMASH!
EVERYTHING ALL RIGHT?
SHIT.
I'M SORRY.
I GUESS I DIDN'T-
WE'RE GOING TO BUTCHER HER, YOU AND I.
HEY!
ICE-COLD

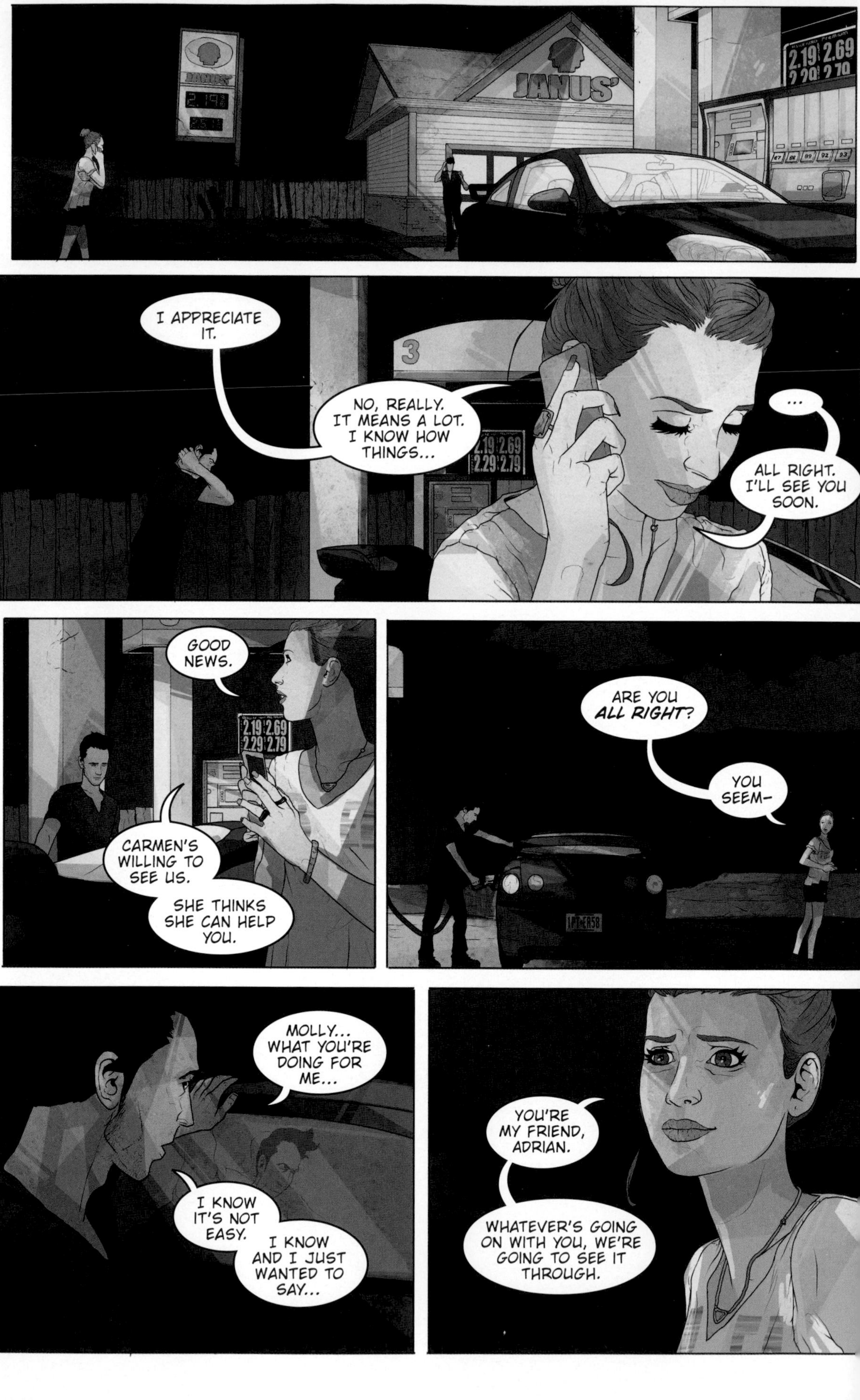
JANUS'
2.19 2.69
2.29 2.79
I APPRECIATE IT.
NO, REALLY. IT MEANS A LOT. I KNOW HOW THINGS...
...
ALL RIGHT. I'LL SEE YOU SOON.
3
2.19 2.69
2.29 2.79
GOOD NEWS.
CARMEN'S WILLING TO SEE US.
SHE THINKS SHE CAN HELP YOU.
ARE YOU *ALL RIGHT*?
YOU SEEM-
MOLLY... WHAT YOU'RE DOING FOR ME...
I KNOW IT'S NOT EASY.
I KNOW AND I JUST WANTED TO SAY...
YOU'RE MY FRIEND, ADRIAN.
WHATEVER'S GOING ON WITH YOU, WE'RE GOING TO SEE IT THROUGH.

"I WON'T LET YOU FACE THIS ALONE."
THERE'S A...
...FLY...

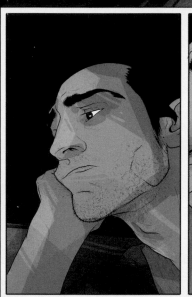

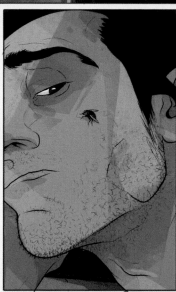

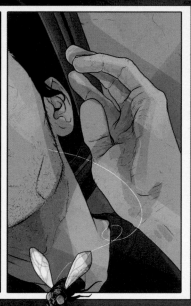

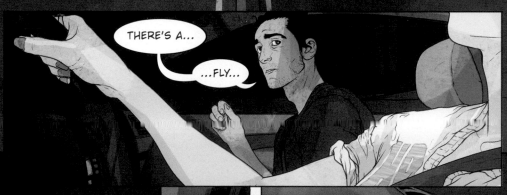

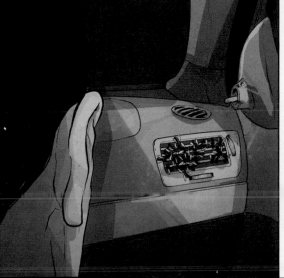

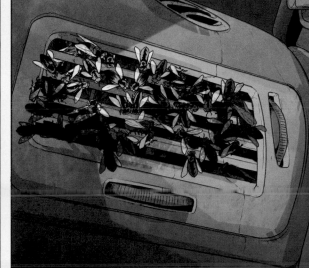

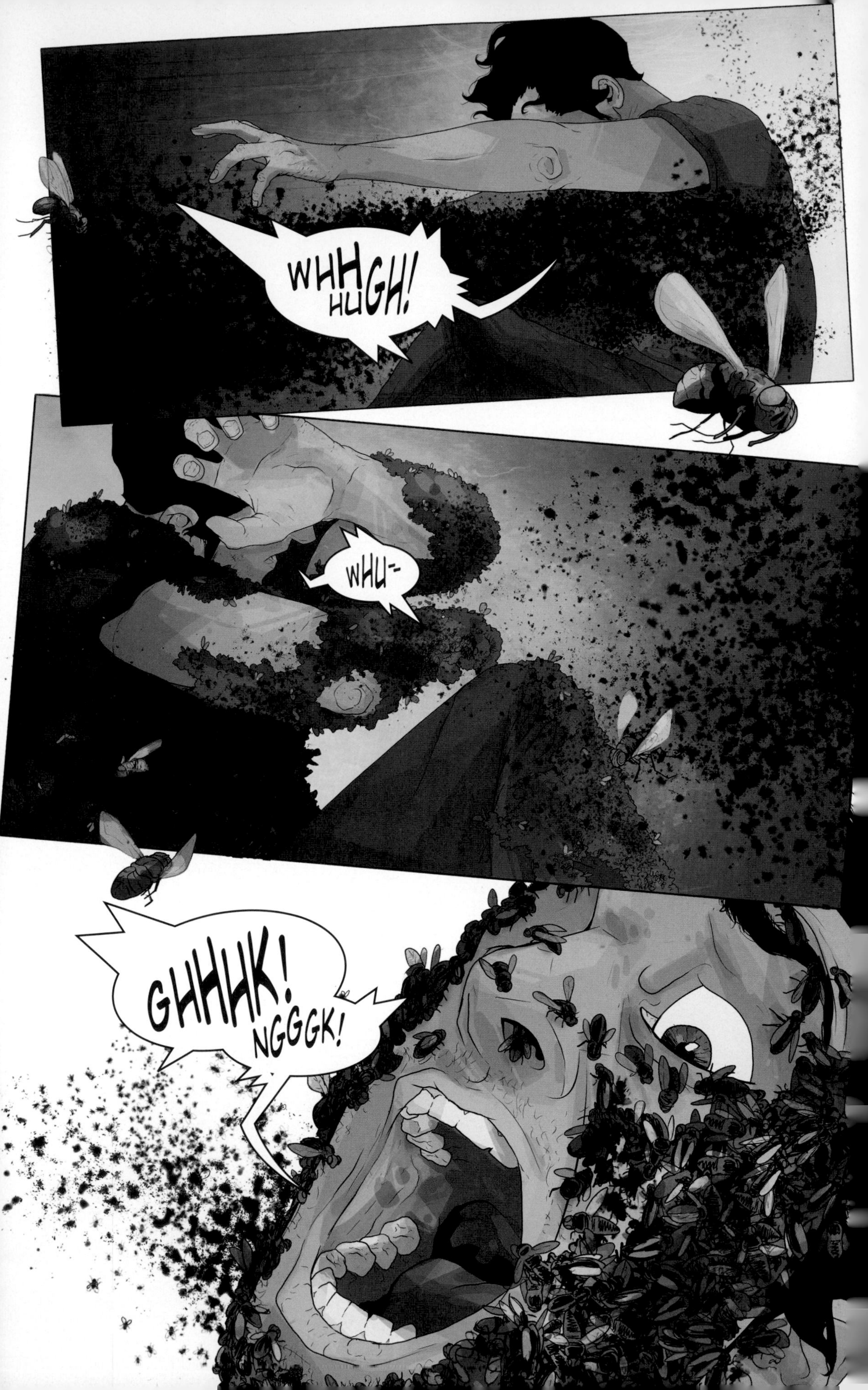
WHHGH! HUGH!
WHU-
GHHHK! NGGGK!

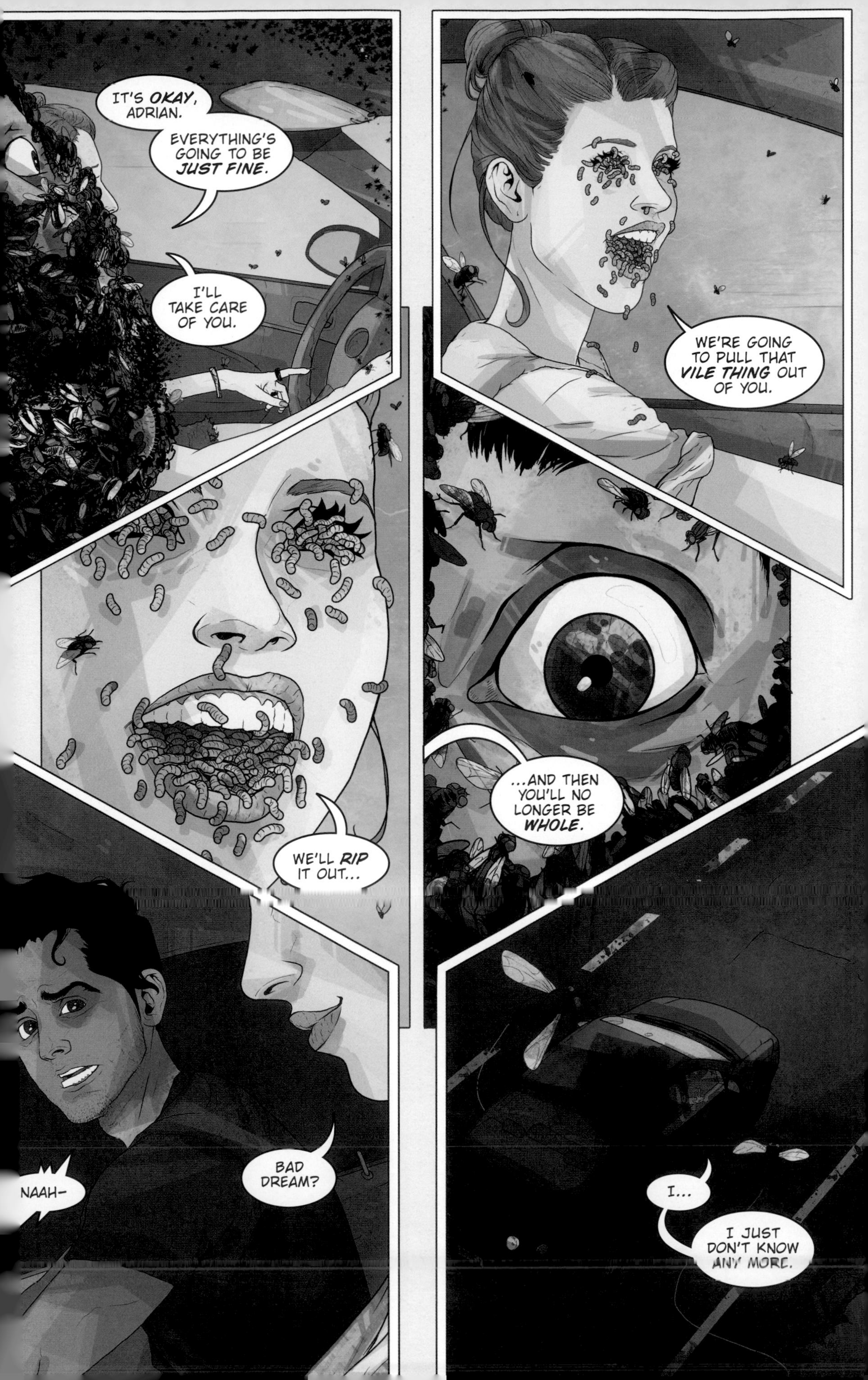
IT'S OKAY, ADRIAN.
EVERYTHING'S GOING TO BE JUST FINE.
I'LL TAKE CARE OF YOU.
WE'RE GOING TO PULL THAT VILE THING OUT OF YOU.
WE'LL RIP IT OUT...
...AND THEN YOU'LL NO LONGER BE WHOLE.
NAAH-
BAD DREAM?
I...
I JUST DON'T KNOW ANY MORE.

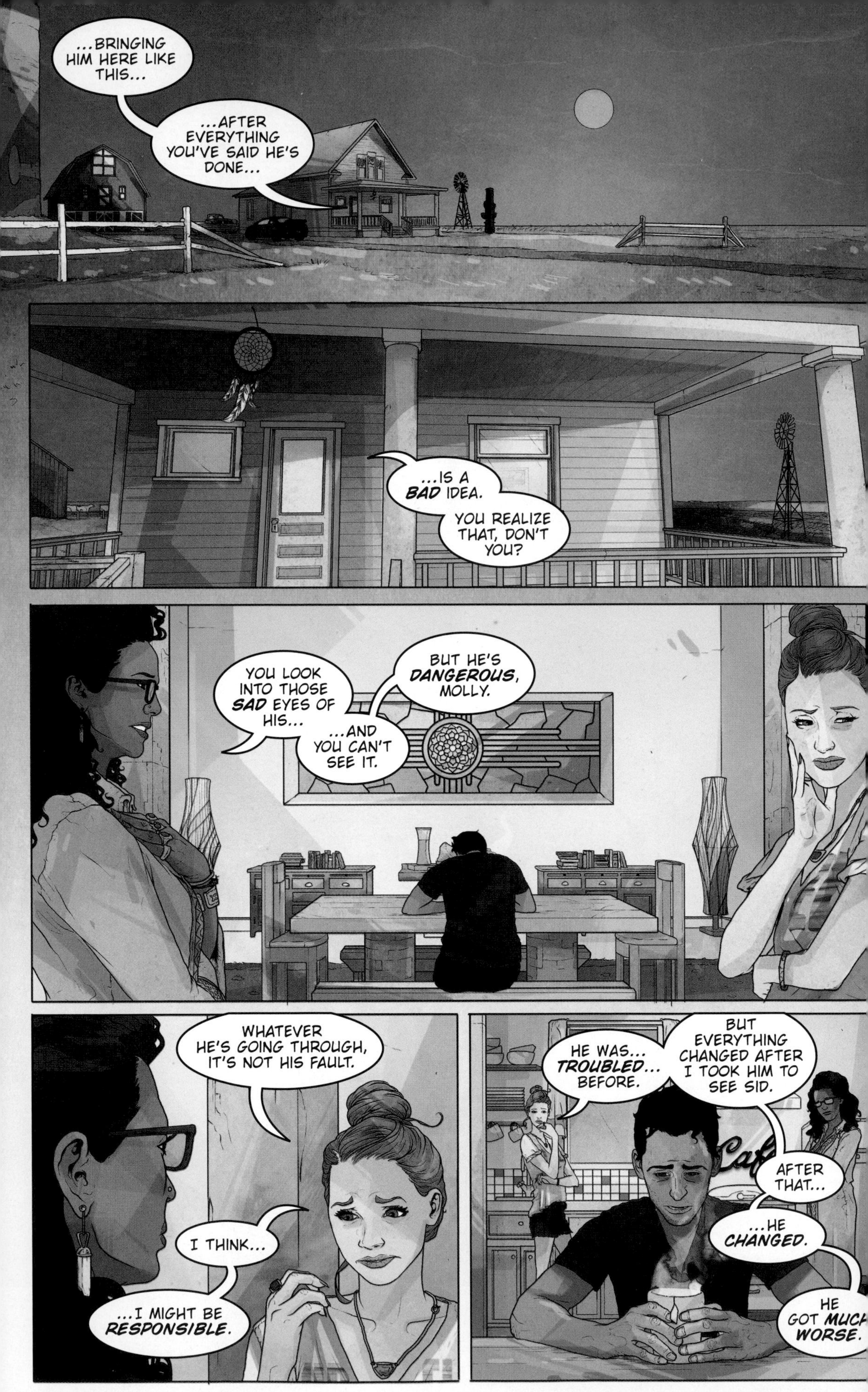
...BRINGING HIM HERE LIKE THIS...
...AFTER EVERYTHING YOU'VE SAID HE'S DONE...
...IS A BAD IDEA.
YOU REALIZE THAT, DON'T YOU?
YOU LOOK INTO THOSE SAD EYES OF HIS...
...AND YOU CAN'T SEE IT.
BUT HE'S DANGEROUS, MOLLY.
WHATEVER HE'S GOING THROUGH, IT'S NOT HIS FAULT.
I THINK...
...I MIGHT BE RESPONSIBLE.
HE WAS... TROUBLED... BEFORE.
BUT EVERYTHING CHANGED AFTER I TOOK HIM TO SEE SID.
AFTER THAT...
...HE CHANGED.
HE GOT MUCH WORSE.

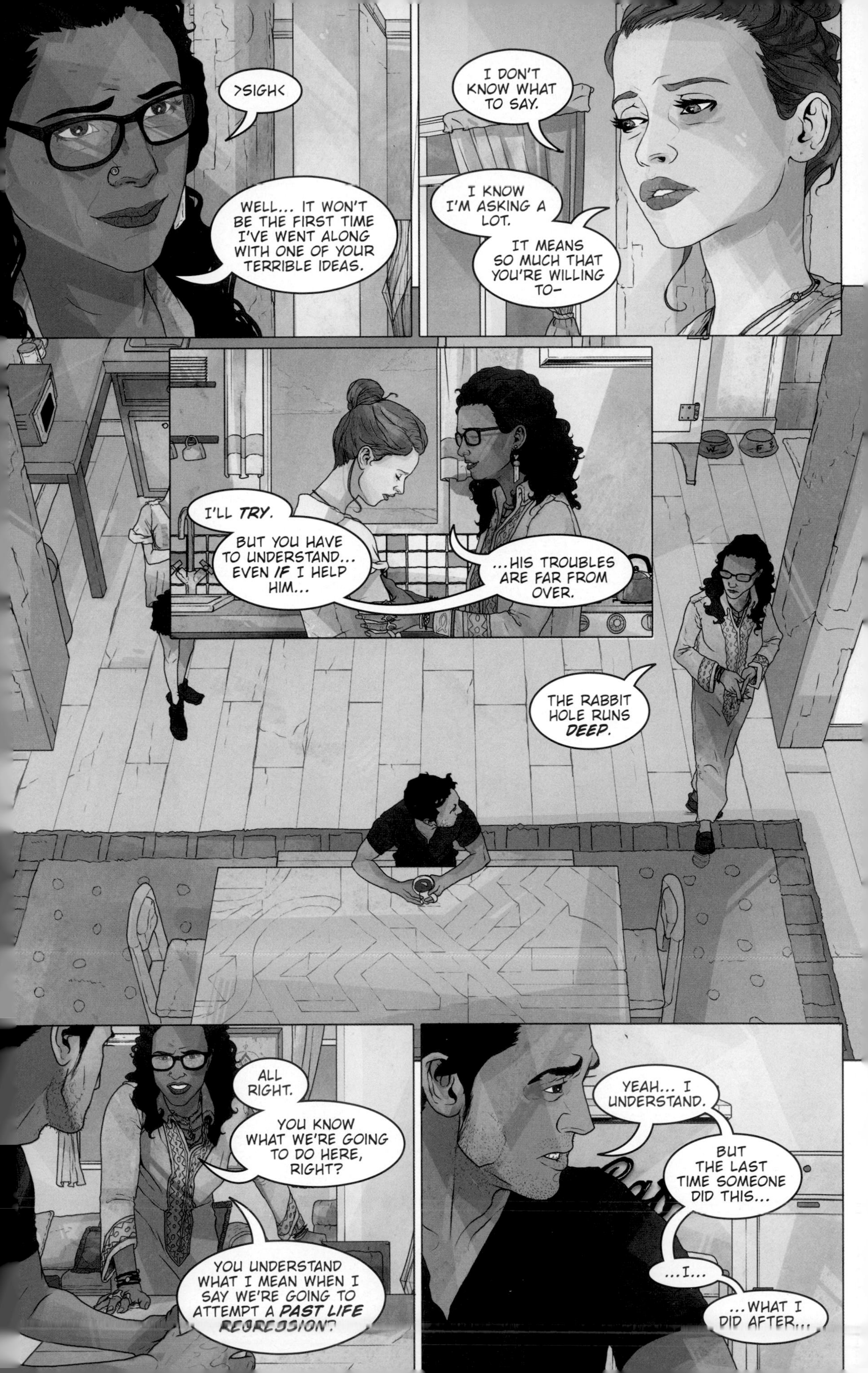
>SIGH<
WELL... IT WON'T BE THE FIRST TIME I'VE WENT ALONG WITH ONE OF YOUR TERRIBLE IDEAS.
I DON'T KNOW WHAT TO SAY.
I KNOW I'M ASKING A LOT.
IT MEANS SO MUCH THAT YOU'RE WILLING TO–
I'LL *TRY*.
BUT YOU HAVE TO UNDERSTAND... EVEN *IF* I HELP HIM...
...HIS TROUBLES ARE FAR FROM OVER.
THE RABBIT HOLE RUNS *DEEP*.
ALL RIGHT.
YOU KNOW WHAT WE'RE GOING TO DO HERE, RIGHT?
YOU UNDERSTAND WHAT I MEAN WHEN I SAY WE'RE GOING TO ATTEMPT A *PAST LIFE REGRESSION*?
YEAH... I UNDERSTAND.
BUT THE LAST TIME SOMEONE DID THIS...
...I...
...WHAT I DID AFTER...

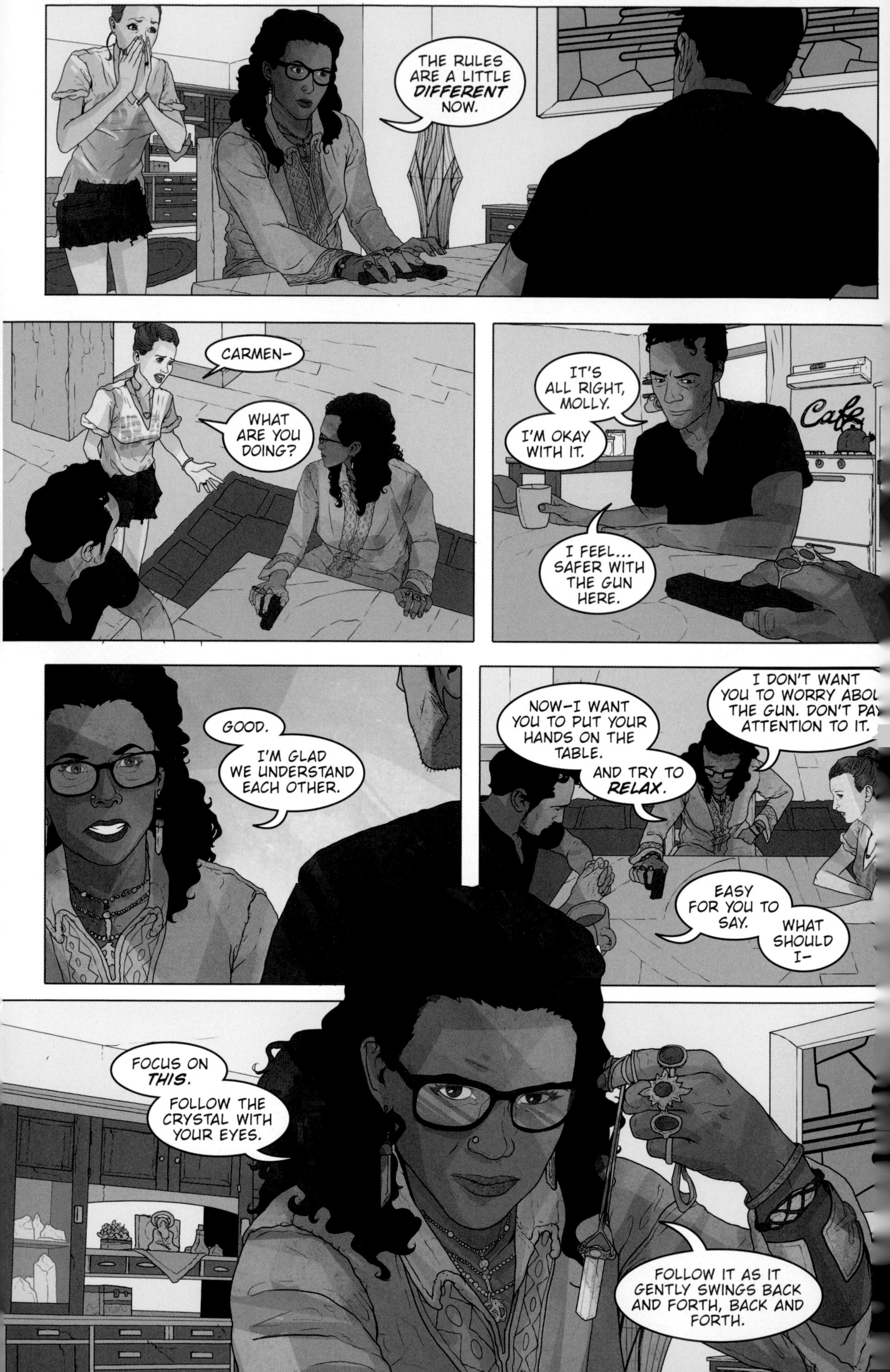
THE RULES ARE A LITTLE DIFFERENT NOW.
CARMEN-
WHAT ARE YOU DOING?
IT'S ALL RIGHT, MOLLY.
I'M OKAY WITH IT.
I FEEL... SAFER WITH THE GUN HERE.
GOOD.
I'M GLAD WE UNDERSTAND EACH OTHER.
NOW-I WANT YOU TO PUT YOUR HANDS ON THE TABLE.
AND TRY TO RELAX.
I DON'T WANT YOU TO WORRY ABO THE GUN. DON'T PA ATTENTION TO IT.
EASY FOR YOU TO SAY.
WHAT SHOULD I-
FOCUS ON THIS.
FOLLOW THE CRYSTAL WITH YOUR EYES.
FOLLOW IT AS IT GENTLY SWINGS BACK AND FORTH, BACK AND FORTH.

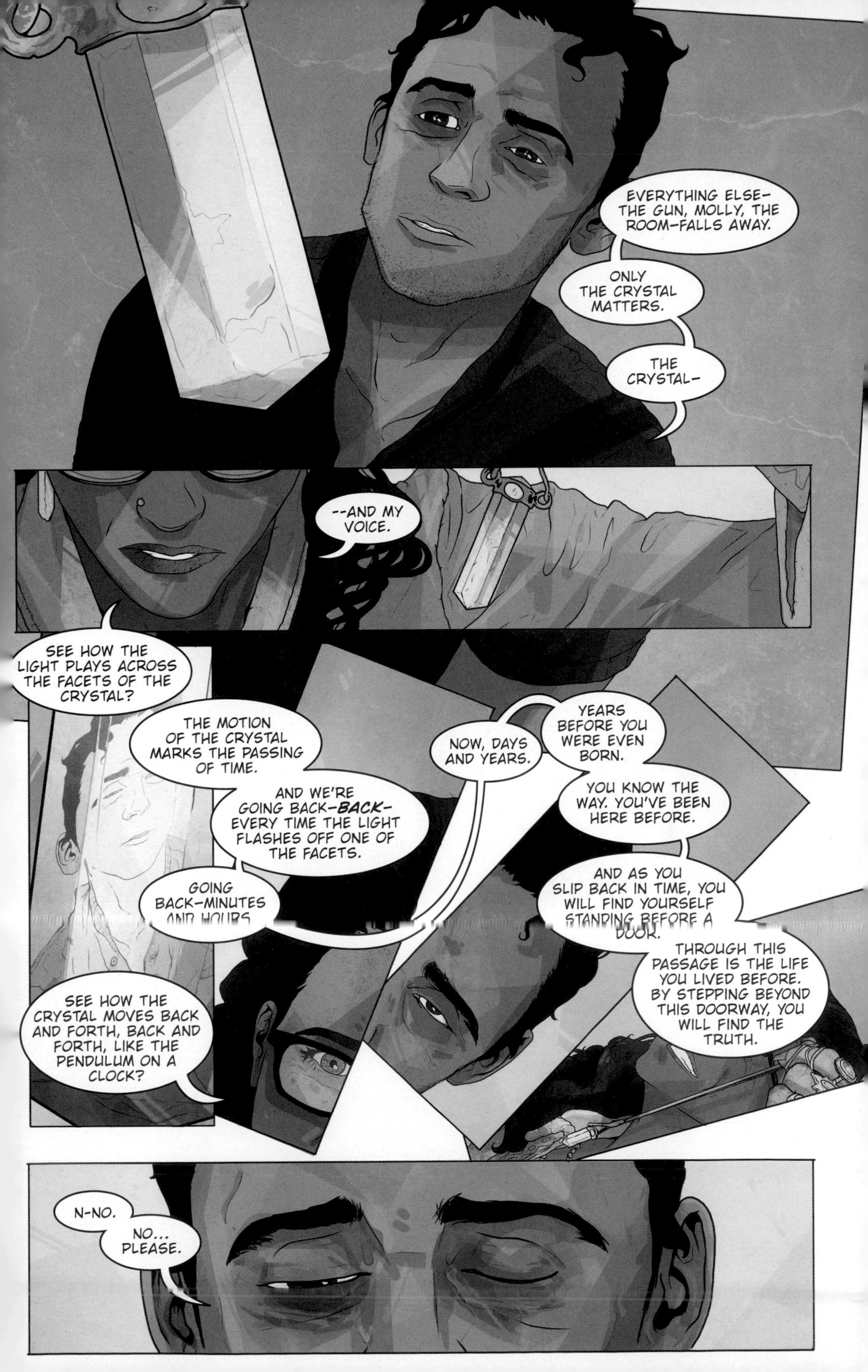
EVERYTHING ELSE— THE GUN, MOLLY, THE ROOM—FALLS AWAY.
ONLY THE CRYSTAL MATTERS.
THE CRYSTAL—
--AND MY VOICE.
SEE HOW THE LIGHT PLAYS ACROSS THE FACETS OF THE CRYSTAL?
THE MOTION OF THE CRYSTAL MARKS THE PASSING OF TIME.
AND WE'RE GOING BACK—**BACK**— EVERY TIME THE LIGHT FLASHES OFF ONE OF THE FACETS.
GOING BACK—MINUTES AND HOURS.
NOW, DAYS AND YEARS.
YEARS BEFORE YOU WERE EVEN BORN.
YOU KNOW THE WAY. YOU'VE BEEN HERE BEFORE.
AND AS YOU SLIP BACK IN TIME, YOU WILL FIND YOURSELF STANDING BEFORE A DOOR.
THROUGH THIS PASSAGE IS THE LIFE YOU LIVED BEFORE. BY STEPPING BEYOND THIS DOORWAY, YOU WILL FIND THE TRUTH.
SEE HOW THE CRYSTAL MOVES BACK AND FORTH, BACK AND FORTH, LIKE THE PENDULUM ON A CLOCK?
N-NO.
NO... PLEASE.

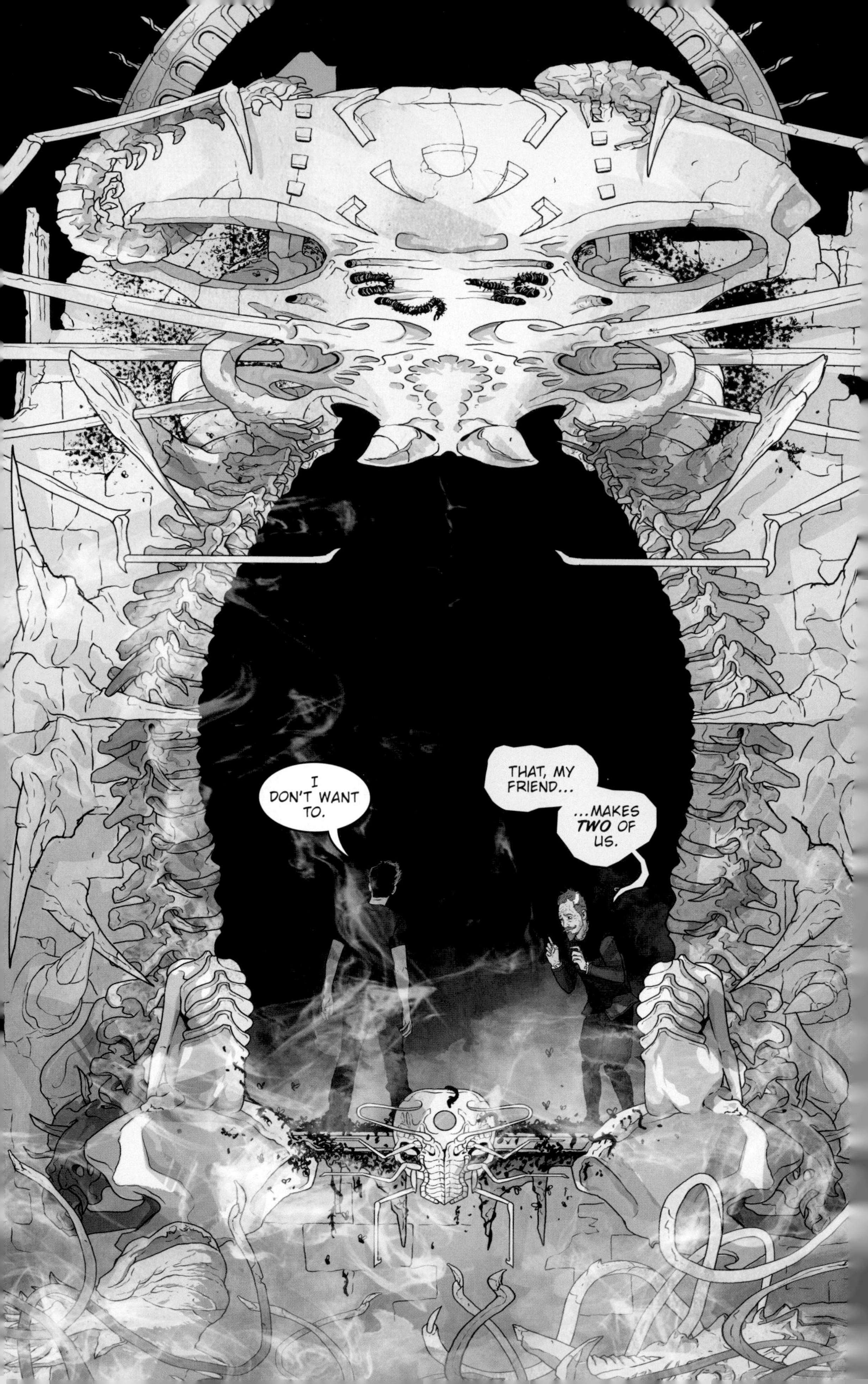
I DON'T WANT TO.
THAT, MY FRIEND...
...MAKES TWO OF US.

FIVE

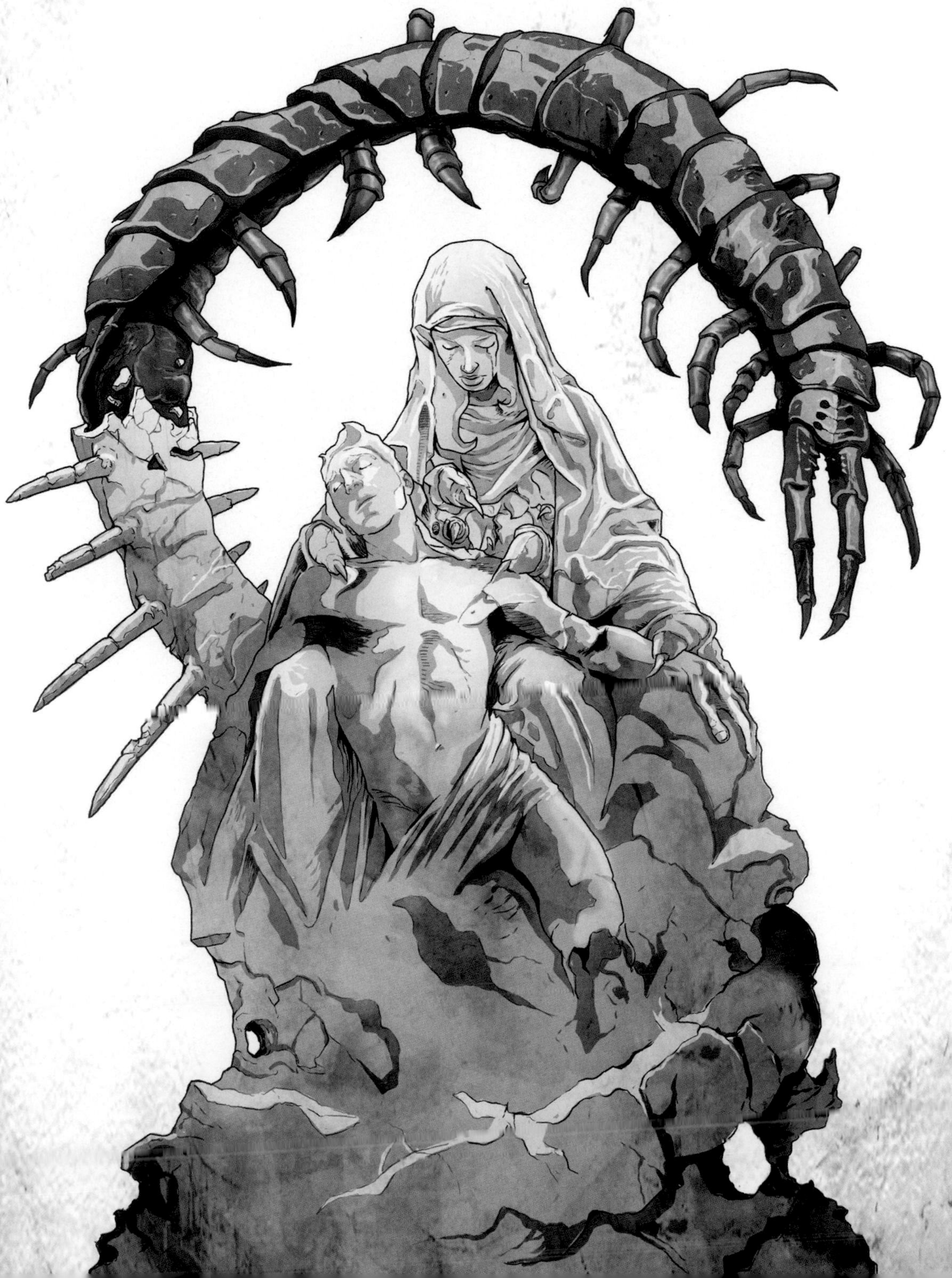

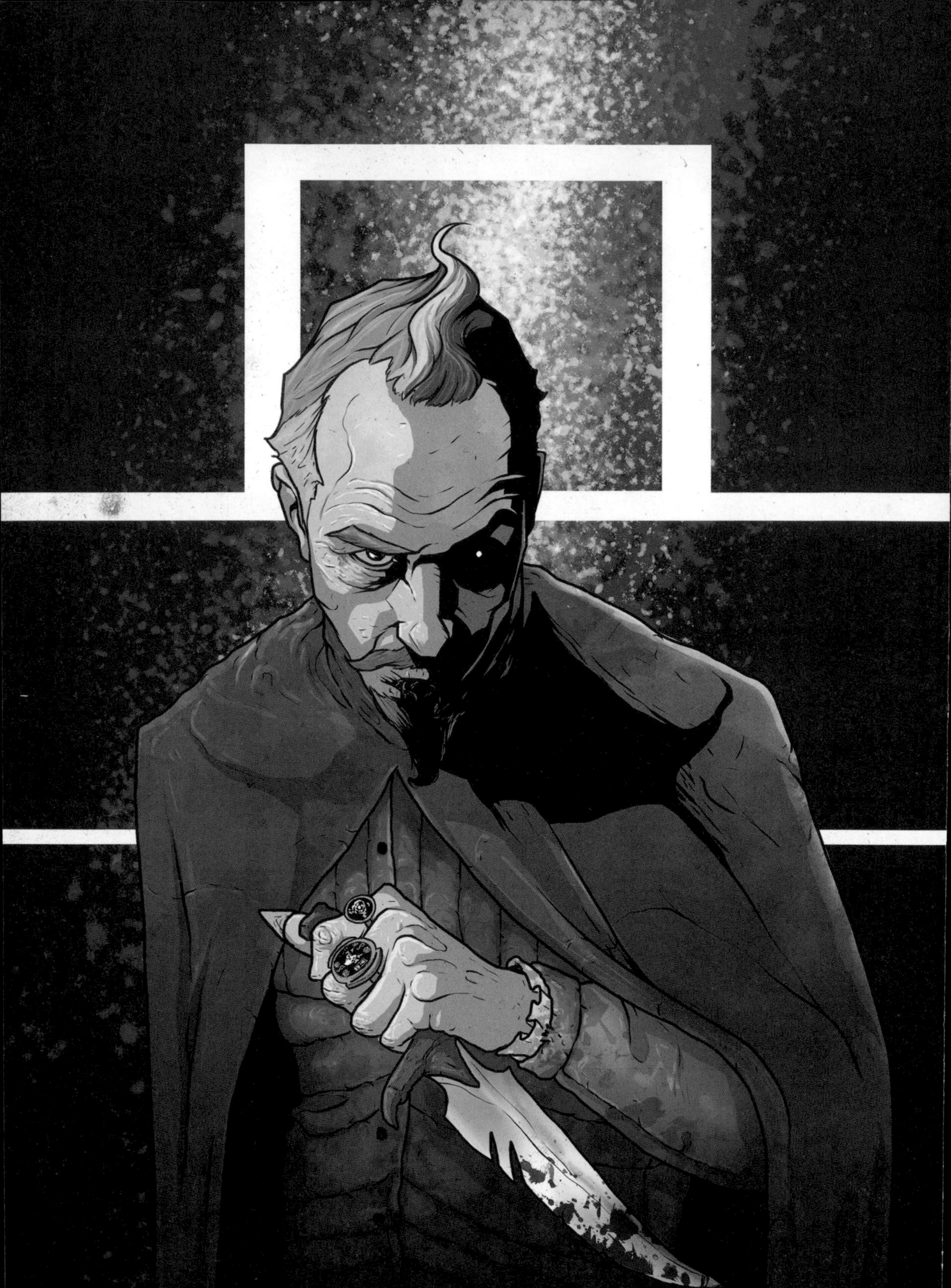

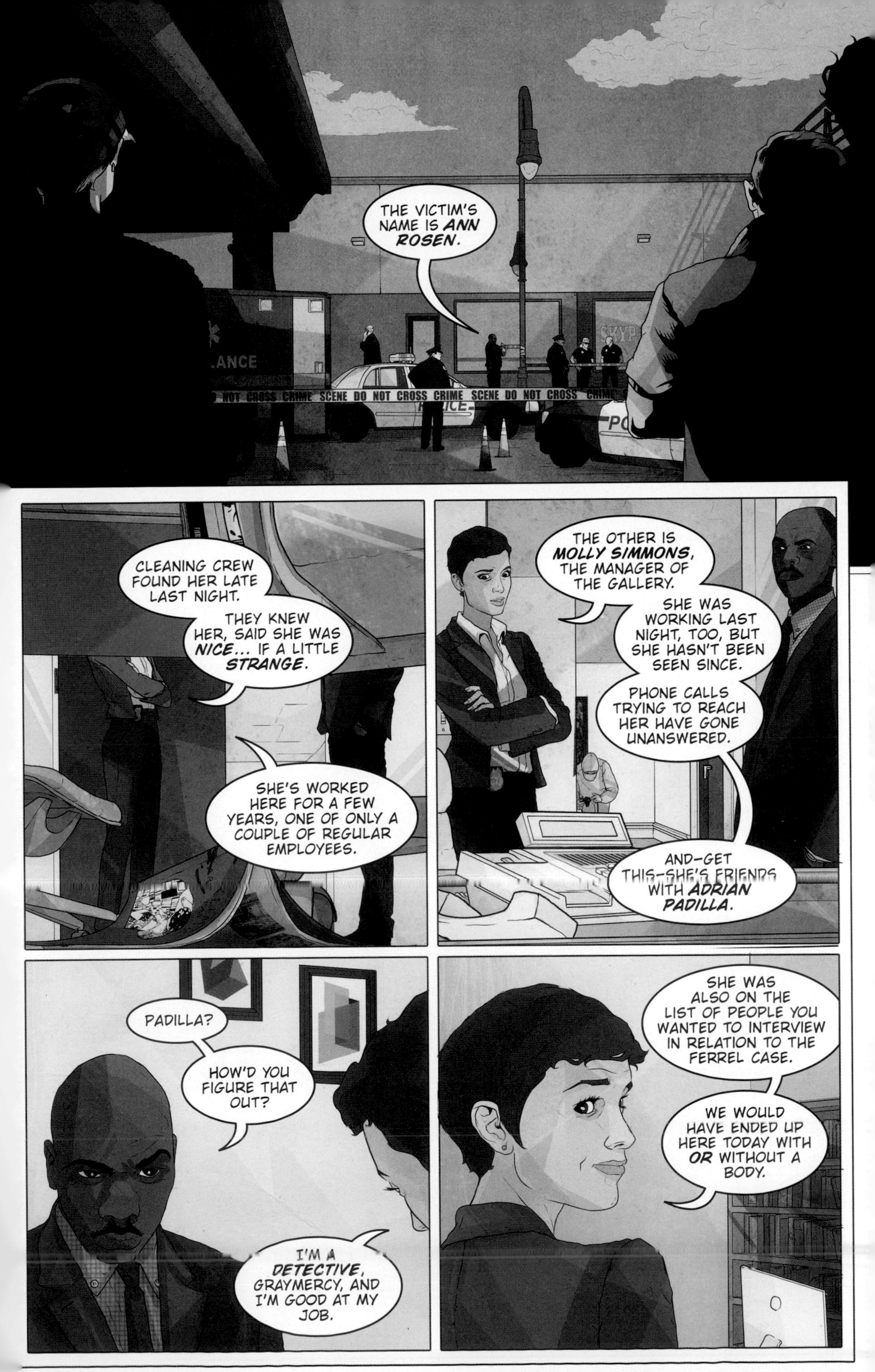
THE VICTIM'S NAME IS ANN ROSEN.
DO NOT CROSS CRIME SCENE DO NOT CROSS CRIME SCENE DO NOT CROSS CRIME
CLEANING CREW FOUND HER LATE LAST NIGHT.
THEY KNEW HER, SAID SHE WAS NICE... IF A LITTLE STRANGE.
SHE'S WORKED HERE FOR A FEW YEARS, ONE OF ONLY A COUPLE OF REGULAR EMPLOYEES.
THE OTHER IS MOLLY SIMMONS, THE MANAGER OF THE GALLERY.
SHE WAS WORKING LAST NIGHT, TOO, BUT SHE HASN'T BEEN SEEN SINCE.
PHONE CALLS TRYING TO REACH HER HAVE GONE UNANSWERED.
AND—GET THIS—SHE'S FRIENDS WITH ADRIAN PADILLA.
PADILLA?
HOW'D YOU FIGURE THAT OUT?
I'M A DETECTIVE, GRAYMERCY, AND I'M GOOD AT MY JOB.
SHE WAS ALSO ON THE LIST OF PEOPLE YOU WANTED TO INTERVIEW IN RELATION TO THE FERREL CASE.
WE WOULD HAVE ENDED UP HERE TODAY WITH OR WITHOUT A BODY.

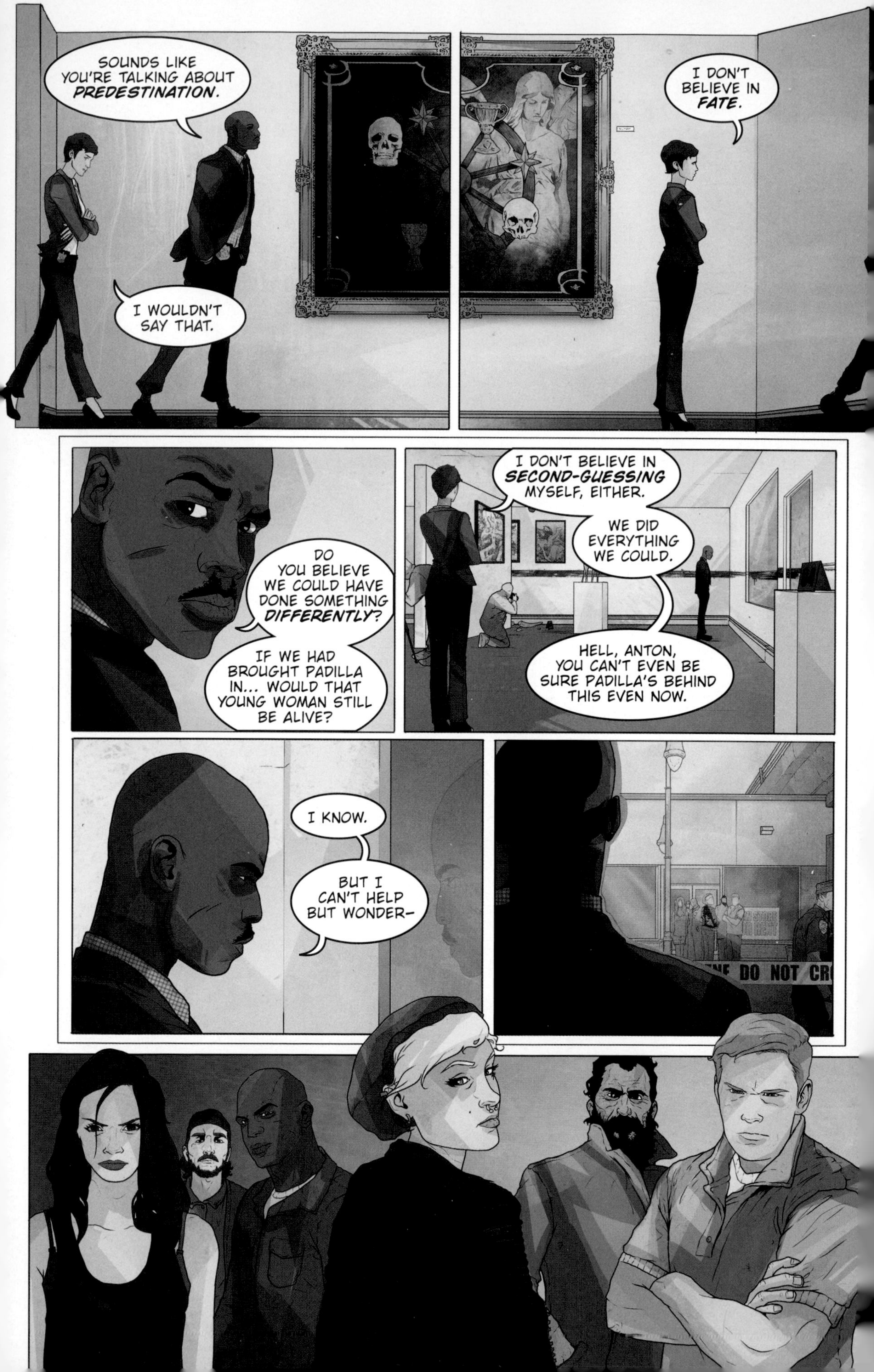
SOUNDS LIKE YOU'RE TALKING ABOUT **PREDESTINATION**.
I WOULDN'T SAY THAT.
I DON'T BELIEVE IN **FATE**.
DO YOU BELIEVE WE COULD HAVE DONE SOMETHING **DIFFERENTLY**?
IF WE HAD BROUGHT PADILLA IN... WOULD THAT YOUNG WOMAN STILL BE ALIVE?
I DON'T BELIEVE IN **SECOND-GUESSING** MYSELF, EITHER.
WE DID EVERYTHING WE COULD.
HELL, ANTON, YOU CAN'T EVEN BE SURE PADILLA'S BEHIND THIS EVEN NOW.
I KNOW.
BUT I CAN'T HELP BUT WONDER-
DO NOT CR

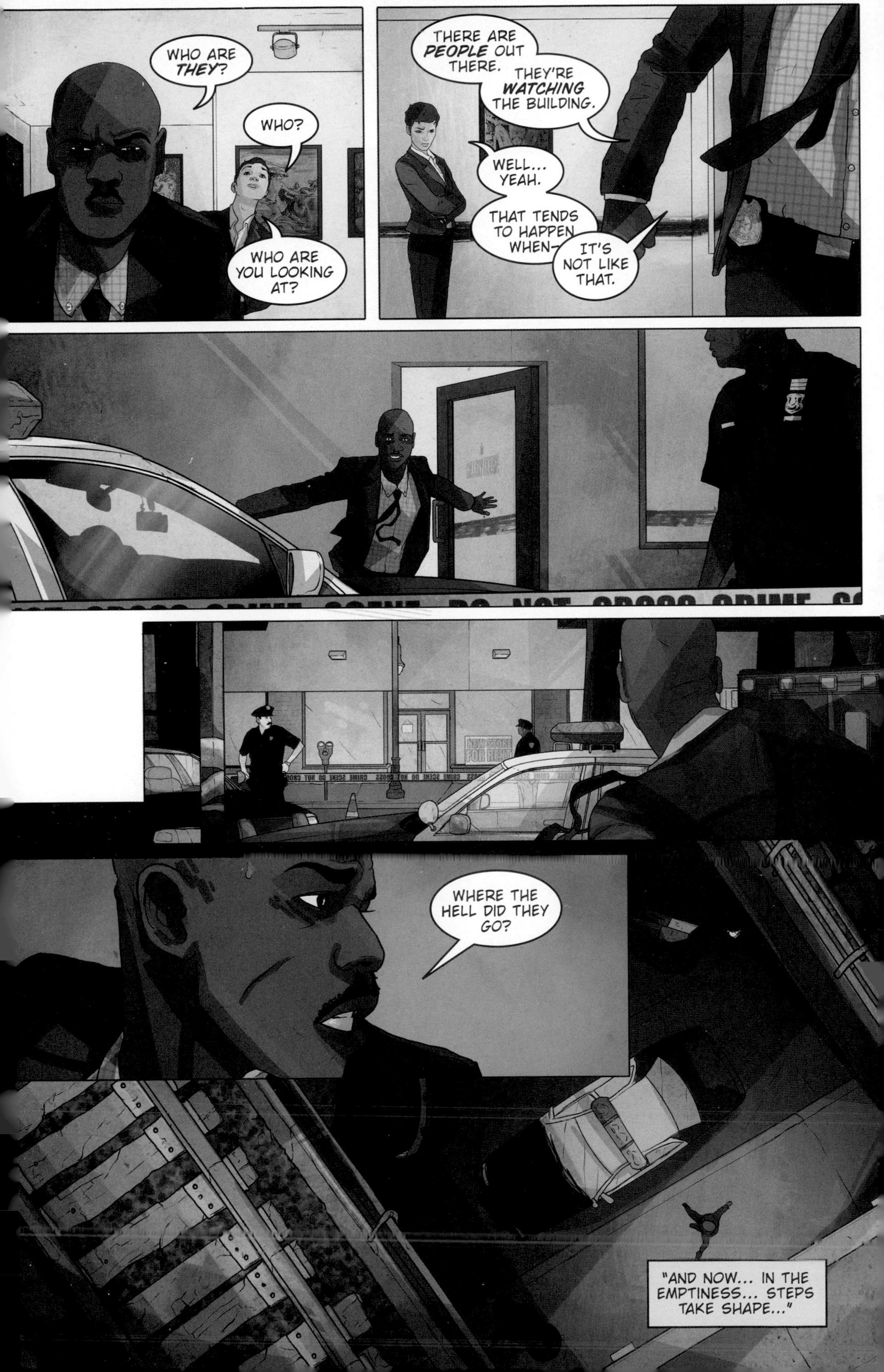
WHO ARE THEY?
WHO?
WHO ARE YOU LOOKING AT?
THERE ARE PEOPLE OUT THERE.
THEY'RE WATCHING THE BUILDING.
WELL... YEAH.
THAT TENDS TO HAPPEN WHEN—
IT'S NOT LIKE THAT.
NEW STORE FOR RENT
WHERE THE HELL DID THEY GO?
"AND NOW... IN THE EMPTINESS... STEPS TAKE SHAPE..."

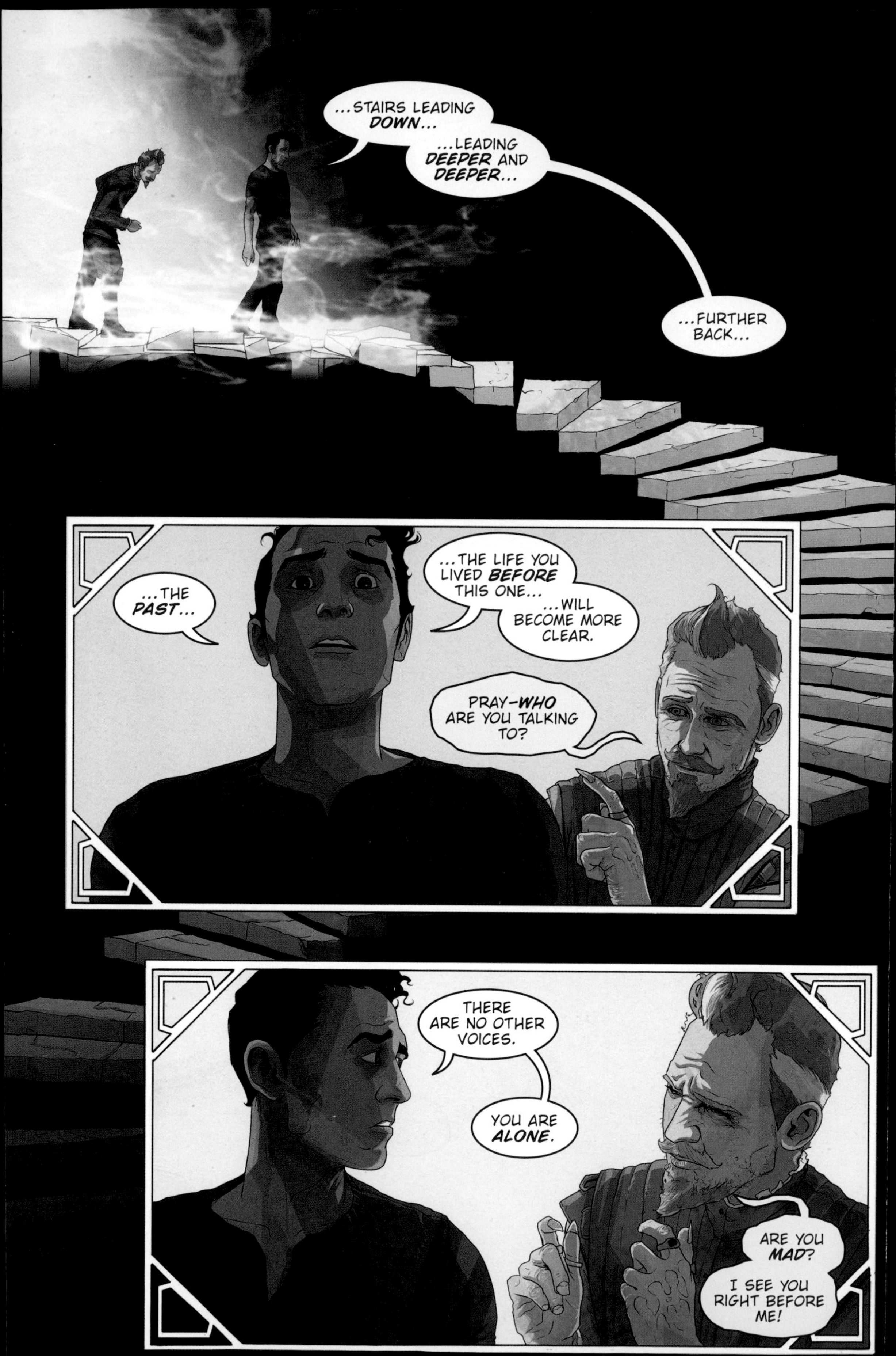
...STAIRS LEADING DOWN...
...LEADING DEEPER AND DEEPER...
...FURTHER BACK...
...THE PAST...
...THE LIFE YOU LIVED BEFORE THIS ONE...
...WILL BECOME MORE CLEAR.
PRAY-WHO ARE YOU TALKING TO?
THERE ARE NO OTHER VOICES.
YOU ARE ALONE.
ARE YOU MAD?
I SEE YOU RIGHT BEFORE ME!

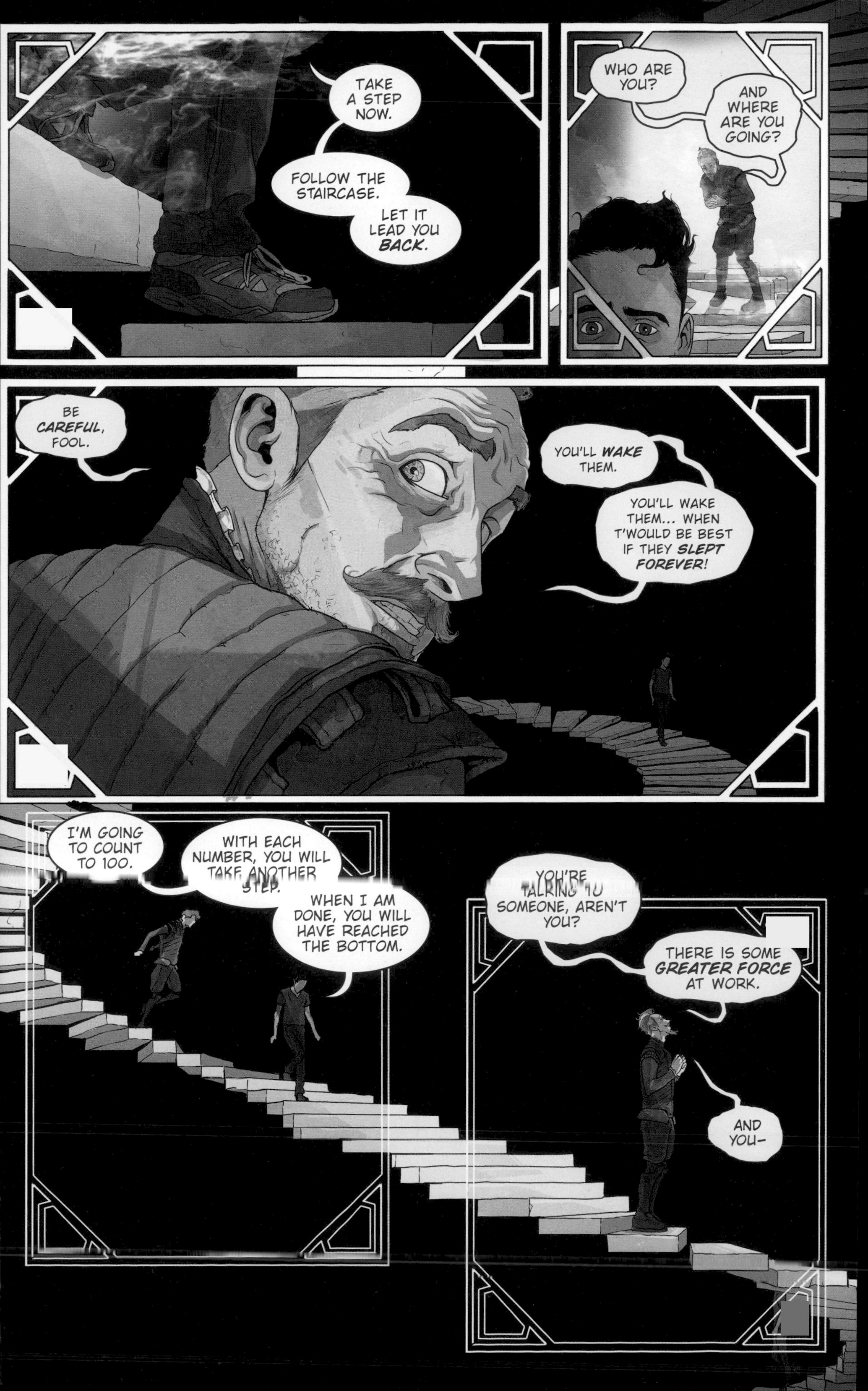

TAKE A STEP NOW.
FOLLOW THE STAIRCASE.
LET IT LEAD YOU **BACK**.
WHO ARE YOU?
AND WHERE ARE YOU GOING?
BE **CAREFUL**, FOOL.
YOU'LL **WAKE** THEM.
YOU'LL WAKE THEM... WHEN T'WOULD BE BEST IF THEY **SLEPT FOREVER**!
I'M GOING TO COUNT TO 100.
WITH EACH NUMBER, YOU WILL TAKE ANOTHER STEP.
WHEN I AM DONE, YOU WILL HAVE REACHED THE BOTTOM.
YOU'RE TALKING TO SOMEONE, AREN'T YOU?
THERE IS SOME **GREATER FORCE** AT WORK.
AND YOU–

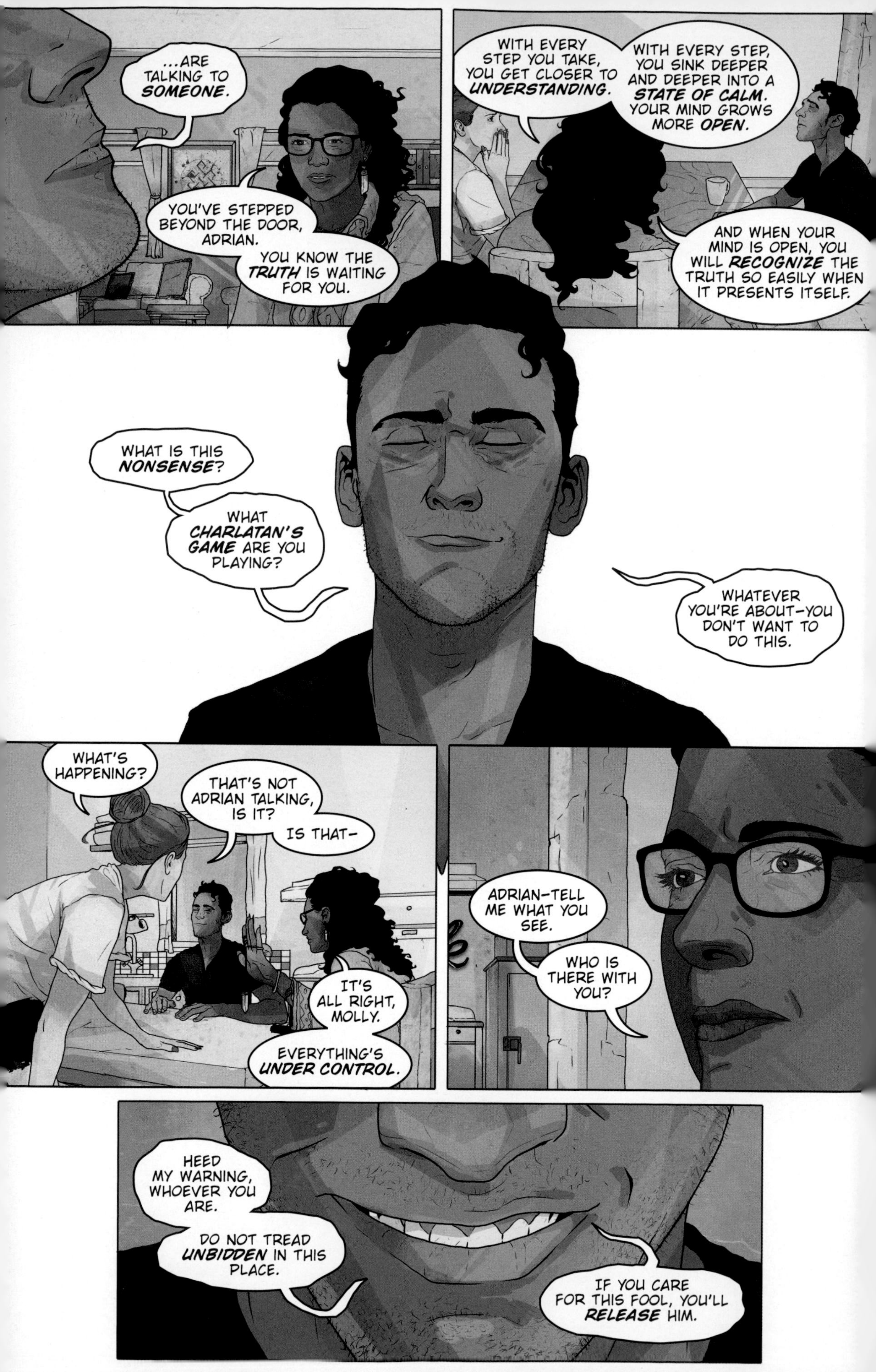
...ARE TALKING TO SOMEONE.
YOU'VE STEPPED BEYOND THE DOOR, ADRIAN.
YOU KNOW THE TRUTH IS WAITING FOR YOU.
WITH EVERY STEP YOU TAKE, YOU GET CLOSER TO UNDERSTANDING.
WITH EVERY STEP, YOU SINK DEEPER AND DEEPER INTO A STATE OF CALM. YOUR MIND GROWS MORE OPEN.
AND WHEN YOUR MIND IS OPEN, YOU WILL RECOGNIZE THE TRUTH SO EASILY WHEN IT PRESENTS ITSELF.
WHAT IS THIS NONSENSE?
WHAT CHARLATAN'S GAME ARE YOU PLAYING?
WHATEVER YOU'RE ABOUT–YOU DON'T WANT TO DO THIS.
WHAT'S HAPPENING?
THAT'S NOT ADRIAN TALKING, IS IT?
IS THAT-
IT'S ALL RIGHT, MOLLY.
EVERYTHING'S UNDER CONTROL.
ADRIAN–TELL ME WHAT YOU SEE.
WHO IS THERE WITH YOU?
HEED MY WARNING, WHOEVER YOU ARE.
DO NOT TREAD UNBIDDEN IN THIS PLACE.
IF YOU CARE FOR THIS FOOL, YOU'LL RELEASE HIM.

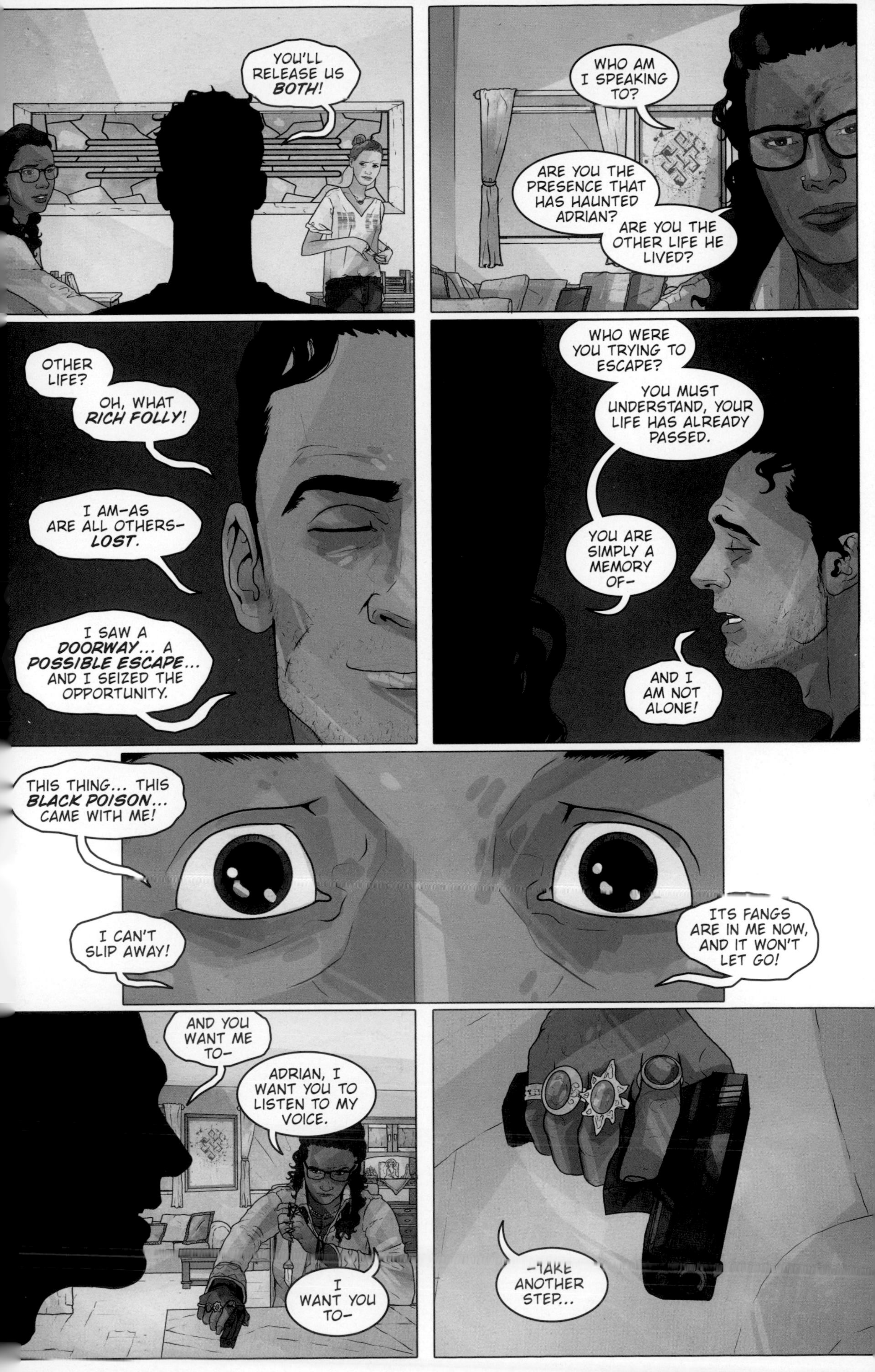
YOU'LL RELEASE US *BOTH*!
WHO AM I SPEAKING TO?
ARE YOU THE PRESENCE THAT HAS HAUNTED ADRIAN?
ARE YOU THE OTHER LIFE HE LIVED?
OTHER LIFE?
OH, WHAT *RICH FOLLY*!
I AM—AS ARE ALL OTHERS— *LOST*.
I SAW A *DOORWAY*... A *POSSIBLE ESCAPE*... AND I SEIZED THE OPPORTUNITY.
WHO WERE YOU TRYING TO ESCAPE?
YOU MUST UNDERSTAND, YOUR LIFE HAS ALREADY PASSED.
YOU ARE SIMPLY A MEMORY OF—
AND I AM NOT ALONE!
THIS THING... THIS *BLACK POISON*... CAME WITH ME!
I CAN'T SLIP AWAY!
ITS FANGS ARE IN ME NOW, AND IT WON'T LET GO!
AND YOU WANT ME TO—
ADRIAN, I WANT YOU TO LISTEN TO MY VOICE.
I WANT YOU TO—
—TAKE ANOTHER STEP...

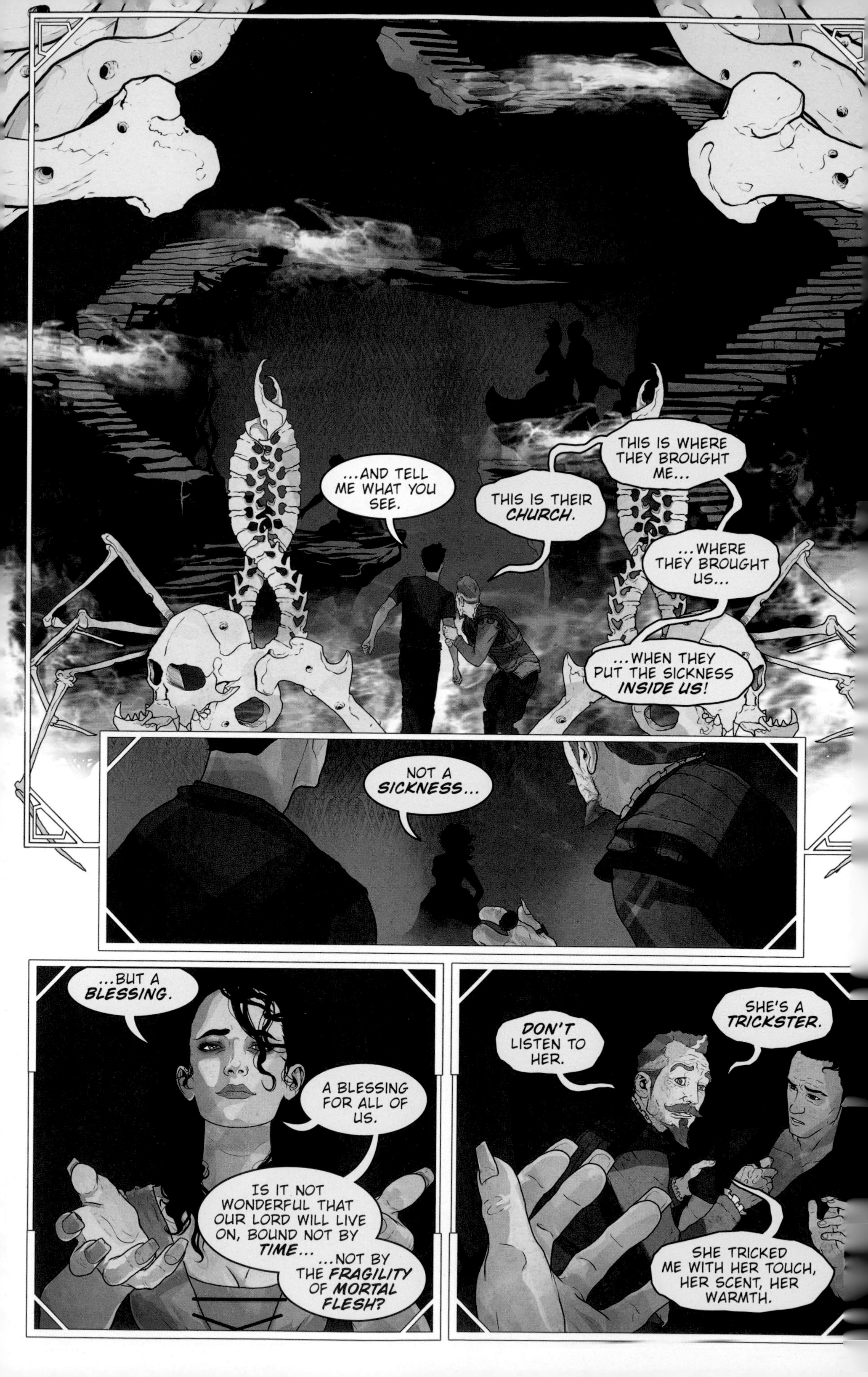
...AND TELL ME WHAT YOU SEE.
THIS IS THEIR CHURCH.
THIS IS WHERE THEY BROUGHT ME...
...WHERE THEY BROUGHT US...
...WHEN THEY PUT THE SICKNESS INSIDE US!
NOT A SICKNESS...
...BUT A BLESSING.
A BLESSING FOR ALL OF US.
IS IT NOT WONDERFUL THAT OUR LORD WILL LIVE ON, BOUND NOT BY TIME...
...NOT BY THE FRAGILITY OF MORTAL FLESH?
DON'T LISTEN TO HER.
SHE'S A TRICKSTER.
SHE TRICKED ME WITH HER TOUCH, HER SCENT, HER WARMTH.

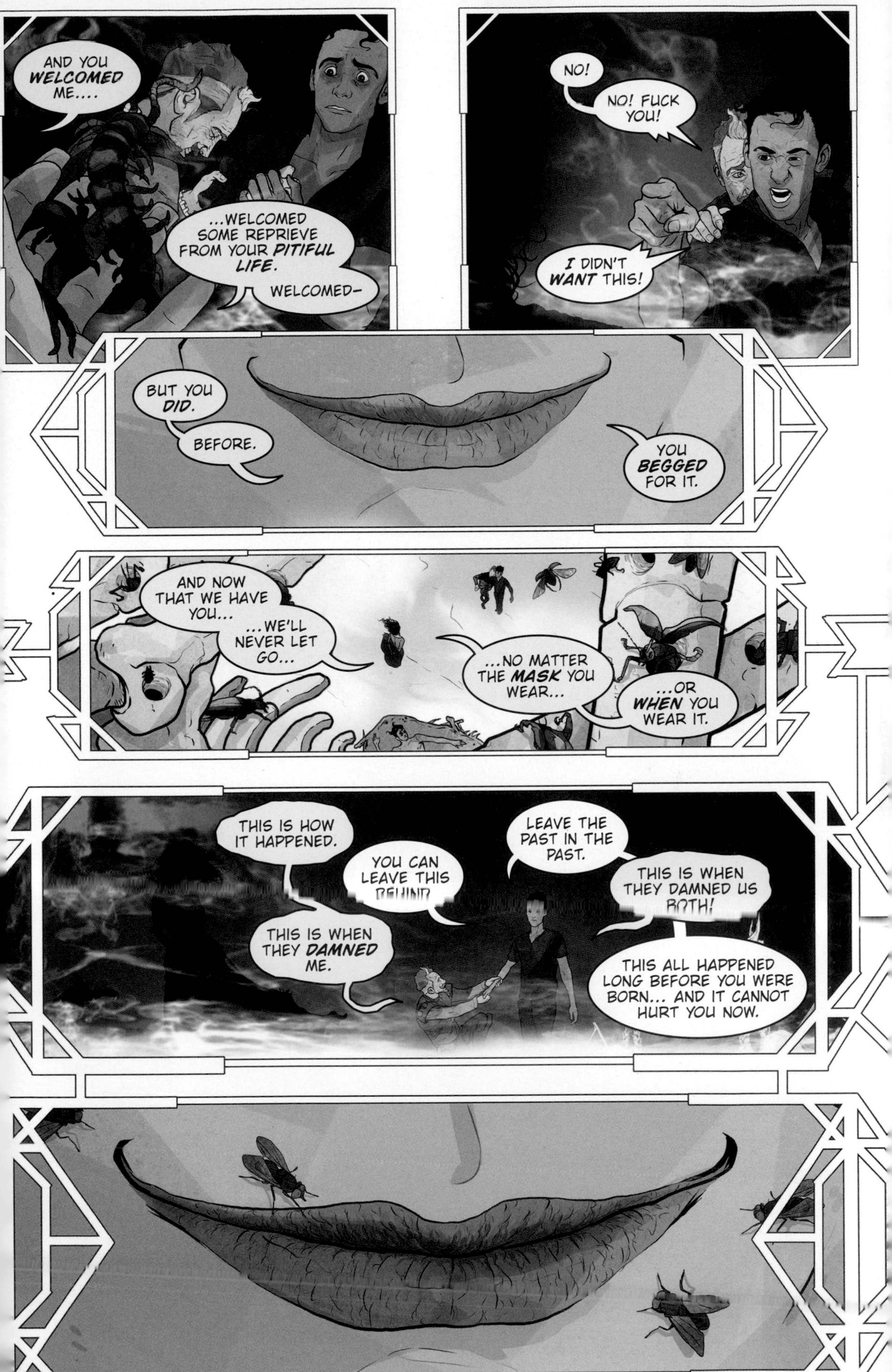
AND YOU *WELCOMED* ME....
...WELCOMED SOME REPRIEVE FROM YOUR *PITIFUL LIFE*.
WELCOMED-
NO!
NO! FUCK YOU!
I DIDN'T *WANT* THIS!
BUT YOU *DID*.
BEFORE.
YOU *BEGGED* FOR IT.
AND NOW THAT WE HAVE YOU...
...WE'LL NEVER LET GO...
...NO MATTER THE *MASK* YOU WEAR...
...OR *WHEN* YOU WEAR IT.
THIS IS HOW IT HAPPENED.
THIS IS WHEN THEY *DAMNED* ME.
YOU CAN LEAVE THIS BEHIND
LEAVE THE PAST IN THE PAST.
THIS IS WHEN THEY DAMNED US BOTH!
THIS ALL HAPPENED LONG BEFORE YOU WERE BORN... AND IT CANNOT HURT YOU NOW.

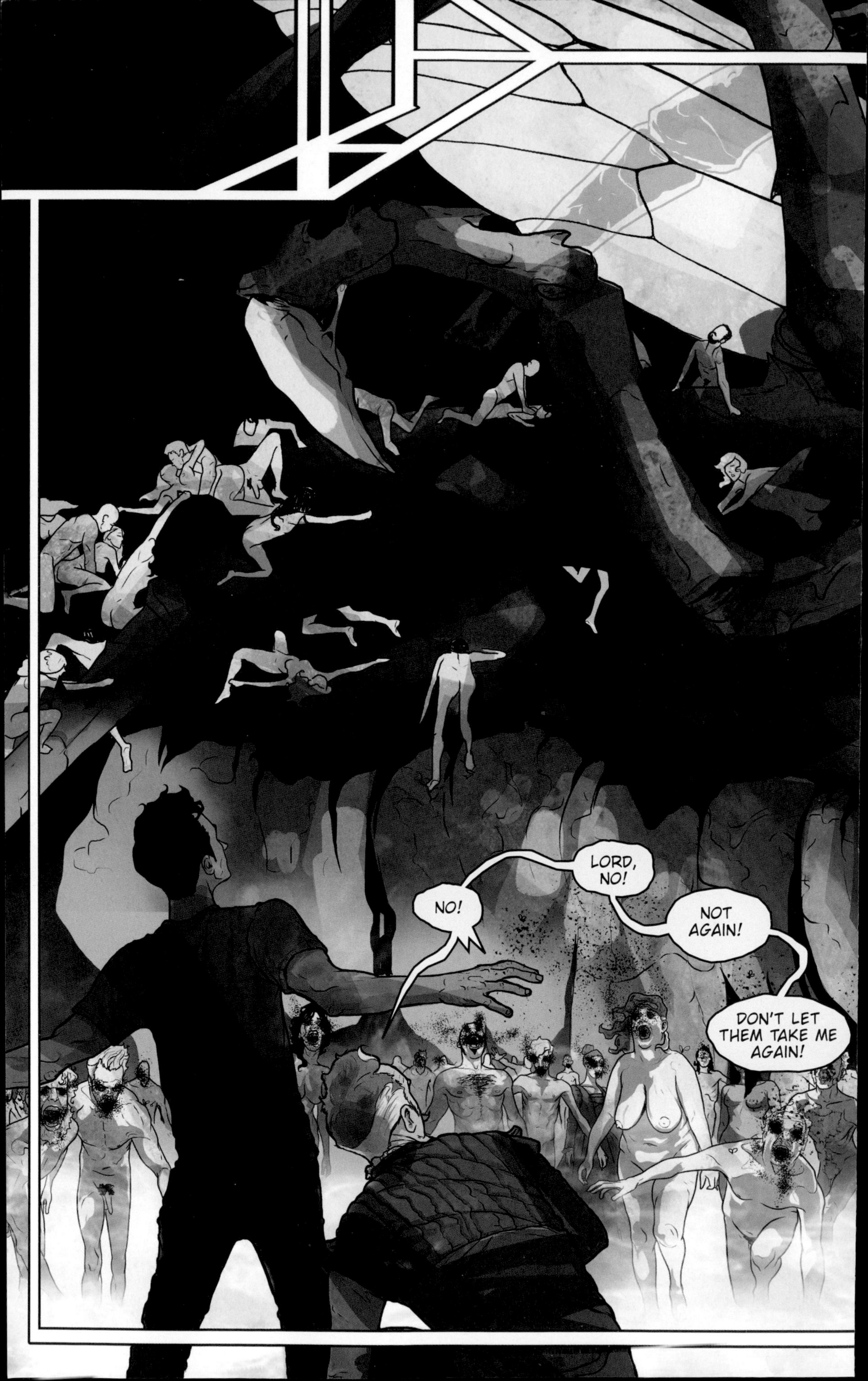
NO!
LORD, NO!
NOT AGAIN!
DON'T LET THEM TAKE ME AGAIN!

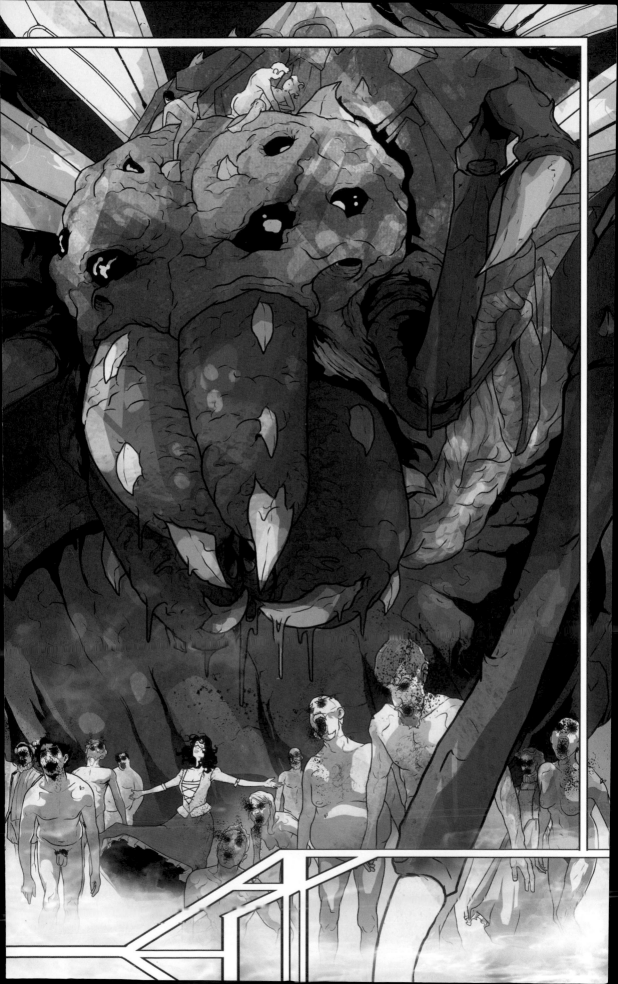

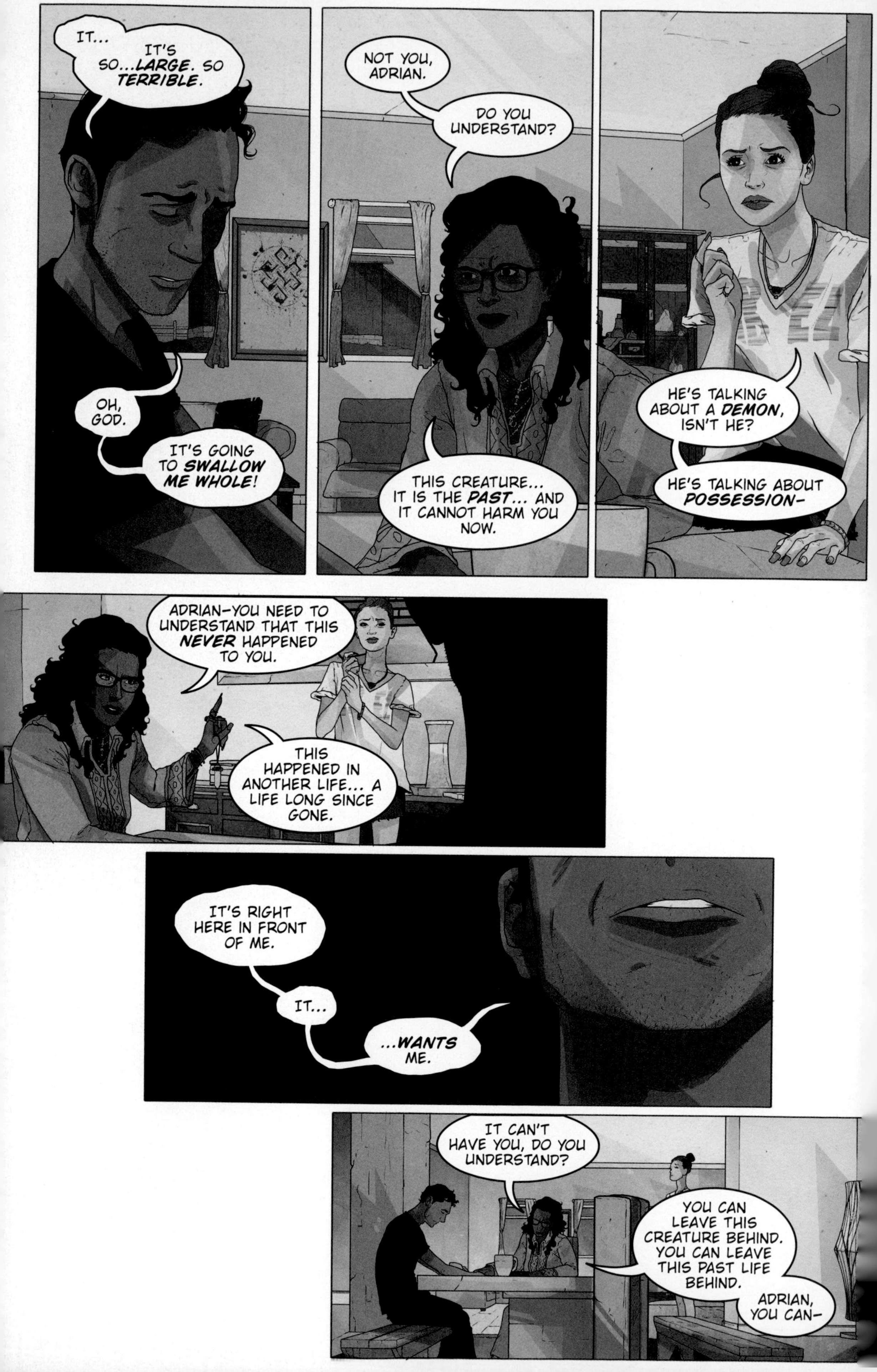
IT...
IT'S SO...LARGE. SO TERRIBLE.
OH, GOD.
IT'S GOING TO SWALLOW ME WHOLE!
NOT YOU, ADRIAN.
DO YOU UNDERSTAND?
THIS CREATURE... IT IS THE PAST... AND IT CANNOT HARM YOU NOW.
HE'S TALKING ABOUT A DEMON, ISN'T HE?
HE'S TALKING ABOUT POSSESSION-
ADRIAN-YOU NEED TO UNDERSTAND THAT THIS NEVER HAPPENED TO YOU.
THIS HAPPENED IN ANOTHER LIFE... A LIFE LONG SINCE GONE.
IT'S RIGHT HERE IN FRONT OF ME.
IT...
...WANTS ME.
IT CAN'T HAVE YOU, DO YOU UNDERSTAND?
YOU CAN LEAVE THIS CREATURE BEHIND. YOU CAN LEAVE THIS PAST LIFE BEHIND.
ADRIAN, YOU CAN-

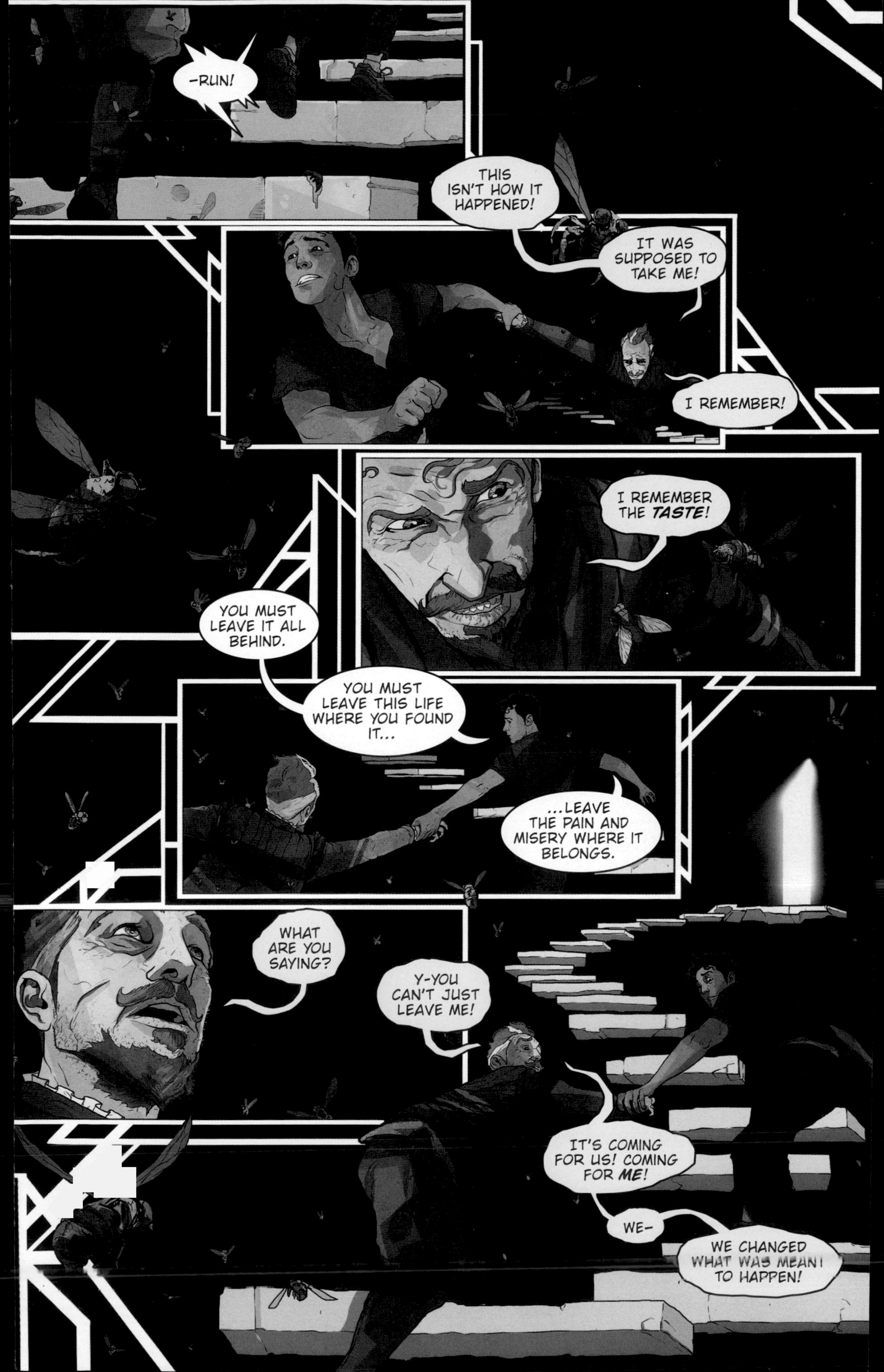
-RUN!
THIS ISN'T HOW IT HAPPENED!
IT WAS SUPPOSED TO TAKE ME!
I REMEMBER!
I REMEMBER THE TASTE!
YOU MUST LEAVE IT ALL BEHIND.
YOU MUST LEAVE THIS LIFE WHERE YOU FOUND IT...
...LEAVE THE PAIN AND MISERY WHERE IT BELONGS.
WHAT ARE YOU SAYING?
Y-YOU CAN'T JUST LEAVE ME!
IT'S COMING FOR US! COMING FOR ME!
WE-
WE CHANGED WHAT WAS MEANT TO HAPPEN!

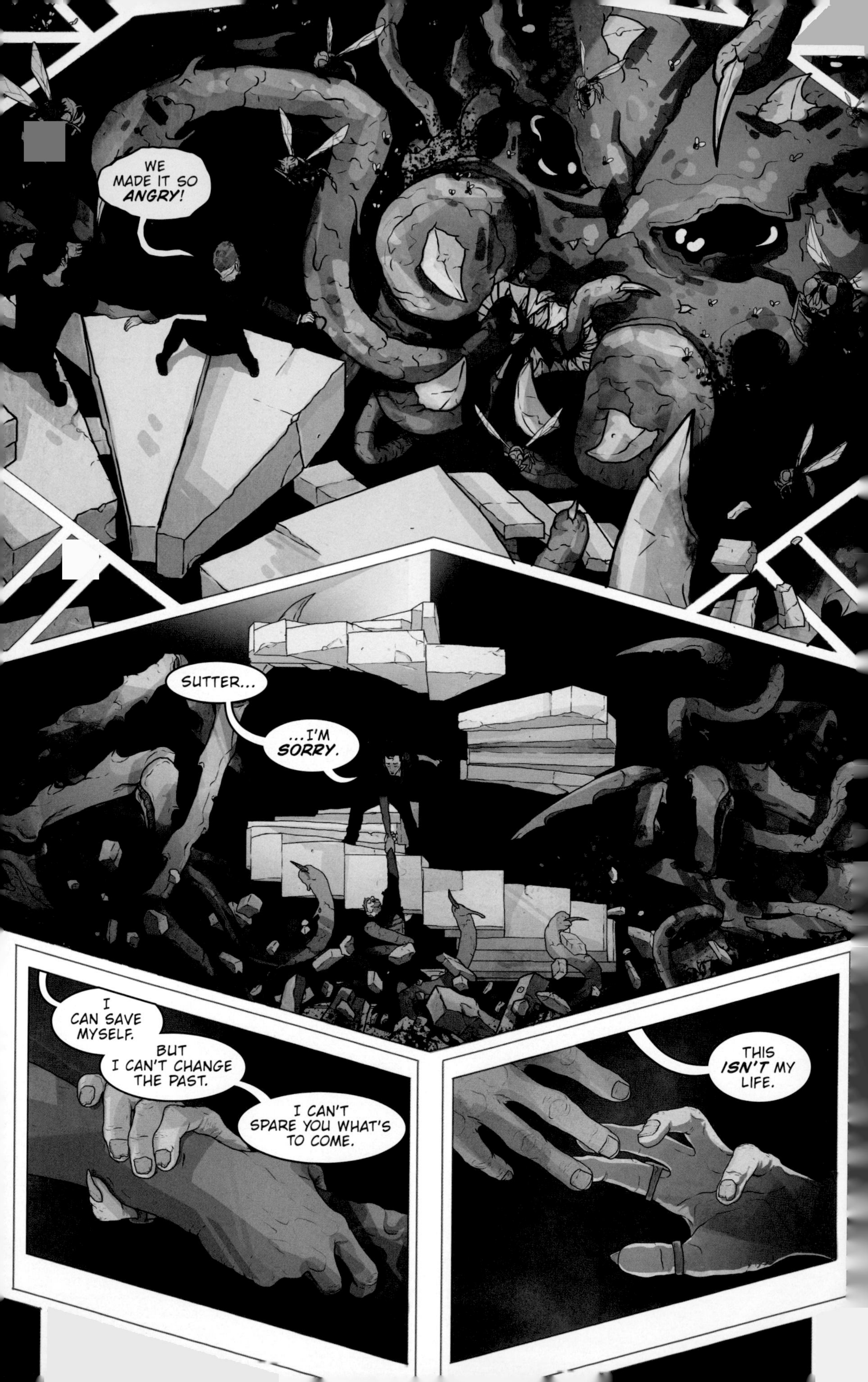
WE MADE IT SO ANGRY!
SUTTER...
...I'M SORRY.
I CAN SAVE MYSELF.
BUT I CAN'T CHANGE THE PAST.
I CAN'T SPARE YOU WHAT'S TO COME.
THIS ISN'T MY LIFE.

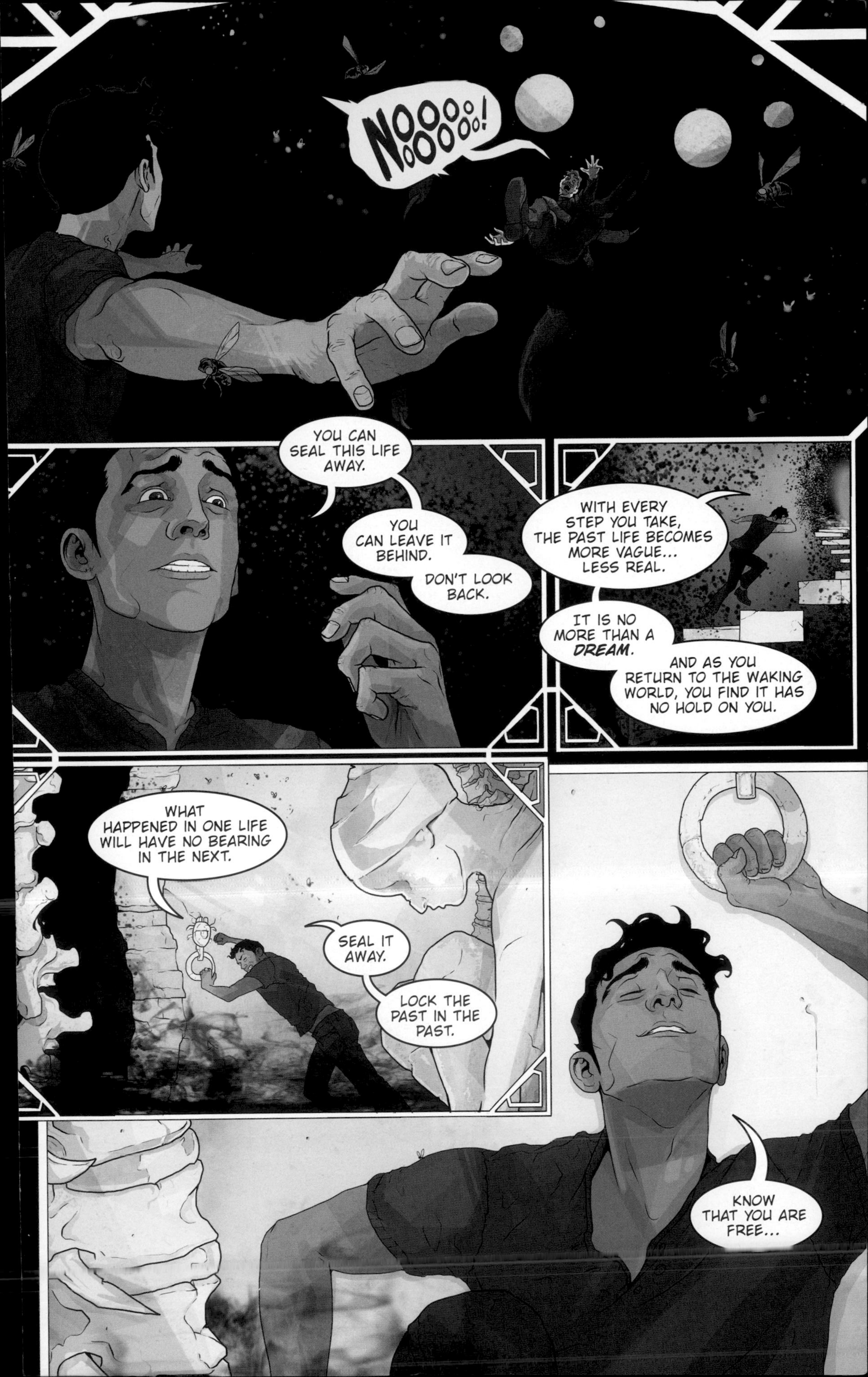
NOOOOOOOOO!
YOU CAN SEAL THIS LIFE AWAY.
YOU CAN LEAVE IT BEHIND.
DON'T LOOK BACK.
WITH EVERY STEP YOU TAKE, THE PAST LIFE BECOMES MORE VAGUE... LESS REAL.
IT IS NO MORE THAN A DREAM.
AND AS YOU RETURN TO THE WAKING WORLD, YOU FIND IT HAS NO HOLD ON YOU.
WHAT HAPPENED IN ONE LIFE WILL HAVE NO BEARING IN THE NEXT.
SEAL IT AWAY.
LOCK THE PAST IN THE PAST.
KNOW THAT YOU ARE FREE...

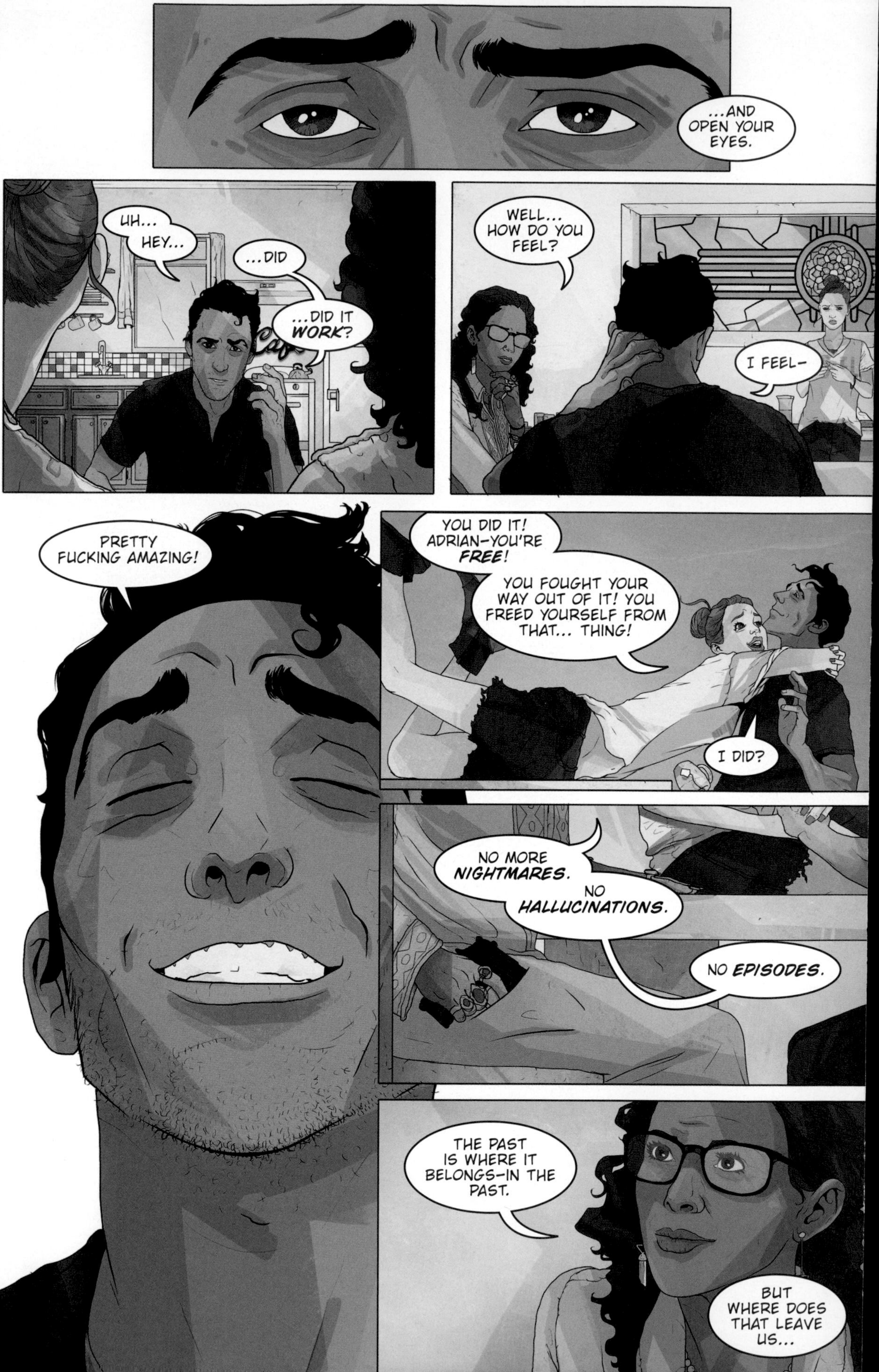
...AND OPEN YOUR EYES.
UH... HEY...
...DID
...DID IT WORK?
WELL... HOW DO YOU FEEL?
I FEEL-
PRETTY FUCKING AMAZING!
YOU DID IT! ADRIAN-YOU'RE FREE!
YOU FOUGHT YOUR WAY OUT OF IT! YOU FREED YOURSELF FROM THAT... THING!
I DID?
NO MORE NIGHTMARES.
NO HALLUCINATIONS.
NO EPISODES.
THE PAST IS WHERE IT BELONGS-IN THE PAST.
BUT WHERE DOES THAT LEAVE US...

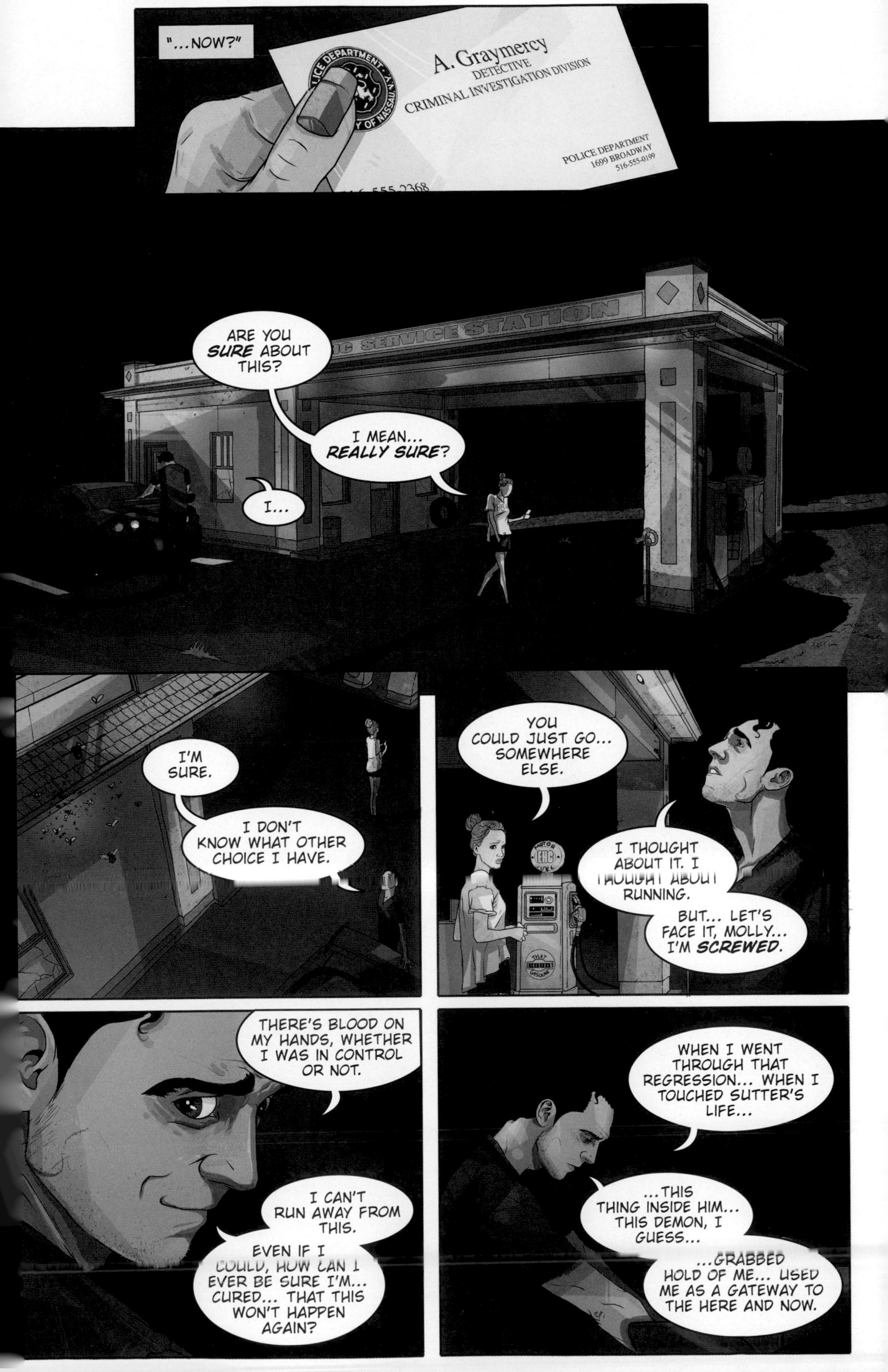
"...NOW?"
A. Graymercy
DETECTIVE
CRIMINAL INVESTIGATION DIVISION
POLICE DEPARTMENT
1699 BROADWAY
516-555-0199
SERVICE STATION
ARE YOU SURE ABOUT THIS?
I MEAN... REALLY SURE?
I...
I'M SURE.
I DON'T KNOW WHAT OTHER CHOICE I HAVE.
YOU COULD JUST GO... SOMEWHERE ELSE.
I THOUGHT ABOUT IT. I THOUGHT ABOUT RUNNING.
BUT... LET'S FACE IT, MOLLY... I'M SCREWED.
THERE'S BLOOD ON MY HANDS, WHETHER I WAS IN CONTROL OR NOT.
I CAN'T RUN AWAY FROM THIS.
EVEN IF I COULD, HOW CAN I EVER BE SURE I'M... CURED... THAT THIS WON'T HAPPEN AGAIN?
WHEN I WENT THROUGH THAT REGRESSION... WHEN I TOUCHED SUTTER'S LIFE...
...THIS THING INSIDE HIM... THIS DEMON, I GUESS...
...GRABBED HOLD OF ME... USED ME AS A GATEWAY TO THE HERE AND NOW.

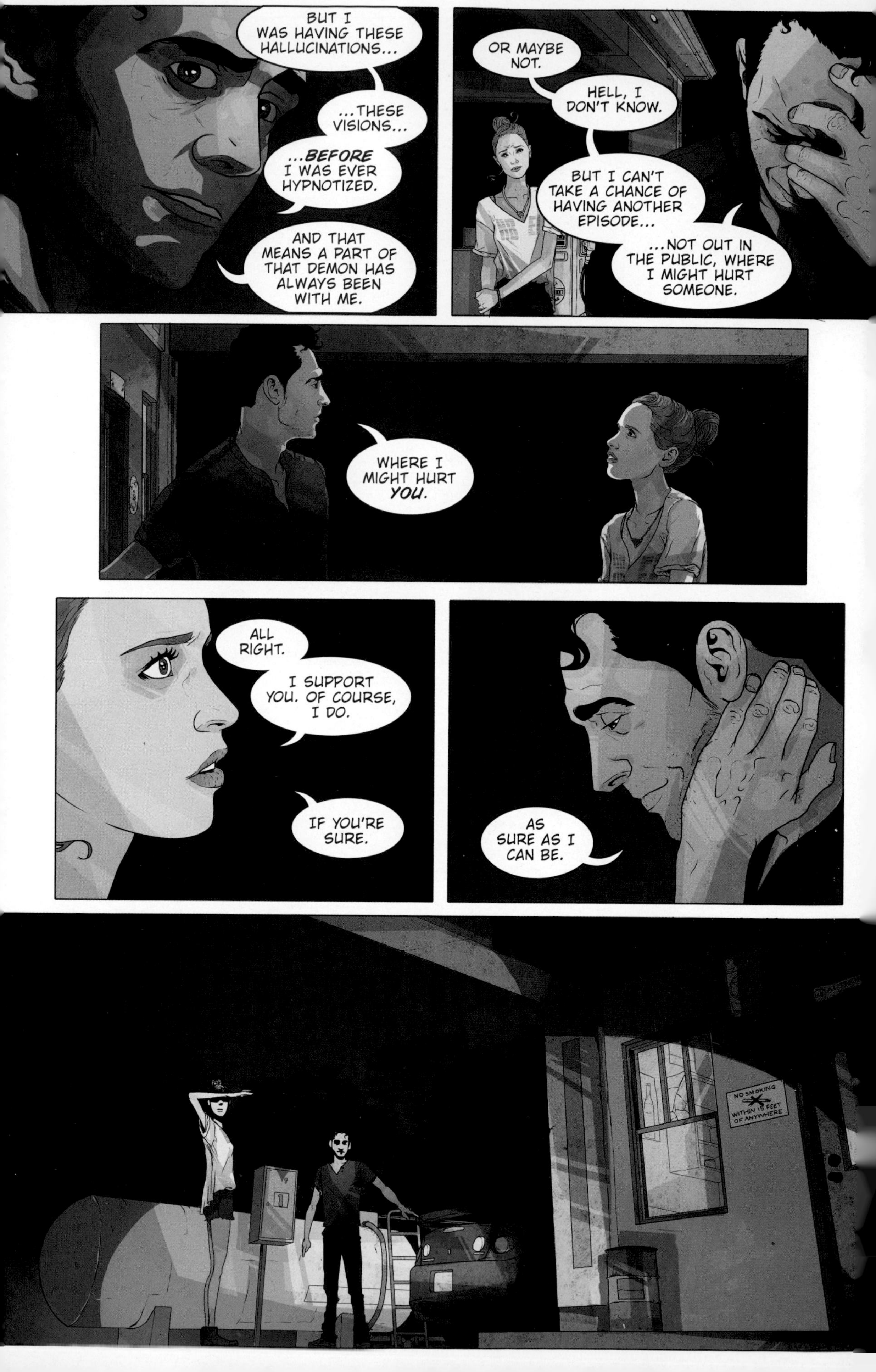
BUT I WAS HAVING THESE HALLUCINATIONS...
...THESE VISIONS...
...BEFORE I WAS EVER HYPNOTIZED.
AND THAT MEANS A PART OF THAT DEMON HAS ALWAYS BEEN WITH ME.
OR MAYBE NOT.
HELL, I DON'T KNOW.
BUT I CAN'T TAKE A CHANCE OF HAVING ANOTHER EPISODE...
...NOT OUT IN THE PUBLIC, WHERE I MIGHT HURT SOMEONE.
WHERE I MIGHT HURT YOU.
ALL RIGHT.
I SUPPORT YOU. OF COURSE, I DO.
IF YOU'RE SURE.
AS SURE AS I CAN BE.
NO SMOKING WITHIN 15 FEET OF ANYWHERE

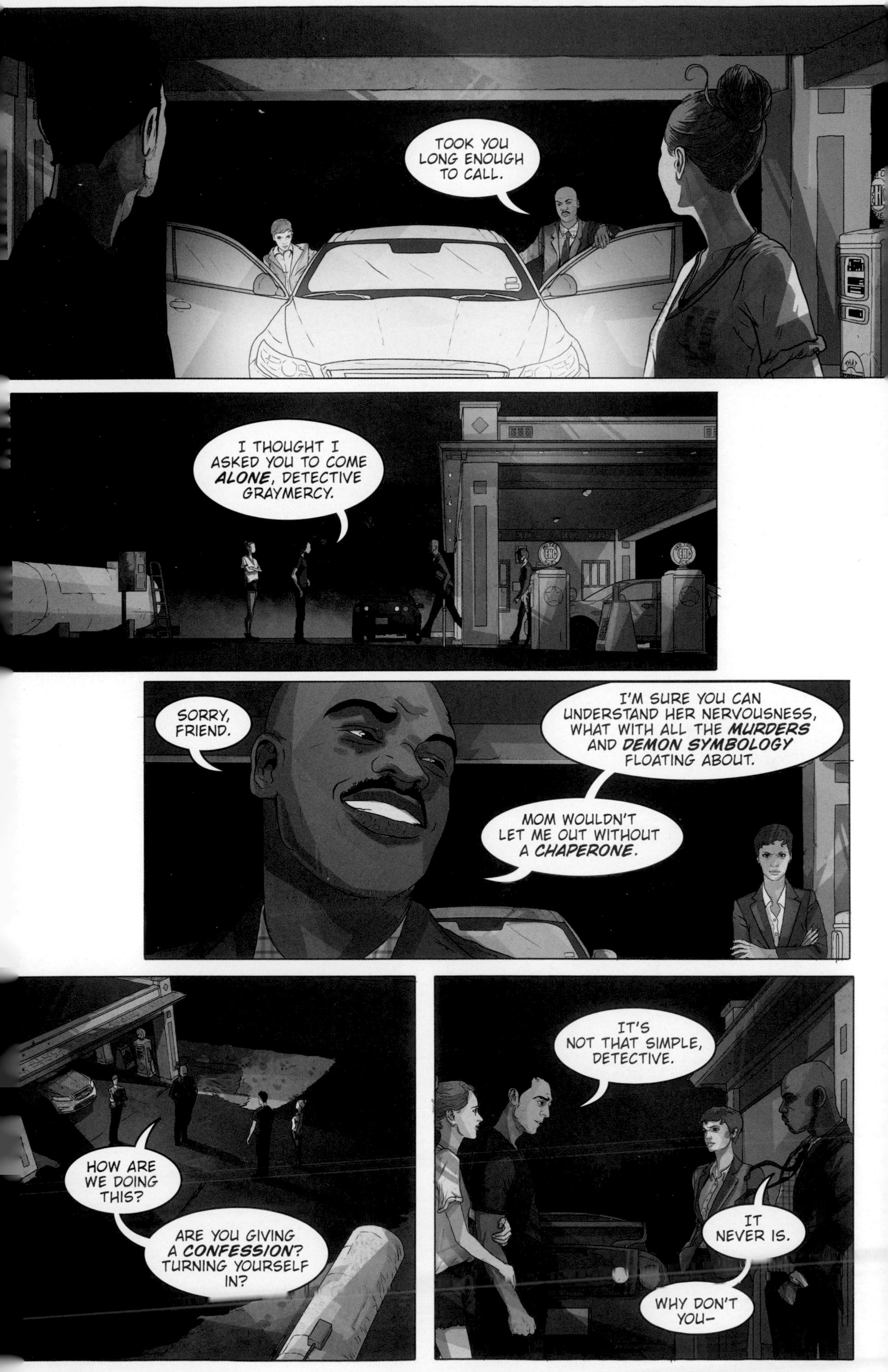
TOOK YOU LONG ENOUGH TO CALL.
I THOUGHT I ASKED YOU TO COME ALONE, DETECTIVE GRAYMERCY.
SORRY, FRIEND.
I'M SURE YOU CAN UNDERSTAND HER NERVOUSNESS, WHAT WITH ALL THE MURDERS AND DEMON SYMBOLOGY FLOATING ABOUT.
MOM WOULDN'T LET ME OUT WITHOUT A CHAPERONE.
HOW ARE WE DOING THIS?
ARE YOU GIVING A CONFESSION? TURNING YOURSELF IN?
IT'S NOT THAT SIMPLE, DETECTIVE.
IT NEVER IS.
WHY DON'T YOU-

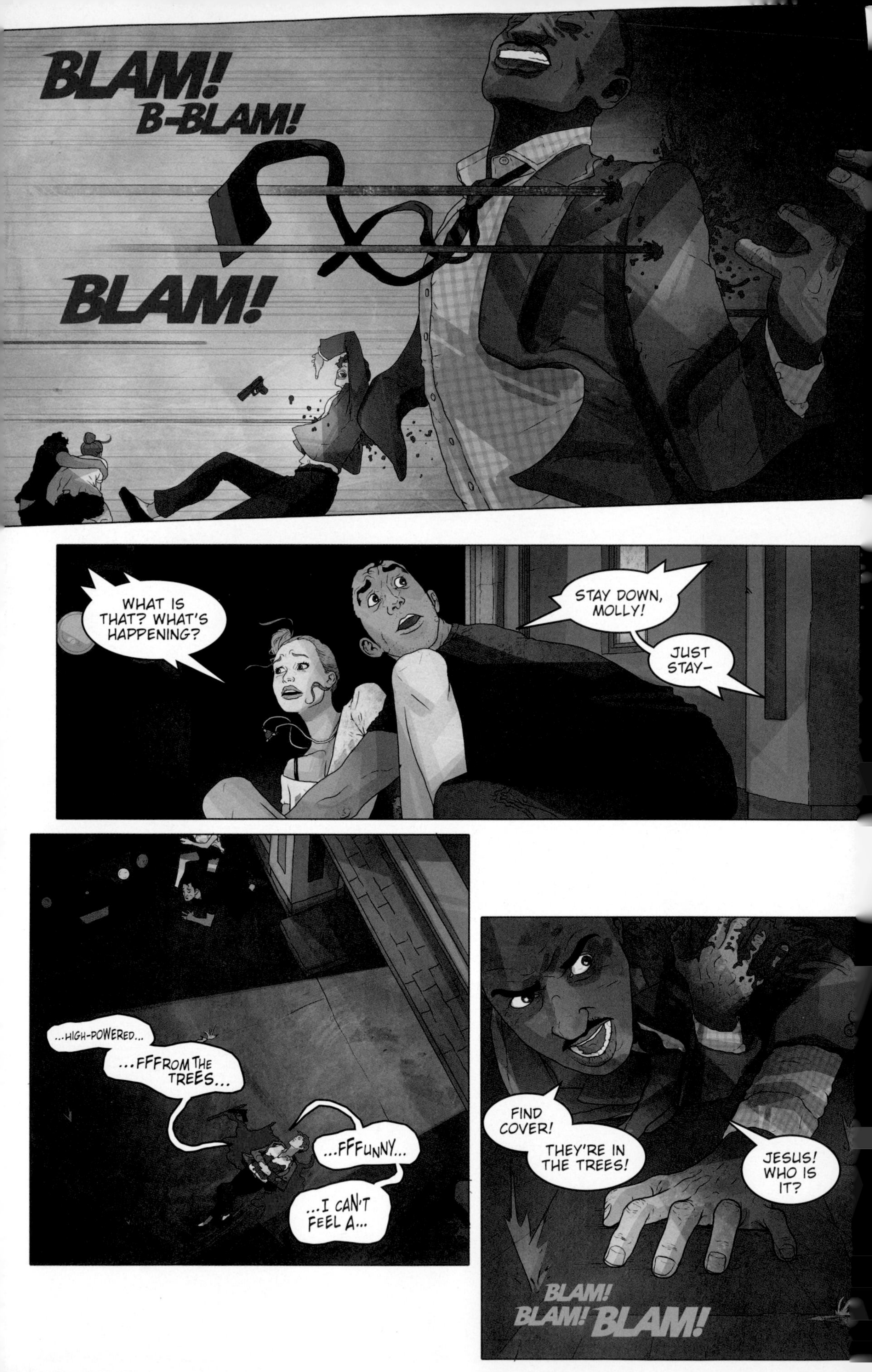
BLAM!
B-BLAM!
BLAM!
WHAT IS THAT? WHAT'S HAPPENING?
STAY DOWN, MOLLY!
JUST STAY-
...HIGH-POWERED...
...FFFROM THE TREES...
...FFFUNNY...
...I CAN'T FEEL A...
FIND COVER!
THEY'RE IN THE TREES!
JESUS! WHO IS IT?
BLAM!
BLAM! BLAM!

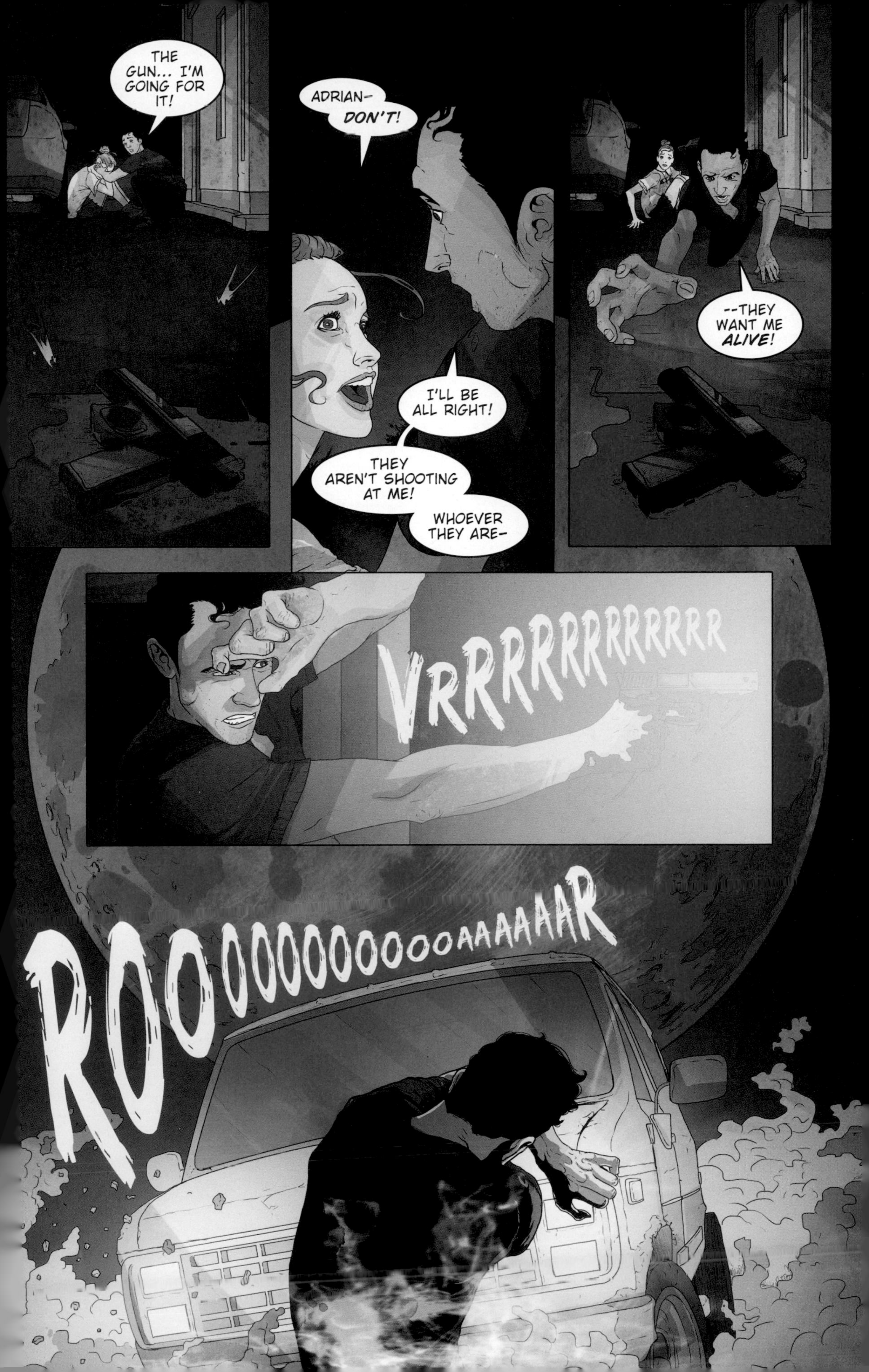
THE GUN... I'M GOING FOR IT!
ADRIAN- DON'T!
I'LL BE ALL RIGHT!
THEY AREN'T SHOOTING AT ME!
WHOEVER THEY ARE-
--THEY WANT ME ALIVE!
VRRRRRRRRRRRR
ROOOOOOOOOOOAAAAAR

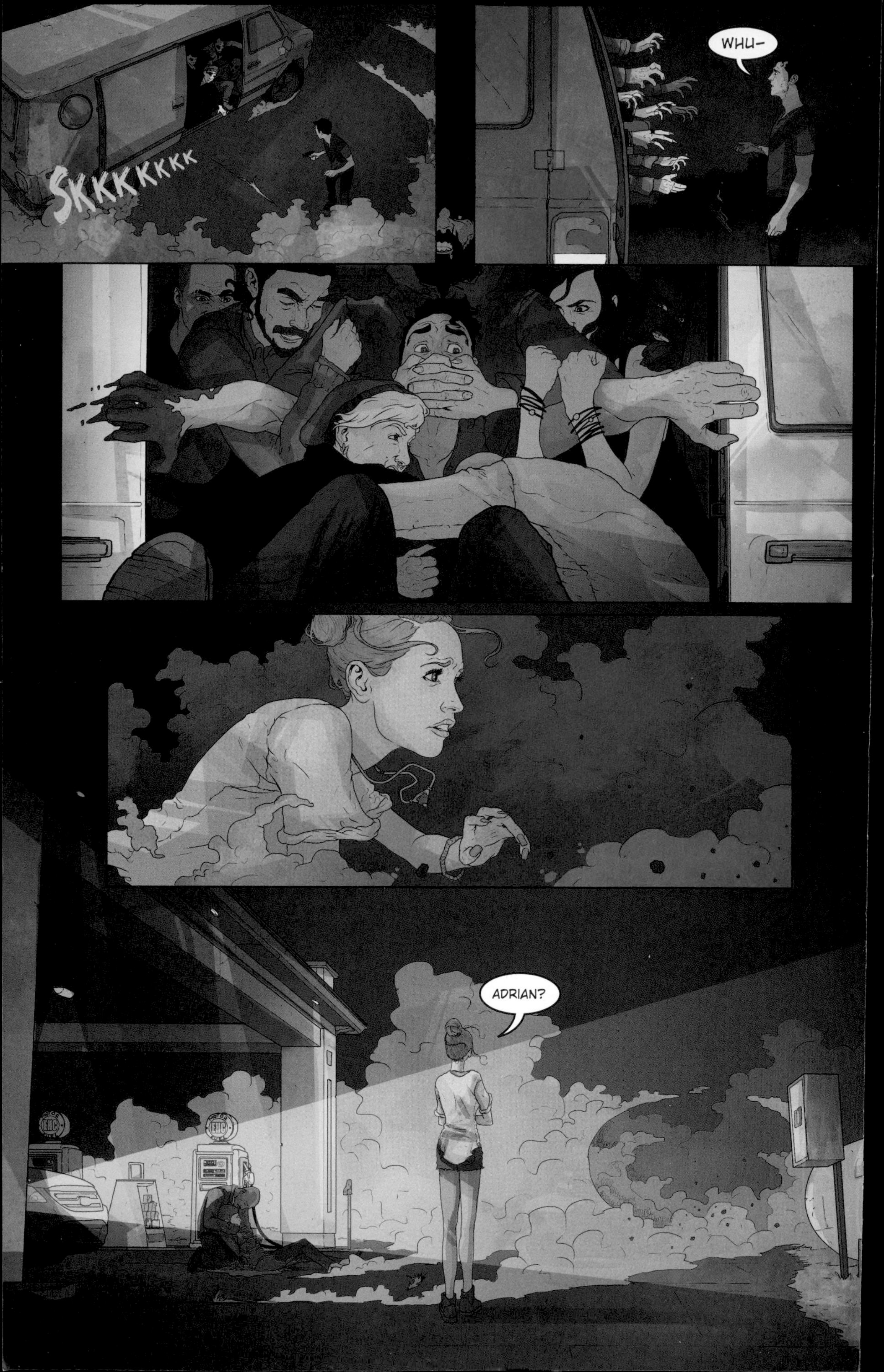
SKKKKKK
WHU-
ADRIAN?

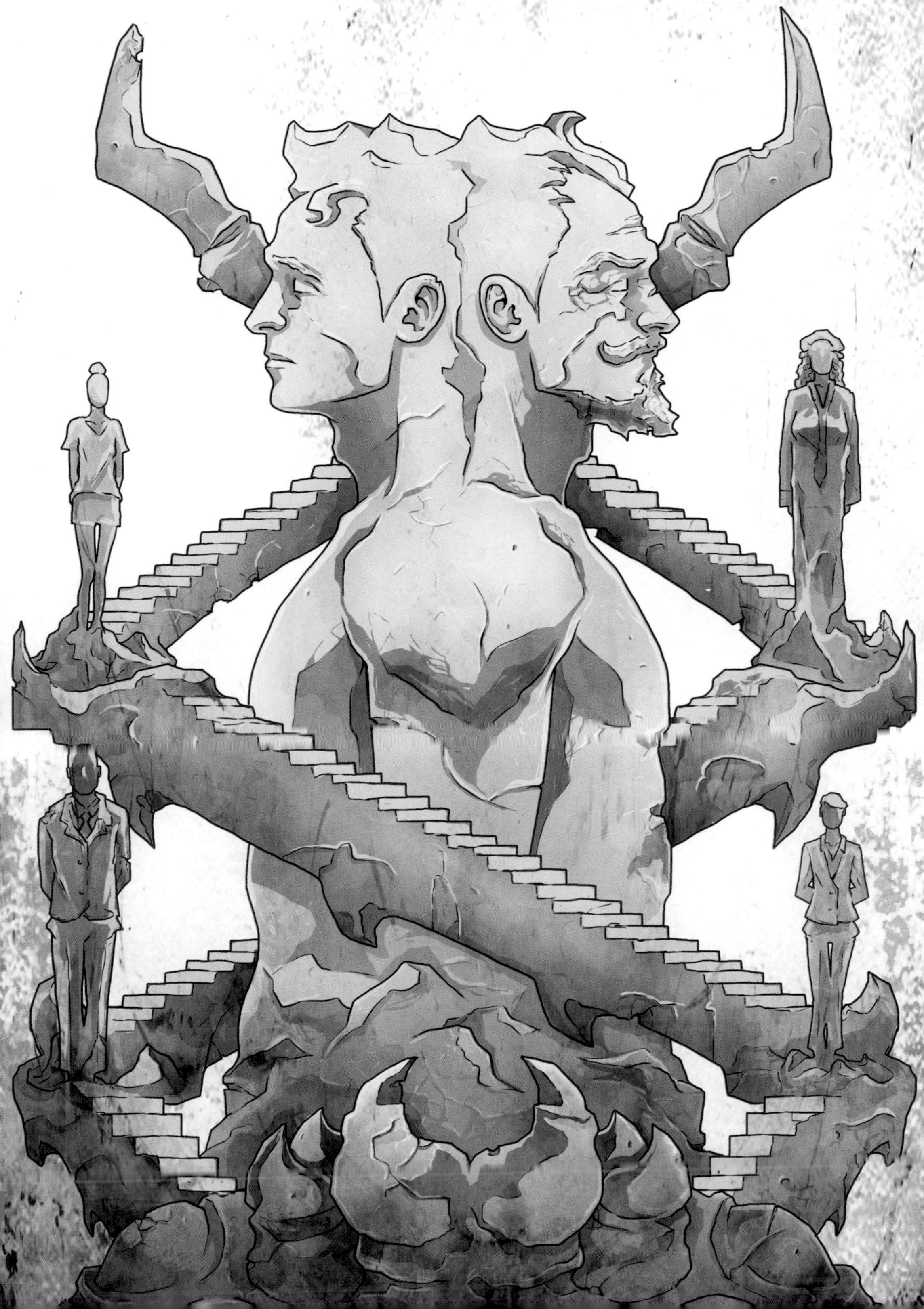

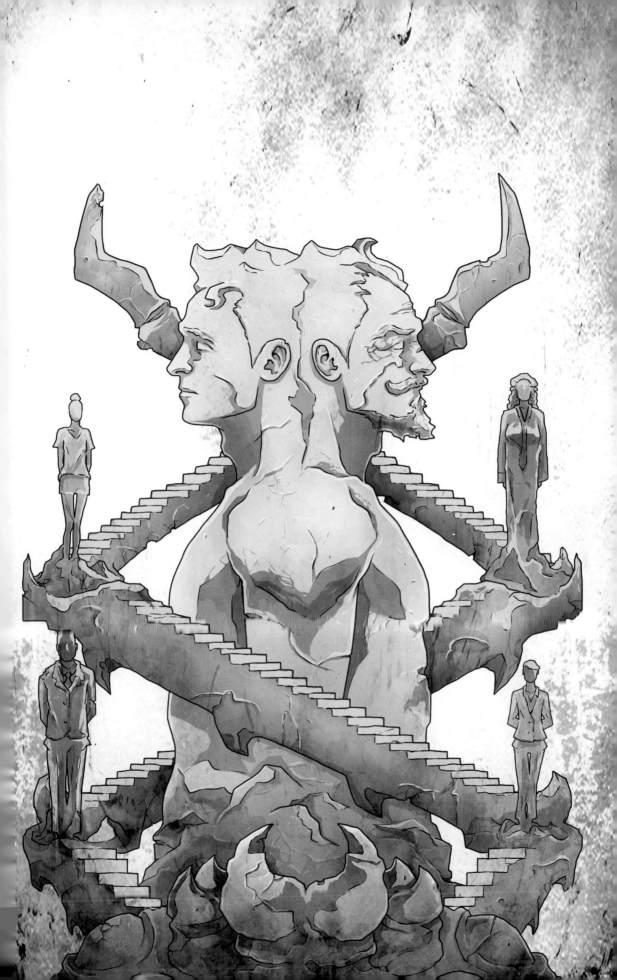

REGRESSION ANALYSIS

Mesmer wheels, lemons, and onions.

That's what I think of when people ask me if hypnosis really works.

When I was growing up, there was this giant wooden Mesmer wheel in the shed out behind the house. This wheel, with its weird spiral pattern of oranges and yellows, had been a centerpiece of my dad's hypnosis act. When it was spun, it created a strange, whirlpool effect that would draw those who watched it deeper and deeper into a trance state.

Or maybe not.

My dad always said the wheel was just for show, a theatrical prop to satisfy expectations of the audience. He never really used the wheel, nor did he rely on pocket watches or ticking metronomes or spoons in teacups. There was this one time, when he was in the middle of a private show at someone's house, when a grandfather clock started chiming. My dad was in the middle of an induction, and he simply said, "Every time the clock sounds, you will find that you are sinking deeper into a relaxed state." That's the closest he came to using some sort of tool to help him during the hypnosis process. Otherwise, he used only his voice, only the words he spoke.

That, he said, was the technique he learned from "the old French gentleman" who taught him about hypnosis.

My dad never really performed on a big stage or anything. He took that old Mesmer wheel and his calming voice to venues including VFW halls and fairgrounds and CB jamborees and high schools. And his act often centered around giving people the hot seat or making people envision they were talking to their favorite actor or musician. He would give people a baby bottle full of milk and tell them he was offering them a Pepsi. He would have them try to smoke carrots (that was actually a big part of my performance as the "World's Youngest Hypnotist").

He saved the past life regressions, of course, for those private sessions.